THE BELLS OF BALANGIGA

THE BELLS OF BALANGIGA

Eleonor Mendoza

iUniverse, Inc.
Bloomington

The Bells of Balangiga

iUniverse books may be ordered through booksellers or by contacting:

iUniverse
1663 Liberty Drive
Bloomington, IN 47403
www.iuniverse.com
1-800-Authors (1-800-288-4677)

ISBN: 978-1-4759-1145-9 (sc)
ISBN: 978-1-4759-1147-3 (hc)
ISBN: 978-1-4759-1146-6 (ebk)

Library of Congress Control Number: 2012906187

Printed in the United States of America

iUniverse rev. date: 04/14/2012

To those who have fought for the freedom of my native land, I am not alone in eternal gratitude.

To those who have painstakingly chronicled history for all of us to know and learn, thank you so much for they have not been lost.

May the memory of those valiant souls be always in our hearts.

Contents

Part Three

Part Four

Appendix

Illustrations

PART ONE

I

December 15, 1940

Cabanatuan City, Nueva Ecija Province

Philippines, Commonwealth of the United States

Lieutenant Jack Stewart sat ramrod straight as Private Smith drove the open jeep toward the hardware store. A horse-drawn passenger carriage called a *calesa* in front of their jeep took its time to let them pass. Smith sighed, but for once, Jack did not mind. He focused on the task ahead. He planned to make his military family proud of what he would accomplish in this country where his father had served in the army for several years.

Nueva Ecija was among the provinces comprising the central plain of Luzon, the breadbasket of the country. Cabanatuan was the capital city, and the main street was a narrow two-lane road called Rizal Avenue. The rather small town had taken on a sprawling look recently because of the new military buildings and installations. The townsfolk were quiet and observant; right now, the place was silent.

It was only a short drive from their barracks. It was not necessary for a lieutenant to come just to buy some lumber and hardware supplies, but Jack was assigned to gather intelligence on the Japanese-owned hardware store. It was a cloudy day and a little cooler, but Jack still felt an ennui he had to shake off. He was beginning to appreciate the siesta-time tradition the Spaniards had passed on to the Filipinos.

"It's 2:00 PM. Now I know why people need a nap at this time," Smith said, as though reading Jack's mind.

Smith parked the jeep in front of the hardware store and went in, but Jack took his time purposely, lighting a cigarette while he studied the store. The hardware store was in a two-story building that looked like a wooden box with two wide windows upstairs, none on the first floor store. The store still looked dark even though the doors were open all the way, revealing the cement floor.

As Jack climbed out of the jeep, he noticed a young lady walking along the sidewalk, carrying a large bunch of flowers. She was a bright picture on a cloudy day with her red sweater, navy skirt, and the orange, yellow, and red flowers. She looked up in surprise as she sensed his gaze, her pretty face framed by soft bangs. She quickly looked down.

Abruptly, a young Japanese man came out of the store, broom in hand, pretending to sweep the sidewalk. His eyes were on the young lady too.

"Good afternoon," the young Japanese said.

"Good afternoon," she answered without looking, her gaze still down. She strode briskly to the far side of the sidewalk and continued in the direction of San Nicholas church.

Jack dropped his cigarette on the sidewalk, stepped on the embers, and went inside the store.

"Good afternoon! I am Mister Seichi Mifune, and this is my son, Yoshiro," the owner said.

"How do you do? I'm Lieutenant Jack Stewart. We're together," Jack said, pointing to Smith.

They all shook hands. Jack took out his list, and they checked off what was available. The store was surprisingly well equipped.

In spite of the two rows of long fluorescent lights on either side of the ceiling, Jack had to let his eyes adapt to his surroundings, before he could pick out some saws, hammers, nails, and other small metal equipment from the display rack on the right. On his left, there were piles of plywood, baskets of grain, and some farm utensils.

"Ahh! We need one more box of nails," Smith said, scratching his head.

"I have some more in the back," Mr. Mifune said.

"Here it is!" Yoshiro said as he put down the box, along with their other purchases.

As the pile on the floor accumulated, Smith again scratched his head. "This might not all fit in the jeep!" he said.

"I can get someone to deliver the rest, if you like," Mr. Mifune offered.

"Let's see first," Jack answered.

With the help of some ropes, Jack and Smith were able to fit everything into the jeep. Mr. Mifune and his son were very helpful.

Too helpful? Jack wondered as Smith eased the jeep back onto the road. Jack had found himself being careful with his answers, suspicious that Mr. Mifune was such a good conversationalist.

Jack felt the jeep slowing as Smith waited to make a left turn.

"Drive toward the church," he suddenly told Smith. "Please."

Smith's brows went up, but he said nothing as the jeep continued down the road.

"The store is dark because there are no windows on the lower floor," Jack thought aloud. "Is that the same with other stores?"

Smith adjusted his cap but said nothing. Jack glanced sideways and realized that this was Smith's way of saying, 'no comment'.

"So we're here," Smith said, wondering what was going on as he parked the jeep in the church plaza.

"I won't be long, wait here," Jack said as he jumped out of the jeep and went into the Catholic church.

He dipped his hand in the holy water and made a quick sign of the cross. He knelt and prayed as his eyes searched for the young lady.

A middle-aged nun with a vase of flowers came out of the sacristy, followed by the beautiful young lady he saw earlier. She carried another vase of flowers. An older lady was right behind them, moving toward the front, and she motioned for the vases to be put in their places on either side of the altar. The older ladies were slightly surprised to see a soldier in church, and the young lady glanced at him, but they went on with their task.

Jack took a backward glance as he went back to the jeep. The young lady was also looking back at him.

The supplies that Jack and Smith bought for the barracks were adequate. Several soldiers helped unload the supplies and take it to the supply shed. They were finished for the day, so Jack and Smith slumped on the bench outside the shed and drank water from their canteens.

"I'm almost sure those were not just storekeepers," Jack said softly, his right hand brushing back a lock of his brown hair blown by the breeze.

"Maybe," Smith replied between gulps of water. "It's hard to tell."

They looked across the campground to where the marching field was a haze of dust. It was now past 4:00 PM. They could hear the sergeant barking orders about how and when to fire. The trainees were asking each other and started arguing. The Filipino soldiers in training were using wooden mock rifles, and the sergeant grew hoarse pointing out the differences between the real and the mock guns.

"Dismiss!" barked the sergeant.

Smith moved sideways in his seat as the sergeant wearily sat down beside them.

"This is going to take a long time," the sergeant said.

Jack had a lot to sort out that night. Here he was in a country that his dad had a great affinity for. He wondered if they would be able to finish training the Filipino soldiers by the target date of the War Plan. Even if some Filipinos did not seem serious and there was much absenteeism, Jack had also come across the competitive, smart ones, and they were good. His job of training the new recruits was going well, but there were not as many soldiers as General MacArthur would like, because there was not enough funding.

Those men are not just storekeepers, Jack thought as he tossed in bed.

He had a grudging admiration for the aura of military precision that Mr. Mifune and his son displayed. They were courteous and polite at a level that could only be seen among the well bred in this country. Jack thought of the other Japanese stores in Manila and the Japanese men working on domestic jobs. This was a time of impending war, and Jack could not prove his suspicions, but he felt that something was wrong.

I'm getting paranoid! They speak English well because they have been to the States, although why did Mr. Mifune not want to say how long? They seemed relaxed. Why am I not relaxed?

Young and restless, he felt some guilt about not missing his girlfriend, Liza. She was blonde, blue eyed, and pretty—the most popular girl in their high school class. He had been the class president and was considered the smartest in the graduating class. She was the prom queen. They were the most envied pair in town.

Jack's family in Virginia had several traditions; among them was going into the military. Like his father, Jack went to West Point, finishing among the top 1 percent of his class.

Jack had gone to West Point because it was expected of him, but when he began to study history and strategy, he became curious about the world and how things work. On his home visits, he began to notice that Liza did not follow his trend of thought, and it was better to talk about benign things or they would not understand each other. Later still, he started getting bored with their conversations. On their last meeting, she had suggested they should marry. Jack made a lame excuse about not knowing how long his next assignment would be, and they left things at that.

When he was assigned to the Philippines, he was glad to get away and also happy about the adventure that lay ahead. His dad had been on several tours of duty in the Philippines and loved it.

Thinking it would be an easy assignment, he had not paid much attention to the briefing about local customs and traditions. Now he found himself reading everything and asking around. He had been laughed at after saying "roast pork" instead of "lechon."

Most Filipino traditions had been acquired from their more than three hundred years of Spanish colonization, and it seemed that Filipinos cherished this instead of hating it. Life here was slow, and Jack thought these attachments to the past slowed the people down even more. Some practices were downright impractical—like the Misa de Gallo, or nine days of dawn Masses before Christmas.

Jack thought about attending these Masses. Being Catholic, he would not mind going to church ... but at dawn?

Maybe just once, for the experience, he thought. *If I can get up early, I'll go. If not, too bad.*

Jack did not fall asleep quickly. He was thinking of too many things at once, from the impending war to what happened that day. He knew his intelligence report only contained observations and impressions, nothing concrete enough to justify a search warrant for the Mifune store. Finally he admitted to himself that he would rather think of the young lady he had seen earlier in the afternoon. The startled look in those big brown eyes stayed on Jack's mind the whole evening. Now he was planning to go to a dawn Mass.

Surprise of all surprises, he did go to church. It would have been dark at 4:30 AM without the streetlights, but it was only two days after the full moon and even if the large Spanish stone church cast a shadow toward the rectory, the church plaza looked bright from the moon glow. The people were arriving on foot; his jeep was the only one parked on the lot. Colored streamers had been strung from the central pole in front of the church to the pine tree by the convent and into some vendor stalls along the street.

Jack stood in the back pew, and from there he saw the young lady enter the church with the elder lady he had seen earlier, along with an older gentleman. He surmised they must be her parents. There were also other people who seemed to be relatives, like a big, extended family.

Jack actually enjoyed the short, simple Mass. There was no sermon. During the chilly dawn, he thought about God, and a sense of peace came over him. It was still dark when the Mass finished at 5:00 AM; in this country, the sun rose at 6:00 AM and set at 6:00 PM.

The families came out after the service with the members greeting each other, the younger ones kissing the elder's right hand for a blessing, and the ladies kissing the cheeks in greeting. The children excitedly went ahead of the elders to the vendor stalls to buy rice cakes.

It was only in this season that vendors, even from out of town, would come to sell different kinds of rice cakes so early in the morning. The streets close to the church plaza were lined with vendors selling treats that were traditionally available only in this season, like the *puto bumbong*. The churchgoers bought them to take home for an early breakfast.

Jack listened to the low hum of excited voices from people buying and selling rice cakes. He got caught up in the excitement and wanted to try all the varieties at once. He went toward the vendor stall where the young lady's family was buying rice cakes.

"Excuse me, I don't know which ... which ones are good?"

The father smiled, and the mother answered.

"They're all good. Try a few at a time, so you can remember which is which. The *puto bumbong* and the *bibingka* are a good start."

The mother helped him with his purchases, and then she turned to her husband, adjusting her shawl at the same time. As though on cue, the father spoke.

"I'm Doctor Carlos Mendez. This is my wife Clara and our daughter Victoria."

"I'm Lieutenant Jack Stewart," Jack answered, shaking hands with the father. He saw the mother blink, look at him with wonder, and quickly hide it all with a gracious smile.

She shook hands with him, but the daughter just nodded and smiled faintly from a distance.

Jack looked her in the eye, when suddenly he felt his heart beat faster. He had been hoping they could all talk longer, or maybe they would invite him for breakfast. Suddenly, he felt awkward.

"Thanks for your help. I'll be seeing you around," he said.

He might have turned red. He could still sense his rapid heartbeat, and he hoped against hope they did not notice. Somehow, he was able to get back to his jeep and drive back to his barracks.

II

Now Jack knew the young lady was a Mendez. He learned that her family owned a house across from the government buildings on Rizal Avenue. Her father was a doctor, and her mother was a pharmacist. Their daughter, Victoria, was called affectionately as Neneng. Their drugstore occupied the lower floor, and the family lived on the second floor.

On one end of Rizal Avenue was the church, and across from it was the school; on the other end was the U.S. military camp, and nearby were the government buildings. In the center of town was the plaza, and behind it, the market. Important people and businesses were on this avenue.

Each day from then on, Jack hoped to see Neneng. After his work of training troops was finished for the day, Jack would cruise in his jeep around town for a chance to see her, but he did not have any luck. It was not everyday that he could go to church at dawn; there were times when he had to start briefings and other work quite early. He was getting frustrated, but he refused to believe he was becoming lovesick.

Jack was no stranger to visiting pretty women. A month ago, his CO had invited Jack to join him for dinner in the big Spanish house just outside of town, the residence of Humberto de Silva. The daughter of the house was a beautiful *mestiza* called Marites, short for Maria Theresa. She was very nice to him, and they all had a wonderful conversation. The next week, she invited him for dinner alone, and he came. After dinner, they went out on the patio for some fresh air, and she had kissed him. For some reason, Jack was not moved by the kiss, but he did promise to call again sometime soon.

But he got caught up in the troop training at the camp and had not seen Marites again. That was different. Now there was somebody he would very much like to see, but he was uncertain exactly how to go about it. He had better ask someone how to do this.

The first person he decided to ask was Teban the singing cook. Jack was the army recruiting officer one morning when an overweight man stood next in line. When Jack looked up from his desk, Teban smiled.

"I can cook," Teban had said.

"Have a seat until I can ask if we need another cook." Jack suppressed the urge to sigh. He was busy, and the applicant in front of him was a bit overweight to be a soldier, but he had hopeful, gentle eyes, and Jack found himself wanting to help this person.

The camp could use an assistant cook, and Teban was in. Later on, Jack found out that Teban had come looking for a job several times. Teban once farmed a plot of land inherited from his parents. It had been enough, and he was a happily married man who liked to sing with his wife. Then his wife delivered their firstborn. The midwife had said there was a problem, so the wife was rushed to the hospital. Both the wife and the baby died. Teban pawned his farm to pay the hospital bill, but later he lost the farm too. He was in dire straits and grieving when, on an inspiration, he started applying as a cook at the camp. Cooking was something Teban liked to do, and after getting a job that he liked, he started to sing again. He always gave a heaping serving to Jack at the food line, to Jack's embarrassment.

Jack hovered around the mess hall after supper, waiting for the soldiers to leave. Teban was usually the last one cleaning up. When it was clear, Jack went toward the kitchen and sat on a stool. Teban looked up and waited.

"Sir?"

"Teban, what are ladies here like?"

"Huh? They're nice."

"How do you meet ladies around here?" Jack asked.

"Oh! At parties, in church, in the market," Teban replied.

"What happens after I've met somebody I like?" Jack persisted.

"Have you been introduced, sir?"

"Yes!" Jack was getting impatient.

"It's important to be introduced by proper people, and the family has to approve," Teban said.

"Teban, I want to court a particular lady," he finally said.

Teban burst out laughing. Jack was acutely embarrassed and glared at the cook. He looked around and saw a Filipino private.

"Out!" Jack said to the private. He turned back to Teban and glowered. "What's so funny?"

"Sir, there are rules, and it will take a long time." Teban stopped laughing and struggled to look serious.

"Try me," Jack said with his jaw jutting forward.

"You have to visit the lady in her house, with or without flowers, sir," Teban said.

"I'd like to take her out for a date," Jack replied matter-of-factly.

"There's no dating here!" Teban said.

"So how do people here get married?" Jack asked.

"That's what I said, it takes a long time—some take years and years!" Teban said.

"I don't believe you!" Jack said.

"That's the way it is here," Teban said with a shrug.

Christmas was in the air, and Jack missed his parents and sister, but getting preoccupied with Neneng blunted his homesickness. He thought of Liza with a sense of guilt, and he finally resolved to settle his feelings by writing to her.

On Christmas day, *parols* brightened every light post along Rizal Avenue, and Nativity scenes were on display in stores. The *parol*, or Christmas lantern, was the traditional décor of the season. Made of finely chiseled bamboo sticks crafted into the shape of a star, globe, or something more ornate, the framework would be covered with colored craft paper with a light bulb placed inside. The *parol* would take the color of the craft paper when it was lighted. Filipinos took pride in making not only bigger ones, but also the most beautiful.

There was much joy in the streets as groups of young people visited with each other and paid respects to their elder relatives and godparents.

In the plaza, decorative streamers cascading from the stage roof to the electric posts surrounding the plaza, gave the appearance of an open fan. Two huge *parols* were on center stage, and *parols* of different motifs hung on every post.

The American band from the camp was putting on a show at the plaza. The patriotic brass band played the John Philip Sousa marches so well that the plaza was filled early with eager townsfolk. Groups of young people arrived with friends, relatives, and even babies.

Jack saw Neneng listening to the music with a group of her cousins. Neneng was at the center of the group, wearing a red and white printed dress with puffed sleeves. Jack was a little dismayed that she looked quite young. A cousin was holding a baby, and it seemed like they took turns as the baby was chubby. Neneng was next as she held the baby and rocked him with the music. Another cousin took the baby's hand and swayed with the rhythm.

She looks so juvenile. Jack hesitated. *Would she be right for me?*

He missed his family this Christmas, but somehow seeing Neneng with her cousins was enough. He strode toward them and pretended to enjoy the band with her group. She kept her distance, but he could at least explain the compositions and hear some shy answers from her.

"Hello!" he said.

"Hello!" she answered back without looking at him.

"This is the 'Hands Across the Sea,'" he said as if talking to himself. "Do you know about the composer, John Philip Sousa?"

She shook her head but continued to sway slightly with the rhythm.

He came closer, then suddenly he noticed the fragrance coming from the flower on her hair. "What's this flower?" he could not help asking.

She looked up startled, then blushed, but somehow said, "Sampaguita."

Jack blushed too, realizing he was a little too close.

"Oh! I was talking about John Philip Souza," he said, trying to get back on track. "He was the leader of the U.S. Marine Band, and he composed these marches."

"I see," she answered as a new march was being played.

"This is 'The Liberty Bell,'" he said.

"Thank you!" she answered.

Is this all she is going to say? he thought. *Never mind.* He deliberately came closer and offered to take the baby cousin from her hands.

As he took the baby, their hands touched, and he felt her shrink back. On the other hand, he felt the electricity and was elated at the touch. He stayed with them, pretending to just be friendly. He spoke with the cousins but stood near her. He felt happy.

The group of cousins walked home afterward. Jack wished he had not come in his jeep!

He was determined to see her the next day. He bought a bunch of flowers and parked his jeep in front of the Mendez Pharmacy. The house faced east, and on its left side was a partially roofed space where their car was parked. The car was on a cemented drive, but around it on the partially shaded entryway there were a lot of flowering plants, mostly orchids and bougainvilleas. There was a smaller gate for the path leading to the staircase and a bigger gate for the car.

Jack let himself in through the open smaller gate and tried to stay calm, suppressing the urge to take the stairs two at a time. He knocked at the door and was surprised to see an old lady open the door. The old lady was surprised too.

"I'm here to visit Neneng," he blurted out.

"Claring!" she called instead of answering him, but she looked at him curiously and remained where she stood.

The mother came out of the kitchen. "Hello, Lieutenant!" she said, looking surprised.

"Good afternoon, Mrs. Mendez, I've come to visit Neneng."

She looked taken aback, then said, "I'm sorry, Lieutenant, but not yet. She cannot receive visitors until she's eighteen."

Jack was almost too shocked to speak.

Mrs. Mendez also hesitated for a moment; then she spoke gently, "I'll give her the flowers, but she doesn't turn eighteen until February. After that, you may visit her." She took the flowers and smiled. "Thank you!" she added.

Jack could not imagine how he got back to the camp, he could hardly speak.

That evening, Teban saw Jack looking despondent as he ate quietly. Teban sought the Mendez's maid at the market the next day and found out about Jack's embarrassment. He put in a good word for Jack and resolved to be more helpful.

Three days later, Teban approached Jack.

"Excuse me sir, I have some information."

Jack looked at Teban and groaned.

"Sir, I talked to Juling, the Mendez's maid and put in a good word for you. Miss Mendez will go back to college in Manila after January six, the Feast of the Three Kings. While she is here, she helps in decorating the altar for the feasts, and she has lessons with the piano teacher. Sometimes they have a picnic by the river, and sometimes she takes a walk with her cousins."

"Thank you," Jack said, his spirits not lifting.

"I have her address in Manila, if you want to write her," Teban finished.

Suddenly, Jack was all smiles.

For the next couple of days, Jack tried to hang around where he might be able to see her. If she ever glanced toward him, he would wave, but she only smiled and kept her head down without waving back.

The Feast of the Three Kings fell on a Monday. Jack was glad that the CO decided to call it a holiday, for he wanted to see Neneng. Jack arrived on his jeep as their car was being loaded. He parked behind Dr. Mendez's black Ford as the father was placing a large suitcase in the trunk.

"Good morning, sir," Jack greeted the father first.

"Good morning, Lieutenant," the father said, straightening up after placing the suitcase.

"Please call me Jack, sir," Jack said.

"Jack it is then," the father said and shook his hand.

Jack smiled and turned to Neneng, who was holding a smaller bag in her hand. "Hello! May I help you?" he said.

She smiled and nodded. Without waiting for a reply, he lifted the bag from her hands. Their hands touched as he did so, but she did not shrink away this time.

"Have a safe trip!" he said, looking closely at her and willing her to look at him.

"Thank you!" she said and smiled.

The mother came, and the family got in the car. Jack stood beside his jeep and waved good-bye. The family waved back.

Jack wrote to her every week, but there was no answer. When February came, he sent flowers for her birthday and was thrilled that he could now start visiting her.

Finally, he received a brief note:

Dear Lieutenant Stewart,

Thank you for the flowers. It is not proper for me to write.

—Victoria Mendez

I've had it! he muttered to himself, flabbergasted.

So he went on with his work, keenly following the news of the war in Europe, but now and then he would sigh—he was still thinking about her. *The school year ends in mid-March*, Jack thought as he counted the days until she could be home again.

III

On March 24 she arrived.

Jack could hardly wait to visit her and consulted Teban.

"Sir, tomorrow at 1:30 PM would be fine," Teban pronounced with a nod.

"Why?" Jack was irritated at another rule.

"Sir, she has to put things away when she arrives, then she rests. The next day, sometime after lunch is OK."

Jack realized there was some logic to the rules sometimes, and he followed Teban's instructions. Jack arrived as instructed with a bunch of roses.

Her mother welcomed him. "Hello, Jack, it's nice to see you."

"Good afternoon, Mrs. Mendez," Jack said with a grin.

He was ushered through the hallway into a large room, where the dining and living room areas were not separated by a wall. The intricately carved wood furniture was livened up with bright cushions that gave the room a warm, cozy feeling. Close to the window facing the street was a higher table with a pair of chairs on each side.

"Where would you like to sit? I'll call Neneng," Mrs. Mendez asked as she moved toward a door. Jack hesitated only a moment then took a chair near the window.

"Neneng, you have a visitor!" Mrs. Mendez said, gently knocking at Neneng's door. Without waiting for a response, she went toward the kitchen.

From where he was, Jack could see the street below with the passing *calesas* and a few cars. Across the street, pedestrians walked on the sidewalk in front of the Government Office. He noticed that this was an advantageous position for watching parades and other events, and that was why the houses in the avenue were prime locations. The window panels were made of capiz shell and wood mullion, while printed cloth curtains framed the window from the sides. The windows were open all the way to welcome the gentle breeze that came now and then and added to the charm of the room.

There were four bedrooms that opened into the living area, and Neneng's was the one on the right, facing the street. The hallway also led to the kitchen and bathroom. A console piano and a china cabinet were set against the wall; hanging above it were paintings and family pictures.

Jack made mental notes of all this as part of his self-discipline in awareness. He figured out that like most houses, this one had two storys, but this house was bigger and had cement outer walls.

He had just sat down when he realized he could not account for a rocking chair just off the dining area, adjacent to a small table. Then the old lady came out.

Jack got up quickly. "Good afternoon," he said.

"Good afternoon," she answered and sat on the rocking chair. She adjusted her eyeglasses and started reading the newspaper on the table.

Is that lady just going to sit there? Jack thought.

Neneng came out of her room wearing a pink dress. She wore no makeup, and instead of bangs, her hair was parted on one side. She walked to the chair opposite him, and then she finally looked up with a shy smile.

"Hello!" he said, getting up and giving her the roses.

"Hello!" she said, adding, "Thank you!"

She took the roses to the kitchen and reappeared with them in a vase that she placed on the dining table. She came back with a smile and sat down across from him.

Jack was pleased. He was about to reach for her hand when he heard something.

"Ahem! Ahem!" grunted the old lady.

He was hoping she had fallen asleep!

"Can we go for a walk?" he ventured. "I don't want to disturb her."

"My grandmother is supposed to be here." She suppressed her giggle with a smile.

He was surprised; next, he heard a knock on the door.

"Good afternoon to you too, Mr. Mifune," Mrs. Mendez answered as quickly as she opened the door.

"Please call me Yoshiro," the approaching visitor said.

Yoshiro Mifune was tall, though slightly shorter than Jack, well-built, and looked nicely dressed in a white shirt and dark pants.

Mrs. Mendez nodded as she gently touched her daughter's shoulder and took the flowers he was carrying.

"I'll put these in a vase," she said and left.

"Thank you!" Neneng said.

Jack and Yoshiro acknowledged they had met before as Yoshiro took the seat beside Jack. Jack cleared his throat several times, trying to hide his consternation.

They started talking first about safe topics.

"It certainly is getting warmer by the day," Jack said.

"This is our dry season," Neneng answered.

"This year, the weather has been good for the rice harvest here and also in Japan," Yoshiro started. "Rice is very important in Japan. To us, rice is not just food. Our elders believed that in every grain there is a god, so we have to eat all the rice. It is precious, it must be respected, and it should not be trampled on. We even have festivals that celebrate the planting season. We use more of the white, round, sticky rice; but here, I'm learning to like the longer grain that is not so sticky. I've tried the brown rice, but not the black or red kind."

Neneng nodded as though respecting Yoshiro's background.

"I've heard that my cousins in Mindanao have tried the red variety that grows there. I haven't tried it myself," she said.

"I saw the schoolchildren dance the 'Planting Rice' in one of the program presentations recently, then another dance simulated the winnowing of rice. It certainly seems to be a big part of life around here," Jack said.

He was glad, however, when Neneng explained about the water buffalo pulling the plow.

Don't tell me I have to read up for this, Jack thought.

He changed the topic to Filipino customs because he wanted to learn more about them; besides, he wanted to hear what Neneng had to say rather than let Yoshiro dominate the conversation with his knowledge of rice varieties. He was surprised by how articulate Neneng was and how much she knew about everything around her.

So she's smart under that façade of shyness, he thought.

The maid served them tea and some pastry, and then she came back to remove the tray. Still the two men doggedly persisted with their small talk, neither willing to let the other outlast him. Neither would give in until Mrs. Mendez finally came back at five o'clock.

"Gentlemen, we will see you again, but right now, I need my daughter to help me in the kitchen," she said.

Jack said little to Yoshiro as they both left. He had a headache. *What if Yoshiro visits every day when I can't because of my work?* he thought. When he got back to camp, he looked around for Teban.

"She will have many suitors, sir! I should have told you that. I heard there will be a *harana* tomorrow evening, but whoever does the *harana* can only see her. They don't have much chance to talk," Teban said.

"What *harana?*" Jack said.

"Sir, a *harana* is in the evening if you cannot visit during the day. A suitor comes alone or with some friends who can sing, and they serenade the lady in front of her window. Afterward, the mother will let them come in and serve drinks, then they leave," Teban said.

I can't believe this! There's another custom I haven't heard about. There's no way I can do a serenade, Jack thought.

That evening, the serenade was composed of four men. The suitor was Jose, a young man studying to be a teacher. Somebody else sang the poignant words of the *kundiman,* the songs of love and suffering that were so much part of their way of life.

> *Ako'y anak nang dalita*
> *na tiguib nang luha,*
> *at nariritong humihibik*
> *na bigyan nang awa ...*

(I am a poor son, full of sorrow, here I come to plead for your mercy)

Jack had a busy day and was unable to visit, so he watched from his jeep that evening and only half understood the song. He was starting to realize what disadvantage he was facing.

As soon as he got the chance, he asked Teban about the songs.

"They are called *kundiman*, sir," Teban started. "These are songs about love, some happy, some sad." Then Teban began to sing. "*Hanggang sa hukay, iibiguin ka hirang.*"

Jack was surprised how well Teban could sing.

"What does that mean?" Jack asked.

"Until my grave, or like, until I die. It means I will love you for as long as I live. That's my favorite with my wife." Then Teban sat down and wiped a tear.

Jack patted Teban's shoulder and left quietly.

"I heard the *kundiman* during the *harana*," Jack mentioned to Neneng on his next visit. He was the only suitor this time.

"It's a beautiful song about love. It affects everyone, rich or poor; sometimes the songs are happy, but most are sad," Neneng replied thoughtfully.

Jack found himself listening for the songs, trying to understand them, and he identified his feelings with it. He visited Neneng as often as he could, without frills. By now, he knew that the proper visiting hours were from early afternoon until about five o'clock. The serious suitors came on Sunday afternoon, as though declaring that their free time was hers. Visiting on weekdays was also done, but the suitor had to be careful not to wear out his welcome.

Jack wondered if she could tell the suitors apart; he could only remember Jose because of his *harana*. She had quite a number of Filipino suitors aside from him and Yoshiro. Every now and then, all the suitors would be seated in the living room area making small talk. The Filipinos would inadvertently fall into talking in Tagalog, but Neneng would explain what they were saying to him and Yoshiro and then steer the talk back to English. Jack admired her sense of fair play and her skill at keeping the men in order. On days when Jack was by himself, he told her about his family.

"I have a younger sister in Virginia, most of the men in our family either manage the plantation or go to the military," he said.

"My father and grandfather are doctors, I want to be a doctor too," she responded.

Jack was feeling hopeful, although still not certain where he stood. He also told her about his younger sister, Penelope.

"She's a good girl, she's spoiled, and she knows she's beautiful."

"I envy people with brothers and sisters; it's not the same as having cousins. My mother is my best friend," she answered.

Jack received word that his father had just arrived on assignment to the Philippines, so Jack visited him in Manila in early April. Jack was eager to exchange notes about the world turmoil and about his work with his dad. Jack was glad to hear that things were fine back home. He received from Penelope a set of handkerchiefs on which she had embroidered his initials, and she also sent him a cryptic letter that his letters were received.

When he came back to Cabanatuan, it was like an alien place. April was the hottest month, and it was Holy Week. The officers and the trainees were mostly grouchy. By Wednesday, the singing of the *Pasion* startled the grunts, who loudly complained.

"What is going on here, Teban?" Jack asked that evening.

"Sir, the *Pasion* is about Jesus Christ's passion when he died for us on the cross. It is the same tune every paragraph. We sing it during Holy Week, like tomorrow they will sing what happened on Holy Thursday in the bible. The Gamez family has a new loudspeaker and invited their cousin from Pampanga, who sings the *Pasion*. When the de Leons made their singing louder on the speaker, the Gamezes made theirs louder still."

By Thursday, the *Pasion* was being blared full blast by the loudspeakers, and the recruits did not show up. Jack went back to the administrative building to work on some reports. He saluted Colonel Dillon, who was on the way out.

"I should have just made this a holiday too. The recruits are observing this as a holiday," Dillon said, shaking his head.

Then it became quiet. From Thursday afternoon to Good Friday, the town was eerily quiet. Fourteen altars were located along the Avenida that were 'Stations' in the 'Way of the Cross'- the practice of commemorating Christ's passion, from the time he was condemned to death, until he was laid in the sepulcher. The priest led the Friday morning 'Way of the Cross' which was attended by many. People walked back and forth to the church; there were no vehicles on the road. Throughout the processions, the church services, and praying the Way of the Cross, the townspeople seemed genuinely intent on contemplation and prayer.

Jack watched the evening 'Via Dolorosa' procession go by and was surprised with the people's religious fervor. He realized that in spite of their history of being oppressed, Filipinos practiced their religion as a way of life; and Jack was humbled.

By Saturday, there was some activity in the city, so Jack hopped on his jeep after noon to visit Neneng. She was standing in front of their pharmacy with several baskets of calla lilies and other flowers on the floor. Mrs. Mendez came out of the pharmacy shaking her head.

Jack parked his jeep and asked, "Can I help?"

"We are still waiting for Dr. Mendez to be free and take us with these flowers to decorate the church," she answered.

"I can bring you there instead, if you like," Jack offered.

"That would be a great help. Thank you, Jack," Mrs. Mendez answered and signaled Juling from inside the Pharmacy.

They loaded the flowers into the jeep, and the two ladies sat in the front seats with Jack. He was glad to have Neneng sit between him and Mrs. Mendez since the jeep was full. After helping the ladies unload the flowers, Jack was about to leave them at their work when Mrs. Mendez invited him to their home for Easter lunch.

The church bells peeling on Easter brought joyful anticipation to Jack, and he was not disappointed. Aside from him, the other guests were the two priests: Fathers Gabriel and Ramos. Jack tasted the Chinese ham he had heard about, and he liked the unusual sweetish-salty taste.

"The church seems much fuller than I expected, maybe the people are worried of the coming war," Father Gabriel commented. "I'm afraid the Japanese are quite strong in Asia."

"The Americans will protect us, we are ready. What do you think, Jack?" Dr. Mendez said.

"War is imminent. Our troop training here is going well, but apparently not in other regions. All in all, it is still less than the numbers MacArthur would like."

"Let's talk about happier things, it's Easter," Father Ramos said. "Mrs. Mendez promised to give us the rest of the Chinese ham, and that's all I can think of."

The men laughed and then moved to the living room to smoke their cigarettes. Jack glanced at the ladies supervising the coffee and desserts, while he listened to Father Gabriel talking about some peasant discontents. Jack observed that Father Gabriel was the cerebral type with strong convictions, and Father Ramos was more happy-go-lucky and easy to get along with.

Later on, Jack dropped off the priests at their convent. Even if he did not have time alone with Neneng, he had begun to feel accepted and more comfortable. He was whistling when he drove back to camp.

IV

When May came, Jack was glad of the pleasant surprises. It was cooler, fruits and flowers were in abundance, and there was so much going on.

May was a time for fiestas. Almost every week, or several times a week, there was a fiesta in one town or another. The whole town would be in celebration. The day would start with a Mass at the church, followed by a procession for their patron saint; then townspeople would hurry home to welcome guests from near or far. Every home, no matter how humble, would welcome guests they did not even really know, and feed them. Invitations were not needed. The big meal was usually a buffet lunch without much conversation, for people just ate.

After lunch, the younger people spilled over to the streets, excited to visit with friends and meet town visitors; the younger population who were in college would usually be home with a lot of invited friends.

By afternoon, there would be a program at the plaza, preceded by fireworks. If no program was scheduled, then there would be an amateur hour where people entered a singing contest. The unpromising singers would be eliminated by the bong of a bell struck by the judge when the contestant was out of tune. After weaning the undesirables, the better singers would be asked to sing again for placement in the top. There were money prizes with corresponding value.

The town fiesta of Santa Monica was May 4. Neneng was busy practicing for a dance presentation for the eve of the fiesta. Jack watched the rehearsal and the performance at the auditorium of the school. He saw she had a male partner who was also a suitor.

Jose again! Jack thought.

The number was called *"Panuelo Dance,"* and Jack looked closely whether she would indicate a preference for her partner, but apparently she would not. He tried to catch her eye, but he realized she was too shy to look at anybody in particular in the crowd.

We are all in the same boat, he observed dryly.

He watched her graceful dance and imagined her in his arms, but the dance ended with her just giving him a glimpse, then she hurried away.

On St. Monica's feast, the church was very full with a lot of out-of-town visitors. The CO had declared a holiday. A maid from the de Silvas had arrived the day before with a note for Jack. It was an invitation for a fiesta luncheon from Marites. He had quickly apologized that he already had another commitment.

Jack was going over to the Mendez's house for lunch. The pharmacy was closed, but groups of people arrived continuously via the side entrance to the house. In the garden by the garage, every available space was lined with different kinds of chairs: plain wood, wire and plywood, benches, etc. Some people were still chatting, but most were already eating. Upstairs, the living room/dining area was lined with chairs all along the walls, and people sat with full plates on their laps, their drinks in glasses on the floor.

Neneng ushered Jack to the buffet table, but she was too busy with the guests.

Jack was getting used to these feasts. He took some *lechon,* the roast pork that was the centerpiece of each big celebration. Jack took some meat with a spoonful of *sarsa,* along with some reddish brown skin that he was sure would be crispy. He next spooned some rice into his plate, then decided that he would try a little of the *escabetse, adobo, morcon,* and the noodle that was called *pansit.*

Gotta watch it! Jack thought, realizing that he had been eating more in this country than back home. Surprisingly, he had not gained weight, perhaps because of the hot weather, or just his work. Nevertheless, he resolved not to overstuff his plate to an embarrassing degree.

He talked with Neneng's cousins, who lived next door. Their mother was Pacing, the youngest sister of Dr. Mendez. Jack was more relaxed as he conversed with Andong and Linda, for they were more carefree and less reserved. Linda was older, and Andong was Neneng's age. Both were black haired and short, as their father Fermin and their mother Pacing were also short in stature. Sometimes they asked for his advice; sometimes they let him tell them about America. They never talked about anything serious before, until now.

"I'm going to finish engineering next school year," Andong said.

"I'll help Mama with her sewing this year, instead of finishing my teaching degree," Linda said.

"I thought you were hurrying to finish?" Jack asked, knowing this was different from what he heard last.

"My bro in college will go to the army, but he will finish his degree first so he can become an officer," Andong explained. "His father is a colonel, and that's his advice. Linda here is thinking whether she should go to pharmacy instead since the Mendez Pharmacy has no Mendez left if Neneng becomes a doctor."

"That's a good plan," Jack said, wondering how the coming war would affect it.

"Tell me if I should enter the army now," Andong asked.

"I don't know. War is imminent, and it will be hard on everybody. You're still young, better ask your father," Jack said, and sympathizing with Andong, he patted his shoulder.

Andong nodded. They seemed agreed to drop the topic, and Andong went for another helping of *leche plan*. After that, he asked. "Would you like to come with us and watch the amateur hour at the plaza? Neneng is still busy."

"I think I'd better work on some report instead, thanks," Jack said and went over to Neneng and Mrs. Mendez to say thanks and bid good-bye.

After the town fiesta, Neneng and some friends taught catechism every afternoon of the week in church. There was no private school in town. The teachers learned most of what they taught from the private Catholic schools they went to in Manila. The more motivated ones did their own reading, aside from whatever family guidance and tradition they had.

Their students were children of different ages, boys and girls. The teachers divided the students by age groups and accordingly taught the equivalent of four grade levels. A few were well dressed with shoes on; but most arrived in whatever clothes they happen to be wearing, and their feet were clad in slippers. They would come to church in the afternoon bringing flowers placed in either tin cans or bottles with water. The flowers were usually from their own garden.

The teachers herded their students to four sections of pews and usually started with a prayer. The lesson came next, mostly an abridgement of Christian doctrine given as a series, the level of explanation depending on the grade level being taught. After the lesson, the children would line up and have a procession, bringing their flowers to the statue of the Blessed Mother.

They would sing hymns and leave their flower offerings at the foot of the statue. This offering of flowers was called the Flores de Mayo (Flowers of May).

The last part was often what the children really liked most. They would be made to line up on their way out and be given some candy by their teachers. As though this was the focal point of the afternoon, children would then go on to play at the church plaza, or they would go home and play some more.

Since Jack could visit on weekdays when his work was done early, he found out one day that Neneng was still in church doing the Flores de Mayo. He took the opportunity to help out and gave handfuls of candy to the delighted children.

"The candy ran out!" Lourdes, one of the catechism teachers, told Neneng reproachfully.

Neneng could not help but snicker. Jack was looking around flabbergasted. He had been too generous in giving the children handfuls of candy—no wonder they lined up in front of him!

"I'll buy candies for tomorrow!" he volunteered.

He bought several bagfuls and donated it. The catechists laughed at his consternation, but the children decidedly went to his line whenever he showed up.

Toward the end of May, usually the last Saturday of the month, most towns would celebrate the Santacruzan. A maiden would be chosen, either for her beauty or in a money contest, and she was crowned the Maria Elena. This came from the Catholic tradition of about 300 AD when Emperor Constantine's mother, Helene, found the Holy Cross on which Jesus Christ was crucified. The Maria Elena would be crowned queen and her escort was called Constantine.

As the month drew to a close, a prominent councilman asked the CO if Jack could be his daughter's escort as Maria Elena. The CO said yes. Reporting for the procession in his dress uniform, Jack was embarrassed to see that he had to escort Marites, the Spanish mestiza he had been avoiding.

She had a reputation for being a flirt, and Jack felt she had set her cap for him. Trying to be a good escort without giving her ideas would not be easy. Moreover, Jack worried about what Neneng would think.

Jack stood ramrod straight beside Marites throughout the procession, oblivious of the biblical personages preceding the float, hardly understanding the repetitive singing of the *"Dios te salve, Maria."*

The procession officially ended as the Maria Elena and Constantine entered the church. The children, however, did not bother to go inside. They ran straight for the church plaza, eager for the games to begin.

There in the center was the *pabitin*—a large square of interlaced bamboo sticks from which hung toys and candy treats. The center of this was connected to a rope running from the top pole to the ground, so it could be raised up and down to bait the children.

When the *pabitin* was lowered, the children grabbed the dangling goodies, only to be frustrated as the *pabitin* was raised. Up and down the *pabitin* went, and the children scrambled beneath it to grab as much as they could. Some got hurt, others fought over the treats, but most just enjoyed the treats and fun.

Climbing a greased, long bamboo pole was next. This was usually a boy's game. So many children tried to climb it only to slide down after reaching a certain height. When a skinny, unkempt boy started, people quietly watched as though rooting for him. He did succeed— grasping the pouch from the top that contained money—and tears fell from his cheeks as he slowly climbed down. Unable to see clearly, he fell from a low height. Neneng was quickly there to help him, for she recognized him as the son of a poor lady who was half deranged.

"Thank you!" he said, and he ran off.

Neneng let him go, knowing he had not been in the other games for he was dirty and unkempt.

The sack race had the usual amount of mishaps: several kids collided trying to hop fast toward the finish line. Neneng was there quickly, checking their bruises, helping them find slippers, and giving each a candy to make them feel better.

The adults watching were having as much fun as the children competing for the prizes. In the middle of the noise and laughter was Neneng, preparing one contestant after another, distributing prices, picking up fallen children.

Jack took Marites home in his jeep. He realized that he enjoyed doing things with Neneng, and he would like to help out with the games and prizes. Her protective kindness to the little children touched his heart, and he looked forward to laughing with her over little silly things that children do. Instead, he had to take Marites home first. He did not quite know how to say it, so he drove rather fast and helped her come down the jeep.

"Will you come in, Jack?" she asked.

"I'm going right back to help Neneng, I'm sorry. Thanks anyway," he said and quickly left.

He went right back to the church plaza, uniform and all, and waded through the milieu of noisy children. He gave Neneng a hand distributing candies, even to some children who had already received some. The children already knew he gave more, so they flocked to him.

He glanced at Neneng, who seemed a little subdued.

Is she jealous? he thought.

He did not have a chance to speak to her. She and her cousins put away all the props afterward, and they walked home.

She's avoiding me, he thought, worried that she would be going back to Manila soon.

He visited her that Sunday, but he could not be alone with her.

The next day, hungry and tired from a training exercise, he took a quick shower, ate a chocolate bar, and visited her. This warm afternoon, her cousins were gone and her Grandma was snoring in the rocking chair. Almost impatient to start talking to her, he chewed on the dumpling that the maid had put out for him.

She suddenly looked up.

"There's a paper at the bottom!" she said.

"What?" he mumbled between bites.

"There's a paper at the bottom of the *siopao!*" she repeated and looked concerned.

He looked blankly at her as she suppressed a giggle. She reached for the other dumpling in front of him and turned it upside down to show the square paper at the bottom.

At that instant, he grabbed her hand and did not let go even when she pulled away. She looked at him, close to panic. Instead, he leaned forward and held her hand to his chest.

"Let go," she said.

"I love you," he said, gazing at her. "Tell me you love me too."

"Jack, please!" she pleaded.

"Say you love me," he countered.

She was about to cry, so he finally let her go. Thank God Grandma kept snoring.

He was afraid she might leave, so he sat down and tried to explain.

"I had nothing to do with being an escort, the CO ordered me, and I didn't even know what was supposed to happen."

She looked like she was pouting. He got up and walked toward her.

"No!" she said, startled.

But he had already pulled her close to him. She gave him a shove, but he disregarded it and held her close.

"Jack!" she said in panic.

Suddenly, he heard Mrs. Mendez greeting Yoshiro.

Not again! Jack thought as he went back to his chair.

For the rest of the afternoon, Jack doggedly stayed until he and Yoshiro were shooed away by Mrs. Mendez once more. Jack left feeling anxious, knowing Neneng would be going back to school soon.

The news that some high officers were coming for a visit was met with enthusiasm. People in the town were eager to show their best. There was going to be a reception, a banquet, and before that, a program of dances and songs.

To keep civilians from wandering deep in the army compound, a makeshift stage and an outdoor banquet pavilion were hastily constructed close to the camp administration building, which was the largest building close to the gate.

Neneng was with her group of friends practicing a different dance, called the *La Jota Balunguena*.

Jack watched them practice while he helped bring in chairs for the audience. When they finished the practice, he saw she was alone arranging some props behind the stage. As she smiled shyly at him, he approached her and held her by the waist.

"I love you," he said.

"Jack!" was all she could say, but she did not push him away.

"Darling!" he said, catching his breath.

Suddenly, a loud clanging sound startled everyone. Somebody had dropped the gong.

Neneng broke loose. "You'd better go," she said, and she glanced back as she hurried over to help a hapless male dancer in a half-naked costume.

V

The evening was electric with anticipation. The honored guests included Jack's parents, but he had refrained from telling Neneng this. He was going to surprise her! The important people in town were all going to come. They were advised to wear "national dress."

The *barong tagalog* was the national dress, as proclaimed by President Quezon. Traditionally made out of pineapple fibers, the cream-colored cloth was delicate and gossamer-like. For this reason, the *barong* was worn over a sleeved, white undershirt.

Long ago, the Indios (the Spanish name for the natives) were made to wear something that signified their conquered status. To ensure there were no weapons or stolen goods, the authorities required that they could see through the shirts: it could not be tucked in, and there could be no pockets. In time, however, the Filipinos started decorating the front with embroidery, and the expensive ones became status symbols. It became the dress code for diplomatic and social functions.

The women used the *pina* cloth for a gown with butterfly sleeves and a rather low-cut neckline—this was the mestiza dress.

The silent contest for beautiful gowns was on again. Rumors and intrigue caused discord among the vain matrons. Tan Commercial store had sold out its pina cloth last fiesta; but Pacing, Carlos's sister, had bought three pieces from Pasig, which were all sold out before Mrs. de Silva's maid arrived. Rebecca de Silva had to send her maid all the way to Pasig, the province known for clothing materials and embroidered specialties. Half the town made silent bets that the seamstress would not have enough time to sew it.

The fireworks started thirty minutes before the program. A clear, moonlit sky magnified the bright silhouette of streaking lights bursting with a flash of varied colors. The noise from the fireworks mingled with the excited voices of guests arriving in the well-lit program pavilion.

The ushers seated all guests on time; then the lights went off. A hush fell on the audience as a light shone on the band. The American national anthem was played, followed by the Philippine hymn.

The presentation was like a chronology of Philippine culture, starting with the Igorot Dance. For the Spanish period, Marites de Silva was eager to perform her flamenco dance, and she prevailed. The fiery performance, the swishing of her skirt, and the click of her castanets left a lot of men agape with admiration.

Jack Stewart, however, was oblivious. He kept looking at the program, awaiting the La Jota Batanguena, in which Neneng was going to dance.

For this dance, the ladies wore the Maria Clara dress, popularized long ago and named after the love interest of Jose Rizal, the Philippine national hero. It had a white loose top with long bell-shaped sleeves, over which a gossamer-like embroidered shawl was pinned in front. The long skirt featured alternate white and black stripes running vertically.

Jack sat at the row for junior officers, right behind his parents. He was so proud of Neneng, and he gazed at her lovingly. This time, when their eyes met, she did not quickly look away.

Jack was ready to jump as soon as the program was over—he quickly sought out Neneng.

"I'll be right back for dinner," he said without looking at his parents.

"Let's get some fresh air for a minute, just a little while before dinner starts," Jack said to Neneng and caught her hand.

Surprisingly, she let him lead her, even if she shook off his hold on her hand. "There are people," she said softly.

He led her to an arbor a distance from the side entrance. Even before they could reach it, he took her in his arms and kissed her. She seemed to faint at first, but soon she answered his ardent kiss and embraced him back.

"My darling!" Jack said happily.

The dinner gong was loud, and it sounded repeatedly, as though prodding the laggards to come to the table.

If only time could stand still, Jack thought, unable to fight the ringing noise. "I'm going to introduce you to my parents, they're here," he said. He grabbed Neneng's hand and led her back.

She gently withdrew her hand as they entered the pavilion.

The makeshift pavilion was a simple structure with a galvanized iron roof and strong posts on all corners, but it looked very festive. The sides were open, but streamers and garlands of flowers looped around the ceiling and all over the sides. Torches had been lighted all around it like a tropical paradise. The fragrance from the flowers wafted with the cool evening breeze as it blew the streamers into a constant dance festooned with lights. Inside, the guests and the officers mingled before dinner, chattering and laughing, a beautifully dressed array of the well-to-do and the intelligent.

Clara Mendez looked regal in her mestiza dress, her complexion showcased in the traditional low cut dress that also displayed her shoulder. The pina material of her gown was the most expensive version, and the all-over embroidery added to the cost. She had looked wistfully at the gown in Manila last year. She smiled and decided it was too expensive, but Carlos had seen her look and decided to buy it for her. Because she felt some guilt, she had not worn it until now. Clara readjusted the butterfly sleeves higher on her shoulder, feeling the cold breeze.

Beside her, Carlos wore his best *barong tagalog,* looking dignified and content. The intricate embroidery on the front and sleeves was elegant. He, too, shivered when the breeze blew.

Clara's hair was in a bun, and for good measure she decided to put the gold decorative hair comb called *payneta* on top of it. She had inherited the *payneta* from her mother, and this was only the second time she had worn it. Earlier, she had sensed an eager anticipation from her daughter, and as though caught in a contagion, she found herself really dressing up. She even wore the gold medallion necklace that accented her beautiful neck.

The de Silvas were across the room, and Clara just waved. She was glad that Rebecca had her new gown, but Clara could sense the dagger looks Marites had been pointing at Neneng. Clara stood erect beside her husband, a fan on her right hand, as they conversed with Mr. Quitos. A year ago, he had warned them that there might be locusts. The usually pessimistic man was always the first to call on them if there was bad news. This year, he was a happy man blessed with a bountiful harvest.

"Part of it will go to the American stockpile here in Cabanatuan," he said importantly.

Carlos Mendez nodded. "One fourth of the Fuentes and the Luna harvest go there too," he stated simply. The fear of war was in every conversation now.

Clara felt someone was watching her intently, and she turned around, one brow up, wondering. She looked up to see a man in a colonel's uniform looking at her. She paused and her eyes widened in disbelief.

"John?" she whispered.

Colonel John Stewart came forward quickly and took both her hands, to the surprise of Dr. Mendez.

"Clara, I can't believe this!"

"John!" she said again and paused, half-confused. "It's you!" She quickly recovered and turned to her husband. "Carlos, this is John Stewart. We met when we were children in Balangiga, Samar. Meet my husband, Dr. Carlos Mendez."

John Stewart seemed to hold Clara's hand a trifle longer before he released it. He shook hands with Carlos and introduced his wife. "Meet my wife, Doris."

Doris came forward with a quizzical look. "How do you do?" she said and shook hands.

Carlos introduced Colonel John and Mrs. Doris Stewart to the circle of friends around them.

"Well, we must invite them to our house, if they are old friends, Clara," Carlos said.

"Why, of course!" she answered.

"I'll be out of town tomorrow, so how about the day after, for supper?" Carlos continued.

"Excellent!" John Stewart answered. "I'll be showing Doris the town and the environs tomorrow. The next day is fine with us."

"Good!" Carlos said as they all started for their seats in the long banquet table.

There were several long banquet tables, arranged in rows. Except for the head at each table, there were no set places for the others. At each head of one table were the generals, at another, the mayor and the parish priest. At their table, the camp CO, Colonel Dillon, sat at one head and Colonel John Stewart at the other.

Jack and Neneng arrived almost breathless just as everybody was heading for their places. Their parents acknowledged them and guided each to sit with them.

The convivial chatter was only interrupted by the hushed silence of prayer before the meal. As the aroma of food wafted with the breeze, everybody sat down in anticipation of a wonderful feast.

On Colonel Stewart's right was Dr. Mendez, then Clara; Doris Stewart sat on his left, followed by Jack. Neneng sat next to her mother, farther to the right, across from Jack and his mom. Neneng looked radiant, and she half smiled at Jack when they exchanged tender glances.

Jack glanced at his dad as the latter passed off on the *lechon*. His dad did not seem to be himself. Next he saw Clara Mendez wipe a tear surreptitiously. For some reason, his dad was quiet, and he seemed to keep glancing at Mrs. Mendez.

She, on the other hand, focused her attention to the couple on Jack's left. The conversation was about the delicacies of the region, especially rice cakes.

"Yes, a lot of our rice cakes and delicacies are cooked with coconut milk; most use white sugar, others will specify brown sugar. We use a lot of sweet rice; sometimes we add root plants, or even fruits, as you will see in the *para los dos*. By using a different method of cooking, sometimes the same ingredients will turn into something else. You'll be surprised at the variations. They're all good," she explained to Mrs. Green.

"How about the banana leaves? When do you use them?" Mrs. Green asked.

"We use them for the *suman*, like the one we have here," Clara pointed, "also for the *bibingka*, tamales ..." She did not finish what she was saying.

"Oh yes, Jack has a girlfriend back home," Doris said loudly. "She wanted to get married after Jack finished at West Point, but time was so short and he had to leave for his assignment. I suspect she's been secretly planning details all this time Jack has been away."

"Mom!" Jack said and looked at Neneng.

Doris had been talking to Carlos Mendez, but her statement was said a little too loudly and clearly, and a lot of people heard her.

There was a sudden quiet at the table. Most people knew the Mendez family and they felt uncomfortable. At the other table where Marites sat with her parents, the clink of flatware falling on the floor could be heard. The American guests, however, were oblivious of the ongoing romance.

"How about the coconut leaves?" Mrs. Green asked, for she was determined to try some cooking here.

"We use them for the rice called *puso*," Mrs. Mendez said, struggling to keep the conversation going.

The rest of the dinner banquet was an agony the Mendez family endured without losing their composure.

Jack shot a pleading glance at Neneng, but she pretended to be busy eating and never glanced at him again for the rest of the dinner. Jack was fuming by the time the banquet was over.

He went to Neneng as people were leaving, but she did not look at him and just held on to her mother.

"Neneng!" he started. He caught her hand, but she just shook her head and tugged at her mother's arm so they could leave quickly.

Jack was happy to see his parents, but they had not really talked yet. They were all busy sizing each other up, asking about each other's health and exchanging news of other family, friends, and home. He had been saving his news about Neneng for last, like it was something precious.

He had written Liza six months ago to explain that he was sorry, that he had fallen in love with somebody else. When there was no answer, he had written again two months ago. He had also confided to his sister, but for him, matters of the heart were not discussed with parents.

He could not believe this was happening. Jack was worried about how to patch up this misunderstanding with Neneng. Even if he was upset with his mom, he knew she meant well, and he tried to control his frustration.

"I've already broken up with Liza," he said without preamble as soon as they reached his parent's quarters.

"Jack, you can't!" Doris said. "She's planning things!"

"I've written her twice to explain this. I'm in love with Neneng, and I'm going to marry her!" Jack said.

Doris looked at her son, bewildered.

"Jack! That's just not being done! You're not going to marry a Filipino!"

"Yes, Mom, I will," Jack said, determined.

He looked at his dad for sympathy; instead, his dad looked dazed. Frustrated, Jack left them for his barracks. He could not sleep.

Neneng did not know how she got home. She had clung to her mother's arm as tears flowed freely onto her costume. Numbed, she felt her mother ushering her to her room.

"Goodnight!" Clara said to her husband with a knowing glance.

"Goodnight!" Carlos said with a blessing after Neneng kissed his hand.

Clara followed Neneng to her room and sat with her at the edge of her bed. Neneng was crying more audibly now, uncontrollable sobs rocking her body as she gasped for air. Clara embraced her daughter.

"My dear," she said.

Neneng embraced her, and Clara tried to hold her daughter steady from the uncontrollable crying. Clara was crying too.

"My dear," Clara said again.

"Mama, I love him!" Neneng cried.

Clara let her daughter cry, stroking her hair and holding her up as Neneng's sobs came out like spasms of pain. It was a long while before the sobs finally became shorter.

Weak from her spent emotion, Neneng clung to her mother. Slowly, Clara helped Neneng get ready for bed, putting aside both their gowns. Clara had been quiet most of the time as she struggled to suppress her own emotions. Neneng sensed this and looked at her with a question.

"There is something from my past I'll tell you more about at another time," Clara said. "John Stewart and I were childhood friends in Balangiga. We grew up planning to get married, but we were parted. Sometimes things don't turn up like we hope. Pray to God for strength that your wound would heal."

Clara held Neneng's chin, and only then did Neneng see the pain in those eyes.

"Let's get some sleep." Clara embraced her daughter and reluctantly left the room.

VI

Clara went to her bedroom and heard Carlos's intermittent snoring. She lay on her side of the bed and closed her eyes, wanting to sleep quickly and ward off the memories, but they came unbidden as vividly as if it was only yesterday.

She was eight years old, still dressed in her Sunday clothes, running in the direction of the nearby American garrison. They were playing tag, and the other children were scattered in different directions to avoid being tagged by her cousin Dolfo. Suddenly, she saw a tall American boy watching them. Startled, she tripped and fell. He was immediately beside her and carried her toward the shade of the mango tree.

"I'm alright!" she said, embarrassed at being carried like a cripple by a stranger.

He looked closely at her ankle. "I suppose you're OK! I'm John. Colonel Stewart's my dad," he said proudly. "We're visiting the troops here."

"Ah … ah … My name is Clara Luna, and my father is the camp doctor," she said.

The other children crowded around them and introduced themselves.

"I'm Diego," her older brother said.

"I'm Dolfo," her older cousin said.

Tonyo, Paco, Anita, and Tomas introduced themselves too.

John surprised them by remembering most names; he only missed Tomas. John did not play tag with them, but later on, when Dolfo challenged him to a wrestle, John won. Later on, they played chess, and Clara got bored so she went upstairs to their house and helped her mother in the kitchen.

The family lived on the second story of a wooden house; the first floor was rented by a Chinese retail store. There was a staircase in front and another staircase in the back that led directly to the yard where the children played.

That evening, John and his dad, Colonel Paul Stewart, joined the family of Manuel and Faustina Luna for supper. Dr. Luna had invited the colonel.

John was twelve years old. His mother had died in a car accident when he was nine, and from then on, his father took John with him during summer vacations. His father's older sister took care of John during the school year. They were from Virginia. Some of the family took care of the plantation, others went to the military. John was going to the military.

"What does Clara call you?" John asked Diego with a puzzled look during supper.

"I'm her Kuya, meaning older brother. It's her sign of respect, since I'm two years older. She's supposed to obey me, and I'm supposed to protect her," Diego answered seriously.

The parents smiled, and Clara nodded.

The next day and for the whole week, John was back every morning to play with her brother and other friends. Since she was younger and a girl, sometimes she was included, oftentimes not.

For the *patintero*, Diego carefully explained to John how the game was played.

"*Patintero* is a game of two groups. The first group will try to let its members penetrate the square lines of the opponent and come back; the opposing group will guard the horizontal lines and one vertical line and not let anybody in. The first group will try to enter without being tagged. You avoid being tagged by just letting your feet hang on the line. The first group tries to come in by using taunts and diversions so they can score a goal, or home. You can enter on either side of the vertical line as long as you get to the deepest square and come back."

Looking at John's facial expression, Diego drew a diagram in the dirt. "You go here like this, see?" He traced the path with a stick.

"There are four of us, including Anita," Dolfo said, knowing that Anita was tomboyish and could run fast.

"OK, there are four of you, Clara will be our fourth," Diego said.

Diego and Dolfo shook with *papel, guinting, bato* (paper, scissor, stone). Dolfo's hand was shaped like a scissor to Diego's paper, so Dolfo's group was going in first.

Diego put John in the last horizontal line since he was not sure yet how the game was played.

Anita was overconfident. As Dolfo taunted Diego, she ran inside, but Paco caught her.

Now it was the turn of Diego's group to go in. John was still confused exactly how it was done, so he watched Diego and Paco taunting Dolfo, one on each side.

Dolfo was taller than Diego. Dolfo stretched out his arms and tried to catch Diego. Unable to go in, Diego ran back and forth from his side to Paco's side to taunt Dolfo. Dolfo pursued Diego, and Clara, seeing the opening, suddenly ran inside. Tonyo saw her and tried to tag her.

"Kuya! Kuya! Ahhhhhh!" she screamed, extending one foot into the line, her whole body away from the square.

Tomas was on the vertical line and joined Dolfo and Tonyo, who were trying to tag Clara. They stretched out and almost lost balance.

Diego ran swiftly to the first square on the other side, then all the way to the deepest square and was coming back. When John saw him coming back, he did the same thing. Paco followed, but when he got to the last square, Dolfo and Tonyo saw him and tried hard to tag him.

Clara was now free to run to the farthest square and all the way back to the last square before Dolfo tried to stop her. Paco made home, and as Dolfo ran back to catch him, Clara made home too.

Diego's group was the biggest winner, and they all jumped up and down and made all kinds of whoopee sounds. Dolfo was angry, and he went home.

Most of the children had a wonderful time just playing tag, hide and seek, catching dragonflies, or climbing fruit trees; but Dolfo started to have a simmering dislike for John, who became good friends with Diego. Diego stopped the others, who called John "Amerkano! Amerkano!"

On the day they played tug-of-war, it got worse. Dolfo was older, but he and John were of the same height. Dolfo challenged John to a tug of war, and John won. Clara was watching.

Frustrated, Dolfo challenged Diego, who was two inches shorter and three years younger. Then he thought better.

"Let's make it a group. Paco! Tonyo!" Dolfo called.

The two went behind him to pull. John stood behind Diego, but there were only two of them.

"Clara is your third," Dolfo said, laughing.

She glared at him.

Before Diego and John could align to pull, Dolfo started to tug at the rope. Diego and John scrambled to pull and keep the knot on the center.

It had rained the night before, and there were puddles of water all over the yard. The boys were all slipping in the mud. When Clara saw the knot moving the other way, she suddenly ran behind John and pulled on his waist as hard as she could. He was startled and tugged hard on the rope.

They all fell backward as the rope gave way, and the knot was on their side. John fell toward Clara, and Diego fell on John. Clara was screaming, and she had mud on her legs and skirt.

"We won!" Diego exclaimed as he got up.

"We won!" John said, brushing back the brown hair that kept falling to his forehead. All of a sudden, the three of them were laughing their hearts out.

By the time they got sober and decided to go upstairs to their home, their mother gave them a light spank on their bottoms.

"Hmph! Get changed!" she told them, but she was more gentle to John. "Wash up John and change into Diego's clothes, you're dirty." She was giving John's clothes to the *lavandera* (washing woman), when her sister-in-law Luming arrived.

"We need some rice," Luming said.

Faustina kept a straight face and led Luming to the kitchen. Luming left with a sack of rice.

Once, on a Sunday, the Luna and Stewart families had a picnic a little way out of town by the stream. The fathers were talking about politics and war, and Paul Stewart was glad to talk to somebody who spoke English and whom he respected.

"The American troops should soon have proper accommodations instead of using your town hall. I hope the townsfolk understand that it is our duty to keep order and to protect you from pirates. I am sorry there are still clashes with rebels, for America hopes to be friends with the Filipinos."

"It is not easy to explain that to the rebels," Manuel replied. "Many of them think that the oppressive Spanish regime has been replaced by another. They have yet to encounter a kindly American like you."

They probably agreed on a lot of things for they often nodded their heads at the same time. Clara stayed close to her mother and helped prepare the food. After lunch, they had a swim.

"What's upstream?" John asked.

"Let's go find out!" Diego answered.

"Kuya! What about Mama?" Clara meant to tell him to ask permission first.

"You stay here!" Diego said confidently.

Diego and John went exploring. They came back hungry, but the mother was mad at them.

"You two!" she said. "Why can't you stay still? I was worried about you!"

They sat forlorn. Clara came over and handed each a sandwich she had made for them.

"Thanks!" they both said.

By mid-August however, John had to go back to school. His dad brought him back to the States.

For some reason, the rains became sparse in Balangiga, and a season of drought occurred that 1901. The farm crops were not enough for the town, and the townspeople and the soldiers at the garrison began to compete for what food was available.

Most people had backyard vegetable gardens; the Luna family preserved fruits and stored food to make them last, but they were careful too. The fishermen were a lot of help, since even the farm animals were so scrawny. The water buffaloes ate withered grass.

Dr. Luna was the only doctor in Balangiga and for several miles around. Often, another town would ask him for help. One Saturday when their father was out of town, the family woke up to the loud tolling of church bells. The bells rang and rang until the children thought they would go deaf. Then the air was filled with war cries, shots, and the horrible screams of people being killed!

Diego and Clara cowered in fear and hugged their mother. They stayed upstairs not knowing what to do. They locked the doors and closed the windows. They heard indescribable screams of fear and agony, followed by the sound of running and shouts in the street. They peeked from the window and saw the Philippine rebels chasing American soldiers to kill them. Some soldiers ran to the shore and used *bancas* or swam across the sea.

When the gunshots were over, they heard the moans of the wounded, but the rebels were oblivious to that. The rebels were bloodied but triumphant, and they ran up and down the street savoring their victory! It looked so terrible, and Clara and Diego were mesmerized.

Their father was not home, and their mother kept the house locked, but the children peeped from the side of the closed windows. For a while, it became quiet, and their mother told the maid to prepare breakfast. She warned them.

"We better eat, we don't know what is happening and we must be ready for anything."

Diego and Clara ate very little. The maid was trembling.

There was an uneasy silence and they stayed indoors, not knowing what to do. They finished one rosary, but after that, Faustina could not keep her children from peeping through the side of the window. The rebels were walking proudly up and down the street, and some women came out to talk to them.

Suddenly there were gunshots. American soldiers were arriving in boats, and they started firing at the rebels even before they came ashore. After the soldiers landed, they chased the rebels, who were mostly armed with bolo knives. There was fighting everywhere: the shores, the streets, the town square, and the backyards. Faustina grabbed her children from near the windows, and they laid flat on the floor. Some shots hit the side of the house!

It took a while before the shots became fewer, then it stopped. They felt relieved, and then suddenly the screams and wails of women pierced the air. There were so many dead men in the streets. There was blood all over, some fresh, some caking in the heat of the sun.

The family stayed upstairs. They could hardly eat, for all they wanted to do was peek from the window sides and listen. They could hear the women mourning their dead husbands.

When night came, they all stayed in their mother's room, including the maid. Their mother told them to hide under the bed if somebody came. They roped together several blankets so they could escape through the window if necessary. They could not sleep until it was dawn, and then they could not get up until it was almost noon.

A series of loud knocks startled them. They did not want to open the door because they were so scared. The knocking continued for a long time until Faustina decided to investigate. The maid knelt like she was ready to die.

"Ponting, this is Luming!" Dolfo's mother said.

Only then did they open the door. There stood Dolfo's mother, looking angry.

"Celso was killed. I have no money."

Luming wanted them to help bury her husband Celso, and she almost demanded it. Faustina hesitated, unsure if it was safe yet.

"The battle is over!" Luming said with an air of contempt, instead of looking grieved.

Faustina looked askance at her sister-in-law. Their husbands were brothers, but Celso's family always came demanding that something be given to them. Faustina decided to give Luming some money and before evening, they buried Celso. So many dead were being buried, but there was no priest. The priest was also out of town when this happened.

Other families just dug a grave in the cemetery and said their own prayers. With the money from Faustina, somebody dug the grave and Celso had a coffin. Dolfo did not help much. He talked and talked and boasted that when he grows up, he would get even with the Americans for killing his father. Except for Dolfo, everyone else was crying and sad after the funeral.

Faustina kept her family at home the next couple of days because they were afraid of everybody. The maid brought them information in bits and pieces since she was the only one allowed to leave the house.

The rebellion had been staged by Filipino rebels under General Lukban. The town mayor had told the American captain of the garrison they needed more men for fear of the Muslim pirates from the south, who might come to harass their town. In reality, all the newly hired Filipinos were rebels ready for battle.

The night before, a procession of women brought some coffins to the Balangiga church. When the American sentry asked about the coffins, the women said the bodies were of people who had died of cholera, so the Americans did not open the coffins.

Actually, the coffins contained bolos and armaments for Lukban's men; and the women in the procession were Lukban's rebels, dressed as women. They waited in church for the signal the next day.

The ringing of the church bells at 6:00 AM was the signal. The chief of police was himself a rebel, and he hit the unknowing American sentry with a rifle butt, then cut him with a bolo. The rebels ran toward the garrison, where the Americans were sitting down for breakfast. They cut down the ropes holding up the tent and massacred the soldiers, who were too surprised to fight back. The three highest-ranking officers were all killed.

Some Americans were able to fight back, killing some rebels, but they were cornered and with nowhere else to go. The survivors ran to the shore and used *bancas* or swam across the sea. Even those already wounded tried to swim, screaming in pain as the salt water hit their wounds. They swam toward the shore of the American garrison at Basey, Samar.

Captain Bookmiller, the commander at Basey, was outraged. He and his men loaded up boats and swiftly arrived at the shores of Balangiga. They shot the rebels frolicking on the shores and came to town with blazing guns. Angry and vengeful soldiers chased the rebels down the street. Among those killed was Celso, Dolfo's father.

Of the seventy-four Americans in Company C, forty-eight died, including the three officers. Twenty-six survived. When the report of the incident reached higher authorities, Brigadier General Jacob Smith issued an order that the Filipinos should be severely punished, to make Samar "a howling wilderness." He declared that all men who could possibly bear arms be killed.

He was asked to clarify the age of males that should be killed.

"Ten years and above," Smith said.

Major Littleton Waller, the marine officer, executed this order literally. Another wave of American soldiers arrived to exact this punishment.

The townsfolk thought things were quieting down, and so did the children, who were at their vegetable plot that morning. When Clara and Diego heard a group of American soldiers rushing from the garrison, Clara quickly turned and ran up the stairs. Diego was farther from the house, and since he was cut off from running home, he turned to run toward the coconut trees. A bullet hit him in the head. Clara was on top of the staircase when she heard the shot. She turned in time to see him fall. She ran back to where he was.

"Kuya! Kuya!" she cried, but he was dead.

Their mother came running downstairs, but it was too late. They screamed and cried, but nobody could help them. They remained there, mourning and too shocked to move. It was past noon before the heat and the flies made Faustina realize they had to wrap Diego in bed sheets. They put him in a little cart with the help of the maid, and they made their way to the cemetery. The maid used the plow, and Faustina and Clara tried to help too. They dug a spot near the grandparents, far from Celso. The women had to bury the dead; there were no men left.

Manuel Luna arrived on his horse and wondered at the eerie somberness and the scenes of devastation as he entered the town. He tied the horse to a post near their house and worried that there was nobody at home. He ran across the plaza and saw dead bodies, which finally made him realize what had happened. He ran toward the church, but it was quiet. Then he heard the crying from the nearby cemetery.

He found his family as they were finishing the rosary. He screamed and cried like he would go mad. They all cried for some time until they had no more tears. It was getting dark when they slowly walked home, exhausted with grief and hungry.

For several days, the soldiers burned hundreds of houses, destroyed crops, and even killed the *carabaos* (water buffalo). They took the three bells from the church as their war booty, and they burned the church. The town was in shambles. The market was empty. Worst of all, the soldiers obeyed the order to kill not only the men but even the boys ten years and older. The women and children who were left were beside themselves in mourning.

Dr. Luna would have been killed too, but the new captain recognized him as the doctor who once treated him.

Dolfo, however, was alive. He saw the soldiers coming and hid in their house. His mother Luming frequently went to Manuel Luna's home to get food. Dolfo was kept hidden for months. Later on, Dolfo came out looking pale and sickly, instead of the usual bully that he was. Once he got better, he boasted that he would get even with Americans one day.

Manuel's family was devastated by Diego's death. Manuel said he was not going to treat Americans anymore, but soon they came and ordered him to report to their hospital.

There was a strong enmity between Americans and Filipinos. It took a while for the townspeople to rebuild the church, and this time there were no bells.

Later on, the Filipinos realized that some Americans were bad, but most were good. The Americans realized that the Filipinos just wanted to be free. The Filipino-American war was declared over by 1902, but Balangiga was one of those places that took a very long time to forget.

VII

Clara tossed and turned in bed as the past she had tried to shut out for so many years came rushing back. She heard the cock crowing to herald the dawn, but she felt exhausted and once more closed her eyes.

After the insurrection was declared over, the Americans started reforms that were good in many aspects. With time, the Filipinos gradually responded to their benevolence.

Clara's family was still quite wary of Americans, and they were somber in dealing with them. Clara frequently remembered John when she saw children playing, and especially when they visited Diego's grave.

John and his father, Colonel Paul Stewart, visited Balangiga and the Luna family four years after the massacre. Clara could not look at John, for he and Diego had been very good friends. Both of them felt a mixture of shame and anger at what happened.

John was a young man then, and he sought to speak to Clara in private and held her hand. "I want us to remain friends in spite of everything," he said.

Clara could not speak and just cried. He waited and looked at her until she looked at him and nodded.

John went on to study at West Point. On his summer break, he joined his dad in the Philippines and visited Clara.

Dolfo, however, was always lurking in the background, devising obstacles so John could not see Clara. Dolfo was her first cousin, but like his father, he was not nice at all.

Manuel Luna's family helped support Dolfo and his mother, but those two always complained. Dolfo resented his uncle for trying to discipline him and telling him to make something of himself. Dolfo preferred to hang out with his friends drinking *tuba* (an alcoholic drink from coconuts). Worse, Dolfo began to look at Clara in a funny way, making her uncomfortable, so she avoided him.

Clara's parents sent her to Manila for college. She usually came home on summer vacations and on Christmas break.

One day in January, Manuel died of a heart attack. Clara came home for her father's funeral and felt more discomfort with Dolfo and her Aunt Luming.

Manuel Luna had left quite a number of properties and a good income for his family, but Dolfo started subverting the tenants. The Chinese couple who rented on their first floor left because Dolfo would get things from their store without permission, and he did not pay. Another Chinese merchant rented the space, and they soon complained too. Dolfo would collect from them without authority and pocket a portion for his own.

The tenants on their farms were harassed by Dolfo, but out of fear, only a few complained to Faustina. One tenant was badly beaten by Dolfo just because there was not enough food to serve to Dolfo and his friends. Faustina found out what he was doing only much later. Next, Dolfo tried to run their lives.

Faustina started barring him from coming to her house unannounced, but he just laughed. Their house was just next door.

When John arrived that summer, he knew Clara was eighteen. Even if she seemed young, he wanted Clara to commit to him, like a fiancé, but they did not have a chance to really talk.

Dolfo blocked all his attempts to see Clara. John would find trash thrown his way, or he would get doused by buckets of water. Whenever John was visiting Clara, Dolfo would come upstairs and make all kinds of noise, even if her mother told Dolfo to leave.

One Sunday, as Clara was coming out of church with her mother, John approached them. "Mrs. Luna, Ma'am, I know Clara is now of age, and I'd like to speak to her alone. I assure you I have the best intentions for your daughter," he said.

Before Faustina could say anything, John took Clara's hand and guided her to a horse drawn buggy he had rented.

"John!" was all she could say, too surprised to do anything else.

"Get in!" he said firmly, and she obeyed.

They rode the buggy without speaking for quite a while as Clara glanced sideways at him. He looked very serious, so Clara sat far away from him. She noticed they were far from town.

"Where are we going?" she asked.

"Remember where we once had a picnic?" he said. "You don't have to sit so far away," he added with a sigh.

She was taken aback, and with a side glimpse at him, she sat more comfortably at a lesser distance. He reached for her hand, held it for a while, then let it go.

A few minutes later, they were on the bank of the stream where they once had a picnic, a long time ago.

John had brought a picnic basket with food and drinks. Clara was surprised that he had planned for this. He helped her come down from the buggy, and his touch seemed to burn her. He quietly took the basket and brought it under the shade of a tree. He spread a cloth and sat down. After some hesitation, she sat down too.

"I don't know where I'll be assigned next, I might not be able to visit you next summer," he started.

"Oh!" she said, but she could not hide the tears that slowly fell.

She sensed a movement, and suddenly he was holding her by the shoulders.

"I'd like us to marry now, or very soon, Clara. I love you, I think you know that," he said.

She was startled and looked up into his eyes, then she became thoughtful. He drew her close and kissed her on the lips. She caught her breath and half withdrew, but all the years of pent-up longing was bursting to be released.

John was now kissing her eyes, her throat, and soon she was kissing him back. Her arms went around his neck, shyly at first, and then they were holding each other tightly, passionately, as time stood still.

"Oh, John," she whispered. "I love you. I love you so much!"

"My darling!" he said in between kisses

When finally they paused, he took a ring from his fifth finger. It was a gold wedding ring with diamonds, ornate in an unusual way that other people might not think of it as a wedding ring at first glance. John put it on Clara's left fourth finger, but it was loose and could only fit on her right middle finger.

"This was my mother's. My father let me have it to give to the woman I love. Now you are mine. I will love you forever," John said.

Clara looked at the ring with tears in her eyes. "I will always love you, John, forever and ever," she said solemnly.

As they looked into each other's eyes, they were filled with emotion and kissed again. They clung to each other, and time stood still. The clouds had covered the sun as though conspiring with them, and they held each other, dreaming together of their future.

A sudden burst of light brought them back to reality as the clouds finally moved away from the sun. The sun was setting, but not until it painted the sky with brilliant hues of orange, pink, and red.

"Oh!" Clara said.

John pressed her hand as though they felt a blessing from Mother Nature. They stood in happy silence, gazing at the horizon, but it was over too soon. John looked from his watch to the dying embers of the setting sun. They had been gone for quite a while, and darkness would spread fast. They had eaten all the food.

Hurriedly they picked up their things and loaded it back to the buggy. This time, Clara sat close to John as he possessively put one arm around her, holding the horse reins with mostly one hand. He glanced sideways and smiled at the blissful look on Clara's face.

"We can marry now or next year," John said. "Let's ask your mother's permission now. Do you want a big wedding, dearest?"

"No," she said. "If you have to leave soon, let's keep it simple."

"I'll come for you after my next assignment is settled. What is it?" he asked as he glimpsed a crease on her brow.

"My mother, I'll miss her. She had been talking about going back to her relatives, since my father died," she answered.

"One day, when you and I are settled, she can come live with us," John said, knowing how much Clara cared for her mother.

"That would be wonderful," Clara said, moving closer to John and holding his arm.

They arrived home feeling very happy, and Clara ran upstairs excitedly.

"Mama! Mama!" she called.

Mrs. Luna came out to see her daughter and John bouncing up the stairs. She breathed a sigh of relief. "I've been worried. Where have you been?"

"With John! We are going to get married!" Clara hugged her mother, who hugged her back.

"You're still very young," Faustina said. "Are you sure?" She looked from Clara to John.

"Yes, Mrs. Luna," John said. "We can get married tomorrow or as soon as possible, so I can come for her when I know my next assignment."

Faustina was still taken aback. She looked from one excited face to another and sighed.

"I will ask the priest tomorrow and let you know," she said. She looked at her daughter with mixed emotion, feeling happy for Clara yet beginning to realize she would lose her daughter.

"We'll just have a simple wedding since John needs to leave soon," Clara said.

"Then I'll come for her when I know my next assignment," John repeated.

Faustina gave up trying to talk over the two chattering lovebirds.

"I'm just inviting my good buddies and my CO, I'll write my dad," John said.

"And I'll just invite relatives and some friends," Clara said happily.

"You have my blessing, dear. I'm so happy for you both," her mother said.

John joined them for supper before he left reluctantly.

"Until tomorrow," he said, kissing Clara lightly on the lips and pressing her hands.

Then something very terrible happened.

VIII

Clara woke up with a start. The memory of Balangiga had come back to haunt her; her attempt to forget had been futile as her love for John came surging back. No real sleep came—instead she struggled to still her sobs.

From lack of sleep and the emotional upheaval of the night before, Clara was already tired before she could get started. She dragged herself to the kitchen and started cooking, knowing she had to prepare for the next day's party. She sent Juling, the older maid, to the market for other ingredients. She looked at the progress of the young new maid, Tessie, stirring the soup. Clara realized she needed extra help. She ran after Juling, who was leaving by the back staircase.

"Call Agapita," she said.

Neneng hadn't really slept because she cried through the night. She got up late and dazed, her eyes swollen. She went to the kitchen and tried to help. She started chopping some onions and suddenly felt angry.

Clara observed her daughter chopping with vehemence.

"Those are just onions dear," she gently reminded.

"I don't want to see him!" Neneng said petulantly.

Clara stopped stirring the pot and sat beside her daughter. "Your father has already invited their family to the dinner before the problem arose, it will not be proper to change that. However, we can say your Uncle Emong sent for you to help with the tenants settling their accounts."

Neneng nodded and smiled. Clara felt relieved.

After lunch, Neneng left with her grandmother for San Nicholas, Gapan, where she made herself useful in her uncle's house. She was to return after the house party.

Jack came to visit that afternoon but was told by the maid that Neneng was not home.

The day of the party was busy, with Clara ordering the help to do last-minute cleaning, arrange the table setting, and finish cooking another dessert.

The Stewarts arrived promptly at 5:30 PM. Carlos greeted them and made them comfortable in the living room area.

The men talked about the coming war while they sipped wine. Doris Stewart was excited to learn about the different dishes as she sniffed the aroma from the kitchen. Clara indulged her curiosity by explaining the different spices used with each food.

Jack looked around expectantly and answered only in yes or no, even if the others tried to draw him in the conversation. He looked from the china cabinet to the piano and back again to the door of Neneng's bedroom.

Soon they sat down. John Stewart was guided to one end as Carlos Mendez sat at the head on the other end of the table. Jack sat on his father's left.

The table was laid with food dishes they were supposed to pass around. There was the usual *pansit, adobo, morcon, escabeche,* and *sinigang.*

Jack liked *sinigang* and noticed that his dad took a good serving of it too. He had looked forward to this dinner in anticipation of seeing Neneng. He finally asked, "Where is Neneng?"

Clara tried to look noncommittal.

"Her uncle sent for her because he needs help with the tenants coming in to settle their accounts. My mother went with her," she replied.

Clara was immediately sorry she had mentioned her mother, aware that her mother had looked after John like a son. John Stewart looked at Clara as though he wanted to say something.

Jack opened his mouth ready to protest, and then he just nodded. He was silent for the rest of the evening and stopped eating. Clara and Doris talked about the different fruits to try to draw Jack into the conversation, but Jack stayed quiet. The women chattered as much as possible to hide the discomfort Jack seemed to be in.

Neneng returned the next day with her grandmother. She was silent and distracted. She went from the piano to her room to helping in the kitchen, and then back to her room to read. She did not accomplish much because she often cried and was miserable.

Jack went to visit Neneng every afternoon he was free, but he was not able to see her. Her room remained closed, and the maid relayed all kinds of excuses.

The next week, Jack learned his unit was going to move up to the Cagayan Valley. He went to see Neneng, but was told she was not well. He demanded to see Mrs. Mendez.

"Po! Po!" Tessie, the younger maid, called helplessly.

Clara came out of the kitchen and looked at Jack. The maid shook her head and left.

"I'd like to talk to Neneng, even if through a closed door, Mrs. Mendez, Ma'am, if you don't mind."

She looked at him with sympathy and allowed him to proceed. He knew where her bedroom was, and he knocked.

"It's Jack! I'd really like to speak to you. I'm leaving for Cagayan tomorrow!"

There was no answer.

"Neneng! Please! I've not even had a chance to talk to you about this!"

Jack knocked again. There was only silence. Jack felt very frustrated and sad, then finally he turned away.

Clara Mendez gently touched his shoulder and let him go.

Jack went back to his barracks and decided to write Neneng.

June 4, 1941

My darling,

It is true that I had a sweetheart when I left Virginia last year, but I did not get engaged because I had doubts about my commitment. When I first saw you, I knew this was different, and before December was over, I had written Liza asking to be set free, for I was very much in love with you.

You may think that I had not been straightforward with you, but I did not even know where I stood, whether you would love me too. In our first kiss, I had not even imagined how happy I would be in your love. Please say you had forgiven me.

Love,

Jack

Neneng read the letter brought by Teban and threw it in the trash. She was hurt for the first time in her life. She had been almost impervious to the attention of her suitors, but with Jack she had felt comfortable like he was a friend sharing in her activities. She only felt the stirring of emotion when she saw him escorting Marites. Their newfound love made her feel like she was walking on clouds, and how happy she had been. But it was so brief! How abruptly and suddenly was that happiness shattered!

If only she could turn back the clock to when she felt nothing for him, for now she was in a daze and could not think of ever being happy again. She had heard of so many girls falling for married soldiers, and she thought she would not be like that. Would she have fallen for a married man? They were all sorry tales.

Neneng was used to being sought after; instead, Doris Stewart looked disapprovingly at her, her look of shock so plain to see. Neneng thought she was better than that, but apparently not. She was still inexperienced about love, but being an avid reader, she believed in an ideal kind of love. She thought that her family and the family of the man she would marry should be very amiable toward each other—not like this, like she came from nowhere.

She did not really know Jack's character. Courtship in her country being what it was, she liked him from what she saw, and she believed what he said. But how many other things had he not said? She was numb from analyzing the situation.

Her mother had mentioned that she almost married Jack's dad, and they had been parted. Things had happened so fast, and her mother had yet to tell her the story. Neneng resigned herself to her fate. She resolved to forget Jack, the sooner, the better.

The next morning, Jack's unit marched out of Cabanatuan. Jack was riding a jeep toward the end of a long line of troops. As the troops passed by the Mendez house, Jack looked intently up at the upstairs window and knew that Neneng was watching from behind the curtain. His jaw was set, but his heart was heavy. He was really mad at her now—yet he could not help the tear that fell unbidden on his uniform.

Earlier that day, he decided to write her as soon as he woke up.

"I'm really mad at you now!" he wrote. He told Teban to bring it to her. Then he changed his mind and told Teban to wait. "I love you very much, no matter what happens," he wrote. Jack gave this to Teban too. Teban brought both letters to Neneng.

The next day, Neneng began to pack. Her father drove her back to school the day after that.

Neneng caught her father looking sideways at her. She had been assisting in his clinic whenever she was home on vacation. He had complimented her natural aptitude for it, but that won't be enough if she allows herself to be distracted because of Jack.

"I will study well, Papa," she said, holding his hand.

Carlos smiled at his daughter and squeezed her hand too.

Two days later, Colonel Stewart came knocking at the Mendez residence. He had something to find out. The maid told him the family was in a church gathering—only Mrs. Luna was home.

"I'd like to see Mrs. Luna," he said.

When he was shown in, Faustina Luna got up from her rocking chair and looked up.

"Mrs. Luna, I'm John Stewart, it's been a long time." Before he could finish, his voice broke, and he held the old lady in his arms.

Faustina looked more frail and older than he remembered. He remembered her like a second mother who cared for him and treated him like a son.

"John! Oh, John!" she said, but overcome with emotion, she just cried and could not say anything else.

"I've been wanting to know—" John started.

She continued to cry and shook with emotion. John held her tight, and his eyes filled with tears.

"Mrs. Luna," John tried again, but the old lady was still shaken with sobs.

"John!" was all she could say.

After a while, John realized he was too shaken to face anybody. This was not going to work; he had better leave.

"Good-bye," he said, gently kissing the old lady's forehead. She just nodded and stayed in her chair, still crying.

IX

Colonel John Stewart was assigned to fill in for Colonel Dillon as CO at Cabanatuan, when Dillon had to attend to some family emergency. It was a very warm August day (1941), and John was hoping for some respite after inspecting the troops and recommending some changes. A knock on his door derailed his trend of thought.

"Come in," he said as he put a marker on his outline. He looked up as a visitor was ushered in by the secretary.

Clara Mendez looked startled when John looked up. "Oh! I thought Colonel Dillon was the CO?"

"He's still out of town," John said, getting up. "How are you, Clara? Dillon will be back soon, and I'll return to Manila," John spoke quickly, sensing Clara's hesitation. "Please sit down," he added.

"Fine, thank you," Clara replied and sat on the edge of the chair, looking tense. Clara Mendez looked confused and took a deep breath; then she began.

"I've had some suspicion about Mr. Mifune, but I thought I was imagining things. Last night, Mrs. Cortez's son had a very high fever so she came to our house for help. Dr. Mendez was still in Bulacan, but at her pleading, I came with some medicines to see what I can do. With some medicines, we were able to bring the temperature down and I decided to go home. I hadn't realized that I'd been there for hours. It was almost midnight, and I had come without a servant, but I decided to go home alone, anyway.

"I thought it was pretty safe, and I walked noiselessly across the plaza. I was about to cross the avenue when I heard soft voices from the Mifune store. For some reason, I hid myself and watched. A small truck was in front, and a military looking man was bringing large crates into the store. It didn't look like ordinary hardware. That's really all Colonel, good-bye."

She bowed quickly and got up.

John had been taking notes as she spoke, then he put his pen down and looked up.

"What happened that night, Clara? I just want to know," he said.

Clara was already at the door, her hand at the knob, ready to flee. She looked back at John and told her story.

"When you left, I was very happy, making plans with my mother. Suddenly, Dolfo arrived! He had been looking for me all afternoon and was very jealous, thinking I was with you.

"He confronted me.

"'Where have you been?' he said angrily.

"'You have no right to ask her like that!' my mother answered for me, very offended.

"Dolfo was blinded by jealous rage. He came toward me and shook me by the shoulders. 'Where have you been?' he repeated.

"I just stared at him, so shocked by his violent behavior that I couldn't answer. He shook me repeatedly and screamed at the same time.

"'Where have you been?'

"'Let her go!' my mother said, at the same time pushing him away.

"With the force of an enraged animal, he pushed my mother away, and the force made her fall backward against the wall. Dolfo looked like a madman, but I seemed to wake up.

"'Let me go! You are bad!' I screamed. When he would not let go, I fought free and slapped him! 'John and I are going to marry!' I screamed at him.

"'I will kill him!' Dolfo answered angrily. He pushed me back, and I fell toward my mother. 'You won't have the dignity to face this town! I'm going to tell them that you are disgraced!'

"'John!' was the only thing I could say. I was thinking of warning you.

"Dolfo knew my father had a gun. He went to the cabinet and found it. He turned as he left. 'I will kill him and both of you if you try to leave the house!' he said.

"I helped my mother get up, and we looked around disbelieving. My mother and I embraced in the room and did not move until he had left.

"I was shaking with both anger and fear, but my mother was thinking. She looked determined, and she started to go over our cabinet where we had our titles, jewelry, and money. She quickly packed them in cloth sacks, along with a few clothes.

"When our servant, Marta, arrived from visiting her sick niece, I wrote a message for you.

"'Bring this message to John,' I told her.

"It took her a while to come back and make a report. 'Dolfo is watching the house. I pretended to go back to my sick niece to bring medicine. I left John's message with the guard, because John has been called to the next town. He will be back in the morning.'

"My mother decided that when Dolfo leaves his post, we will slip out, go to your camp, and get refuge. She also decided to bring our papers, money and jewelry. We waited as our maid, Marta, watched for Dolfo to leave. It was an agony of waiting until before dawn, when she signaled us to come out.

"We quickly left and went to your camp. The guard said you had not yet returned, so we hid in the shadows of a nearby tree. The sun was just beginning to rise when there was a sudden commotion in the camp gate.

"An army vehicle had arrived in a rush; the noise from its screeching tires startled us. Then groups of soldiers were gathering and talking excitedly. We went there to see what it was about.

"'Stewart was ambushed! He's dead!' We heard it repeated from one soldier to another.

"I was stunned. I felt like I died too, but my mother held me close and made a decision.

"'There's nothing more for us in this town,' she said. 'Dolfo will terrorize us and make you marry him, or your reputation will be destroyed.'"

Clara was crying. John was already at her side and embraced her.

"My darling," he said, kissing her tenderly, then with a passion that she returned.

"Oh, John!" she cried.

After a while, holding on to him, she continued.

"We took the first bus that came, and continued until we got to Catbalogan. From there we went by boat, then bus, until we reached Manila. We traveled continuously until we reached my mother's hometown in San Nicholas, Gapan (Nueva Ecija). Her brother Felipe was good to us. Later on, my cousin Celestino would take care of our properties in Balangiga. My mother helped in the family business of grinding *palay* for the farmers. I went to college in UST to finish pharmacy."

Clara looked at the ring that John had given her. "My happiest memories are with this ring, it has given me strength to go on with life."

John held her hand with his right as he kept his other arm around her. He told his part of the story.

"After I left you that evening, I arrived at camp and found the other soldiers getting ready. There was news of a possible pirate raid in the next town. I was among those sent to reinforce the garrison there. It turned out that it was possibly a false alarm, but we stayed there until dawn just to be sure. When we returned, our army vehicle was ambushed by gunfire. Without seeing our attackers, we returned fire. I was seriously wounded, one soldier died. When I regained consciousness at the hospital, I asked about you, but nobody could tell me what happened. The two gunmen were Dolfo and Tonyo, and they were dead too.

"I went to your house when I recovered, but Dolfo's mother was there and hostile toward me, blaming me for the death of her son. For five years, I visited the Philippines every free time I had, looking for you. In the end, I thought Dolfo killed you and your mother, and nobody knew. My dad and aunt were anxious for me to marry and forget. They thought Doris was very suitable, and I just went along. She had been a good mother to my children."

"In Manila, I met Carlos, who was studying medicine," Clara said. "I told him that I had loved once before, and I did not want to be courted anymore. He persisted for ten years, and finally, I married him. He's from Cabanatuan, so we moved here. He is a good, decent man."

Then, as though realizing the present, she moved away from John and wiped her tears.

"We each have our own families now. Good-bye John," she said sadly and left.

John could not move for a while, he felt weak with the revelation. That past was so fresh in his mind, and he could not let Clara go; but he knew he must. He sat on his chair, shaken, as tears rolled down his cheeks.

It took a while, but with a sigh, he knew he had to give an order. Mr. Mifune's store would have to be searched.

For Clara, there was no surprise the next day when soldiers searched Mr. Mifune's store and found boxes of weapons. The whole town thought it was a long time coming, but nobody knew how it finally became real. The Mifune father and son were sent to prison.

X

In June 1941, Neneng was back in Manila to continue her studies. She wanted to be a doctor, but she felt that too many things happened on her last vacation. She tried hard to shut out the memory of Jack. Although naturally smart, she had to put in an extra effort to stay focused. She hid her tears from her friends, but they could tell she was suffering. She left the room whenever the radio aired love songs, especially the *kundiman*.

Jack was immersed in his next assignment. The war in Europe was raging, and it was just a matter of time until the Philippines would be involved. Staying busy eased the pain, and he tried hard to forget.

It was October 1941 when Jack was able to get a long enough leave. He went to Manila and stayed with his dad. Both of them knew Jack would use this opportunity to see Neneng.

"Your godfather's son got hold of me, and I was able to get back to him. Would you like to join us for lunch tomorrow, Jack?" John asked.

"Tomorrow is Sunday, mind if I pass? That's when most people visit, and I hope to see Neneng."

"I understand, son. I'll give him your regards."

Colonel John Stewart had attended an earlier Mass at Fort McKinley and did some paperwork in his office. Fort McKinley occupied a huge area of land south of the Pasig River. It was the USAFFE headquarters for the Philippine Department, the Philippine Army, and the Far East Air Force. It was a busy place where specialized artillery training was being conducted.

Although the entire army was working for a state of readiness in case of war, John had become aware that their ammunitions and supplies were not geared for war. The guns were old, even from the First World War, and did not work right. Worse, some bullets did not match the guns.

John drove south from Manila to meet with his godson at the officers' club in Nichols Air Base. He went there in good spirits, only to come back crestfallen. He learned that the air force also suffered from lack of supplies, mismatched parts, and nonfunctioning equipment.

He needed to put this information in tomorrow's meeting agenda. He planned to prepare the facts and the data that night.

Neneng went to college in the University of Santo Tomas, which was run by Dominican priests and had been founded since 1611. UST occupied an entire block, bounded in front by Espana Street, behind by Dapitan Street, and Forbes Street and P. Noval on either side.

Her dormitory was along Forbes Street, about half a block from Dapitan Street. It was ran by a well-to-do old maid, Miss Castro, who was reputed to be strict and charged a good price. The food was good and the *dormitorianas* were well-to-do. The ivory colored Spanish-type house was bordered by an ornate iron fence with a gate for cars and a smaller gate for people.

Jack walked through the garden path beside the parked Ford and smelled the fragrance from the blossoming jasmine, roses, bougainvillea, and canna lilies. This was his fourth time to try to see Neneng, but he had not been successful. Miss Castro was polite and even asked if Jack would like some coffee. Neneng's dormitory mates were all nice, and some even flirted with him, but the answer was all the same. Neneng was always out—visiting friends or somewhere else. He knew it was a lie, but there was nothing he could do.

Jack was feeling low as he went back to his dad's quarters at Fort McKinley. He wondered if he would ever see Neneng again; his feelings alternated between despair and anger. His short leave has ended; he would be going back to the Cagayan Valley. He was almost done packing when he heard his dad come in. Father and son were mindful of seeing each other when they could, as though the threat of war brought forebodings they could not put a finger to.

One look at Jack, and John sat down in the nearest chair.

"She wouldn't see me!" Jack said unnecessarily. Then something occurred to Jack. "There's something unusual about you and Mrs. Mendez, Dad. You haven't exactly helped me out, if you are old friends."

Colonel Stewart stood up and paced the floor. He put his cigarette out in the ashtray, then sat down, as though limp.

"I have nothing against you being involved with Neneng. I think I love her already as a future daughter-in-law, if it should happen. You see, a long time ago, I was about to marry her mother."

Jack put away the shirt he was folding and sat down. He looked at his dad with the questions on his face.

Colonel Stewart narrated his story of Balangiga as though in pain.

"I didn't know what really happened … neither of us did, until Clara Mendez came to my office. I'm not going to lie to you, son. I never knew I still feel very strongly toward her. She seems to know that too. She's going to avoid me, and I will keep my distance, because we each have our own families now. You have my word that I will remain faithful to your mother. It would not be proper for me to visit. You will have to do this yourself."

The revelation overwhelmed Jack, and he sat down, unable to sort out his jumble of thoughts. After a while, he stood up and finished packing.

"I'll be OK, Dad. Take care! I love you!" Jack embraced his dad.

"Be careful, son, I love you!" Colonel Stewart embraced his son and watched him leave with a heavy heart.

XI

The threat of war hung in the air as December came. The Filipino ebullience at Christmastime evaporated. People shopped, but they were more discreet in buying. They looked for something really useful, in case of war. The *parol* was on display, but there was less caroling.

For students, the semestral exams came up just before they could go home on Christmas break. As usual, the students were cramming, Neneng and friends among them.

December 8 fell on a Monday, but even if they had heard Mass just the day before, they had to hear Mass again; the Feast of the Immaculate Conception was a holiday of obligation for Catholics. In the University of Santo Tomas, there would be no school that day.

"Wake up!" Neneng shook Delia.

Being less religious, Delia was trying to get away without hearing Mass again.

"Me first!" Maria said as she grabbed a towel to go to the shower.

The usual bickering always occurred when everybody tried to get dressed at the same time.

Neneng and her friends scrambled out of their dorm on Forbes Street and turned right on Dapitan. It was a little cold, and most of them wore sweaters. They were entering the UST campus when they noticed people on the streets talking excitedly.

"I wonder why?" Delia asked nobody in particular.

They all paused.

"Extra! Extra! Pearl Harbor was bombed!" the newspaper boy shouted at the top of his voice.

"My God!" most of them exclaimed, looking at each other.

Not knowing what else to expect, they decided to proceed to the Dominican church toward the P. Noval side of the campus. The church was full, but the people were subdued.

The priest saying the Mass cut everything down to the essentials. There was no sermon, as though he was in a hurry. Several priests came out to help in the communion. It was quite a short Mass, considering the Feast day. Then toward the end of the Mass, the priest spoke.

"Pearl Harbor had been bombed! Let us all pray for God's mercy!"

He gave a blessing to each column of pews.

The people came out of the church with a mixture of apprehension and fear. Some went home in a hurry. Others formed groups talking about the events, while others just milled around, uncertain of what to do, and just listened.

The girls hurried back to their dorms in a state of confusion. Miss Castro was crying and did not know what to say. Some sat down on the parlor chairs while others just stood by in apprehension. They were looking forward to an extra day of studying, but instead they turned on the radio at full blast.

"Davao City was bombed at 6:30 this morning!" the radio announcer emphasized.

"Ladies and gentlemen, more areas in Luzon seem to be under attack, several areas, as a matter of fact! Right now, however, there is so much confusion, we are awaiting confirmation of exactly what has happened!" he continued.

The girls looked at each other, now more fearful.

"Are we going to have exams or not?" Delia asked, making everybody more confused.

"Tuguegarao has been bombed!" the radio cracked.

"I'm going home!" one of the girls, Maria, said.

"I don't think there's any exam, I'm packing," Neneng said.

There was a rush to go upstairs to their rooms. There were usually three or four beds in a room, the twin beds arranged close to each other with a narrow aisle between. Everybody was in a panic state of packing, getting out their bags and suitcases, separating their books and notes, and colliding between the beds.

"My toothbrush!" Maria said.

Back and forth, they stumbled on each other.

"Baguio! Yes, Baguio has been bombed!" the radio updated.

The girls were crying loudly and wiped their tears with their sleeves. A crumpled heap of white fell on Neneng's feet.

"Whose are these?" she asked.

Maria came forward without speaking and rifled through the pile. She took what was hers and left the rest where they were. Neneng picked up the rest of the uniforms and put them on the bed.

The college ladies in the University of Santo Tomas wore white uniforms. The cut varied with each college; some had colored stripes, an embroidered emblem, or some means of identification on the lapel. The dormitory girls paid for a washer woman to do the laundry and iron their clothes. Just the same, there were varying degrees of sloppiness, and it usually got worse during exam time.

Delia came forward and transferred the uniforms from her bed to another. "We don't know how long the war is. We better take our beddings," she said.

The dormitory required them to bring two sets of bedding, but they did not usually have to pack those if they were coming back. Now each one of them went back to their beds, stripped them of linens, and repacked.

Finally, they finished, sort of, and most of them sat on the beds. Every now and then, somebody would get up to retrieve something from where it had been almost forgotten.

"How do we go home?" Norma, another girl, asked.

"I'm sure my father will come for me!" Maria said.

"Can I ride with you?" Neneng asked.

"Sure, we're both from Nueva Ecija!" Maria answered.

"If my father arrives first, you can ride with us," Neneng said thoughtfully.

The girls talked about the different means of going home.

"Don't take the bus, or you'll be stranded," Amy advised, since she was the eldest in the group.

As though tired, they sat on the beds, fanned themselves, and took deep breaths. After a while, they started getting anxious again, for nobody had arrived to pick anyone up yet.

Miss Castro was glued to her chair, listening to the radio downstairs. Beads of perspiration made streaks on her makeup as her usual preoccupation with her appearance was forgotten. Gloria the maid had been waived away several times.

"The food is already cold!" Gloria said loudly.

"Huh? Warm it again!" Miss Castro said irritably and went up the stairs quickly. She was feeling hungry now.

"Let's eat something first!" she said.

"Oh! We haven't eaten lunch!!" Maria and Delia chorused.

"No wonder we can't think!" Amy could not help saying as all the girls hurried downstairs to the dining room.

"I'll wait for word from some relative, it's impossible to go all the way home to Davao now," Delia said.

"Don't worry. You can stay with me," Miss Castro said.

Only then did the other ladies realize that Miss Castro did not really have relatives around. They touched her shoulder in sympathy while Maria hugged the older lady. They also tried to cheer Delia up.

"Somebody will come for you," Neneng said hopefully.

Davao was on the island of Mindanao. It took Delia more than four days of traveling by boat to get to Manila. Neneng and Amy sat beside Delia and pressed her hand, for they were all feeling helpless. No proper lady would travel alone during times like these.

By four o'clock, Norma's car arrived. She was going home to Bulacan, so she took Amy with her.

Neneng and Maria waited anxiously, beginning to perspire. When Carlos Mendez arrived, Neneng bolted out of the door and ran toward her father at the garden path.

"Papa! Papa!" she cried.

Carlos looked haggard and embraced his daughter.

"I can take people going our way toward Cabanatuan. The Japanese are bombing more towns, including Iba and Tarlac!" he said.

Maria did not wait; she brought her bags out quickly and loaded them in the trunk.

"Good afternoon, Dr. Mendez, I must have a word with you!" Miss Castro had been waiting. "What will I do with the students? Where will I go? What shall I do? The Japanese might bomb Manila next!"

Carlos Mendez stopped in his tracks and put down Neneng's suitcase. He was suddenly embarrassed for not sympathizing with Miss Castro.

"Let's talk about it in the parlor," he said.

To his surprise, tea had already been prepared, and Miss Castro motioned for everybody to sit down as the maid served tea and a flaky dry pastry called *otap*.

"Let Delia stay with you until you are sure she can travel safely to Mindanao. Her parents might send somebody to fetch her. You two can look out for each other."

"I'll advise you to stay in this house, otherwise other people will come to vandalize it or take it away from you. Store food and look around for resources you might still be able to buy at the market, once everybody settles down. If you can't hold things together, come to Cabanatuan or send out a word for help, and I'll do something about it."

Miss Castro sighed with relief, reassured there were people she could turn to. She embraced Delia, and both smiled through their tears.

Neneng followed her father with her bags; then on impulse, she ran back to kiss Miss Castro and Delia again and say good-bye. Maria came out of the car too and did the same, kissing cheek to cheek, unable to voice their fear of what the war might bring.

As soon as the car reached Laong Laan Street, the chaos started. The main streets heading to the provinces were clogged with cars, calesas, and other transportations going in different directions without any semblance of order. There were no policemen, for the dominant worry was survival; even the law enforcement officers were busy taking care of their families.

Everybody just wanted their own business done without regard for others. The first reaction was to go home to their families. There were so many collisions and near collisions, it was hard to avoid being bumped or bumping into another car. A horse lay sprawled on the street after a calesa collided with a speeding car.

Carlos Mendez quickly swerved to the left to avoid another car. It was unfair to mix slow calesas with speeding vehicles. Their car window was open, but the noise of horses neighing, people tooting their horns, other people running and screaming in the streets was unnerving. He cranked the handle to close the window a bit, but it was so warm! He swerved again to avoid getting bumped; he just missed hitting another car!

When they reached the highway, the cloudy day became prematurely dark from the dust and confusion. They had to slow down, only to be startled every so often by cars coming from the opposite direction with reckless speed. Carlos wondered if they would get home in one piece. Neneng's knuckles were white as she held on to her seat. For once, Maria was silent, closing her eyes now and then when she thought a collision was about to happen.

By the time they reached Nueva Ecija, it was past 8:00 PM, and they dropped off Maria at San Isidro. Carlos and Neneng graciously refused the offer to join Maria's family for supper, they were just anxious to get to Cabanatuan. Sweating and tired, Dr. Mendez finally parked his car in front of their house.

Clara came running down the stairs and embraced her husband and daughter. She had been sick with worry and could barely catch her breath in relief and excitement.

"Fort Stotsenberg was bombed at noon!" she said.

Carlos looked at Clara and paused to think in spite of his exhaustion. Fort Stotsenberg was in Pampanga, the next province, and it was the base for the U.S.-Philippine airplanes and the home of the elite Philippines Scouts.

Clara herded her husband and daughter upstairs and told the maid Juling to warm the food quickly. After Carlos finished bringing the suitcases to Neneng's room, they all flopped into the dining room chairs, and Carlos talked of the trip home.

"Eat!" Clara ordered as she helped Juling serve them their meal.

It was already ten o'clock, but the two just sipped the water; too exhausted to eat.

"The soldiers are getting ready for combat! Some are being deployed to areas that have been bombed! The Filipino civilians are signing up as soldiers, but they have to be trained first!"

Clara was speaking fast, updating them of what had happened in town while Carlos was gone. She shoved the rice in front of Carlos and blinked when he did not move. In her excitement, at first she did not realize that the two had been through a stressful journey without food and water.

"Eat," Clara repeated gently this time. She sat down to let the two take their time eating and just be with them.

"We will stay in town and help the people and the soldiers, but that will not be easy when the Japanese come," Carlos finally said.

He had eaten little, as though he had forgotten what food was for. Clara placed the water closer to him and put food on his plate.

"The de Leon family was very vocal about putting the Mifunes to death. The mayor had to post more guards in the prison to protect them, as ordered by Colonel Dillon. Later on, Mr. Mifune and Yoshiro were moved to the camp barracks. I was able to buy more food and dried goods as soon as the stores opened, but when we heard that the Philippines was being bombed, the stores closed," Clara said.

They sat around listening to the radio after the two ate, but the announcers were revising which towns were hit by bombs. The family was getting confused, and it was already so late. Exhausted and confused, they went to bed.

There was a sense of restlessness the next day. Everybody listened to the radio, only to hear some announcers picking up an airwave battle with other announcers who had a different data. People changed radio stations every few minutes.

"There are more casualties at the bombing in Tarlac!" one announcer said proudly. "I have reliable information from a witness."

"Manila is being bombed!" the announcer from another station said, panic audible in his voice.

People poured into the streets and into the plaza, gripped by fear. Somehow, there was comfort in talking. Those who were confused listened to groups debating with others on what was best.

Clara went to the market with Juling to see what was still available. She targeted the dry goods and bought most of the sugar and salt that was available, plus a lot of spices, especially the paprika and bay leaves. Juling gave her a conspiratorial look, and she turned to see the servants of de Silva arriving. They left quickly; they were lucky to be there first.

Her mother Faustina was anxiously waiting when Clara got home. There was a message from her Kuya Emong in San Nicholas.

"You can come here if you think it will be safer for you. We will tell the farmers to continue planting rice, because no matter how long the war is, we all have to eat."

More bad news came the following day. The Japanese had landed in the northern Luzon area of Aparri and Vigan. By December 20, the main Japanese invasion force under Lieutenant General Masaharu Homma landed in Lingayen Gulf, on the northwest area of Luzon.

On December 24, Philippine President Manuel L. Quezon, his family, and war cabinet were evacuated to the island fortress called Corregidor in Manila Bay.

Christmas was a somber affair. The Mendez family continued their tradition of attending the nine days of Misa de Gallo and the midnight Christmas Mass, Misa de Aguinaldo, but the feasting was pared down. Their *noche buena*, the midnight Christmas meal, was just *pansit*, soup, and *bibingka*. Their food preparation was reduced to what was necessary.

They had sent for their Kuya Emong so they could be together and talk about what to do. They agreed to increase, if possible, the amount of rice to plant.

"Those relatives in the city might need help," Emong said, always thoughtful of his whole family.

Clara smiled. Her Kuya Emong was wiser and more forward-thinking than most of the brood he had to look out for. In his low-key way, he just got things done.

"We will let Rafael build a chicken house, and Fernando will raise some pigs," Emong said.

"We don't know how or what food supplies will come, so we will eat properly without waste," Carlos said.

"We will plant vegetables near our houses, and I'll preserve the fruits," Clara added.

The family of Carlos Mendez was from Cabanatuan; they were mostly landowners of properties in the commercial district. His sister Cora lived in Bulacan, but his brother Tasio and his sister Pacing lived in Cabanatuan. The siblings who were not so well-off relied on the rent to supplement their incomes. Since Carlos was their eldest, the brother and sisters came to Carlos's house to air their fears and ask for advice.

"Elder brother, what is the best thing to do?" Pacing, the youngest sister, asked.

"The Japanese are not here yet. If you plan to move, do it now. If you want to stay in the city, be careful. I don't know which is better."

"If you want to go to San Nicholas, the house is big," Clara added.

The food was ready. They ate their supper together, each one sighing now and then. A desultory talk of saving what was more important could not even be resolved.

"The property titles are here. Our problem is how to survive until the war is over. I don't know how long this will last," Carlos said.

One morning, there was a burst of gunfire near the town's school, across from the church. Some people hid and peered through their windows. Others came out to the streets and wondered what the noise was. The rumbling noise of tanks and trucks became louder as a column of Japanese troops came into view.

The only resistance was a group of policemen standing near the statue of General Antonio Luna in the school yard. They fired their pistols and were killed on the spot by the enemy. The Japanese army had arrived in Cabanatuan.

They marched down Rizal Avenue while people lined the streets in awe and fear. Behind the infantry, the jeeps and tanks churned the dust and made the watchers cover their mouths and noses. One platoon after another marched to take over in each government building; the soldiers had their guns drawn. There was no resistance.

By the time the Japanese army advanced to Cabanatuan, the American soldiers had already left for Bataan. The civil servants fled their posts and hid at home. The townspeople were relieved they did not kill Mr. Mifune and Yoshiro; otherwise, they would really have suffered.

The Japanese marched into what used to be the American training camp and occupied it like it was theirs to start with. They released the Mifunes and saluted them: the colonel and the lieutenant.

The people who had been clamoring to kill the Mifunes, especially the de Leon family, went into hiding.

Clara felt some trepidation as she wondered if Colonel Mifune guessed about her report. She remained calm externally and watched for any sign that he knew.

Neneng also became apprehensive. Now that Yoshiro has the upper hand, would it be his turn to abuse power? She hoped not.

A subdued apprehension settled in the provinces because people did not know what to expect. Sporadic clashes occurred between the Japanese and the U.S.-Philippine forces that did not make it to Bataan.

Carlos Mendez and his family planned to move to San Nicholas, Gapan, but they procrastinated as there was an upsurge of sick patients needing his care. Carlos sympathized with patients who had no money but paid him with chickens, eggs, or any food; but he also ended up being called to the Japanese camp to help treat the wounded.

"This is going to give me a problem," Carlos said to his family that evening. "I'm afraid of being called a collaborator, but I have to obey the order."

Clara and Neneng held his hand and each said a prayer.

The group of Japanese soldiers who picked up Carlos had also visited Farmacia Mendez and taken all the bandages and other surgical supplies. As soon as they left, Clara called Juling softly.

"Watch the store and tell me if someone is coming."

"Ma'am?" Juling's question was met by a sign to be silent.

Clara started getting boxes to horde medicines, especially the quinine. She took the Vino de Quina that her mother liked to take for stomachache, fever, and whatever else ailed her. She took it upstairs and hid three bottles at the back of the glasses in the china cabinet. She looked for boxes in the rooms and came hurrying down to pack more medicine. She was perspiring and feeling tense when Juling made a sound.

"Somebody's coming!" Juling said softly.

Clara got up, wiped her perspiration, and fanned herself with the cardboard from a box. "How warm it is!" she said.

Mr. Quitos appeared in a crumpled shirt with blotches of dust on one sleeve and his collar.

"We just arrived from San Isidro. I was almost apprehended on suspicion of being a guerilla. We are leaving tonight for the mountains. Where is Carlos?"

"He was fetched by Japanese soldiers to help out with the wounded," Clara said in a hushed voice, looking beyond at the street.

"You'd better leave soon too!" Mr. Quitos said. After a hesitating look around at the street, he left quickly.

Just then the church bells rang the noon hour. Clara closed her eyes, then forcibly stared ahead. Then she prayed the Angelus as Juling watched her.

PART TWO

XII

A simmering grievance pervaded Germany after the Treaty of Versailles was signed in 1919 to end World War I. The punitive terms exacted by the Allies were later met with defiance by the rise of Adolf Hitler, who led his country to Nazism.

Italy was under the fascist regime of Benito Mussolini, and in Japan, radical factions advocating imperialistic expansion had taken hold.

Russia was a communist state, and the neighboring countries of Yugoslavia, Bulgaria, Hungary, Czechoslovakia, and Romania aligned with Germany to avoid the spread of socialism. Treaties and alliances were being signed by different countries with questionable moral hold.

In 1938, the German-Austrian Anschluss was proclaimed; followed by the Germans marching to Austria, then to Czechoslovakia. In 1939, when the Germans marched to Poland, England and France entered the war because of a previous alliance with Poland. In 1940, the Germans invaded France.

Whereas the European powers had once raced to spread their influence through their colonies in Asia and Africa, they could no longer protect their holdings.

Japan pressured the Vichy government to allow it to occupy French Indochina in June 1940, prompting the United States to impose an embargo of steel exports to Japan. Later, U.S. President Franklin D. Roosevelt also imposed an embargo on the war materials that Japan had been importing, including petroleum products, oil, and aluminum.

In 1941, the U.S. government froze Japanese assets; the Dutch government in exile and England also did the same. Now Japan deliberated to get the oil from the Dutch East Indies by force.

By mid-November 1941, the U.S. and Japan were struggling in their effort to avert a breakdown of diplomatic negotiations. Talks were on overtime as Japan basically wanted the United States to leave it alone while it expanded its influence in Asia. The Japanese ambassador requested an extension of the talks to late November, and then to early December.

On November 19, 1941, Tokyo used a low level code J-19 to advise diplomats in Washington that in case of emergency and loss of international communications, they should be on alert and listen to shortwave radio. If they heard the words "east wind rain" in the middle of the news broadcast, they would know that relations with America were in danger. If they heard the words "north wind cloudy," it referred to Russia; and if they heard "west wind clear," it referred to Great Britain. The United States Signal Intelligence Services (SIS) became preoccupied with listening for this wind code information.

Decades earlier, the SIS had gotten off to a rocky start. In World War I, the director of military intelligence recognized the genius for cryptology of Major Herbert O. Yardley. Yardley was moved to New York. In six months, Yardley broke the code the Japanese developed in 1919. This was instrumental in helping the United States make Japan agree to the limitation of naval tonnage ratio at the Washington Naval Conference in 1920.

In 1929, when Secretary of State Henry Stimson found out about the "black chamber" run by Yardley, Stimson thought it was unethical to spy on "friendly" countries and shut it down. Out of work, Yardley published two books that told of his discoveries. When the other countries learned of this, U.S. intelligence gathering was set back.

Although the United States did not have many people working in Intelligence, the SIS broke the Japanese Type A Code in 1936. They called the machine that broke it the Red Machine. When the Japanese changed their codes in 1938, it took the SIS group until September 1940 to break the new codes. They classified the machine that broke the code as Purple, and they called the entire code designations Magic.

There was no Purple machine in Hawaii, but there was one in the Philippines at Fort McKinley. Although the Army Section in the Philippines received the messages, they had to bring it to the navy section, and it was processed at Corregidor for interpretation. The navy did not give the information to General MacArthur's Army Section.

On November 27, U.S. Armed Forces Chief of Staff General George Marshall sent a communication to the commanders of Pearl Harbor, Manila, Guam, and Wake Island that war was imminent.

Around December 1, 1941, successive messages were intercepted from Tokyo to the Japanese Embassy in Washington. Some took time (December 3–5) to be decrypted. First, the Japanese Embassy was told to destroy the codes and the Purple machine; then they were instructed to contact the naval attache for the special chemicals that would ensure the documents were properly destroyed. The message was repeated.

As of December 1941, the SIS had broken six hundred out of the 1,280 Japanese diplomatic codes they had intercepted. Japanese naval intelligence codes were harder to break; only 10 percent were broken at the outbreak of the war.

The tireless work of Colonel Wolf Frederick Friedman and Lieutenant Colonel Frank B. Rowlett with the SIS group, and later Captain Joseph Rochefort, a combat intelligence officer with the navy, were critical factors in decrypting enemy codes.

Aside from the SIS group, the breakthrough was known only to the top-level members of the War Cabinet and the president. There was a system of signing for the documents after reading them, returning them to the messenger, and after the messages had made the rounds of the top brass, the documents would be destroyed except for a single copy. There was an atmosphere of suspicion and a need to keep the reports from the hands of those with socialist sympathies.

By December 3, 1941, President Roosevelt, General George Marshall, Secretary of War Henry Stimson, Navy Secretary Frank Knox, and Secretary of State Cordell Hull were aware that the Japanese embassies had been instructed to destroy their intelligence decoding machines. General Marshall again sent messages to the U.S. forces. The War Cabinet waited with apprehension for U.S. intelligence to notify them that the winds code had come through.

Although Marshall had been regularly sending intelligence communications to the Pearl Harbor command, as in any bureaucracy, each department was protective of its own turf. There was rivalry between army and navy and between layers of officers conscious of their own ambitions. There arose the question of whether the information intended for someone ever reached that person at all. Add to that ineptitude and incompetence, and the U.S. had a problem.

One important message, known as cable 519, had crucial information that would have re-emphasized to the Pearl Harbor command to be on alert. Sadly, on later investigation, this was found to be sitting on the desk of the G2 officer of the Hawaiian Department, supposedly an intelligence liaison who did not even have top-security clearance.

Nevertheless, the assistant G2 told the staff conference about it on December 6, during the weekly intelligence estimates, already three days after the message was received. Later that afternoon, the FBI agent for Hawaii told this assistant they had intercepted a phone call from Tokyo to Hawaii asking about fleets, sailors, searchlights, aircraft, weather, hibiscus, and poinsettias. This assistant told the G2 colonel to alert Lieutenant General Short. They told him they would wait for him if he could be in the headquarters in ten minutes. He got there and told them about it, but the two were not impressed.

On December 6, a fourteen-point ominous message that had been urgently decrypted sat through the night on the Washington DC desk of the G2 assistant to the Far Eastern Section, while he went home to read a novel.

This message was the Japanese government's instructions to its diplomats. The final message instructed that Japan was breaking off diplomatic relations with the U.S. The G2 officer did not understand this meant war. He delivered the message to War Department officials at 9:00 AM on December 7.

Upon seeing it, General Marshall urgently sent the message to the Pearl Harbor Command. His assistant assured Marshall that it would be delivered in an hour. There was a delay, however, and Marshall was not told about it. The War Department radio had been unable to reach Pearl Harbor since 10:20 AM Washington DC time. The encrypted message was then sent by commercial cable via Western Union to San Francisco. From there, it was sent by RCA commercial radio to Honolulu. In Hawaii, around dawn that Sunday, the teletype hook-up between the RCA office and Fort Shafter in Hawaii was not operating. RCA sent a messenger boy on a bicycle to Fort Shafter for General Short after 7:00 AM (1:00 PM Washington DC time).

On December 7, 1941, at 1:00 PM U.S. Central Time (7:00 AM Hawaii time; 2:00 AM, December 8, Philippine time), the Japanese ambassador was scheduled for a meeting with Secretary of State

Cordell Hull. The Japanese ambassador arrived late; by then, Pearl Harbor was already being bombed. The ambassador was confronted with the news. He apologized and left.

The messenger bringing the cable to General Short in Pearl Harbor took cover in an air raid shelter when the bombs fell. When he delivered the cable at 11:00 AM, the bombing was already over.

The Pearl Harbor Command should not have been caught by surprise, but they were. Even with the failure of communications to come promptly, war had been in the air. Instead, miscommunications plagued the chain of command. Add to this the misunderstanding that arose because the Standard Operating Procedure (SOP) of July 14 was revised by General Short on November 5, 1941. In it, Short reversed the order of importance on alert readiness. What was number one, the highest form of readiness, was now number three, and number one was an alert on sabotage. Although Short said he notified Washington, this revision was received four months after the bombing of Pearl Harbor.

The U.S. War Department had been aware of the importance of an air warning system that helped England during the Battle of Britain. They sent Commander William E.G. Taylor, who had been through the experience, to Hawaii in order to set up a system.

The army had no permanent radar installation, but it had five mobile sets in use. That would have been adequate, but General Short claimed there were not enough trained personnel to man it for twenty-four hours. The radar worked only from 4:00 AM to 7:00 AM, making it difficult to train plotters and operators for more than three hours per day. There was a meeting to address some problems between the army and navy on November 24, especially for an aircraft identification system. The problem was not resolved.

On December 7, at 7:00 AM the radar station was operating, with radar operators who were being trained. At that time, B-17 bombers were scheduled to arrive at Pearl Harbor. From one hundred miles away, the operators saw the Japanese planes coming, but without a system of identification, they could not tell friend from foe.

The navy also did not have its radar system on, because when the ships entered the port, the radar did not work because of the surrounding hills; also, the radar caused havoc with local civilian electronic communications. The army did not know this, and the navy did not know that the army radar system worked only a few hours a day.

The mindset of the average soldier, the lookouts, and the focus of the defense systems did not expect the first wave of attackers that arrived at 7:53 AM on Sunday, December 7. Japanese fighter planes came first, followed by level bombers, then dive bombers and torpedo bombers. The first wave lasted fifteen minutes. The Japanese used about 233 aircraft in the attack.

The second wave arrived at 8:50 AM with about 120 planes. Later investigation would disclose that when the first Japanese bombers appeared, roughly 25 percent of the navy's anti-aircraft batteries, consisting of 780 guns, were manned and firing. Within seven to ten minutes, all the navy's anti-aircraft guns were manned and firing.

The same could not be said of the army. Of the thirty-one anti-aircraft batteries under army command, twenty-seven of them were not in position or supplied with ammunition until after the attack ended.

Thus, eighteen U.S. ships, including four battleships—USS *Oklahoma*, USS *West Virginia*, USS *California*, and the USS *Arizona*—were sunk or incapacitated. One hundred sixty-four aircraft were lost, 124 crippled. Wheeler Field, Kaneohe Naval Air Station, Bellow's Field, Ford Island, and Ewa and Hickam Field were in shambles. There were 2,403 dead and 1,178 wounded.

By serendipity, the USS *Enterprise* was out in Wake Island delivering twelve fighter planes to reinforce it. This was the flagship of Vice Admiral William Halsey of Task Force 8. Bad weather had delayed its return to Pearl Harbor. As it was coming back, some of its planes saw the Pearl Harbor attack and joined in the melee. Four were lost, some probably by friendly fire. Two other U.S. carriers were also not in Pearl Harbor on Dec. 7: the USS *Lexington* and the USS *Saratoga*.

Lieutenant General Walter C. Short and Admiral Husband E. Kimmel would later be relieved of their commands.

Since the Philippines at that time was a Commonwealth of the United States, it was thought that the U.S. Naval fleet in Pearl Harbor was established not only to assert the U.S. presence in Asia, but also to protect the American Commonwealth.

Three hours after attacking Pearl Harbor, the Japanese started bombing the Philippines.

XIII

Since 1938, the upheaval in Europe caused nations to be alert for impending war. The first president of the Philippine Commonwealth, Manuel Quezon, asked General Douglas MacArthur to be the field marshal of the Philippine Armed Forces.

MacArthur had retired in 1936 after serving as U.S. Army chief of staff. He had been in the Philippines before and had a brilliant career. Arriving thus in the Philippines, MacArthur wanted four hundred thousand soldiers trained by April 1942. However, the Great Depression was still ongoing, wrecking havoc on worldwide economy. The Philippine Commonwealth did not have enough funds, equipment, or supplies, and less than half of prospective soldiers were being trained.

When World War II broke out, U.S. President Franklin Delano Roosevelt recalled MacArthur to head the United States Far East Armed Forces. MacArthur stayed at the Manila Hotel, where he also had his office.

By then, eighty thousand Filipino soldiers were available to defend their country; and there were fifteen thousand American soldiers in the islands. There was also food preparation—about ten million pounds of rice were stored in Cabanatuan.

However, the ammunition and equipment of the U.S. and Filipino soldiers were not geared for battle. The supplies were inadequate and mismatched, and most were obsolete. The airplanes and their maintenance were not adequate. Whatever was handed to the newly trained Filipino soldiers was wanting too. The Philippine Scouts, composed of elite U.S. and Filipino soldiers, was the only group that was fairly equipped and trained.

Aware of the imminent threat from Japan, U.S. strategists had already devised plans in their war rooms. The first plan was called Rainbow 5. This plan was in effect when war broke out. It called for the defense of the Philippines by attacking the enemy as the invasion force lands on the shores. Major General Jonathan Wainwright would command the North Luzon Force; Major General George Parker would command the South Luzon Force; and Major General William Sharp would command the southern Philippines, including Mindanao.

The bombing of Pearl Harbor crippled the very defense the United States had envisioned for control of the Pacific. At 3:00 AM, December 8, Philippine time, only minutes after the attack on Pearl Harbor, the radio operator in the Philippines communicated to the Philippine Command that Pearl Harbor had been bombed.

Major General Lewis Brereton of the air force ordered his pilots to get ready, but no order came from MacArthur's office. Brereton went to the Manila Hotel, where General MacArthur had his headquarters. Brereton wanted his pilots to counterattack on the Japanese base in Formosa (later Taiwan) since he thought that it would be the source for air assault on the Philippines.

By some accounts, Colonel Richard Sutherland, MacArthur's chief of staff, did not enable Brereton to see MacArthur. The reason was that MacArthur was in communication with President Quezon, and they were of the opinion that the Japanese would not immediately attack the Philippines. MacArthur was also in conference with Admiral Hart.

At the Manila Hotel the night before, there had been a party that lasted into the wee hours of the morning. The pilots who needed to fly the airplanes at Fort Stotsenberg (later renamed Clark Air Base) in Pampanga Province, Luzon, were at that party.

Hawaii time is one day later than the Philippines: 7:53 AM on December 7, 1941, in Hawaii was just before 3:00 AM on December 8 in the Philippines.

Still, at 8:30 AM Philippine time, there were combat planes in the air ready for encounter, but there were no enemies. At 11:30 AM, the pilots in Fort Stotsenberg got their planes refueled while they sat down for lunch. Suddenly, the Japanese planes arrived and strafed all the planes sitting on the airfield.

There were some planes from Cavite Naval Base near Manila that engaged the enemy, and a Filipino captain named Jesus Villamor was among those who fought in spite of the odds.

Unknown to the U.S.-Philippine forces, when they were in the air that fateful morning, the Japanese attack from Formosa was delayed by heavy fog. Just when the Allies sat down for lunch, the fog lifted, and the Japanese attack met no resistance.

Again, on December 9, the Japanese were held down by bad weather. The Allies used the time for whatever they could repair. By December 10, the Japanese planes came back, and the remaining planes could not hold up to the attack. Now the air force was severely incapacitated.

On top of this, the naval base in Cavite was badly damaged. Admiral Hart ordered all remaining ships to go to the Dutch East Indies.

On December 10, two thousand Japanese soldiers landed in Aparri. Most of the Filipino troops were still lacking in training and not yet ready for war; they were easily intimidated by the arriving invaders and got scattered. By December 22, Lieutenant General Masaharu Homma arrived to head the main invading force of forty-three thousand in Lingayen Gulf. Included in this group was the Fourteenth Army, battle hardened in China. The U.S.-Philippine Forces, especially the Twenty-sixth Cavalry of the Philippine Scouts, put up a fight, but was overcome. On December 23, ten thousand more Japanese landed in Lamon Bay, southeast of Manila. The invading force was helped by planes flying from Formosa. The Philippines had no aerial or naval support.

After December 8, the U.S.-Philippine forces worked feverishly to put the war plan into action. The officers came from meetings, briefed the men, drilled, worked on the papers, and checked the supplies. Back and forth, everybody tried hard to come up to the sudden war status. But busy as they were, even if they missed their meals, it seemed they were always behind.

The lower level soldiers did not fare any better. There were misunderstandings in the chaotic rush to get things done; and some orders either did not make sense, or they could not be carried out.

By December 23, MacArthur scrapped Rainbow 5 and ordered War Plan Orange to be put into effect. This alternate strategy called for all Allied forces to go to Bataan and stall the enemy until help could arrive.

After MacArthur moved President Quezon to Corregidor on December 24, MacArthur also moved there with his family and staff.

Corregidor, the rock fortress guarding Manila Bay, had an extensive underground tunnel network called Malinta. There was a main aisle with several perpendicular paths leading to different sections, like offices, living quarters, supply rooms, hospital, etc.

On December 26, MacArthur declared Manila an open city so the Japanese would not come in full assault. It meant there would be no defenses, and civilians would be spared.

From Manila, Bataan was not too far away, but the Allies coming from the northern and southern tips of Luzon had to come from quite a distance. The Allies from Mindanao would not make it.

It was a race against time for the U.S.-Philippine forces to get to Bataan before the Japanese figured out their strategy. On Christmas 1941, some men were not even able to eat or have the chance to greet each other on a great feast day. Sweating, hurrying, and worrying, they had to meet the deadline to get to Bataan.

By December 31, Nichols Air Base, Fort McKinley, the Manila Port Area, and Cavite were all blown up. Some were hit by strafing Japanese planes, but others were destroyed by the Allies so the enemy could not use those resources. The troops coming from the north were especially hampered by the roads that were clogged up by burned and bombed vehicles.

At first, General Homma did not give it much importance when his pilots reported the Allies were spotted going to Bataan. Homma was confident, and the Japanese entered Manila on January 2, 1942.

Meanwhile, the Allies scrambled to get all their forces into Bataan. They even hired Pambusco (Pampanga Bus Company) buses to help move troops and supplies. Layac Bridge was the primary paved connection of the Bataan peninsula to the big Luzon Island. General Wainwright and his men watched anxiously as the weary troops crossed Layac Bridge to what they thought was their safe haven.

Trucks carrying supplies rumbled across the bridge, but some of those were empty, for they still had problems with disorganization and miscommunication. At one point, a soldier asking about two thousand cases of food in Tarlac was told that it was Japanese property. The ten million pounds of rice stored in Cabanatuan (Nueva Ecija) was not brought because of an old law prohibiting its shipment from one province to another. An oil supply was left behind because when somebody asked about it, he was given the run-around.

There were three hundred barge loads of ammunition and food sent from Manila that were lost or misplaced in transition. Ammunition brought by the trucks were not enough; some were obsolete. Vehicles had to drive without lights so the Japanese could not detect the troop movement. Some trucks driving without lights at night would get lost, but if they drove with lights on, the military police shot out the lights.

One truck driver arrived in Bataan and saw there was not enough food, whereas he knew there were a lot of food boxes in the Port Area. He drove back to Manila and hauled food back to Bataan. He was able to repeat this; the third time he ran into a Japanese patrol.

Through the night of January 5, 1942, and into the early hours of January 6, the Twenty-first Division headed by Brigadier General Mateo Capinpin held the rear until all the troops had gone across the bridge. The tanks covered the retreat, and when the tail end of the formation rumbled over the bridge, Capinpin's men withdrew across the bridge and waited.

The Allies had put bombs on the steel girders of Layac Bridge under the direction of Colonel Ray O Day. Captain A. P. Chanco held the trigger to demolish it. Once they had all cleared out, Wainwright gave the approval, and soon the steel bridge collapsed to the chasm below.

Like any anticlimax, some tanks arrived after the bridge had been blown, and their soldiers abandoned their tanks and crossed on foot. Other tanks went farther below the river and were able to cross to Bataan.

The eighty thousand soldiers—sixty-five thousand Filipino and fifteen thousand Americans—collectively heaved a sigh of relief. Bataan was going to be their sanctuary, but they did not know what awaited them.

XIV

Lieutenant Jack Stewart looked at his watch anxiously. It was only 9:00 AM this cloudy day of December 29, 1941. He was in a convoy of jeeps and trucks from Northern Ilocos that snaked its way down the zigzag Baguio highway. Recent rains had made the roads difficult for travel.

The U.S. officers had not finished training the soldiers who were supposed to keep the enemy from landing on the beach. The enemy did land, and now the strategy was to head for Bataan. Since they were among those coming from the northernmost areas, and they had to avoid the coastal roads swarming with enemies, Jack doubted they could make it to Bataan in time.

One of the trucks with a load of ammunition was struck by a large falling boulder. The other vehicles screeched to a halt as more rocks came cascading down the mountainous highway.

"Krupski is hurt!" the medic said.

"Bauer, you drive!" Colonel Folwell ordered.

Krupski was bleeding from the glass that had shattered from the front windshield. The boulder had fallen on the front hood, and the engine was smashed.

"This truck ain't moving!" Corporal Bauer said.

"Transfer the supplies! Move faster!" Colonel Folwell was getting impatient.

Another truck came forward and moved the disabled one out of the way. The men were sweating and hurrying to transfer the weapons, and they sighed in relief as they returned to their vehicles.

The commotion and damage preoccupied the men. As the engines were revving up to resume their trek, a few men looked up when they heard approaching planes. Most men only heard the planes when they dived to strafe them.

Bombs fell on the trucks, causing ear-splitting explosions of ammunition and oil tanks. Gunfire rained on soldiers as they jumped out of vehicles and ran for cover.

Private Burke had just started the jeep, and he hit the brakes so hard that Jack bumped his head on the dashboard. Jack shook that off quickly and jumped out, heading for the ditch. He took cover and returned fire, but he only had a revolver.

The Japanese planes strafed their convoy several times until all the trucks exploded with a deafening BOOM! Jack looked at the jeep he had just jumped out of. The captain still sat there, but he was immobile with blood all over his face.

Jack and the other soldiers fired back mostly out of wanting to retaliate, even if it was ineffective. They were getting slaughtered without the means to fight back. It seemed like a very long time before the strafing stopped. Pinned where they had taken cover, the Allies had been silent after the useless guns they fired ran out of bullets. The enemy must have presumed them dead as the planes flew away.

Jack and Lieutenant Eduardo Buendia each walked around the perimeter of the scene. There was no sense in cleaning up the mess; the planes might come back. The road was littered with the carcasses of wrecked metal, and the smoke made breathing difficult.

They started removing the bodies from the roadway and into a clearing. Private Hart finally moved from where he lay on the road and helped. Slowly, some bodies started moving.

Jack saw Corporal Bauer stand up from a grassy knoll where he had run for cover. Bauer massaged his neck and looked relieved. He touched his forehead and stared at the blood in his hands. Looking around, he walked to a lopsided mirror on the side of a wrecked truck, tore his sleeve, and bandaged his head with it.

"Attaboy," Private Hart said.

"Shaddup!" Bauer growled.

It was hard not to grieve the loss of friends, but they had to hurry too. There were fourteen men left out of the entire convoy. The first gravesite they dug was not enough; they ended up filling three. They were all sweating and tired by the time the last shovelful of earth covered the third patch.

Jack led the prayer on the first site, Lieutenant Buendia on the second, and Corporal Bauer on the third. They sprinkled water from their canteens on each, imitating what they had seen priests do.

"For dust thou art, and to dust thou shalt return," Private Hart intoned when their service was over.

Corporal Bauer gave Hart a long look, but Buendia already answered.

"It's true."

They searched whatever was left for food and ate hungrily by the shade of a flame tree. Finally, they assessed the damage. Jack and Buendia were the highest-ranking officers left. The general and the colonels, majors, and captains were all dead; even the doctor had died as the medic van plunged into the ravine below and exploded.

They gathered whatever food and serviceable supplies there were and loaded them into the only two vehicles that could still function: two beat-up jeeps. They loaded them up to the passenger seats.

"We're here," Jack said, pointing on the map.

"We can take cover in the mountains while we assess if we can make it to the rendezvous," Buendia said.

"Let's get off the road here and head toward this mountain. Pretty soon, some traffic might make more vehicles available for us to join the main command," Jack said.

Their regiment had received the order to move to Bataan belatedly. Now it was even harder to get there. Except for the alternating drivers, they all walked behind the jeep, every now and then giving it a heave as they made their own path among the shrubs and trees of the mountain slope.

Their radio was not working, but Private Bender promised he could get it working soon. It rained the next couple of days, and the men's anxiety worsened with the weather. They found a shallow cave, but it was their supplies they prioritized there. The men made do with makeshift tents made out of the canvas cloth they had with their supplies.

When the sun came out, the first static news was unintelligible, but Bender continued working on it and cursing. At last they heard some news—Japanese propaganda for them to surrender. The next day they heard from Bataan.

"If Layac Bridge has been blown, the only way for us to join in Bataan will be by boats from Zambales," Jack looked at Buendia.

"All the surrounding areas are teeming with Japanese," Buendia responded.

"It might be wiser for us to sit here and wait for another chance. If we run through the Japanese gauntlet, it will be useless if none of us survive," Jack said.

They agreed to stay where they were and followed the events on the radio. They improved their living conditions by building huts out of the trees and shrubs around them.

XV

The Bataan peninsula juts southward of the Zambales and Pampanga provinces, on the Luzon mainland. It is thirty miles long and fifteen miles wide. Its eastern shore is surrounded by Manila Bay, while the western and southern sides are bounded by the South China Sea. The beach on its southeast tip is only two miles across the sea from Corregidor.

On the southern tip of Bataan was the Mariveles Naval Base. A ship passing between the tip of Bataan and Corregidor would sail to Manila. South of Manila, along the coast, and north of Corregidor, was Cavite, where a U.S. Navy base was located.

Bataan has two large volcanoes, Mount Natib and Mount Samat. In between these volcanoes was a horizontal road. There were two more roads, one on the east, along the coast, and another one, albeit incomplete, on the west. Aside from these apparently unscaleable volcanoes, there were towns, beaches, banana plantations, jungles, and rice paddies.

Ten miles south of Layac Bridge, the Allies drew a horizontal line of defense. It ran through a banana plantation called Abucay and on through Mauban. They called this the Abucay-Mauban line.

Major General Jonathan Wainwright's group oversaw the retreat, and the men were tired. Major General George Parker's group was still fresh; they had tanks, twenty-five thousand men of the Fifty-first and the Fifty-seventh Philippine divisions, and the elite Philippine Scouts. Wainwright's group was going to defend the west, and Parker was going to defend the east side of the peninsula.

The Japanese Forty-eighth Division pursued the Allies to Bataan. These were battle-hardened men who had fought in China. Not realizing the impact of the Allied strategy, General Homma sent the Forty-eighth Division to Java.

On January 11, 1942, the Japanese attacking the Allied stronghold were overaged soldiers and not as well trained. Lieutenant

General Akira Nara commanded the Japanese assault. He divided his forces into two groups: two infantry divisions attacking frontally from the Layac area; and another division that would go west, through Mount Natib, and then south, to encircle the Allies. This latter group would have to scale Mt. Natib, complete with their equipment and supplies.

As early as January 8, General MacArthur realized the insufficiency of their food supplies. He ordered that the rations for the Allies be cut by half.

When War Plan Orange went into effect, John Stewart's infantry division was among the first to move out. He was aware of the disorganization and miscommunication problems.

"I told you there were trucks full of food that we left behind there!" the private argued.

"Well, we don't have it. That's all!" the cook answered impatiently.

"Cut it out!" Lieutenant Dawson could not help intervening.

John commanded one regiment stationed along the Abucay-Mauban line. The shortage of food was beginning to tell on his men. One of his battalions lost ground the previous night, but now they were on the verge of retaking it.

"Captain Torres was just taken to the hospital, Colonel," Lieutenant Dawson reported. "He is dehydrated from his dysentery."

"Thank you, Lieutenant," John said, when suddenly a barrage of gunfire erupted in their direction, cutting off several trunks of banana trees.

The officers ducked for cover and returned fire. Most of them used their revolvers, and only then realized their machine gunner had just been killed. A private crawled quickly to the machine gun, and as the exchange continued, the gap in the barbed wire showed where the enemies were coming from.

Lieutenant Dawson threw a grenade into the spot, but there was no explosion. John threw his, and after the explosion, there were several dead enemies on the ground. There was only a brief pause, then more enemies stepped over the bodies of their dead comrades to resume the attack.

"Come on!" another private challenged as he set out with his bayonet.

A sergeant beside him lifted a machine gun to his waist level and fired continuously.

It took over an hour, but they were able to hold their position. They had been caught by surprise, thinking their scouts would warn them, but those sentinels were dead, their throats had been stealthily slashed the night before. Sweating and grim, with guards on the perimeter, the other soldiers buried their dead.

"Not all the grenades are working right. In case of doubt, throw another one; that is, if we have any more," John commented.

Lieutenant Dawson was still shaken from his near miss. His hand grenade was one of those duds that had not worked right.

The next day was more of the same. Relentlessly, the Japanese attacked the defense line and took advantage of the gaps that opened up.

Just as the fighting was most intense, a messenger arrived from the western defense line. The Japanese infantry division that scaled Mt. Natib had suddenly arrived and attacked. They startled General Wainwright's men, and the Allies could not match the ferocity of the newcomers.

On January 23, 1942, the Allies had to retreat to the second line of defense, the Bagac-Orion Line, ten miles farther south. The men were weary of falling back, but John knew it was just from pride. Dismantling their tents and carting out their ammunitions, the men piled past the stalks of banana trunks.

"It was better among the bananas!" complained a private.

"Uh!" a corporal slapped his forehead, killing a mosquito.

They were in a jungle area with moist undergrowth. The murmur of a nearby stream lighted up some men's eyes.

"We can fill our canteens!" one private said.

The others just grunted. Most men had been made aware that daytime biting mosquitoes might be carriers of dengue (Philippine hemorrhagic fever), and nighttime biting mosquitoes were carriers of malaria. They were supposed to avoid going to those places where mosquitoes abounded. They marched until they reached a mountain slope with craggy rocks.

John nodded in acknowledgement as his regiment crossed paths with the Fifty-seventh and the Forty-fifth Infantry Divisions of the

Philippine Scouts. John knew those men would be taking on the enemies on the eastern flank.

The Philippine Scouts had started as a group of Filipino soldiers helping the Americans during the insurrection. They knew the terrain and scouted for the Americans. The tradition of soldiering was strong, and these men were better trained than the new recruits who signed up just before the war.

But whether they were Americans, Filipinos, Philippine Scouts, or new recruits, they were all human -hungry and sick at varying degrees of severity. A report stated that more than half of the men were sick from various tropical illnesses, but John doubted the accuracy of the report.

Men suffered not only from malaria and dengue, but also from dysentery, which was being spread by flies, and from starvation, which made things worse. Men were fighting even if they were sick, just as he was. He had started having a fever the night before, but he had put off a visit to the hospital.

The Japanese attack continued with some brilliant strategy at times. Some of their hit-and-run units infiltrated Allied lines, deluding the Allies into thinking there were more enemies out there. Some Japanese units had audaciously advanced way ahead of the rest and ended up as isolated pockets in Allied territory. One such group of one thousand men under Colonel Yoshioka was reduced to five hundred men with no food and little water. They were dug in and surrender was never in their minds. By February 10, however, they received an order to retreat.

"Sir! They're gone!" a corporal said apprehensively to Captain Delgado.

"Who? What!" Captain Lauro Delgado was mad after realizing who had gone.

John Stewart turned from reading a memo. Captain Delgado was coming toward him, with the corporal following close at his heels.

"They must have crept out of their foxholes last night; our soldiers did not see anything! We were surprised the foxholes were so quiet this morning," the corporal continued excitedly.

"We cannot afford these mistakes!" Captain Delgado said and threw away the cigarette he had once looked forward to smoking.

John Stewart patted Captain Delgado's shoulder. They were all getting edgy. Even here at the Bagac-Orion line, the second line of defense, the enemy attacked incessantly. Now their one chance to corner one of the 'pockets' have just vanished.

At the officers' meeting, most of them realized they were really spreading themselves thin. There was another pocket in the center of the Eleventh Division, and another down the gorge of the Cotar River. The enemy came from different directions.

Worse, Japanese soldiers on boats had started arriving on the southern beaches. They landed at Quinauan, Longoskawayan, and Agloloma points, as well as the tiny peninsula between the Anyasan and Salaiim rivers. The Allies have to assign units to the beach area to stop the enemy forces from building a beachhead. This usually tied up the defense units as the enemy holed up in caves and rock outcrops, refusing to surrender. The Allied defense line was spread thin.

As enemies charged in wave after wave, the Allied boats, minesweepers, and airplanes from Corregidor helped. It took time, with most episodes resolved with all enemies killed and no prisoners taken, for the Japanese did not surrender.

The Allied air force units also suffered severe losses. One squadron that was deployed at Cabcaben airfield had been reduced to 16 from 107 P40 planes; there were only four of the P35 planes left out of fifty-two. By the end of January, more were lost.

If the soldiers were hungry on half-rations, they became hungrier still when their ration was cut another half, into quarter-rations in early February 1942. More soldiers were sick, and supplies were running very low. Malnutrition and starvation were now on the equation.

One morning, the bright sun added to the stifling humidity even before the men got breakfast. The officers were about to start their briefing when a burst of machine gun fire came out of the forest nearby. Not having much time to think, everybody picked up their weapons and charged toward the melee. A huge assault was on. The front soldiers were already wiped out, and the enemies were surging forward.

"Ugh!" the corporal beside John let out a grunt as he fell backward, lifeless.

John dropped his revolver and picked up the machine gun that fell from the corporal. He charged forward as he pressed the trigger, and he belatedly realized he was isolated out front with only two other Allies on either side of him.

"Cover!" Captain Delgado said, and John rolled toward a rock several feet behind him.

"Go!" John said, as one by one, they took turns to return to their main line of defense.

The respite was brief. Machine gun fire was soon reverberating from the woods ahead of them; then it was not from the jungle anymore. The enemy was advancing on the clearing, and there were hordes of them.

Picking up more ammo with one hand, John raised his other hand to signal a retreat. "Fall back!" he shouted.

He formed an imaginary line with several officers holding off the enemy while the others retreated past the kitchen, past the tents, and deeper into the slopes of Mount Samat.

"They're still coming!" John said, looking at his machine gun. He had used the last round already. Now they were getting weapons from the dead nearby.

"We might just get butchered!" the corporal beside him whispered what was in everybody else's mind. They were all sweating now.

"We're near the camp of the Eighty-eighth Field Artillery Regiment! Keep firing!" John shouted back.

"Last round, I'll cover," Captain Delgado said.

"I'll take the next," John said with a sigh of relief. He had just grabbed another machine gun.

Suddenly, they heard a burst of machine gun fire from the kitchen. The mess sergeant was running toward the enemy without cover. The sergeant had picked up a machine gun from a fallen soldier and went charging by himself. The enemy was startled only for a while, then they recovered and cut the sergeant down.

"No!" cried a corporal.

"Calugas!" Delgado turned in time to recognize the mess sergeant.

Sergeant Calugas fell with the blood bursting from his chest. He bought with his life the short respite that gave John and his men enough time to retreat.

On the Japanese side, Lieutenant General Masaharu Homma was not having it easy either. In February, during a staff meeting, Homma burst into tears and fainted; by March, he was summoned to Tokyo. Homma requested more troops, tanks, and other support. With the addition of fifteen thousand men, the infantry attack force now numbered fifty thousand soldiers.

Meanwhile, Philippine President Quezon had already left Corregidor by February 20, 1942. He was taken by submarine to Antique, in the Visayas, and then moved to Mindanao. There were still American airplanes able to fly to and from Mindanao, since Mindanao was not fully occupied yet. From there, Quezon was flown to Australia, taken by steamer to California, and subsequently transported by train to Washington DC.

President Roosevelt ordered MacArthur to leave Corregidor. On March 11, MacArthur left with a heavy heart for Australia.

"I shall return!" MacArthur vowed to the Filipinos.

Major General Jonathan Wainwright was promoted to lieutenant general (March 1942) and was now the Commander of Allied Forces in the Philippines, stationed in Corregidor.

Major General Edward King was the highest-ranking officer in Bataan.

XVI

April 3 was Good Friday, but continuous bombardment of the Mt. Samat area by the Japanese burned the campsites and incinerated a lot of men.

In the jungle where John had to command sick, starving men, those who could, helped move the wounded to the hospital three miles away. The air was thick with the dust and smoke coming from fires following the bombardment. The acrid smell of burning flesh permeated the air.

John was lucky to be alive, but his dysentery was getting bad, and he was almost sure he had malaria. Mosquitoes buzzed them day and night; and the flies feasting on dirt and dead meat spread bacteria.

By now, three-quarters of the Allied troops were sick from malaria, dysentery, dengue, or other diseases. Since their food ration had been quarter-rations since February, a lot of them were malnourished already. They had eaten an assortment of horsemeat, monkey, snakes, cats, mice, and lizards; some soldiers had gone fishing and ate fish. Most of the sick men went back to fighting as soon as they could in a valiant effort to forestall the enemy advance. They stood on the frontlines in varying degrees of illness.

Those suffering from malaria fought in between their delirium, impatient with their illness, for the hospital had been out of quinine for several weeks. The last available quinine was in liquid form and administered in a shot glass. Those suffering from dysentery often had no control over where they relieved themselves; the flies that alighted on their stool also swarmed on whatever food was left.

John wished he could forget it was April, but the next day when the sun shone so bright, and the heat was so stifling, he felt he was already in hell.

"It's Easter, you fool!" he scolded himself.

He managed to make the sign of the cross and said a short prayer. Another bomb fell just to his right, and he jumped along with some men into the nearest foxhole.

A series of blasts on top of Mt. Samat forced the dazed Allies out of their foxholes. They had to retreat all the way to the San Vicente River. The Japanese came in droves and blasted the Allies indiscriminately. John envied them for having a lot of ammunition, for he and his men were getting stingier with theirs. With their supplies running low, they were going for the sure kill.

The Allies counterattacked on April 5 and 6, and Major General Edward King planned another one.

"We will counterattack tomorrow!" he said.

His men, however, were weak from disease and malnutrition and practically out of ammunition. Their tanks had already run out of fuel. The continuous bombardment was nerve-wracking for the Allies, and some vulnerable solders were driven to the verge of insanity. They dropped their weapons and, with a bewildered look, ran down the mountain slope toward the beach.

Filipino civilians living around Mt. Samat had also started evacuating to the beach, away from the bombing. The transport boats trying to evacuate the nurses out of Bataan and into Corregidor were at Mariveles beach too.

Still hidden under camouflage in the jungle were a few remaining U.S. airplanes. The planes that could still fly were ordered to fly to Del Monte, in Mindanao. Airmen who had no airplanes had to join the infantry.

General King issued his counterattack order on April 7, but on April 8, he realized its futility and cancelled it. He knew this would be difficult for General Wainwright, still hoping in Corregidor, but King ordered his men to destroy their weapons.

"I'm not surrendering," a captain muttered to his men.

Several officers talked among themselves and decided to go to Corregidor by small boats, leaving some lower-ranked soldiers feeling abandoned. After some second thought, however, about two thousand soldiers who did not want to surrender decided to go to Corregidor. When the boats ran out, they took their chances and swam the two miles to the other island.

Like getting more punishment from above, the earth in Bataan suddenly trembled that evening: an earthquake struck at 10:00 PM on April 8.

On April 9, 1942, at 6:00 AM, Major General Edward King surrendered Bataan.

"Bataan has fallen!" Newspaper headlines read.

The radio announcers were beside themselves in reporting the news to a stunned world.

XVII

Jack's group gathered around the radio with a tense foreboding. Since being isolated from the main force in December, they had settled in their primitive dwellings and augmented their supplies from ambushed convoys.

Their radio conked out now and then, but they were aware of the starvation and disease in Bataan. They had near-misses as they gave vent to their frustration by ambushing enemy convoys one after another.

By April 1942, it was obvious that the Allies in Bataan were in a precarious position. Easter passed with Jack praying fervently the Allies would somehow prevail. No miracle happened; instead, the constant bombing could be heard on the radio. The blasts made the listeners jump just from hearing it. Jack's group heard about the counterattack and another one coming; then they could not believe it when the order to destroy weapons was given.

"There's an earthquake!" the radio announcer said. "My God!"

It was about 10:00 PM after a tense day. The announcer's voice registered surprise, then anger and a question as to why they were being punished.

Jack's group could hear the rumble of the earth shaking, the rattle of swaying metal, the hissing sound of frustration, and the cursing and praying of soldiers.

Most of them barely slept that night, and everybody gathered around the radio before sunrise. Radioman Private Bender had awakened much earlier to work on the radio. This warm, sunny day, there was no static. The men gathered around the radio with a sense of dread.

As the sun rose on the horizon, the men held their breath and listened. There was only silence instead of the sound of battle.

"We are surrendering!" the hoarse voice on the radio whispered.

"My God!" said Private Bender.

"Oh no!" Jack said.

"*Putang ina!* (s.o.b.)" another private cursed.

Most men stood immobile, as though in shock; some brushed away tears. A sense of bitterness pervaded, followed by anger and despair. Slowly, some soldiers tried to eat a semblance of breakfast while others prayed, and still others walked around aimlessly.

Jack went back to his cot and sat there for a long time. He presumed his dad was in Bataan and knew that surrendering would not suit him. Jack worried that his dad would get killed putting up a fight even if it was futile.

"Please God! Have mercy!" Jack prayed.

"If only we were able to train more men, if only we had enough time to really train them, if only ..." Jack thought as his tears fell.

XVIII

John watched as Sergeant Beck waved the white flag and walked with his other hand up in a gesture of surrender. Beck talked with the Japanese colonel, but afterward, he seemed to be taking his time and looking at other units as he came back. John looked thoughtfully and then realized why.

"Throw away all objects you have taken from any Japanese!" the sergeant hissed.

All the way up the line, the soldiers passed the word quickly and rid themselves of any objects they had taken from dead enemies.

A private emptied his pockets, but the corporal next to him did not. John gave a signal to Captain Delgado, and the corporal got elbowed. The corporal emptied watches and rings from his pocket.

The Japanese colonel walked confidently toward Brigadier General Casey and took the latter's gun. Then he shouted his orders to his men, gesticulating and pointing at different directions.

"Raise your hands in surrender!" Brigadier General Casey said, alarmed that a Japanese private had just struck a corporal with a rifle butt.

Quietly, the Allied prisoners raised their hands. Some looked around bewildered. Most looked angry, with their jaws set and teeth clenched, but some were bowed with tears in their eyes.

"You!" a Japanese private pointed at a private and signified by motions for him to pick up the rifles and set them in a pile.

A dozen more men were ordered to do the same.

"Ugh!" They turned to see a corporal on the ground, bleeding from a bayonet wound.

A Japanese private had made him empty his pockets, and the corporal had Japanese money on him. Several more soldiers suffered the same fate.

Some Allied soldiers complained of their hunger to no one in particular; they could see how intimidating their captors were. Their last quarter-ration had been yesterday, and after a sleepless night, they were marching in a direction pointed to them by bayonets. Like rivulets from the mountain slope, the lines of Allied prisoners were headed toward Mariveles Beach.

What first sounded like the hum of distant buzzing bees became louder as the soldiers marched.

"It's from somewhere down below," whispered Captain Delgado.

The curiosity registered on the prisoners' faces, but they did not ask. Soon they found the reason on the beach. Twenty five thousand Filipinos dislodged from their homes by the bombing, were now on the beach. They had evacuated with their bundles of clothes, food, and utensils. Most were talking hysterically to each other, and others were shouting out to their families to stay together. Little children did not realize the dangerous situation. They ran back and forth, thinking it was fun.

A Japanese private pointed one civilian inland, but as soon as the civilian was far away, he circumvented back to his family.

The mass of humanity was breaking into pandemonium, with the Filipino civilians calling out to members of their family, while the Japanese barked their orders to the Allied prisoners, who could not understand. A lot of Allied soldiers could not care less; they stood bewildered, not paying attention to anybody.

Finally, a young Japanese colonel saved the day. He fired several salvos into the air. After the shrieks of the Filipinos died down, and the dazed POWs looked at him, he pointed inland and pushed one civilian in that direction; then he pointed toward the seaside and pushed one POW in that direction.

The word passed down the line, and the prisoners started to line up. The prisoners were told to register and keep track of their units, but many were slow to follow instructions. Some were apathetic, not wanting to accept the reality of surrender, yet staring at a predicament they did not want to face. They stood with shoulders stooped and heads down, hiding their tears. The agony of defeat was hard to swallow.

Oh God! Have you abandoned us? John asked in prayer. *Forgive me, Lord!* He surreptitiously wiped away tears. *There is nothing to be ashamed of, we have fought beyond the call of duty, no matter how weak and sick we were.* Then with some despair, John thought, *Is death better than what's next?*

For a while, the lot of them just stood there, like mindless robots; the men milled around looking for their friends, pointing each other to their individual units, distracted by the face of comrades that mirrored their despair.

They watched the approach of a tall, good-looking Japanese captain who was accompanied by fellow lower-ranked soldiers with drawn bayonets. They made way as he seemed to be approaching Brigadier General Casey, John's immediate superior.

"Form in groups of one hundred to three hundred, by units, and register over there," he pointed. "And please pass the word around," he told General Casey in clear English. With a casual salute, he was gone.

Sergeant Beck usually met news like this with a scowl, but even he was impressed by the captain. With a nod from Casey, Beck started ordering.

"Come on! Form by platoons, then into companies! Move it before we get baked by this heat!" Sergeant Beck cupped his hands to make his loud voice carry farther.

"Delgado!" John signaled to the captain so the latter would take the lead of another unit. With a nod, Captain Delgado went forward with another group.

Out of the chaos, a semblance of order took shape. Whatever humiliation and anger the soldiers felt, it gave way to the instinct to survive, to stay together and make sense of what was next. It was past noontime when John's unit extricated themselves from the beach.

"Are they gonna feed us?" a private asked.

"Dunno," Captain Black answered without interest.

John had tried to distribute the good leaders of his regiment evenly, now he braced for those who would need more help. The heat was terrible. The soldiers stunk, and they were hungry; some soldiers just wanted to lie by the wayside to die.

Corporal Lange was slumped on the wayside when a captor shoved him with a rifle butt.

"Get him up!" John ordered his men, then he turned to the Japanese major. "You can't do that!" he said, stepping forward. The Japanese major just ignored him.

Captain Lopez edged from behind and tugged at his sleeve.

John saw there were more soldiers slumping on the wayside. "Let's get them up," he said quietly.

The soldiers helped the sicker ones by holding them up by the waist. The heavier cases needed two men to hold them up by the shoulders.

"Water!" Corporal Lange said weakly as John propped him up.

A hand stuck out a canteen in front of them. John looked in wonder at the giver.

"Thank you!" Lange said.

John gave the corporal his drink and gave the canteen back to the Japanese captain, who just nodded.

They were all silent for a moment, realizing one act of human kindness, and then they resumed their march.

"Wait a minute! What's he doing?" Sergeant Beck hissed.

A Philippine Scout was lying on the roadside, almost dead, and a Japanese soldier was bent over and feeling for the pockets. Not finding anything he liked, he took a ring off one finger.

A Japanese lieutenant was nearby and saw it. The lieutenant slapped the Japanese soldier and returned the ring.

Lopez grabbed the Philippine Scout off the roadside. "Let's go!" he said.

The Scout, Private Robles, was not fighting anymore, but the others did not want to give up.

"Try! Please!" John said, since his hands were full already.

Robles only mumbled. General Casey gave Robles his hand, weak as he was, and the two started walking slowly.

Their group staggered on and only realized they were on the slopes of Mt. Samat when they tripped on the jutting stones and rocks. They went past Hospital #1, which was now patrolled by Japanese guards, and when they passed by a previous camp site, they slowed down to look around the bombed-out remains of ammunition crates, oil barrels, and decaying bodies. As the acrid and putrid smell hit them, they hurried out of there and were soon near Hospital #2.

Hospital #2 was being evacuated. Sick patients stood helplessly as their captors ordered them to leave.

"Out!" a Japanese soldier shouted in English.

A U.S. general was being ordered by a Japanese private. Brigadier General Reynolds supported himself on a post, while the POWs looked at each other, aghast.

John gave his charge to Captain Black and stepped in front of the general. "We'll take him!" John said to the captor.

"Private Pedro Santos, sir," a short, dark Filipino private said as he stepped forward and helped John.

Other POWs were already helping the patients to their feet. Some could march with support, but so many more were really bedridden. The simplest thing to do was for two men to lift the cot from either end and just to walk on with it; but they did not have enough cots.

The next best thing was to tie two ends of a blanket on each end of a bamboo pole, like an ugly hammock that was darkness inside. The sick patient had to content himself inside this, as each end was carried on the shoulders of two marching men. The patient inside was shaken whichever way the bearers walked.

Brigadier General Reynolds ended up in a blanket cot that John and Sergeant Beck were carrying. The general's dysentery was bad— he was very thin and dehydrated. John gave his canteen to the general; then Sergeant Beck gave his, to no avail. Nobody else had food or water, for they had not been fed. The general's diarrhea was full blast, soiling the blanket and dripping through the path that John and the other soldiers had to tread on.

Ahead, Sergeant Beck stumbled on a stone outcropping, loosening his grip on his end, and the body in the cot was about to fall. John pulled his end but stumbled on a stone too, and the three of them tumbled to the ground.

"Sorry, General!" John peered inside the blanket.

There was no sound. He reached for the pulse, but General Casey touched his shoulder.

"Let's just go!" Casey said.

John looked up to see a captor with a drawn bayonet coming their way. Sergeant Beck and John quickly resumed their march.

"Lopez!" John said.

Captain Lopez turned just in time to catch Brigadier General Casey from falling forward.

The day was too long, the hunger and thirst gnawing in their bellies, those without resolve staggering on. More of the weaker soldiers lost their balance, and the stronger ones had their hands full keeping the weak away from the bayonets that would stop their struggles. After seeing too many remains of bombed-out camps and wreckage, the POWs shifted their gazes away from the memory of their futile struggle. They just marched and tried to keep each other's spirits up.

They had gone past the rice paddies, and the road was now nearer the coastline. A soft breeze blew as the sound of waves lapping against the shore grew more audible. The fishermen's boats silhouetted against the far horizon made John long for fish. He mentally checked their location.

As though reading his mind, Brigadier General Casey asked. "Where are we?"

"We have passed Orion and Pilar," John said.

"When are they going to feed us?" Corporal Lange said in a weak voice.

"Dunno." Captain Black's tone made John look up. Black was becoming apathetic, just when they needed each other's help.

"Easy, son!" Casey answered.

The sun had already set, and it was dark; yet even in the darkness, they marched, stumbling and cursing. The men grumbled softly, but no food nor water came. They marched through the night, and except for a short rest, they did not sleep.

"We're in Balanga! Won't they feed us still?" Corporal Lange was persistent.

"Maybe they will," John said weakly.

"Food!" exclaimed some voices from the front.

"Thank God!" John answered.

The prisoners felt relieved. Those with charges put their patients down first. John and Sergeant Beck put down their patient near a tree. There was no sound as they opened the blanket. Reynolds's face was ashen, his lips parched, and his lifeless eyes stared unseeing at the skies.

All around them, other soldiers reacted to the loss of the patients they were carrying.

"Let's line up for food first!" Captain Lopez said after a pause.

John and General Casey nodded in assent, knowing they had to be practical.

Their last ration was the day before the surrender, and some had not even been able to eat their ration. The eagerness showed in their faces, only to be replaced by dismay. There by the roadside, and scattered in several places, were large vats of "food." It consisted of rice cooked with plenty of water and some salt. It was rice gruel, a kind of porridge, and the Filipinos called it *lugaw*.

One soldier offered his turned-over helmet and was struck on the head with a rifle butt. The captors did not intend to give them much, but they did not really have anything to serve their food with. The prisoners in the front who stood in confusion were shoved out of the line. The quick thinking ones came up with their palms together, turned up.

"Oooohh!" One soldier dropped some of the porridge on his shirt, for it was hot. Quickly, however, he slurped what was on his hand and picked the food from his shirt as he walked away. He would have gone back the line, but the guards were watching.

The next in line resolved not to drop his food, no matter how hot. Down the line the word passed on what to do, and not to try for seconds either, or some might not be fed. Other soldiers put back in line the ones who had not been given food yet.

Water was another problem. It was another long wait, and they were not allowed to fill their canteens. Private Santos volunteered for the general and John.

"Thanks, Pedro!" John said. "We will bury General Reynolds in the meantime."

They all knew they had to save time, or they might not get another chance. In a clearing near an acacia tree, they started digging. They had no shovel, so their helmets had to do. It was a fairly adequate grave but not satisfactory by usual standards, for it was less than four feet deep. They had to pound the helmets on the parched ground with stones and roots, the clinking noise catching the attention of the guards. They were all sweating profusely, their heavy breathing audible, and they felt hungrier still. Beck clambered up the grave with a grunt.

Slowly, they lowered the body without the blanket, for a lot of sick men would need it.

"Our Father," John started the prayer as the men gathered around. "Eternal rest grant unto him, O Lord ..." Nobody answered, so John answered too. "And let perpetual light shine upon him. May he rest in peace. Amen"

"Amen," the others answered.

XIX

"Sir, let's put Corporal Collins there," Private Santos whispered.

He motioned to John that he would shoulder the other end. Collins was suffering delirium from malaria so they rolled him into the hammock.

"We're not moving yet," John observed.

Some activity seemed to be going on beyond an acacia tree, so they put down the cot and sat on the ground. Private Santos went over to check what was going on.

"Stay away from there!" Santos said, hurrying back. "Our soldiers are digging several gravesites, and some of the diggers are being bayoneted and pushed in along with the dead."

"Let's see about that!" Beck angrily got up.

John held down Beck's shoulders, knowing it would be futile. Their group decided to stay on the other side of the acacia tree, content to lie down whichever way. In the darkness they laid mostly still, sound asleep after their exhausting march.

By morning, there were bodies that did not move—the men who were dying, who, after a lull of sleep, did not wake up anymore. Captain Black, Robles, and Lange had made it off the slopes of Mt. Samat, but now they lay immobile.

John woke up feeling hot and weak. He looked around and saw Beck pick up Black's lifeless body by the shoulder. Beck looked at Santos, who was still hesitating. Santos then reluctantly picked up the dead captain's legs and followed Beck to the gravesite. Santos hurried back.

"I'm not going back there," he said, afraid that he would be pushed into the grave himself.

Beck had come back wordlessly, picked up the dead body of Robles, and brought it to the gravesite. He seethed with so much pent-up anger that the Japanese private, looking at his enraged countenance, let him pass. Beck brought the body of Lange last.

The food and water they got was never enough; some men were becoming reckless and went back surreptitiously to fill up their canteens. John was glad when the columns ahead of them started to move.

They picked up their cots and moved again. This time, Santos and Beck carried Collins, while John assisted General Casey. Onward they marched past little towns and marshlands, along paved and unpaved roads. Some roads with gravel were painful to walk on for those soldiers who were barefoot.

"We passed Abucay!" Beck said.

"We passed Pilar?" a corporal whispered from behind Lopez, making the latter turn.

Lopez double-stepped beside the corporal, catching Espinoza before he keeled over.

"Espinoza has malaria," Lopez said, noting the fever and the corporal's yellowish pallor.

John was glad Lopez was there. He himself was almost in a stupor, walking without thinking. He knew that Pilar was long ago, but said nothing. Most of the men could not think anymore from hunger and exhaustion. John could hear Espinoza talking to himself in a rambling way and was thinking it may be cerebral malaria.

"It's so hot!" Santos complained.

"It's April," answered John.

Most men had their desultory talk in the morning; nobody really wanted to talk after midday. With the heat and lack of water, their lips cracked from dryness. When they tried to lick their lips, they tasted the dust and sweat. Their activity was limited to their staggering walk.

John counted five prisoners bayoneted as they slumped on the road. He controlled his temper as he had to reach out and catch Espinoza by the waist. Lopez had tripped, and Espinoza fell down along with him. Espinoza was shaking with chills and fever, but he could be bayoneted too, regardless of his malarial attack.

"Aw! Aw!" A chorus of sounds could be heard farther up the road.

The prisoners suffered from lack of supplies. A good number of them had gone barefoot during the march. On a newly asphalted road past Layac, their feet were getting burned by the asphalt. Some POWs made a sprint past the obstacle. A number of them were smart enough to march on the shoulder of the asphalted road. Some captors were not letting the POWs choose.

"Get them on your backs!" Beck said, elbowing his way to the center, the cot and Santos right behind him.

A lot of those with boots helped, but many were too weak to take on more of a load. The prisoners helped each other, but there was only so much they could do. They had to move on. John sympathized with the men whose soles would get burned.

They passed a dreary area with no sign of habitation, and for several miles, the men walked slower. Under a cloudless sky, the sun was making their helmets feel like burning pans. One by one, the prisoners took off their helmets.

Just in time! A load of Japanese soldiers were having fun in an open truck. Most POWs stood aside on the road to let the truck pass. Some captors had a sadistic idea as the truck came slowly toward marching prisoners, and several laughing captors started hitting the helmeted soldiers with their rifle butts.

"You SOB!" screamed a fallen POW.

"D— it!" screamed another bleeding soldier.

"Take off your helmets!" shouted a major from the front of the column.

Too late—a lot more POWs got the treatment. Some were stunned, and they slumped on the wayside. Their comrades had to help them up, or they might get the bayonet. Sometimes those who could help had their hands full; others just marched on, not needing help and not helping out either.

Beside John, General Casey grunted, planning to address the situation. Suddenly, a rumble of tanks came from behind. Most prisoners just stepped aside to let them pass, but one soldier was slumped, unaided on the road. The third tank backed up, ran over the soldier, and left the flattened body on the road.

Beck gave his side of the cot to Lopez and walked back to the fallen body. John and most of his unit halted to see what they could do. Two Japanese soldiers came forward and pointed their bayonets at Beck.

"Let it go, Tom!" John intervened quickly.

Beck backed off just in time, for two more guards were coming. He went back to his place; a huge, burly man with a kind heart, but without a weapon and surrounded by his enemies, he was powerless. His head bowed in frustration, he turned back to hide his tears. The men could see the streaks on his cheeks.

There was only silence for a while, as in a stalemate where the opponents are fatigued. But the marchers behind them were surging forward, as though pressing them on, so with their heads bowed, John's group marched again.

They reached an area where Filipino civilians stood by the roadside, others peering through their windows as the columns passed. The Filipinos had come out like standing witnesses to their ordeal. They were mostly older couples, women, and children. Some villagers were barefoot, others wearing slippers; the younger ones wore threadbare clothes, for at least they could get away with less modesty than the older ones. A lot of the older ladies still wore the customary long printed skirt, topped by a cotton blouse with bell sleeves and an accompanying shawl.

At first, the villagers were just solemn watchers, as though communing with them to give them strength. Some of the older ladies started praying loudly, and women were openly crying. Then, as though by sudden impulse, the villagers decided to take some risk. Young men and children came running to the roadside with pails of water and some food.

"Water, Joe!" A tin can full of water darted out from among the crowd. John did not even think. He grabbed it, took a gulp, and passed it to General Casey beside him. Lopez gulped water from another tin can and motioned to Santos to give it to Collins first. Beck grabbed another and passed it on to Santos.

Lopez was suddenly alert to more possibilities.

"Beck!" Lopez handed Espinoza to Beck's other arm so his hands could be free.

Lopez quickly gathered food and continuously passed it on to the next soldier beside him. The tin can dipped several times into the pail before one of their captors kicked it.

More prisoners got lucky as they moved on, for the villagers were getting braver too. They were flashing the V sign with their fingers. Some women were now stepping forward with some fruits, *puso*, and even chicken.

The stroke of luck was uneven. Some POWs received food; others with strict captors did not. All too soon, the Japanese became aware of what was going on, and some villagers were pushed back with rifle butts. Still wanting to help, other villagers put the tin cups of water and food by the roadside, then they would step back. POWs would pretend to slump and pick up the food.

"They bayoneted a pregnant lady!" The word passed from behind.

Like a hissing telegraph, the prisoners spread the word to the front. The woman had given a cooked chicken to a prisoner, but a nasty Japanese private saw it and killed her.

"These people are not giving up," Beck said, as instead of getting intimidated, the villagers continued to line the roadside and hand out food.

"I have a fever!" Lopez said, pausing and putting his hand on his forehead.

"Hold on!" John said as he moved toward Lopez at the same time he handed Casey to Espinoza.

Lopez keeled sideways, feeling weak and starting to tremble.

"Malaria!" John said as he caught Lopez's shoulder.

John looked up as he sensed a group of villagers surging forward, and an old lady with a long skirt nodded to him.

John looked back, the wonder in his face giving way to hope. Lopez had stumbled, but before John could grab him, an old Filipino woman grabbed the captain and hid him under her long skirt.

"What?" Beck asked, not understanding where Lopez was.

"He went under some old woman's skirt," John said quietly.

"What?" Beck still did not get it.

"Later," John answered, afraid that the Japanese might find out.

When he got the chance, John explained that he saw several of the old women grab some of the stumbling prisoners and hide them under their skirts. It might take a while before it got dark or before the columns of prisoners passed by, but John was sure that those prisoners would successfully escape.

"I wouldn't have thought of that!" Beck exclaimed.

Santos smiled proudly through his tears, unable to say anything else.

There was some spring in their footsteps for a while, until the unrelenting sun set, and they began to stumble unseeing on the stones. They must have sighed in unison, for *lugaw* was again being served. Like it or not, they had to eat it. Beck lowered his end of the pole, and Santos lowered his end too

At a distance from the roadside, there stood a fairly large wooden house. On its right was a barn of sorts. Only the back and both sides were partially covered with *nipa*.

Most men wanted to sleep in the barn, and it became full. With so many sick of dysentery, it smelled bad. There were no trees nearby, just ditches and uneven ground with patches of grass here and there. Close by were some rice paddies; at a distance were *cogon* grass and untilled land. John chose a patch of grass close to a ditch and turned to Beck.

"Let's stay here," John said.

Beck nodded and they lowered each pole holding the cot gently.

Private Santos had rotated to assist the general, and Santos was making eye signals that the general was not doing too well.

"Let's look for water," Beck said, already several feet ahead and looking around.

Lieutenant Foster quickly followed, picking up the canteens of John, Casey, and Collins. Foster had been four lines behind them, but one soldier ahead of him died, and the other two had disappeared. John asked him to relieve Santos when the latter was getting weak.

"I got something!" Foster said triumphantly as he returned, holding up the canteens.

He carefully picked his way back, his shadow from the gas lamp darkening his path. He sat down on the side of Collins's cot, put the full canteens beside him, and quickly fell asleep.

John smiled, too tired to say anything. He stretched on the ground on the other side of Collins and promptly fell asleep with General Casey on his left. It was a very warm, humid evening, but it was heaven sent for the prisoners to be able to sleep at last.

"Up!" John tried to rouse his men quickly. The columns ahead were already moving, and John did not want his captors to notice something. "You'll have to carry the other end, Harry. Feeling better?" John said to the lieutenant, looking at him closely.

The lieutenant opened his mouth, but stopped before he could ask his question. "Right!" he said with a nod.

Lieutenant Foster had delirium from his malaria the other night. He seemed to be a little better this morning and would have to help out. John had assigned General Casey to another corporal from behind them. The other men were either still too weak or they were already helping the other sick ones. Sergeant Beck had not come back. John presumed he escaped. Private Santos was not around either.

They marched for quite a distance along plainer ground on dusty roads with only a few trees within sight. After the scenery changed to sugar cane fields, the next village displayed clay pots at the roadside store.

"We must be in Pampanga!" John said to no one in particular, knowing that the province next to Bataan was Pampanga, known for its clay pots.

There were more Filipinos by the roadside, but the guards were stricter, and very little food got through to the prisoners. True enough, they later passed a road sign marking "San Fernando."

The prisoners marched to the railway station at San Fernando. John watched as two buses already filled with prisoners were just leaving. Newly arriving prisoners were now being loaded in boxcars.

They let Collins get up from his makeshift cot. Collins stood dazed, and John held him by the arm as he covered his eyes from the glare of the noonday sun.

"Thank you, sir," Collins said weakly.

Foster put the cot alongside a heap of similar contraptions. He glanced at the boxcars.

"Isn't that enough?" Foster asked the Japanese private loading them up.

The Japanese private ignored Foster and motioned more prisoners in.

"My God! We're next!" Collins did not want to go.

Foster approached a Japanese private, hoping for some other alternative for the sick men. Instead, a bayonet was pointed his way. General Casey stood unbelieving of this predicament, but he was too weak to protest. Foster climbed into the boxcar and extended his hands to General Casey as John gave a little lift from behind. Next they helped Collins and the others; then John climbed in too. They were standing, packed like sardines, and still their captors were making more prisoners get in.

There were 100–150 prisoners placed in each boxcar. The steel boxcars were thirty three feet long, eight feet across, and seven feet high. Inside the boxcars, men sick with dysentery were pressed hard against others sick with malaria, dengue, and other illnesses, aside from malnutrition and fatigue.

"Can't breath!" Casey said, but there was nothing anyone could do.

The twenty-five-mile ride from San Fernando, Pampanga, to Capas, Tarlac, was a four-hour ride. There were no means to go to the toilet, nor was food or water provided. The POWs were packed so close to each other with no breathing space, and the boxcar windows were closed to prevent escape. The dysentery cases could not help defecating where they stood. Others started throwing up with the stench, but it fell on fellow soldiers, for there was no space for it. After some hours, others also had to urinate. The stench was overwhelming. Their sweat fell on each other, and most of it was warm; but men with impending shock had cold sweat.

When the boxcars opened in Capas, Tarlac, dead men were all over the floor, covered in feces and urine. The ones who were alive scrambled out, throwing up and gasping for air.

John hurriedly jumped out of the boxcar and threw up. Lieutenant Foster looked very pale and weak, clammy perspiration streaking his dirty face. He stumbled out of the boxcar as though unseeing and tripped on John's leg as the latter was still retching on the ground.

"Colonel!" he gasped.

Both men took deep breaths until the sense of panic quieted down. When they looked around, some faces were not there anymore.

"Collins," John said and made a sign of the cross. "General Casey?" John asked and looked around at the same time.

Foster nodded toward the boxcar.

"Longwood," another said beside him, bowing his head.

All around them, prisoners were reciting the names of the fallen comrades, followed by silent prayers for each.

"March!" the Japanese captain said.

The POWs warily got up to form a line. John held Foster up by the shoulder, just like the other prisoners helping each other. John looked grim, shaking off his exhaustion only to face with numbing apathy another march.

Then something happened. Somehow, having reached the nadir of such degrading treatment, a resolve was born not to lose their last vestige of dignity, to be proud of what they had done, even in defeat. John looked around him, and with an effort, stood erect as best a soldier could. Foster paused, and with tears in his eyes, made himself stand straight.

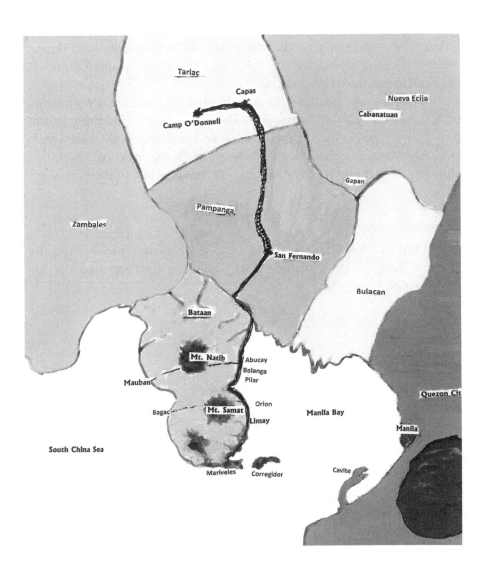

As though united in thought, other POWs around them also paused, then tried to stand erect. They began to walk with a sad, quiet determination on their faces. They did not speak of their utter humiliation, they just wept silently, not bothering to brush away their tears. They had endured the most inhuman treatment, in spite of their illness and hunger, and they were not going to let the enemy get them down. They struggled to walk with pride, walking unaided and almost without seeing, to survive the last eight miles to Camp O'Donnell, the final leg of the death march.

The Japanese guards were mostly officers. There was no beating here. Even the captors were taken aback by the look of these gaunt, dirty, smelly men, looking sorrowful and walking with their heads held high beyond endurance; for even as hope was lost, the men clung to the last shred of human dignity that was left to them.

Out of the 76,000 (12,000 U.S.) prisoners surrendered by General King, 10,000 prisoners (2,300 U.S.) soldiers died on the death march.

XX

Lieutenant General Jonathan Wainwright in Corregidor was grim after receiving news from Major General Ernest King that Bataan would be surrendered. He knew King had done his best. Most of the Luzon forces were in Bataan; but Corregidor, the Visayas, and Mindanao were still in Allied hands. Wainwright resolved that Corregidor would be a beacon of hope, for he would engage the enemy for as long as he could. He felt the burden of not letting his people down as he made the rounds of his troops. From atop a hill, he focused his binoculars on Mariveles beach, on the tip of Bataan. His heart was heavy with the thought of his men who were gathered there when they surrendered. He then focused on the other side. Cavite Naval Base was in enemy hands. Unless a miracle happened, this would not be an ordinary uphill battle.

As the commander of the entire U.S.-Philippine forces, Wainwright had to forestall what seemed to be the inevitable. He would not let the Philippines fall to the Japanese, but how long would they last until help came? He knew the unspoken law of the soldier that obeyed the commander-in-chief. They had to rally the troops, but deep in his heart, he knew no help would come.

He could overhear the soldiers manning the hilly outposts preferring to be at the Malinta Tunnel, not knowing that those in the tunnel wished they were manning the hills. There was no better place; the bombs would rain on them.

After the Bataan POWs were taken to Tarlac, the Japanese focused their attention on Corregidor. The enemy guns were aimed at the island fortress, and shelling was almost incessant, especially on the birthday of Emperor Hirohito on April 29. After all the pounding, the enemy boats started to arrive at the beaches. The Allies continued to fight, but fresh hordes of enemies charged without regard to their mortality. As the Allies gradually retreated, enemy tanks arrived to continue the onslaught, pushing the Allies back to

Malinta tunnel. Cornered and fearing a massacre, Wainwright surrendered on May 6, 1942.

Wainwright was brought before Lieutenant General Homma in Bataan. It was not enough for Homma to accept the surrender of Corregidor, he demanded the surrender of the entire US-Philippines forces. Knowing they were basically hostages, Wainwright surrendered all forces on May 7.

Although the U.S.-Philippine forces in the Visayas and Mindanao were still ready to fight, Major General William Sharp had no choice but to obey the order. They were instructed by the enemy about which focal points to report to, and from there, the higher-ranking officers were segregated.

All officers, from full colonel on up, were separated from the rest and placed in a different housing arrangement at Capas, Tarlac. There were sixteen generals at the time of surrender. They were later transferred by "hell ships" to different work camps in Formosa, Korea, or Japan.

Most of the twelve thousand soldiers in Corregidor were marched through Manila; then sent to Cabanatuan, Nueva Ecija. They were to languish in a prison camp about four miles away from town.

XXI

The prisoners in Camp O'Donnell lived or died in hell. After five days and nights of the death march, they arrived in a camp that had once been used as a training camp for Filipino soldiers. There were no dwelling places for most of the captives. They got burned by the sun, and they got soaked by the rain. The available buildings were used as hospitals for the very sick, for most of them were sick anyway.

There were only two spigots for water. The prisoners promptly lined up and took turns, but there were thousands of men who needed it. Some degree of rationing went into effect, but the weak among them suffered the most.

John had been a full colonel before the war broke out. In Bataan, his regiment had maintained excellent discipline and fought well. He was up for promotion while in Bataan, but that did not seem to matter now. His dysentery got really bad as soon as they reached Camp O'Donnell, so he was in their primitive hospital, disgusted with his own stink. On top of that, he had a high fever, which he knew was from malaria. During his deliriums, he imagined the faces of the soldiers who had died of the disease.

"I'd like to be shot!" he screamed in delirium. He reasoned in a disjointed way that, as a soldier, it was better to die in battle rather than die because of a mosquito bite. "How can I slap a mosquito when I'm shooting at the enemy?" he screamed again.

Captain Lauro Delgado woke up in the middle of the night after hearing John Stewart's screams. *"Punyeta!"* Captain Delgado swore to himself in frustration. Delgado ran from his bunk to close his hand over John Stewart's mouth. "Easy, sir! Easy!" Delgado said.

Colonel John Stewart was not just Delgado's project; Delgado looked up to him as the father he wished he had.

The men were very loyal to John. They were aware that the high officers were being segregated. They decided to keep the captors oblivious of John's officer status, hoping to have a high-ranking officer for a leader. They needed for John to lie low so they took turns watching him. Today was Delgado's watch.

Lying on a hospital bunk bed, stripped to his waist because of his high fever, John was below the radar. In between his bouts of delirium, John regretted the lack of medicines, especially quinine. The doctors came to him, but they had no medicine at all.

John became fixated on the lack of quinine. Long ago, when he visited his dad in the Philippines as a young man, he saw his first case of malaria. It made such an impression on him that when he got back to the United States, he read about malaria and its treatment. By the time he was in the army, John fully knew the implication of disease in war outcomes.

"Get the quinine!" John said. In his worst delirium, John muttered everything he knew about quinine.

Malaria took a heavy toll among the soldiers. So many were dying, their agony made more poignant by what they screamed during their deliriums. The ones with cerebral malaria were quite colorful. Those still well enough to want some sleep were startled by screams, and too often, they could not tell if it was a delirium or if indeed something was going on.

"Airplanes! We are saved!" a soldier suffering from cerebral malaria screamed one night.

Several soldiers ran outside and looked for the airplanes, but there was nothing.

In his sane moments, John figured that the Japanese had a good amount of quinine, and somehow, the Allies must try to get some too. He was too weak to move, lying on a wooden bunk with a torn blanket, but Captain Quitos came by for his routine update.

"All high-ranking officers from full colonel up to Lieutenant General Wainwright have been segregated in a camp in Tarlac. They were later shipped to somewhere, nobody knows, probably Japan, Korea, or Formosa. The high-ranking prisoners in the Camp O'Donnell hospital might later on be moved to Cabanatuan, where the prisoners from Corregidor were sent."

"Captain, please pass on the word that we should try to get quinine whichever way possible. Please," said John and fell asleep.

In the first few days, the prisoners were still in a daze, and there was no order. The line for water from the two spigots was always long and slow. Fights often erupted when a soldier filled more than one canteen. An officer among the POWs had to act as arbiter now and then, for it was true that sometimes the water was for the very sick who could not line up.

Their food was just the rice gruel called *lugaw*. The flies then came like a plague, swarms of them flying back and forth from the dead to the food to the latrines. Now and then, tiny maggots would greet the POWs as they looked aghast at their food. A lot of the POWs were too disgusted to eat it and just went hungry.

A sergeant, however, put his own perspective.

"This is protein I'm eating here, don't think about the worms," the former cook said, and he ate his *lugaw*.

Some soldiers copied his example, trying their best to be practical; others just could not do it—they picked out the wriggling forms and threw them gingerly away.

The officers worked to put order to the chaos. Sanitation was a big problem. Most prisoners relieved themselves wherever, in different places, sometimes too close to where they found themselves sleeping. The foul odor was especially bad on warm, humid days. Bickering and discontent was bad for the morale.

When they first buried their dead, the new arrivals could not think straight; they were still exhausted from the March. Some of the soldiers doing the burying were also weak and dying; they would just keel over and be buried too.

The burial sites were initially too close to their habitation, and they were not deep enough; when it rained, the bodies floated. Finally, Dr. Landsdale and the other POW doctors asked the Japanese colonel for more leeway in burying the dead. They reasoned that the dead must be buried farther away, and they had to be given time to bury them deeper; otherwise, even the captors would be affected should an epidemic break out. The captors approved their request, and the POWs assigned soldiers for burial duty on a rotating basis.

The latrines too had to be dug farther away, and deeper, mostly on the north and south sides of the camp, with additional ones near their hospital. That improved the morale, for there were days when the bad odor was not discernible.

The POWs started a campaign against the flies: swatting them, covering their food, and burning soiled materials. Rules on sanitation were enforced. Most of the prisoners were sick, but they brought the very sick patients to the primitive hospital, even if there were no medicines. The hospital was one place the able-bodied tried not to get near to. It was like seeing the face of death, or rather, smelling it. The stench was everywhere, from the sick bodies, the dead, and the dysentery.

The death toll from illness and malnutrition continued; and the Filipinos had it worse. For every American who died, about forty Filipinos died. The body count from April to July 1942 was 21,684 Filipinos dead, or about 249 a day, and 1,488 Americans dead, or about seventeen a day.

Death was everywhere. Bad as it was, the prisoners tried to make sense of their situation.

John awoke very early after a bout of delirium. He was exhausted and beginning to doze off when he heard a captain ordering the men.

"Excavate another gravesite. It has to be bigger and deeper. Logan, Heller!"

"Sir!" a corporal said as he put a canteen of water to John's parched lips. Next, he put a medicine in John's hand and nodded. The corporal fed John a cupful of rice gruel.

"Thank you, son!" John said with a broken voice.

John presumed he got quinine at last, but he had to wait. With time, he would find out where this came from; right now, he could not jeopardize his luck by asking questions.

He could feel the men caring for him, and he knew he must get well quickly. He was worried that some of them were giving him their share of food, and he must not take advantage of that.

"The men are beginning to compete for work details," Captain Delgado reported.

Delgado sat on the empty bunk across from John. The occupant of that bunk had been a private who died the night before from dysentery and malaria.

"With more work details being set up, we've had more contact with civilians. The word is out about the quinine, and the civilians are helping. There is now an improvement with our malaria patients." Delgado finished his report with a salute.

John was too choked up to say anything.

The next day, it was Captain Blythe who briefed John.

"Some are reporting that the Japanese are giving them a little more freedom, and Filipinos are handing them food."

"Keep getting the quinine," John could not help interrupting.

Blythe nodded and continued. "Quitos's detail was completely wiped out. They did a pretty good job fixing up the wire posts at San Carlos, but one soldier escaped. When the Japanese counted them off and one was missing, the rest were all killed."

The next report was again from Captain Blythe. John was feeling better and sat up, but his brow was raised with an unspoken question.

"Captain Delgado has either escaped or been killed. We are not sure. He went for a work detail, and neither the Japanese nor the prisoners came back. Your suggestion about the quinine is working. We have more quinine to spread around, even if it's not enough. The Japanese are allowing us to bury the dead farther away, because even they could not stand the stench of diarrhea and bodies that decay quickly in the hot sun.

"The flies are better controlled now. Some Filipinos are being allowed to bring water into the camp perimeter. One time, when the guards could not tell the Filipino prisoners from the civilians, they just shot them all."

With the trickle of quinine that started to come in, John willed himself to get better fast. The war was not yet over, and his men needed him. His diarrhea finally stopped, and he knew there were so many soldiers who had done things for him.

"Don't pay attention to the news that a Red Cross truck is coming. Somebody just made that up. Rumors are beginning to fly without any basis. Either the men are deluding themselves, or this is wishful thinking." Captain Blythe shook his head. "By the way, Private Heller died the other day."

"That young man could have done better," John could not help saying.

"Yeah! Well, he lost the will to live. He did not eat his food; when dysentery struck him, it was over." Captain Blythe looked sad.

Captain Blythe later apprised him of another trend. What used to be a trickle of visitors from afar looking for their imprisoned relatives, had become a steady stream. The Japanese would let them stand from a certain distance only. It was difficult to find a specific person, but just the same, the visitors came. They stood from afar and just silently watched.

XXII

Captain Lauro Delgado was reluctant to join a work detail. He had some scruples about getting off with an easy job when others were suffering at the camp. One of the men, however, volunteered his name when the captors were looking for an engineer. There were ten prisoners in this work detail, and they were on their way to the next town to fix a bridge. They had worked on that for a week now, along with another group, and they were almost finished. The Japanese had become friendlier. The four American and six Filipino prisoners behaved well, and there was no attempt to escape.

Their truck chugged and sputtered on the muddy road. It moved too slowly as the men pitched and turned inside, falling off their seats now and then.

"Are they putting down their guard?" Delgado thought.

He counted only four guards when they were picked up. He figured there would be more guards on the work site when they got there. It had rained heavily last night, and although it continued, it seemed to be tapering off.

"How are we going to work in this rain?" asked Corporal Munoz.

"It's tapering off," replied Private Duque.

Their vehicle was traveling slower because of the muddy road, and their guards were getting tense. There was a fear of being ambushed when the vehicle was slow, and there were a lot of accidental killings of the soldiers the guerillas were trying to rescue. Suddenly, the two Japanese guards sitting in front started cursing. From the back seat, closest to the front, Delgado peered through the glass between the guards and saw the problem. A coconut tree had fallen across the road, blocking it.

The two guards in the back of the truck looked at Delgado, letting him take care of it.

"Munoz, Duque!" Delgado ordered the two private soldiers who complained the most.

Delgado needed some quiet while he tried to figure out whether the coconut tree fell because of soil erosion or because guerillas did it.

Munoz and Duque came down from the truck with muttered expletives under their breath. Even before they reached the tree, they stumbled in the mud; when they tried to lift the trunk, they slipped and fell, but could not budge it.

"It's too heavy! It's soaked!" Private Duque cupped his hand to direct his observation to the truck.

Delgado made hand signals to the guard to let him come down. As he jumped down, the rain poured. He signaled for four more men to come down the truck. The two guards in front signaled back without moving from the front seat. The other one hollered to the two guards in the back to send more men.

Instead, the rest of the prisoners all came down. They swished through the mud, complaining as lightning lit the skies. The two guards in the back came down too. They were arguing about the obvious miscommunication and blamed each other. Rain poured in the buckets; thunder accompanied the lightning.

Hardly able to see, Private Duque slipped on the mud and knocked down Captain Delgado.

"What the ...?" Delgado was irritated as he fell.

The first guard came forward and also slipped, his rifle flying in the air. Delgado picked up the rifle; but he did not return it to the guard. The second guard had not seen it and was still coming forward. Sergeant Meeks was right behind him and gave the guard a hard blow on the neck. As the guard fell, Meeks took his rifle and the revolver. The first guard had just gotten up and, seeing the other one on the ground, pulled his revolver. Meeks fired two shots, and the guard slumped dead in the mud.

"Let's go!" Delgado said triumphantly, getting the other revolver from the first guard.

They all ran to the bushes on one side of the road. The two guards in front suddenly realized what was going on. They chased the prisoners, but Delgado and Meeks each put one away.

The POWs came out and inspected the truck.

"Can't use this, but we'll strip it," Delgado said.

They took all the wirings, communications, and other equipment they could carry. They did not hurry, because the weather was so bad, they did not think enemy reinforcement would come.

They walked toward the interior, away from the road. The darkness looked all the same as the rain poured with only a little let up now and then. Each of the men took their share of swearing and frustration as they slipped and fell on the mud with their scavenged equipment. Hours passed, and they walked through several rice fields before they saw an isolated farmhouse. They were all dripping wet as Delgado knocked on the flimsy wooden door.

The men put their equipment on the ground. Obviously, there was no room for it inside the tiny hut. As it took a while without an answer, they looked apprehensively at each other. Delgado and Meeks drew their guns as Delgado knocked once more. A middle-aged farmer hesitantly opened the door and spoke in a quivering voice.

"Please come in! I did not hear you knock because of the rain."

The soldiers went inside guardedly. The water dripping off their pants and shirts fell between the slats of the bamboo floor.

"Don't worry," the farmer said.

An awkward silence fell when the soldiers looked at the inhabitants of the *nipa* hut. The eyes of the wife and four children were wide with fear. The oldest was a teenaged son, not so tall, but his muscles bulged from his tattered shirt. He hovered near the kitchen area, and Delgado surmised that he was close to whatever knife they had. Two younger girls and the youngest boy stood in the corner. It was a one-room hut, and their clothes were tattered.

"Good afternoon to you all!" Delgado said in a respectful tone, smiling.

The wife could only nod, but the children smiled back.

"Cook some rice, Soling!" the farmer said.

The wife moved without speaking, bringing her clay pot to the sink, measuring the rice and water, and lighting up the dying embers under the pot. She took out something wrapped in banana leaves from a clay jar and placed this near the embers to warm it.

She moved fast for somebody who seemed so worn out by work. Against the wall was a wooden drawer from which she took several tattered shirts and cloth pieces. She gave them to her husband.

"Change first into dry clothing," the farmer said.

"Thank you very much!" Delgado said.

He turned to distribute the pieces to his men. They sorted out who could get into the shirts, for they were small. Sergeant Meeks and the bigger guys got the pieces of cloth that they used like capes, for most of them were shivering by now. By turning their backs away from the audience, the men changed their shirts. Each one now went to the window and tried to wring out the water from their uniforms. They then spread them out to dry. Nothing fitted Delgado either so he contented himself by wrapping the shirt over his shoulders and tying the sleeves together.

"Son, get some string beans," the mother said to the teenaged son without turning.

The young man was Isyong. He picked up a battered looking umbrella and went out in the rain. He came back with fresh string beans dangling from both hands. The mother cooked them too. She merely nodded to her husband when the food was ready.

"You can have it! We already ate some of that earlier," the farmer said graciously.

"Thanks a lot!" the POWs chorused.

The aroma of steaming rice brought tears of joy to Duque's eyes. The POWs had not eaten proper rice for a long time. The object wrapped in banana leaves was half of a leftover chicken, and Delgado did the honors of cutting it up fairly among the ten of them. On second thought, he decided to apportion all the rice and the string beans the wife had cooked with some anchovy. He did not want any grudges to come out of this blessing. He gently put each portion on the banana leaves that served as their plates. They ate with their hands.

The table was small. Some sat down, the others ate standing up, while Delgado and Meeks sat down after Duque and Munoz finished.

"Here's more water!" Isyong said.

"Aaaah!" Duque said with a sigh, relishing the sweet taste of rainwater.

The teenaged son smiled as he brought in a pail of rainwater that had been put outside for collection. When the men had filled their canteens, the son filled up their earthen jar in the kitchen. He went out again to connect his pail to a tin trough below a galvanized iron contraption.

"Sometimes guerillas from Mt. Arayat come this way," the farmer said.

"We're that far south?" Meeks asked.

They chatted with the farmer and found out that the Japanese had not been to this area yet.

Having eaten a little more than usual, and feeling warmer, most of the men were ready to sleep soon. The children were already lying down on a mat close to the kitchen area. As the rain steadily poured, it was dark outside, and there was nothing better to do. Nobody cared what time it was.

Lying down on the bamboo floor, shoulder to shoulder and straight like logs, they at least provided warmth for each other. Most of the men snored quickly, but Delgado mused about his courteous greeting that broke the ice.

Somehow, at the critical point of an encounter, her mother's memory had guided him. She was his first teacher, telling him to be courteous and respectful, a sign that he was a friend, not a foe.

Delgado's father was Lucas, the handsome bastard son of a Spanish mestizo. Mostly left on his own, he worked odd jobs here and there. One day, as Lucas helped haul some goods at the market, he caught the eye of a homely looking girl who happened to be there, accompanied by a maid. He started sending flowers through the maidservant.

The young lady was Felicidad, from a well-to-do family, flattered that at last somebody was paying her attention. Her father quickly saw the angle that the suitor was working on and forbade any relationship with that "good for nothing" bastard. The love struck lady paid no heed as she agreed to meet surreptitiously with the young man; and as was true with what was forbidden, she thought she fell in love with somebody wonderful. The two eloped, and the whole town savored the scandal, for the young lady was already expecting a baby.

Embarrassed at his daughter's predicament, but not wanting to completely abandon her, her father arranged a quiet wedding, bought them a small farm in another town of Tarlac, and then practically cut off communications.

Lucas was not much of a farmer. They had enough so they would not go hungry, but no more than that. Felicidad bore Lauro through a difficult delivery and was rewarded with the joy of having a good son.

At first love was enough, and she was content, but their needs increased with the rapidly growing son, big for his age, handsome, and quite smart. Lucas, however, could hardly make ends meet; he took on odd jobs as a laborer, hauling rice sacks.

When Lauro was six years old, Lucas started making him work with him. Gradually and surely, Lauro made a difference in their income. Felicidad was not aware how much help Lucas was getting from Lauro. One day the boy came home with a bruised shoulder from carrying wood and rice sacks back and forth.

"Our young child should not be given such a hard time! I'll just do the work!" she said.

The mother had already been sewing clothes and planting vegetables; now she started accepting cleaning jobs. She worked harder to spare Lauro from being used, and she insisted on him going to school. Her pleasure was in those evenings when she looked into his schoolwork and guided her son. She taught him his prayers and his manners.

"Even if we are poor, we have honor," she repeatedly told her son.

Lucas had no time for genteel considerations. He could hardly make ends meet by his own work; he was glad those two could earn something so he could have time to drink with his friends.

Lauro envied the kids who could just go out and play, for he worked when he was not in school. He grew masculine and strong from the manual labor, and he still excelled in school.

His father died of TB just as Lauro was accepted in the Philippine Military Academy. As a scholar, his schooling was free, and he had a stipend. Lauro visited his mother as often as he could, and he realized that her concern was for him to have the breeding she had, which his father did not have and that money could not buy.

"How blessed I was with my mother!" Delgado thought.

He had not seen earlier through his mother's suffering, her disillusionment with her husband, the love long gone, clinging to her thread of life for her son alone.

When he visited her one Christmas break, they went to the Misa de Aguinaldo (Christmas Midnight Mass). He sensed his mother looking at him with all her love as he sang with the service. She succumbed to TB before summer came. It was her memory that kept him striving for the best, to be a decent person when it was tempting to take advantage of fools. Delgado's tears fell just before sleep came, as he remembered her thin body in his arms, willing her to wake up for him.

The next day the sun was high and shining brightly before the soldiers stirred.

"We'd better move," Delgado said, but he was not sure where.

Just then, Isyong arrived. Delgado's eyes widened. They could have been sitting ducks. They were so tired, and in a friendly house, that nobody had stood guard that night. The teenage boy had left early that morning and contacted a guerilla base two kilometers away.

He had come with instructions on where to lead them.

"Our luck is holding," Meeks said, reading Delgado's mind.

"Have some coffee first," the farmer said.

The "coffee" was toasted rice and coffee grinds, a form of food adulteration meant to prolong the use of the relatively expensive coffee. The "coffee" with *pan de sal* (salted bread) was a treat.

"Thank you very much!" the POWs said effusively.

They were all smiling as they changed into their uniforms and said good-bye. Picking up their equipment, they followed Isyong through the rice paddies and the trees beyond.

"This way," Isyong said.

XXIII

As the Japanese army was arriving in Manila, a lot of civilians decided to flee. Those with relatives in the provinces were able to leave, but those who were uncertain where to go got trapped by the advancing army and ended up staying home.

Lieutenant General Masaharu Homma calculated that a less belligerent approach would be better, so it was quite orderly when the Japanese army entered Manila in January 1942. The Japanese Military Administration was set up. Philippine currency was replaced with Japanese war notes and later with Japanese occupation money. Curfews and blackouts were instituted. Warning posters read: "For each Japanese killed by a rebel, two Filipinos will be shot." The Philippine national song and American songs were banned.

Civilian foreigners were herded for internment to various detention centers: the University of Santo Tomas in Manila, the Los Banos Bilibid Prison, and other confinements. The nurses from Bataan were brought to Los Banos.

The mayor of Manila, Jorge Vargas, was ordered to form a government under Japanese control. Vargas communicated the proposal to the members of the legislature. One-half of the Commonwealth senators and one-third of the lower house cooperated. Out of the cooperating politicians, the Philippine Executive Commission with six department secretaries was formed.

Later on, a Preparatory Commission for Philippine Independence was authorized by the Japanese, ostensibly to grant future independence to the Philippines. The study was headed by Dr. Jose Laurel, and a Constitution was signed and ratified in September 1943. The false Philippine independence was granted by the Japanese to the republic, with Dr. Jose Laurel as president in an inauguration on October 14, 1943.

Jose Abad Santos, the prewar chief justice of the Supreme Court, was supposed to head the government after President

Quezon and Vice President Osmena were evacuated by the Americans. Abad Santos refused to cooperate with the Japanese and fled to Malabang, in Mindanao. He was caught and subsequently executed.

The Japanese instituted systems for governing the populace, including the KALIBAPI (Kapisanan sa Paglilingkod sa Bagong Pilipinas, or Association for the Service of the New Philippines). This association was in charge of selecting representatives from the provinces and the cities to be sent to the National Assembly in Manila.

The Kempetai, or Japanese military police, kept an eye on things. The justices from the Supreme Court down to the lower courts were appointed by the president. The president and all government officials, both civil and ecclesiastic, were under the supervision, and needed the approval of, the Japanese authorities.

Some Filipinos did not need much prodding. They had no principles and cooperated in the name of survival. A group of Filipinos had an association called Makapili (Makabayang Katipunan nang mga Pilipino, or Association of Concerned Filipino Citizens) that was pro-Japanese. A system of distributing food rations—rice, sugar, etc.—to the populace was enforced.

Rich or poor, Filipinos soon found themselves in predicaments that could be called collaboration. A lot of those who acted out of fear, or from lack of will to stand up to aggressors, were understandable, but some rich citizens did not want to jeopardize their holdings, lose their possessions, or be inconvenienced by deprivations. Some businessmen were downright friendly and cooperative with the Japanese, and some politicians and prominent citizens claimed to act as buffer between civilians and Japanese, thus ostensibly saving lives.

Those who acted along grey lines of principle always rationalized their actions, but some actually took advantage of the situation for economic gain and preyed on their more patriotic fellowmen.

In Manila, where there was a heavier concentration of Japanese troops, relatively fewer incidents against collaborators occurred. In the provinces, where people tended to know each other, there were assassinations of so-called collaborators. Collaborators could retaliate and make up stories to settle personal scores, and the Japanese army would take care of it for them.

The average Filipino already had established loyalty to Americans at this point in their history. They reacted to the yoke of oppression by forming or joining active guerilla movements throughout the country. Because of this, the Japanese often rounded up the men in town.

One of the frequent events was the rounding up of people suspected of anti-occupation activities. They would be sorted out by a hooded traitor. The unfortunate ones would be made to stand against a wall. Bursts of gunfire and screams of horror were followed by silence, and the ground would be splattered with blood and bodies that had twisted in pain before dying.

Whenever a guerilla was captured, his comrades tried to rescue him, no matter how difficult. They knew that torture would be employed to make the captive talk. Screams of pain and agony could be heard from far away. Most of the time, the dead bodies hanging from the tree at the plaza showed the marks of what had transpired: fingers broken, nails pulled out, tongues cut off, faces grotesque, the bodies misshapen. Soon it was hard to find any able-bodied young man in town.

A superstition grew that the trees in the plaza were haunted. The older folks would tell the kids that these victims of violence, who were not ready to die, still had a lot of things to tell somebody. People stayed away from those trees at night. Even during daytime, the kids ran quickly past the trees.

On the other hand, there were places where the guerilla leaders abused their arbitrary rule, victimizing innocent civilians. It was a very dangerous game of betrayal and malicious mischief, so some families moved to other places where there was some degree of justice.

In the central plain of Luzon, like the Nueva Ecija and Bulacan provinces, the Hukbalahap (Hukbo Nang Bayan Laban sa Mga Hapon) movement was formed.

It was hard to tell if going to the provinces was better or not, as most of it depended on luck. Some of those who stayed in Manila did not have easy lives, but they survived. Food was scarce, but it could somehow be found, depending on someone's resourcefulness.

The civilians lived on what was available and complied with the food rationing. They devised ways to augment their food supply by planting. They worked somehow, earned money, did a lot of bartering, and hoped they would survive.

Those who lived in strategic areas had an advantage: they could fish along the coast. In those areas where they could have a pond, freshwater fish was available, although by the time it became a steady harvest, they had to give a portion to the garrison. Since both Filipinos and Japanese ate a lot of rice, the people with rice fields had a distinct advantage. Wherever they could, they planted vegetables.

What people used to take for granted was something they hoarded under the occupation. Shoes and shoe materials were not easy to come by. In the provinces, a lot of people went barefoot.

Textile stores had long run out of quality goods. They put out inferior quality cloth that nobody would buy under usual circumstances. Most people did not have enough money anyway, so they just darned their clothes several times over.

Businesses with products that were useful to the Japanese war effort had to give up a portion, if not most, of their products to the occupation authorities. Business owners were wary that sooner or later, depending on how much they cooperated with the Japanese, the guerillas might punish them for collaborating.

Manufactured products from Japan could be found. They were affordable to those who had power and money, which was suspect under the circumstances. Soon however, the have-nots had reason to deride those who could afford such products, because the "Made in Japan" products did not have good quality and were not durable enough.

Some schools functioned, but progress was slow, as both teachers and students were distracted.

The Japanese stepped up their campaign to endear Japan to the Filipinos. Japanese soldiers played musical instruments for children at the plaza, but the parents had already prejudiced their children to stay away from Japanese soldiers because some of them forced their attentions onto some women.

Japanese propaganda filled the airwaves, telling the guerillas to surrender, and extolling the virtues of the Japanese occupation. At first, it was a comedic effort. The Japanese announcers could not pronounce the "l" in "Filipino." Instead, they kept saying "Firipino," which made the civilians laugh. The occupation forces corrected this error and used Filipino announcers and singers to do their bidding under duress.

Since American songs and English were banned, the Filipinos sang more *kundiman*, which somehow united the Filipino thought and longing. One composer attempted to mask his rebellious spirit with a *kundiman* song in which his love for a lady was like the love for the country. It was foiled when a collaborator notified the Japanese authorities. The composer was put in jail, but because of pleas from several Filipino officials, he was placed under house arrest.

The music Filipinos liked most were the more melodious Latin songs with Filipino lyrics. New songs came out in other dialects and became popular. *Kundiman* competitions were held at the plaza, which was a good way to divert peoples' minds from their misery. The occupation forces tried to keep the plaza looking good by stopping the hanging of guerillas in the plaza. They just shot the captured rebels instead.

Religious observations continued, but both sides used the spectacle to spy on each other. The level of influence was proportionate to how compromised the official was as a collaborator. Rumors would spread if somebody was not at the procession. If that person was not seen the next day, he would be presumed dead.

Since most Filipinos were Catholic, the old women prayed for those executed. When they could not tell the good ones from the bad ones, they just said, "Have mercy on us."

Some people started losing their faith; others stopped going to church. The priests wondered how much the people could support them, in spite of their increased workload from deaths and other spiritual and temporal needs. The priests shook their heads and carried on.

Those whose faith did not waver continued with their devotion, feeling they were being tested. Older women with simple lives, their floor-length, old-fashioned skirts almost in taters, continued to trek daily to church and pray harder. Gradually, people learned from looking around them, and they were glad for their own lives. Church attendance increased once more, as people began to pray for the possible and impossible to be granted to them.

Over at the University of Santo Tomas and other detention centers for noncombatants, the incarcerated people lived in overcrowded conditions, and food was not enough. They did not even have enough clothes, blankets, and other necessary things. The townspeople near these centers became aware of their need and started throwing blankets, food, and other things over the high fence for the detainees. Perhaps it was just a little, but it helped those interned feel they were not abandoned. The story was the same with the detention centers in Los Banos and the Bilibid prison.

The years seem to drag slowly, one day at a time, but the spirit of nationalism lived on. People were thin and reduced to a basic existence, but a grim sense of determination pervaded as they decided to fight back and survive.

XXIV

By March 1942, Carlos regretted that he had not moved his family from Cabanatuan to San Nicholas. Clara forgot to complain about the sugar ration and felt anxious instead when Yoshiro started visiting Neneng again. Things were already complicated as it was, and she worried for her daughter, even though she trusted Neneng's decisions. Neneng used many excuses, but she had to see Yoshiro if it could not be avoided.

Meanwhile, Neneng's cousins added to Carlos's worries. Carlos's sister, Pacing, had come to their house late at night and wondered where her son Andong was. Although Andong returned the next day, he was still planning to join the guerillas.

One day, a message was slipped into Clara's basket as she tried to find some spices in the market. She only saw the message when she got home. She quietly showed it to Carlos as soon as he finished with patients in his clinic. The guerilla movement wanted Dr. Mendez to come with them that night. There was no need for a long discussion; the family had been waiting for something like this to happen. They packed their essentials, and Clara prepared the medicines she had taken from her pharmacy. She knew the guerillas could use them.

It was hectic to get so many things done all at once, but her mother Faustina should not be exposed to the hardship of living on the run. Clara gave instructions to Juling. "Tomorrow, early in the morning, take my mother to San Nicholas."

Clara figured if they left that evening, there would be enough time in the morning to spirit her mother away, before the Japanese found out they were gone. They ate a hasty supper; their stomachs were tied in knots as they imagined different scenarios of disaster.

Juling was stationed in the garage area, the boxes of supplies hidden behind the car. Over and over, she practiced what she was going to say if asked where the family was.

"They were abducted by the guerillas!" She repeated this several times, nervous that she might say it the wrong way. She had to say it like the Mendez family was taken against their will.

The family waited with trepidation. The sun had set an hour ago, and when the guerillas still did not come, Carlos began to sweat from the tension. Clara and Neneng sat on the sofa with Faustina, tensely holding hands. Suddenly, there were footsteps and a series of soft, urgent knocks.

As soon as Carlos opened the door, two men came inside quickly and closed the door.

"We had a hard time getting inside the city," the older guerilla said grimly. "The Japanese are on alert because of the ambush! We have to take you behind the plaza in a stealthy way."

The younger one beside him looked scared.

Before the astonished family could say anything, they heard the loud screech of a jeep on the street, followed by running footsteps toward their door.

"Dr. Mendez! Dr. Mendez!" called the Japanese soldiers, knocking at the same time.

The guerillas rushed to the nearest bedroom to hide as Carlos nervously opened the door. Four Japanese soldiers were immediately in front of them.

"Dr. Mendez must come to hospital!" a Japanese sergeant ordered.

"What happened?" Carlos managed to ask, in spite of his trepidation.

"Ambush! Many wounded ... including Colonel Mifune!" the sergeant suspiciously explained.

"I'm coming!" Carlos replied, more for the sake of keeping the guerillas hidden rather than from a genuine desire to help.

Faustina must have held her breath for a long time, for she sat weakly in her rocking chair after Carlos left. Clara held Neneng as they both sighed in relief at the close shave. The elder guerilla came out of the room and peered from the side of one window. He waited to see if the coast was clear, then he picked up one of the cloth sacks.

"Wait! Wait!" Clara raised her hand. "We are not coming unless Carlos is with us!"

The older guerilla was not a man of many words. He looked at Clara, but he did not argue. The younger one shrugged his shoulders. After checking again if the coast was clear, they left.

Clara wondered what kind of outfit that was. She had expected an argument, or at least a change in plans, not just a shrug of the shoulders. She almost felt unpatriotic!

Carlos did not come home until the next day. When he arrived, unshaven and exhausted, he went straight to bed and slept until past noon the next day. He had attended to Colonel Mifune and other Japanese soldiers.

A convoy of Japanese trucks carrying troops and supplies had been ambushed outside of Cabanatuan. More than half of the Japanese soldiers were killed, and most of the survivors were wounded. The hospital had called in anyone who could help. Dr. Mendez was becoming renowned for being a good surgeon, but being called to the Japanese hospital could cause trouble.

Carlos was glad to go home, eat a meal, and have a bath and shave. He had only one day to recuperate, for the next day he was fetched to help in the Japanese camp again.

An old man came to their pharmacy the next day to buy some medicine. For his payment, he gave a piece of paper to Clara: "Dr. Mendez, kill Colonel Mifune."

Carlos was glad he had not been branded a collaborator and shot, but he was still distressed to hear this. Colonel Mifune had a human face: his patient, former neighbor, someone he knew, and for whom there was a mutual respect. He brooded over his predicament.

The next time he was called to the Japanese hospital, he looked for an opportunity. Instead, the other doctors and personnel exuded an atmosphere of humanitarianism and camaraderie. Carlos was not able to formulate a plan.

All his life, Carlos seemed to have made wise decisions. He was a studious, quiet man, observing things around him without making a comment. He stood slightly taller than most Filipinos, his eyes were more rounded, and he was fairly good-looking. However, he was not popular with the ladies since he hardly talked to them—until he met Clara. He first saw Clara in her dorm.

Clara was on her way out to attend a *novena*. He had come to bring a bouquet of flowers for his cousin's birthday. Half obstructed by the flowers, and carrying his books in the other hand, he almost collided with her at the doorway. He apologized profusely just to keep her talking to him while she looked ready to flee. His cousin, her dorm mate, finally came down and amusingly introduced them.

Carlos Mendez was in medical school, and she was studying pharmacy at the University of Santo Tomas. He immediately realized he wanted to see more of her and told his cousin so.

Although Clara was cold to the attention of practically all men, he decided to pursue her. She did not socialize with men; she just studied and went home to her town in Nueva Ecija during vacations. Being from the same province, he was able to visit her whether it was school time or vacation break. He was able to see her in one out of four attempted visits, for she avoided him as much as possible.

From their years in the university until she had her own pharmacy in San Nicholas, Gapan, he visited her, even if his practice in Cabanatuan started to make him busy. She had told him long ago that she had loved once, and there was no need for her to be involved again.

"We can be friends. I think we can live a good life together," he said.

"We can be friends without you needing to visit me," she countered.

Still, he visited until he was thirty-six years old and she was going on thirty.

"We are both getting old. We should not be too old to enjoy the happiness of having children," he pleaded.

At that, she gave him a long, thoughtful look.

The next time he visited, he pursued his topic.

"Will you marry me? It does not have to be a big affair, if you don't want it. I promise to be a good husband."

Tears fell on her cheeks.

"Yes," she finally said.

Carlos Mendez was a contented husband. He came from a Chinese mestizo family in Cabanatuan, and they happen to own a nice tract of land on the main avenue, Avenida Rizal. He was the eldest of four children, and his parents let him have a fourth of their land along the Avenida.

Whereas he had a clinic in their family home along the Avenida when he was a bachelor, when Clara consented to marry him, he razed an old shop that stood on his land, and on its stead, he built a large house. The lower part was cement, and the upper floor was wood. The upstairs area was more than enough for them to live in. On the lower floor, he had three clinic rooms, and the rest was Clara's pharmacy.

Clara sold her pharmacy in San Nicholas, Gapan, and used the money to buy more rice lands. They had servants to do the menial work, and yet Clara could cook, sew, and do many other things aside from managing her pharmacy. She was involved in church activities and community work; the nuns and priests were her friends. She was respected, and people deferred to her judgment.

Carlos Mendez had seen her reaction with Colonel Stewart and wondered if this was the man she had loved once. He found that immaterial now, however, for he had complete trust in his wife.

Their only daughter, Neneng, was a delight with her good sense and graciousness. She was smart but sometimes scatterbrained, and she had a temper that even he could not handle.

He let his wife handle his daughter's fits because they had the same flammable temperament, which came and went as quickly as the clouds cover the sun. They could be arguing one moment, then they would be laughing together suddenly. They liked to sing and play the piano, and they danced well. Neneng had shown an early aptitude to be a doctor. He was very proud of his family.

This order to kill Colonel Mifune caused a dilemma for Carlos because he could not kill anybody. Clara shuddered at the thought and could not come up with any ideas either. Carlos was anxious to start helping the guerillas, but right now, treating the wounded in the Japanese camp was a humanitarian duty. *I'm sworn to save lives! Can't somebody else please do it?* he thought.

In his optimism, he wrote a note and left it in the pharmacy for whoever would pick it up.

It said: "Please let somebody else do it."

Two days later, after the jeep taking him home from the Japanese camp left, a man came out of the shadows.

"Why did you not kill Colonel Mifune?" the voice asked.

Carlos whirled around and only saw a dark figure.

"I can kill a soldier in battle, but I cannot kill a patient," he answered.

A burst of gunshots was heard, sending Clara and Neneng rushing down the stairs.

"Papa! Papa!" Neneng cried.

"Carlos! Oh my God! Help!" Clara screamed.

The blood from his chest was on Clara and Neneng's clothes as they held the slumped figure of Carlos Mendez catching his last breath.

"I love you!" he said; then he died.

Clara Mendez was angry in spite of her grief.

"If we are just going to kill each other, we don't need enemies!" she said defiantly to nobody in particular.

The death of Dr. Mendez was a big event in town, not just because of his prominence, but also because of the convoluted way it came about. Following Filipino custom, the wake for Dr. Mendez was in the living room of their house. He was embalmed and laid in the best coffin. The coffin was on a funeral stand set close to the wall, surrounded by large bouquets of flowers, light fixtures, and lighted candles in stands. A large crucifix was on the wall directly above him, along with framed images of the Sacred Heart of Jesus, the Blessed Mother, and different saints. There were several rows of chairs for the visitors who came morning, noon, and night. In the evening, Father Gabriel came and led the rosary. After the prayers, people sang a hymn together, and then food was served.

Clara tried hard to be more frugal in the spirit of the times. During the day, the visitors were just served tea and *pan de sal, galletas de patatas* (cookies), or *biscocho*.

After the evening prayers, it was customary to serve something heavier. Although the Mendezes tried to pare down the serving, there was still the usual *pansit, siopao, guianatan,* and other dishes. It was wartime, and there was supposed to be a paucity of goods, but different dishes appeared that would not be available anywhere else. Relatives and family friends usually brought food to help out, but Clara thought this was a bit much, considering the times.

Mr. Liong always sent something to serve every evening, usually four large platters of *pansit.* He owned the Eatery down the street, and he had been one of Carlos's patients. Clara was tempted to tell Mr. Liong to stop his kindness, for some gossip-mongers were speculating that Mr. Liong would be courting her next. Clara decided to just be gracious in her attitude rather than muddy the waters.

All the relatives from Clara's side and Carlos's side were in town to help, from cooking to serving and talking with visitors. After the food service was done, quite a number of people stayed on. The superstition was that the corpse should have some company while he was in his coffin, so a vigil, or *lamay,* occurred. Throughout the evening and through dawn, until the next morning's visitors came, there were groups of people playing table games in the living room.

The cousins and younger relatives were protective of Neneng, for even if she cried constantly and her eyes were swollen, she made a valiant effort to receive visitors. Clara, however, was like an automaton—taking care of things and taking care of people. It was only when she laid down to sleep that she let go her emotions, crying silently as she missed the good, steady man who she learned to love in her own way. Now she felt the burden of responsibility in heading her household with a war brewing.

The relatives on Clara's side slept in their bedrooms, wherever they could fit, usually on the floor on a mat called *banig.* The relatives from Carlos's side slept with the cousins in Pacing's house.

It was not unusual for the same people to come everyday for prayers. Aside from the relatives, there were a lot of people who considered themselves close friends and felt like they were part of the family in making visitors feel welcome.

Mr. and Mrs. Humberto de Silva came twice, as though honoring them with their presence. Clara was actually thankful there was somebody who could talk to Colonel Mifune. No doubt Mr. de Silva thought that he was equal to, if not better than, Colonel Mifune. The two men had occasions of laughing together as they talked, and other lesser mortals did not know whether to be afraid or be glad that they got along well.

Although Mr. de Silva was pleasant, his wife Rebecca was condescending to the other ladies. She placed herself in the center of well-to-do women and pronounced her judgment on the events around her. Nobody dared contradict her.

Rebecca was a beautiful Filipina, and having won the prized scion of the landowning Spanish family, she considered herself well above the rest. Humberto had met her in Zamboanga when he went there on vacation. She was the local beauty queen, and they were introduced. Peeved that, for once, she had met a man who was being pursued by women, rather than he pursuing her, she set her cap for him. When Humberto went back to Cabanatuan without committing himself to her, she came to Cabanatuan, accompanied by her mother. A while later, the church bells peeled for their wedding.

For a long time, it was the talk of the town. The townspeople liked to speculate on what went on in that Spanish-style stone house. It stood imposing in the middle of a well-kept lawn. Servants worked to keep it that way; and servants ministered to the family's various whims. The family however, mostly kept to itself, except for the occasional visits from relatives and, later on, from the children's friends. The three children went to school in Manila, and even when school was out, the two young men chose to stay there. Marites used to stay most of the time in Manila too, until she met Jack Stewart, and now she had been coming home more frequently.

Since the hacienda was several kilometers from town, the townspeople did not really know what transpired there. By now most of the servants were imported by Rebecca from Mindanao, and they spoke mostly Bisaya and only a little Tagalog. When their servants came to the *ciudad* for market and other things, vendors went out of their way to extricate information for gossip. Rumor-mongers speculated on what had transpired since Humberto was fifteen years older. Some people would clown around with a woman pursuing a man, and then they would reverse the role, back and forth.

Clara caught the cold, appraising look that Rebecca shot toward Neneng. She tensed with maternal protectiveness, but realized that her daughter need not be alarmed. She asked Neneng to bring the pastries to a group of younger friends while Clara signaled the maid to bring the drinks to the de Silvas. As she headed back to the kitchen, she overheard Rebecca's voice.

"So the priests always come to the Mendez's house during feast days? That's why they declined my invitation last fiesta!"

"It's been like that for a long time, like they are part of the family, you see," Pacing explained.

"Well! I will not bother to invite the priests again then," Rebecca interrupted irritably, and she started fanning herself.

The helpers crowded in the kitchen were peering through the curtains to snoop at the spectacle.

"Why is she fanning herself when it is not even warm?" Tessie the maid said.

"Let me see," the maid of Mr. Liong said and she pushed the curtain back a bit.

Clara decided to ignore a coming attack and brought coffee to the group of matrons. "Maybe we should have a visit after the visitation is over. I'd like to show you my orchid collection," Rebecca said to Clara.

"That would be wonderful, thank you," Clara said, trying to sound enthusiastic.

"I do get busy too, even if you stay much slimmer," Rebecca continued.

Clara was at a loss for words and just smiled. Humberto came over and patted Clara's shoulder as they prepared to leave. Clara slid out of his reach and graciously shook hands.

Neneng acknowledged the departing guests as she stood up from a younger group. She nodded with a smile, hiding the unpleasant feeling left by the guests.

Clara had to admonish the kitchen help and other relatives from peering in the curtains. They whispered their comments as soon as she turned her back. Marites did not come; she was leaving for Manila.

Perhaps Colonel Seichi Mifune really had a good regard for Dr. Mendez, since he came to the visitation twice. This, however, caused awkward moments, which Clara tried her best to minimize. The first time he came, Clara thought he was spying, and she was on her guard. She was surprised that he could talk pleasantly of things in general, and she felt relieved.

Clara met the colonel only once before, when he had come to Carlos's clinic for a consultation. Since then, she had seen him only from a distance, and she kept it that way. She caught him glancing her way several times during the visitation, but she shook that off.

Different rumors circulated. There was a lot of speculation as to who had killed Dr. Mendez, for one guerilla group denounced whoever had killed the doctor. When she was very angry, Clara herself would have taken vengeance with her own hands, but she did not even know who did it. Clara tried to shut off that bitter memory; for next some gossips were speculating on whether she would remarry.

There were some people for whom the event was entirely social. They watched who came, what they wore, or what others did. Most men grouped together according to their sympathies, for as the more serious ones talked about the war, they had to look around for the possibility of betrayal from those they did not know.

The burial was on the ninth day. Carlos's casket was placed on an elaborate hearse, and the profusion of flower arrangements around it left no open space. Townspeople came to the house early, especially the different social groups and associations that staked specific spots on the procession line. The deceased's relatives followed after the hearse; Clara and Neneng walked side by side praying their rosary. By 7:30 AM, the funeral procession started walking from the house to the church.

Colonel Mifune had ordered the car to be available for Mrs. Luna to use for that day, but she declined graciously, saying she would supervise the reception after the funeral.

The church bells peeled as Father Gabriel stood to greet the procession from the altar. Neneng glanced sideways as she held her mother's left arm. Her mother had stopped praying momentarily and closed her eyes when the bells peeled, and then she moved on with distant eyes.

The Mass was quite long, as the mayor and the president of the apostolic group had their say, in addition to Father Gabriel's sermon.

The communion alone was an ordeal, with most of the townsfolk receiving the sacrament. Thankfully, the soloist was able to sing throughout without mishap, wisely singing at a lower pitch and singing less strenuous songs as the communion dragged on.

Father Gabriel blessed the people who attended after the Mass, and with the altar boy beside him, proceeded to lead the procession to the nearby cemetery. Carlos's brother Tasio made a speech as the coffin was pushed in the family mausoleum. A number of people made a spectacle of crying loudly, as though speaking to Carlos, asking him to intercede for them in heaven. Clara and Neneng cried silently, their eyes swollen. Then everybody went back to the Mendez house for lunch.

Former patients came in droves for their good doctor, and Clara resigned herself to accepting graciously the *abuloy* (donations), even if she thought some of those people needed the money or food more than she did. It would be insulting to refuse. The *abuloy* went back to buying food for the guests.

Clara somehow felt a sense of vindication at the show of support they received from the people attending the funeral services. She was touched and humbled. The house was full day and night, even if they tried to serve less. The bitterness she once felt gave way to resignation, thinking that these things happen during a war. Neneng was able to hold her own, right beside her.

Her Kuya Emong had come, and they discussed the possibility of the three women moving back to San Nicholas. Without a man in the family, the women felt vulnerable.

Clara thought for quite a while about the suggestion. Being a traditionalist, and as expected, she was more comfortable with going back to her own kin, rather than staying with her husband's. Right now, she just wanted to sort things out, to go back to some semblance of normalcy. She was sure she and Neneng would stay quiet for a while.

XXV

Yoshiro came to visit after the prayers were over. He arrived in his new uniform as a captain, looking pleased. An air of renewed confidence was in his demeanor, the brown soldier's uniform accenting the fairness of his complexion. He leaned over a vase of gardenias and inhaled the fragrance. He had seen Neneng cut some stems from their garden and put them in vases.

Neneng felt relieved that she did not have to be embarrassed in having to face him when the other mourners were around. Yoshiro seemed excited, and Neneng wondered why.

"Congratulations!" Neneng said with a half smile, wondering what it took to be promoted.

"Thank you," Yoshiro answered modestly.

Not sure if it was safe to talk about his promotion, she hesitated. She looked up and was startled by his gaze, for her brownish black hair and black dress offset her creamy complexion, and she looked quite becoming.

She always kept the conversations on safe topics like customs, literature, and anything other than the war and Yoshiro as a person; so she talked about Filipino writers.

"So my favorite poem is Jose Rizal's 'Mi Ultimo Adios,' have you read it?" she said.

"Yes," Yoshiro smiled, seemingly able to discern her tactic. "I want to marry you!" he said suddenly.

"Ah ... ah ... I'm in mourning for one year; also, I'm Catholic," she blurted out, caught by surprise.

"I will respect your religion," he said gently.

She looked at him, not knowing what to say.

"I'm going to be a nun," she said after a pause.

"I can have you taken if I please," he said and his jaw was set grimly.

Neneng looked at him with a hurt look; then, unable to say anything, tears rolled down her cheeks.

He looked at her for a while; then he stood up. He walked toward her and touched her shoulders. Her head bowed, she cried silently without moving. He left.

"Mama, Yoshiro proposed to me!" Neneng ran to the kitchen as soon as Yoshiro left.

"My God!" her grandmother said as she grabbed a chair and sat down.

Clara Mendez looked startled, then grim. She started to plan at once. "We have to leave this afternoon! We will go to Manila first so it won't be easy to find us," she said. Next she turned to Juling, the maid. "Borrow a pair of pants from Andong."

Clara's mind was racing. The pants from her cousin would be for Neneng's disguise. Clara was all too aware of spies lurking around, ready to give the Japanese any information they could use. She and Neneng quickly packed some essentials into cloth sacks. Clara told Juling to take the sacks with her to Bulacan province and wait in the bus depot.

Faustina watched silently through the commotion, knowing that Clara was struggling through the vivid memory of another time like this. She held her daughter and granddaughter with her aging hands and gave them a blessing.

The two changed their clothes, smudged their faces with flour and charcoal, and came out of the house through the store. They walked slowly toward the church, but seeing a group of people by the plaza, Clara hailed a passing *calesa*. They got off at the church, but the two came in only for a quick prayer, then they went out by the side door. They walked through the back streets toward the bus depot and got on the bus going to Bulacan. Once in Bulacan, they met with Juling and sent her back to care for the grandmother and the house. Juling understood that if she did not know where they were going, she could not tell anybody anything.

Clara pressed the thick eyeglasses closer to her eyes, at which point everything was a blur. She had the habit of bringing it down her nose if she really had to see. Using Carlos's eyeglasses was part of her disguise as an old woman. She added a cane, as though she needed some assistance.

Assisting the old lady was Neneng, dressed like a boy, her loose pants and rumpled shirt covering her figure. The hat hid her hair and completed her peasant disguise.

Clara closed her eyes as she and Neneng sat toward the back of the bus. This was the last week of March, and the heat worsened the smell of chickens on the bus. Dust blown by the wind and passing vehicles settled on their hair, making it stiff and gray.

"I must tell you the story of Balangiga, including what I only learned recently," Clara said.

She was nagged by the idea that not telling her daughter her life story, and about John, was an omission that bordered on betrayal. Too many things had happened recently, and they needed a chance to really talk. She finished her story on the way to Manila.

"Is that why you often start when you hear the church bells?" Neneng asked.

"Yes," Clara replied. "It often brings back painful memories of how our lives changed when those bells tolled."

Clara's daughter always confided in her, and in return, she sensed that Neneng guessed how she felt for John Stewart.

"We are two different families now, and it will stay that way," Clara said. Her face was strained with pain, but she tried not to think of herself. "For some reason, I believe Jack's explanation, simply because time has proven that his father is a man of honor. You must follow your heart about Jack, only time will tell true love. I hope you find happiness." She embraced her daughter.

It was evening when Clara and Neneng arrived in Manila. Luckily, they arrived at her cousin Manolo's home without any mishaps. The startled cousin let them in and fed them.

"We ate already," Manolo said as his wife and children came out to greet the visitors.

They sat around the dining table and exchanged stories about what was happening in their respective towns and the food shortage. It was very late at night when they went to bed, caught up on the news of what was going on, except Clara did not say why they suddenly came.

"We are just visiting," she said, aware that they looked unusual for visitors.

Her cousin understood that something was afoot and played it her way. Clara could not afford to compromise them. Clara planned to be ahead by a day before Yoshiro knew they were gone; she hid their trail in case spies reported their whereabouts. Only she knew where Neneng would be going.

The next day, Clara and Neneng bade good-bye. They smudged their faces with dirt before they left and put on their disguises. They then took a bus to Baguio.

An older cousin had once entered the Carmelite convent. Clara was familiar with this place and knew how to establish contact. So far, the enemy bombs over Baguio had spared the nunnery.

Clara and Neneng pretended to be old, poor people begging for help at the gate. They knocked for quite a while before the gate slowly opened and an old nun peered into the outside world hesitantly.

"Sister, I must see Mother Elena! I am Clara Mendez. Mother Superior knows me." Clara talked fast for an old-looking lady, and she held the nun's hand so the nun could not close the door on them.

"We cannot wait outside for long!" Clara motioned for Neneng to come in already. "Please Sister!" Clara slipped inside as the nun was about to protest.

The old nun was upset and ready to scold them. She faced Clara, but she was stopped by their look of relief and the tears that erased the smudges on their faces. Without saying a word, the old nun motioned for them to follow her.

The Mother Superior was welcoming and sympathetic. She knew Clara's family from way back. She was curious if Neneng had a religious vocation or whether she was just hiding.

"I do not know if she wants to be a nun or whether she's still in love with Jack and will want to marry someday. I don't think she really knows where her heart is yet," Clara said frankly.

They agreed to let Neneng think things out. In the meantime, Clara asked if she could stay too until things cooled down.

The convent was a peaceful refuge; the cloistered area was cool, and the silence was conducive to prayer. In the first few days, Clara was thankful for her chance to reflect, and she and Neneng followed the nuns' schedule.

By the fourth day, Clara was willing to commit herself to some undertakings. She had been helping some older nuns with the cooking and noticed that the roof leaked when it rained.

She offered the Mother Superior the money she had with her to fix the roof. Clara was glad to be of help, for she had guessed that contributions to the convent had not been coming since the war. She helped without overstepping her bounds, and after three weeks, she felt that Neneng was safe.

Clara then left for San Nicholas, Gapan (Nueva Ecija). Nobody recognized her when she walked slowly toward the big house looking like a down-trodden beggar.

As she expected, her Kuya Emong, her mother, the servants, and others had been questioned; but it seemed like things had quieted down after three weeks. With Neneng safe at the convent, Clara would have to send for her mother Faustina to come to San Nicholas. Her Kuya Emong took the early morning bus the next day and came home with the mother that afternoon.

It still did not feel quite safe, so Clara stayed indoors during the day. She was afraid that Yoshiro would find out where she was.

Yoshiro arrived at the Mendez house the day after he had proposed, expecting that Neneng would be unpredictable after their showdown yesterday. He was not prepared to see a frightened servant insisting that Neneng and Mrs. Mendez were in Manila.

Thinking that Neneng was again avoiding him, he insisted that Juling knock at Neneng's door. The door was open, but mother and daughter were gone!

"You are coming with me," he told Juling.

Juling was hauled off to the camp and subjected to interrogation.

Yoshiro's fury was mixed with admiration. Clara Mendez had been quicker and outwitted him and the spies around town.

Yoshiro had come to the Philippines two years before the war broke out. Aside from his military training, he had also finished school as an engineer. His family came from a line of feudal lords, with responsibilities and privileges. They were followers of tradition and ready to uphold Japan's supremacy by learning to compete against the Westerners. That was why he spent two years studying in the United States.

Yoshiro's father was typical of his breed: authoritarian, demanding, and with a faint disregard for women. Yoshiro was aware that geishas were the norm when his father was out with his friends. He wondered if his father's opinion of women had changed since he came across Mrs. Mendez. He sensed an admiration from his father that was not easily given.

Yoshiro had a more modern regard for women that he learned in New York. He became aware that a lot of women were very capable, although the very aggressive ones turned him off. He had dated a number of beautiful Americans.

When he first saw Neneng walking to church, he smiled at what he thought was a little girl who reminded him of his sister. It was on second look that he realized that she was probably only five years younger than he was, only more innocent looking and carefree. She had a fair complexion that could be mistaken for Japanese.

His purpose when he first visited was to just get to know her and pass the time. He was not disposed by nature and circumstance to hang out with other men or socialize with women. When they started conversing, he realized she was a wide reader and could talk well.

Under that veneer of aloof shyness, she was nice but had moods when she was difficult. Unlike most women who preened and tried to get his attention, she actually seemed to think that she was doing a duty to sit in front of visitors. On his first visits, she looked like she would rather be somewhere else or doing something else.

She upheld tradition and was strong in her beliefs. He had watched her explaining to Jack Stewart about coconuts.

"What's a *puso*?" Jack had asked.

"If the accent is on the first syllable, it means heart, if the accent is on the second syllable, it means cooked rice wrapped in coconut leaves," Neneng explained.

"Coconuts! I'm still so surprised what else comes out of the coconut!" Jack had said wonderingly.

"It is a very useful tree," Neneng quickly answered. "The trunk is used as logs for some homes; the leaves are used to wrap *puso* or for baskets, and as roofs. The coconut meat is delicious when fresh and can be dried out for *copra*. We drink the juice. The shell is used for castanets and buttons; half of a coconut we use to scrub floors. We get the *tuba* from it, as well as the *ubod* for the *lumpia*," she finished.

She was almost out of breath, her brown eyes flashing. Jack was startled; but Yoshiro could not help but laugh at her vehemence, and soon all three of them were laughing. That was when he realized he had fallen in love!

It was hard to draw her out. She kept steering the subject to safe topics; besides, Jack Stewart was always there, and it became a race of who could outlast whom.

On one rare day that he had arrived while she played the piano, he had asked her to go on playing, but she refused and got up. He sat instead at the piano stool and played the first movement of the "Moonlight Sonata." Then he opened the seat cover and looked at her piano pieces, flipping through a mixture of mostly Beethoven and Mozart pieces.

"How about this?" he asked.

She pouted at him but reluctantly sat down. She took the Beethoven "Pathetique" and played the first five minutes of the second movement brilliantly. He stood listening appreciatively, and as though lost in thought, he absentmindedly sat down beside her. With that, she lost her composure, and perspiring, she finished in disaster.

"Neneng!"

He heard the mother's reprimand from downstairs.

The grandmother came up from downstairs to sit in her rocking chair. "Humph!" she said.

Neneng got up from the piano seat and moved to the chair by the window. She glared at him.

He belatedly realized that it might not have been proper for him to sit right beside her, for she usually kept her distance from men. He was about to apologize, but she looked funny hyperventilating and glaring at him at the same time. He could not help it, he laughed instead. She grinned at first, then soon they were both laughing!

Yoshiro did not have to mix with people on the streets to get information. He and his father used their courteousness to advantage and found that being helpful to those who came to their store, and advising them on the use of tools, had its rewards.

People talked about things that were useful for intelligence: from supply of ammunitions, to harvests, to build-ups, food storage, and other people. He had found out what happened with Neneng the night of the officers' reception.

He was not sure that Neneng had already committed herself to Jack Stewart. If so, it would be recent, and it was not too late for him. If necessary, they could marry, and she would learn to love him. They would live in the big cities for his work and also to be free from provincial traditions that he was sure could strain their relationship.

Still nothing! The maid had been interrogated closely for two days. Certainly, it was a question of sedition if people suddenly fled from one place to another during wartime. Juling sweated as she sat on a chair with the bright light on her face.

"All I know is that they went to Bulacan. Have mercy! I don't know anything else!"

She kept repeating this until the interrogator got tired. Yoshiro had instructed that she was not to be harmed physically. Juling was put in jail for one more week, while Yoshiro waited for the report from spies. Neneng was not among the Mendez relatives in Bulacan, neither was she in Manila. Yoshiro ordered Juling to be released. Yoshiro was arrogant, but he was not vicious.

I will find Neneng, he thought. *I have the upper hand, after all.*

XXVI

Jack's group became larger as more Filipino civilians joined them. After the fall of Bataan, Allied soldiers who escaped the death march started joining them too. With more men, they built settlements deeper in the mountains.

There were aborigines living in the mountain area, and Jack's guerilla group maintained a friendship with them, respecting their customs.

The Filipino soldiers knew some local farming so now there were lots of *camote, kangkong, saluyot*, string beans, tomatoes, and squash. For rice and meat, they used intermediaries to barter with merchants in the towns; they also received some supply from civilian sympathizers. Oscar, the Filipino cook, ruled the kitchen.

Jack and his men lived simply and became adept at running fast on all kinds of terrain as they ambushed convoys and enemy patrols in the area. They could survive long periods of hunger, ate whatever was available, and felt lucky that only a few caught malaria. They had gotten more quinine from the last ambush, and Jack sent messengers with the surplus medicine to other units.

Most of them adhered to the long-sleeved uniforms and long pants, especially at night. They realized the usefulness of mosquito nets; if without nets, they devised ways to minimize skin exposure when asleep. A civilian doctor, Dr. Yuson, visited their camp every two weeks. So far, his advice on preventive medicine had been useful. There was some wariness on the guerillas' part, so Yuson was blindfolded, coming and going, on his visits.

They had a few cots among their ambushed supplies, but most soldiers made their own wooden bunk beds and placed various salvaged cloth pieces on top as their mattress. Jack had a regular bunk bed. It was hard on the back, but better than a cot after a long day of raiding Japanese convoys.

Their proud evidence of progress was the officers' hut, where Jack and most officers lived. The large *nipa* hut had layers of coconut leaves for a roof, and the walls were open to the outside from the waist up. Their bunk beds were lined in three rows from the window to the center. In the center was a table with lamps, maps, and papers. Chairs surrounded it, and there was a clearing all the way to the open doorway. Every now and then, water dripped down the roof when it rained hard. They placed buckets and tin cans where the water dripped to prevent puddles of mud from forming all over the dirt floor.

Jack and Ed Buendia got along so well they were like brothers; they worked well together by either dividing the labor or taking turns in their command. Both were worried when Sergeant Meier and Sergeant Conde requested permission to marry local maidens and build their own huts. There was an officers' meeting to set down the rules, and permission was granted. The officers could not afford a breakdown in morale, yet they also understood the loneliness of the men.

Boiling their water became a rule after Dr. Yuson lectured them about amoebiasis in this region. Sergeant Meier drove the point home by describing a boy he saw in one village.

"He was thin, small for his age, with yellow eyes and a big tummy. His skin could be yellow too, but it's hard to tell because he was really dark."

Jack and his men wondered if boredom would overtake them, but it was not to be, for keeping order and preventing civilian damage took up their time.

Jack helped himself learn Tagalog after he got hold of a grammar book. Buendia would jokingly check his progress now and then.

In spite of the easy camaraderie among the officers and their relative comfort, a sense of homesickness would now and then come over Jack.

Back home in Virginia seemed so far away. The last gracious way of living he knew was in Cabanatuan. The main street was Avenida Rizal. From the market, he bought fruits like *siniguelas, santol, chiesa, duhat,* and mangoes. He had gotten bellyaches from eating too much at once. Jack remembered the fiestas, the processions, the *harana*, and Teban. It took a while for Teban to learn that Jack did not need a heaping serving at the food line. Teban was a friend who worried about him and his courtship of Neneng. Teban had been left in Cabanatuan when Jack was transferred. *'Where is Teban now?'* he thought.

Jack thought of the Mendez family and Neneng, even if it hurt to think of her. He could not forget Neneng. He had not seen her since the night of the officers' banquet. Her face came unbidden into his mind every night before he slept, and he dreamed of their visits. He felt so hurt that she did not want to see him again. She crept into his mind even during the day when they were not busy. He imagined her when he looked at coconut trees, the sun, the moon, the stars, and everything. Whenever he smelled something fragrant, he remembered the *sampaguita* on her hair.

Buendia relayed to him whatever news tidbits he heard about the Mendezes and Cabanatuan.

Jack learned that Yoshiro had visited Neneng when she came home to Cabanatuan, and Jack was jealous. When he learned that Neneng had gone to a convent, he was first relieved; then he became anxious. He heard that a bomb had hit a convent in Manila, and he was scared for her safety. Jack preferred the evenings after a tiring day, for it was more merciful to be able to sleep without being tortured by memories.

One evening, the rain poured like buckets of water as a typhoon hit eastern Luzon. The guerillas were stuck in their tents as the mud puddles around them got bigger; the dampness and cold added to their low spirits. In a distant hut, Private Bender let his would-be assistant tinker with the radio. The static was ongoing, making some men irritable. Suddenly, the static cleared and a *kundiman* song filled the air. The men smiled.

A famous singer could be heard singing, "Masakit man ang nangyari, hindi kita malimutan" (Even if what happened hurts, I cannot forget you).

Jack marched through the rain, down to the fourth tent where the radiomen were smiling. He turned off the radio and stalked back to his hut.

"Sir?!" protested the assistant.

Bender elbowed his assistant. "He's just lovesick!"

The other soldiers sighed. They had received word that Jack and Buendia had been promoted to captains. They knew Jack was tough in battle, but there were these unguarded moments when he was obviously pining for someone.

Jack reached his hut completely drenched, his hair flattened on his forehead.

"Sorry," he said as the other officers gave him curious looks. He changed clothes and, without saying another word, laid down on his bed. His jaw was set like he was ready for a fight, but inside, he felt miserable from longing. He wished he was somewhere else. He knew that when he was not around, the men would strum their guitars and sing *kundiman* songs.

XXVII

Even if at first the Filipinos were terrified of the Japanese, those who had relatives in the army persisted to know if their loved ones were alive at Camp O'Donnell. People started asking around, and soon, there were people trekking to the camp to look for their loved ones. They would stand for hours from a distance, trying to find the people they sought among the walking. When they could not find them, they devised ways of trying to communicate to somebody they recognized so they could find out if their beloved was dead or alive. Soon there was a network by word of mouth—who was seen there and who was not.

What started slowly as a trickle of stragglers, walking exhaustedly to the camp, became a stream of people coming from afar to visit their loved ones. No talking was allowed, no food could be given; the long conversations were only with eyes that filled with tears.

Like most people, Emong asked around if his brother might be a POW there. Although their family was not outwardly demonstrative with their affection, the blood bond among them was very strong. In the marketplace and among the peasants that worked on their farm, the word was out to find out about Celestino.

Emong lived in an imposing stone family house, the patriarch of his brood after his father Felipe passed away. The clan owned the land far beyond the rice paddies that the eye could see. Emong had to look out for everybody in his clan, including his Aunt Faustina and cousin Clara. Although the relatives of Clara's husband lived mostly in Cabanatuan, Clara had turned to her Kuya Emong when she had to evade the Mifunes.

Among those who were better off, the custom was to turn to your own bloodline; for the rules of propriety were strict, and there was a wariness of non-blood relatives not treating them properly. Thus, his Aunt Faustina and his cousin Clara were now in the big house with Emong at San Nicholas. Emong would otherwise be alone, except for the helpers.

Emong had shown an early aptitude for farming and managing land holdings. He had done well with common sense and good intuition; and now with the war, they still had a steady source of food even if they had to surrender a large part of the harvest to the Japanese.

Their family followed the tradition of the Tagalogs, the dominant cultural group in Luzon. There was a strong Spanish and Chinese influence; their bloodlines determined each generation, and each family had their own hierarchy of elders. The elder ones took care of the younger ones, and docility was the norm.

Emong's wife and son had died in a car accident and he did not remarry. He had two siblings who died in infancy, one sister lived in Mindanao, and his three brothers—Manolo, Vicente, and Celestino—lived in Manila. In this closely knit family, Emong kept in touch with his other siblings and made sure they got enough rice because the rationing was unreliable. He either came by himself, or sometimes Kulas the steward came with him.

Celestino, the youngest brother, was the firebrand. He had finished at the Philippine Military Academy, and he was a lawyer. He taught at the Academy, and he was a captain when the war broke out.

A long time ago, upon hearing that their Aunt Faustina's property was going to be misappropriated by the in-laws, Celestino had gone to Balangiga, challenged the in-law, and sold the properties for his aunt. He did not give any hand-out to Luming, even though by the time of Dolfo's death, Luming had little property left, for she had squandered their inheritance.

"She could fend for herself, after being so evil," he told his Kuya Emong.

He gave the proceeds from the sale of Dr. Luna's lands, house, and other properties to his Aunt Faustina. She invested the money into more rice lands, and she bought a house for Celestino and his wife when he got married. Aunt Faustina had always been close to her nephews, and the bond of this closely knit family was stronger than ever.

Emong found out that Celestino had been in Bataan and was now a POW in Camp O'Donnell. His Aunt Faustina wanted to see his nephew, but she was quite old, and Emong finally convinced her not to come. Clara definitely could not come, for she had to remain in hiding. Her eyes misty, Clara prepared special food for the trip.

To see Celestino, Emong decided to go to Capas, Tarlac, alone. He did not know what to expect, and he did not want to bring attention to himself. Since he was already white-haired, there were checkpoints where he was just waved on. He took the early bus at the San Nicholas terminal but did not go to Capas directly. He decided to go to Pampanga and buy some *bangus*, or milkfish. He then pretended to be a seller of these at Tarlac.

Most people visiting the prisoners had to walk the eight miles from Capas, Tarlac, to Camp O'Donnell. Luckily, some roadside stalls rented bicycles, and Emong was able to rent one.

He was taken aback by the smell of dirt and disease when he arrived. His eyes scanned the thin, weak prisoners who hobbled around, looking for Celestino. Emong's straw hat was not much help, so he fanned himself with it. On his left, he noticed that some Filipino visitors were getting closer to the barbed wire. He moved farther from the group to avoid trouble.

Who will take care of my cousins, or bring palay to Manila? he thought.

After quite a while, he saw Celestino come out of what seemed like the hospital, looking thin, stooped, and tired. Emong looked at Celestino and willed him to look back at him. Finally, Celestino turned, and Emong cried quietly as he looked at his gaunt brother. He stayed for several hours, just looking, as though keeping his brother company.

Most visitors stayed for hours. The lucky ones who found their loved ones stood there to commune with their suffering. In between, the visitors talked among themselves, exchanging notes about the prisoners, about the effect of war in their towns, and about the new Japanese system.

As the sun descended in late afternoon, the visitors began gathering their things, and so did Emong. He waved in the direction of

Celestino. Celestino looked back and talked with his eyes, as though telling him to look after his family. Emong nodded and was about ready to leave when, from the other hospital door, a tall figure came out.

John had been ill for quite a while, and this was his first time out of the hospital. He had been accustomed to being indoors, and coming out to the brighter surroundings made him blink. He had heard of the visitors, and his curiosity was whetted. He was still weak, but seeing those people standing from afar, having traveled from quite a distance, touched him. He waved to no one in particular, and as a breeze blew, brushed back his hair with his fingers. As he stood there, John was overcome by longing, and tears fell on his cheeks. He was a little taken aback by his emotion, and still feeling weak, he decided to go back in.

Emong did not think John saw him, but he was sure it was John. Now Emong had a heavier heart. He wondered whether he should tell Clara.

He put it off only for a day.

"John is in Camp O'Donnell," he said. Emong had heard about Clara's story of Balangiga from her mother. He realized she needed to sort this out herself, and he let her make the decision.

Clara was stunned. She had been praying for her loved ones who had to fight for her country, but she dreaded to know exactly how bad they were faring. She agonized on what to do for two sleepless nights; then she made up her mind.

Clara could not be dissuaded from going to Capas, Tarlac. She reasoned that it would be good to see Celestino, but in her heart, she wanted to see John most of all. She knew she had to prepare for this because she could not be traveling late at night; she would need to sleep somewhere respectable. Clara packed some *galletas de patatas*, cooked *tapa*, *puso*, and bananas.

"Take Kulas with you," Emong said.

Kulas came early, ready with umbrellas, and a *lampara*, a lamp that used kerosene.

Kulas was a distant cousin who was less well-to-do and functioned as a handyman or steward on their farms. He was only slightly younger than Emong, and his age was the reason he was still around, for most young men had either joined the guerillas or had been killed.

Clara wore the housemaid Pilar's clothes and was disguised as an old lady. They started early in the morning and took the bus. They arrived in Capas, Tarlac, at almost noon.

They were prepared to walk the last eight miles to Camp O'Donnell, aware that only a few bikes were available. Most of the women shielded themselves with umbrellas from the hot sun, while the men wore hats. Now and then, people would rest and eat under the shade of trees on the wayside. There was an expectant air, mixed with sadness, as people churned the dust on the unpaved road. The dust whitened their hair, the baskets, and their clothes. As the camp drew closer, the visitors became eager and started hurrying. Even the tired laggards hurried.

Behind the barbed wire perimeter, the visitors jockeyed for the vantage position on a slightly elevated ground to see the prisoners. Their small conversations were mostly about where they came from and who it was that they were looking for. There were no facilities, the ground was barren and rocky, and some women spread their *tapis* (small aprons) on the ground when they had to sit down.

Clara and Kulas moved from one spot to another for a better view of the prisoners. When Clara saw all the suffering, she cried silently, feeling the agony her beloved had to suffer. Kulas saw Celestino first and pointed him out to her. They waved at each other, but Celestino looked sick. A fellow prisoner touched his forehead and caught him by the shoulder. After a weak wave in their direction, Celestino and the other prisoner went in.

Clara was sobbing audibly as her heart went out for her cousin, and she stood there praying.

The crowd of visitors had the same thing in mind. Although some moved from spot to spot for a better vantage point, others were content to stand silently from afar, whether they saw their beloved or not. This was their vigil—to share the pain of those who had fought for their country.

Clara sighed as she searched for John among so many prisoners, all looking sick and thin, their uniforms torn and dirty. Some prisoners were milling around, some in desultory conversation, but most seem to be in one activity or another: ready to load a small bus for a work detail, carrying the dead toward the gravesite, helping the weak ones eat, walking in a daze, or just sitting forlorn in a corner.

It took a while before she saw John: a tall figure in a torn officer's uniform coming out of the hospital door. He came outside as though needing some fresh air then quickly looked up to where the visitors stood. Not recognizing anybody, he waved as though to everybody.

Clara saw John come out, and her heart leaped with joy. Then she saw how thin he was, and she cried.

John turned to another prisoner, who stood alone as though in a daze, gave him some water, and they went inside the hospital together. Then he came out again, looking at the visitor's area as though intent on finding someone.

Clara scolded herself for being a sentimental wreck, and she tried to stand more erect. *I should be glad and content just to see him alive*, she thought.

When John came out again, she was wiping her tears with a handkerchief. She hastily waved her handkerchief, and John waved back. He pretended to stay occupied with talking to other prisoners here and there, but he kept looking up at where they stood and waved surreptitiously. Clara knew he recognized them and waved back, the light reflecting the gleam from the ring John once gave her. She smiled bravely back at him, but overcome, she sat down on a rock. She cried silently as the tears blinded her, but again she stood up as most visitors did, standing for a long time in communion with the suffering of their beloved.

Before long, the sun set, its fiery glow casting a spell on Clara and John as though they were transported to a time long ago, when they looked into each other's eyes and made a vow in Balangiga. How tenderly he had kissed her as he gave her the ring that bound her to him, and how quickly the flame of their passion engulfed them. The memory was too much for Clara; she gasped as she struggled to keep standing.

John, too, was standing transfixed as he looked at her for some time, until the gong sounded for the prisoners to eat. A prisoner nudged John, and he came back to reality. He gave her one long look, waved, and reluctantly went in.

As the darkness spread, Kulas lighted their *lampara*, as most men did. The visitors picked up their things and sadly walked back. Some decided to sleep near the wayside trees, but Clara and Kulas were among those who walked to Capas. They found a place to sleep.

The next day, Clara was quiet on the bus ride home, as though exhausted by emotion. They arrived at San Nicholas in the afternoon, tired, dirty, and hungry. Clara gave her Kuya Emong and her mother only a brief account of the visit, and they understood.

Faustina Luna watched the restlessness that had beset her daughter. She marveled at how John had twice disappeared from Clara's life, only to come back.

When John came to their yard that first day, Faustina instantly liked the tall, wholesome boy. Before long, she admired the noble streak in him, his sense of fair play, and his self-effacing way of getting things done without making a fuss of it. He did not bully, and he did not seem to mind that their playmates were not well-to-do; some wore only slippers or went barefoot. John was the kind who looked at a person, not what they had.

She was taken aback when she first realized that John always knew where Clara was, even if the boys were playing by themselves. After the Balangiga massacre, Faustina thought that it was for the best as far as her daughter's destiny was concerned. There was too much conflict with being involved with foreigners.

Whenever she watched her daughter sigh during their visit to Diego's grave, she thought she would forget in time. But John came back, and every year thereafter, even if it was not easy. When the two decided to marry, Faustina had blessed them, for she knew that not everybody would be blessed with a love like that; but there were others who wanted to usurp it, and Faustina had fought for her daughter's happiness.

Long ago, Clara was a defenseless girl who just cried quietly and was like a zombie that Faustina had to lead from one bus and one boat to another. Clara was in a state of shock, losing her direction after losing the man she loved. Life lost its color, and Clara functioned like an automaton, not enjoying anything, a persistent sadness in her face. She barely ate and cried silently. Her loose clothes gave away the fact that she was getting very thin. Faustina finally addressed her daughter.

"My child, accept the will of God at what had happened," Faustina could not help crying.

Clara had looked at her as though seeing for the first time that her mother was also in pain. They had embraced, and from then on, Clara made an effort to live. Her sense of duty and goodness had always been strong, even if she had no hope of happiness. Clara finished college and later married Carlos, even if there was no love at first. Her daughter Neneng was the first one to really make her laugh and make her alive again.

Faustina had no regrets about her decision to flee Balangiga. She herself had refused to marry a man she did not love. She was a Fuentes from San Nicholas, Gapan, Nueva Ecija, fairly well-to-do, and went for college in Manila. There she had met Manuel Luna, who was from Balangiga, Samar. Manuel was not just a Visaya, but he was a Waray—the inhabitants of Samar and Leyte—and her parents did not approve.

Faustina's other suitor was Ruben, a Tagalog whom her parents had approved of: same dialect, a pure Filipino family, the same background.

Instead, Faustina chose Manuel.

Manuel was the grandson of a Spanish landowner who had married a Filipina. The grandfather had six children who quarreled about the inheritance when he died. The hacienda was divided into six parts, albeit with many complaints. Most of the heirs were not used to a rustic life and were spoiled; they preferred the gaiety in Manila. They did not really know how to run their farm, and when two consecutive seasons of poor harvest occurred, most of the siblings sold their property and left town. Only Manuel's father remained, although he was not much of a success either. When Manuel wanted to be a doctor, Celso, Manuel's older brother, insisted that the cost of Manuel's schooling be charged to his inheritance. Manuel had to study in Madrid, Spain, and very little was left when he returned.

Manuel was a good man, and Faustina was not just a housekeeper. What Manuel earned practicing medicine she saved and invested in farmlands and real estate. She attributed her good business decisions to the Chinese blood from her mother's side. Her household was managed well, with just the right amount of servants, for her mother had trained her to cook, sew, and do everything else at home, so she could properly instruct the servants.

Their prosperity was envied by Celso, who had been careless with his share of the inheritance. With time, Celso, his wife Luming, and their son Dolfo did not bother to hide their resentment of Manuel's family.

Being always busy, Faustina was not given to visiting unless there was a purpose, and she was shocked when the town was deeply involved in the Balangiga massacre that she and her husband were kept out of. She had sensed among the townsfolk that many respected them, but there were also those who envied them, and perhaps they wanted to keep the glory for themselves. Only it did not turn out that way.

She thought of the misgivings she shared with her husband about having to treat Americans when they first came. Her husband felt it was a duty, but both of them worried about the impression this gave to those who had so much antagonism against authority.

Time had proven that the Americans were good; she only wished that Manuel could share the joy of seeing their daughter grown, to approve of Clara and be proud of her.

Clara and Faustina had tried to spare each other from knowing about John. Clara told Faustina about what happened to John that night in Balangiga, but only after Carlos died; and only later did Faustina reveal to Clara that John had come to their house and talked to her.

Clara had not stopped loving John all these years. It hurt so much to see him again when they already had other responsibilities. She had been loyal to her husband and his memory, and now she half-regretted the decision to visit John. She just wanted to see her beloved even from afar, not knowing if they would survive this war. Instead, she now felt his suffering in the concentration camp, and she could not bear it. Perhaps neither did she have the right to it.

Already religious, she resorted to constant prayer: for her cousin to survive; for Neneng and all of them to stay safe; for Jack; and most of all, for John. In her mind, that was what she prayed for, but her heart was grieving for John and for his suffering, and she prayed to God to please let him live, even if she did not have the right to him. She prayed in between her gardening, in between cooking, in between whatever she was doing. She held her rosary if it was around. Otherwise, she counted with her fingers, then would get mixed up. She cried silently at the most unbidden times and at night, and she was often visited by nightmares of Balangiga and this war.

A week after Clara's trip to see John, she and Faustina sat across from each other near the window. On the table in front of them was a pile of torn clothing, socks, and curtains that needed darning. Clara was quiet and seemed to be hurrying, only to have tears fall on her hand.

Clara looked up to see her mother looking at her tenderly; then Faustina came over to hold her shoulder.

"My daughter, our family has loved John as though he was our son, and I can understand the pain you feel," Faustina said.

Clara held on to her mother's arm and suddenly let the floodgates of her misery burst open. Sobs rocked her body as she cried for a long time, becoming short of breath and bent in her chair. Finally, she was spent and spoke in a weak voice.

"I went to visit John pretending I was a friend who cared. I cannot hide the fact that I still love him. I don't have the right to visit again," Clara said.

That moment of facing the truth, admitting her feelings and being able to cry it all out, was like a confession that eased Clara's pain. Deeply religious, a resigned serenity came over her from then on. She stopped the obsessive praying, and she just added one prayer in the afternoon for all the prisoners of war, especially Celestino, John, and Jack, and for her immediate family and all her relatives to survive this travail. In her mind, however, John's picture would always intrude.

PART THREE

XXVIII

Emong visited at Camp O'Donnell several times more. He would wake up very early and rent a bike at Capas, so he could do it in one day, although he would arrive home late and very tired. On his last visit, he was worried that Celestino looked really sick.

On Sundays, they had a routine. Clara would wake up early to hear the first Mass with Pilar. They rode in a *calesa* driven by an old man whose son was in the guerilla movement. Clara usually came disguised as a bespectacled old lady, dressed very poorly, so nobody would notice her. Emong and Faustina heard the later Mass, also riding in a *calesa*.

One morning in July was a little different. After the Mass, Faustina stood waiting near the *calesa* steps. She was getting old and needed help to go up the steps, but Emong was still talking excitedly with the other men in the church plaza. Finally the *kutsero* came down to help her, and she sat on the front seat waiting patiently, wondering what news was keeping Emong. Emong came to their *calesa* and blurted out the news.

"General Homma released the Filipino prisoners! I wonder where Celestino is? Kulas has to ask around! I wonder what happened to John!"

Faustina looked at Emong helplessly. In the first place, she did not have the answer. In the second place, Emong needed to get busy finding out the whereabouts of their men. "Let's go home and send Kulas to find out!" Faustina said excitedly. She wanted to say more, but she decided to stay silent. It was uncharacteristic for Faustina to be impatient, but she was now thinking of several things all at once. She began to worry that Clara might get more involved in the war because of John.

"We will bring the rice to Manila earlier, like tomorrow, so we can find out," Emong said.

Emong had been bringing rice to his brothers' families in Manila. He would come on the bus with Kulas, then take a *calesa* to distribute the bags to each family to supplement their ration. They had several near-mishaps with Japanese soldiers.

Once, on their way back, Emong did not bow deeply enough to the Japanese patrolman and he was slapped. Kulas went to help him, and Kulas was hit on the head with a rifle butt. A well-dressed Japanese gentleman intervened, and the soldier let them go.

They came home indignant but were glad it was not any worse. Emong had a bruise on his cheek, and Kulas had a black eye. Clara and Pilar were busy nursing their injuries, while Faustina walked back and forth, angry and praying at the same time.

Another time, a man ran up from behind them and knocked Kulas down. Emong looked behind them and saw a Japanese soldier preparing to fire his gun. He hit the ground beside Kulas as the bullet hit the man being chased. A trail of blood marked the route of the fugitive. Emong and Kulas waited for the commotion to die down before they continued on their way.

At first nobody was sure where Celestino had been transferred; but later on, his wife told Emong that Celestino was at San Lazaro Hospital. Emong updated his Aunt Faustina and cousin Clara: "Celestino was very sick with malaria and dysentery so he was brought to the infectious disease hospital, San Lazaro, in Manila. He was very disruptive when he had deliriums, for it was hard to control the thrashing of such a big, strong man.

"Celestino was in the building for malaria patients and finally was treated with quinine. When he started to improve, he was able to send word to his family. His wife Anna started visiting him regularly.

"They started taking walks in the hospital pavilions in the spirit of recuperating. Gradually, their walks went farther into the lawn and walkways. One day, they walked like lovers holding hands from the pavilion into the lawn and out of the hospital compound. Celestino had escaped.

"Back at his house in Manila, he could not do much while in hiding. Not far from his house was a collaborator, and across was a councilman whose political color Celestino's family could not tell.

"When the pardon order for Filipino soldiers was issued by Lieutenant General Homma, Celestino figured that he did not really escape from San Lazaro, rather he was let go. He also learned that the Filipino POWs in Camp O'Donnell were first indoctrinated about the Greater East Asia Co-Prosperity Sphere before they were released.

"Now Celestino can come out of his house, but he is getting wary. He thinks Manila is a dangerous place because he could be unwittingly put in a precarious position with the Japanese and end up being either shot or branded a collaborator.

"Maybe he should make alternate plans, it's getting dangerous," Emong finished.

"I'm for moving Celestino and his family here now," Faustina said.

"I agree," Clara said. "I'll start preparing the vacant rooms and clean the closets."

"I talked to the middleman who brings rice to Manila for a fee. He agreed to bring the rice to your other cousins," Emong added.

Celestino's family was moved to San Nicholas. The family preferred to settle at the *kamalig*, the empty barn a little distance from the big house. That was just as well, for Celestino was soon in contact with the guerillas, and it was good that his family stayed mostly hidden.

"The people love Captain Robert Lapham," Celestino said with awe when he finally met the guerilla leader. Celestino told how the civilians would even watch Lapham sleep, because he had earned their trust, and he was a good leader.

The Fuentes families felt blessed that they could now be together to share their little bounty and be together for evenings of relaxation and talk. It felt good in spite of the war, and Faustina would now and then startle them with her insightful opinion. Celestino told them more stories about Camp O'Donnell, but seeing Clara turn pale, he diluted the graphic details, which he only told to his Kuya Emong when they were alone. Even Emong cried.

Although their meals were simple, the taste was not badly off the mark since Clara shared her spices with Anna, Celestino's wife.

They had planted garlic and onions, and Anna could go out to the market now and then. Anna was a good cook and quite gregarious, and the women could be seen quietly slipping from one house to the other, often just to talk or to share whatever the other one prepared.

The children did not go to school, and the adults took it upon themselves to do the teaching. It was a very informal method, but at least they were not idle.

The best part of staying in the provinces was the fresh fruit and vegetables that everybody enjoyed from the garden. Everybody took turns with the watering and removing of weeds. Emong was the boss of the gardening project.

XXIX

The Americans in Camp O'Donnell were stunned by the news. Lieutenant General Masaharu Homma proclaimed the release of the Filipino prisoners at Camp O'Donnell in July 1942. This was in keeping with the idea of a Japanese sphere of influence that included Asians, but not Americans.

About five hundred sick U.S. POWs were transferred from Camp O'Donnell to Cabanatuan on July 5. Since America remained an enemy, the able U.S. prisoners in Camp O'Donnell and the able POWs from Cabanatuan were moved out in "hell ships" to Formosa, Korea, or Japan. Some, however, were sent to the Davao Penal Colony in the southern part of the Philippines.

John had been sent along with the sick POWs to Cabanatuan. When he had recuperated enough, he was transported with a group of prisoners in one of the "hell ships" that ended up at the Davao Penal Colony. He had no idea whether he was lucky or unlucky. He had missed being shipped out with all the high-ranking officers while he was near death from malaria. Another time when officers were shipped out, he had been in a work detail to fix communications systems.

The Davao Penal Colony, or DaPeCol, was a Philippine federal prison in the southern island of Mindanao. It was ten miles northwest of the Davao Gulf and twenty-five miles north of Davao city. Murderers and hardened criminals lived in primitive housing made of lumber and corrugated steel. The colony lay in a clearing of about one hundred by two hundred yards surrounded by jungles and swamps.

When Lieutenant General Jonathan Wainwright surrendered the U.S.-Philippine forces on May 7, the section in Mindanao under Major General William Sharp surrendered on May 10, 1942. The different Allied units surrendered to their respective local Japanese garrisons.

There was disorganization early in the process, with some Allied soldiers being shot for attempting to escape. In units where some succeeded in escaping, several of those left behind were executed instead. Housing a lot of POWs on their way to the penal colony was a logistical problem. The POWs who first assembled in Dansalan (Marawi, Lanao del Sur) were made to march the forty-two kilometers to Iligan, Lanao del Norte. Iligan was the assembly point for Lanao. Then the POWs were sent to Cagayan de Oro, Malaybalay, and then to Davao. Likewise, POWs from other points in Mindanao were assembled at various points on the island before being sent to the Davao Penal Colony.

The first group of POWs arrived at DaPeCol on October 22, 1942. The inmate population of the prison did not easily intermingle with them. On November 6, 1942, groups of POWs from Cabanatuan arrived.

Even in the hell ships, where they were crammed and suffocating, the POWs that came from Corregidor kept their distance from the ones from Bataan. Since the POWs who came from Corregidor were better fed and did not suffer as much as the POWs from Bataan, the former looked with disdain at the scrawny survivors from Bataan. In return, the survivors of Bataan resented those who did not suffer as much as they did, and returned their dirty looks like they were weaklings.

The wariness between the different POWs took a while to wear off, but the criminal prisoners could not care less. They had been there for quite a while and knew how to survive. In the end, POWs and criminals learned from each other and got along without passing judgment on how each of them ended up there.

About two thousand POWs ended up at DaPeCol to farm produce that would supply Japanese garrisons throughout the island. There were one thousand hectares to till: two thirds for rice and the remaining for *camote* (yams), pumpkins, radishes, onions, black beans, Chinese cabbage, okra, tomatoes, peppers, etc.

There were orange and citrus groves, lines of papayas, chicken farms, and *carabaos* (water buffalo). There was a saw mill, a rice mill, a hemp factory, and warehouses. A small railroad was used to transport workers to the rice paddies.

Most POWs thought that working with the water buffalo was a marvel, so they tried it. The slow-moving animal, however, was not easy to master. It would wallow in the mud for a long time rather than work. It was not saddled, so the would-be cowboys fell off its wide shoulders. The *carabao* hair was firm and stuck through the men's clothing, so it was like sitting on thorns. Needless to say, the typical Filipino farmer could ride his *carabao* without any qualms.

The U.S. prisoners formed a system that assigned plots of land to till. Farming time was usually 7:30–10:30 AM and 2:00–5:00 PM. They used mattocks to pick the ground, hoes to break the lumps, and rakes to smooth the ground. Some were assigned to water the plants with five-gallon watering cans, walking back and forth. They transported the farm produce in litters, but sometimes their guards would ride it instead.

The POWs were weak and helpless, but somehow they had to work, for punishment was severe. There was no respect for POW rank as far as their captors were concerned. A Japanese private would not hesitate to beat up a major, colonel, or any POW who made an error or did something to offend them.

In due time, the POWs convinced their captors to let them have mosquito nets. Not that they were real mosquito nets—they were a patchwork of clothes that served the purpose. With less illness, the POWs could produce more food. The latrines were moved farther away and had better disposal.

The POWs wore G-strings and went barefoot every workday. They were careful with their G-strings, even if they had hemp in the colony. Hemp was a rough material and tended to cut into the skin, so they kept the abrasive sections away from constant friction points.

They used their khakis for Sunday service and "grand" occasions—not that their khakis still looked good, but at least they had one decent thing left to wear. Even in their threadbare uniforms, they tried to preserve civility with a prayer service and grace before meals.

The POWs were moved around without preamble. One shipment of the strongest POWs from their camp ended up at the *lasang*, or forest. Another shipment of able-bodied POWs left soon after that, and there was no news for a long time. Later on, those left behind heard from their primitive radio that the hell ship on the way to Formosa was torpedoed by an American submarine. They could not tell who among their friends had perished and who had survived by swimming to the shore.

When POW replacements from Cabanatuan arrived, John could only imagine what might have happened to him there. The new arrivals were scrawnier; and quite a number had either dry beriberi, foot drop, or were going blind.

The POWs at DaPeCol were sympathetic. They had learned to work together by now, resulting in better harvests even if they were still slave laborers. Their nutrition had improved with more rice and vegetables.

The stories from the newcomers were pathetic.

"I just had to get out of there, or I would have really gone blind," a private said.

"You bet I'll eat all the vegetables, even the grass you throw my way. Maybe if my foot drop goes away, I'll be able to work well," another sergeant said resolutely.

He had once been a burly guy who was reduced to a shadow of his former self. When his foot drop got so severe that he could not farm in Cabanatuan, his self-image plummeted.

"If those blood brothers had not been taking care of me, I'd have been a goner. I'd been throwing my food down the latrine when Leon here caught me. I sort of woke up and started hoping again. Now that I'm here, maybe I have a better chance," he said.

The word was out to give those newcomers more food, nutrition, or whatever.

"Give them your yams and pumpkins; those are rich in vitamin A, which is good for the eyes. We don't have carrots," Captain Cooney, MD, said to the others.

The sick arrivals were assigned much easier tasks at first; gradually, the diet, a relative rest, and the better environment showed in their health improvement.

The prisoners knew their produce would feed Japanese soldiers, but this was also their meal ticket, so they settled the problem in their minds. In due time, their farm was producing well, for the rainfall in Mindanao was always better than in Luzon. They rotated the crops and planted more beans in order to have more protein. They became acclimatized to their existence with fewer getting sick, less escape attempts, and more organized labor.

Sometimes monkeys ventured by in nearby trees, and the Japanese would let the POWs eat them. If the POWs raised chickens, they were for the captors only. Once, a corporal tried to smuggle in a chicken to eat. He was caught and beaten up. Another POW caught trying to hide rice in his pockets met a similar fate.

Some higher-ranking officers preferred to just do the organizing and shied away from manual labor. John did both, not wanting to be idle, choosing to rotate among different work areas, liking the diversion that warded off boredom, and hoping to help keep up the morale of the men. He never pulled his rank, and he stayed occupied. As an officer, he could not escape, knowing that the captors would kill several POWs among those left behind.

John and the other officers made up a calendar, and he gradually became aware that he had been in the penal colony for more than a year and a half. He was pensive as he did some lumber work, and having finished hauling the smooth planks on the cart, he asked for Private Cartwright to move it to camp. John had finished early on purpose so he could have time to pick more wood from some of the leftover pile.

He was now very tan and lean, his muscles gleaming as the orange-red glow of the descending sun shone on his sweating body. Stripped to his waist, he chopped more wood so they could enlarge the shack they called their club house.

When they first came to the penal colony, the rainy days when they could not work on their farms were more dangerous. The men got depressed and became troublesome, and two ended up getting shot. Now they used their club house for rainy days, restless evenings, and on Sundays. They had only recently gotten that last concession from the Japanese guards. Their chaplain performed a religious service that was a hodgepodge of Episcopal, Catholic, Lutheran, and Baptist.

In the club, they socialized, played chess and checkers with their primitively carved wood pieces, practiced their group songs, and discussed their theories of where they were in the overall picture of the war. Sometimes their speculations and hopes were so often repeated that they started to believe it. The war would turn in the United States's favor, only their rescuers had not found them yet.

Some men were lucky enough to receive letters from home. It was a badge of honor to wave a letter with your name on it. It was an affirmation that, back home in the United States, people still cared about you.

John watched Captain Cooney reading a letter and felt a tinge of envy. John wondered if his family even knew where he was. He decided to write his family and hoped for the best. Under these conditions, his mail might not be allowed to go out. He did not even know where Jack was.

Close to the clearing near the club house stood a santol tree, the huge trunk crowned with a profusion of tiny white blossoms that would soon turn to fruit. It was practically a legend how it got there. Previous inmates claimed that the wife of a governor had ceremoniously planted it there. Others, however, had a more down-to-earth story.

"Oh! Years ago, a prisoner who just arrived was so sick that he pooped right there and excreted santol seeds!" said one inmate.

"But you don't swallow a santol seed, do you? Isn't that big?" asked Corporal Linley.

"Sometimes I do, especially if it's really sweet," replied the inmate.

The santol was flowering profusely this year, and the inmates swept the fallen leaves from the surrounding trees and burned them directly under the tree. They said that it smoked the mosquitoes and harmful insects away; also, they hoped the fruits would come soon. They did this just before dusk, after their farming was done, as though announcing they were home.

The American POWs got used to it and felt something was missing if they did not smell burning leaves at sunset. They started helping out, throwing twigs and little branches on the fire.

To John Stewart, it had more meaning. He remembered how the people in Balangiga used to smoke the fruit trees at sundown. The women would sweep the fallen leaves and other dirt from the street and light the heap under the mango, chiesa, or whatever tree there was. Usually, the men in the neighborhood would stand around there, chatting and smoking their rolled tobacco. The women would then go inside their houses to cook, letting the men watch the embers die. Some of the children would try to play a little more, but most would hurry home as the darkness gathered.

John was always conscious of his responsibilities. He was sure that his family back in the States was not wanting. His clan had large farms, and their connections with other farmers should ensure a steady availability of food, as long as they were not wasteful. His legal papers were all in the bank, and he had back-up copies in a safe at home. Most of his worry now was about Jack and that communications from them should reach their family back home, somehow.

In his unconscious moments, however, when he thought he was about to die, it was Clara's face he saw. In the depths of his despair, when everything was bleak, a glimpse of glorious sunset brought the memory of his beloved in his arms. He looked forward to the sunset and smell the burning leaves, for it was like being home with a memory—a memory of long ago, in Balangiga, the happiest moment of his life.

XXX

Jack's guerilla camp continued expanding as evacuated families set up dwellings in the perimeter. There was even a pig pen in a far corner, as well as a chicken hutch.

A recent addition was Lieutenant Bantog. He was an engineer who had survived the death march. After General Homma released the Filipino prisoners, he went home to the Mountain Province and was nursed back to health by his wife. He had been reduced to one hundred pounds from malaria and dysentery.

"I am going to fight back, after what they did to us!" he said.

It was from Lieutenant Bantog that Jack's unit heard firsthand the specifics about the sixty-five-mile death march and the conditions at Camp O' Donnell. He added that the American prisoners were mostly shipped to labor camps; only the sick ones remained in Cabanatuan, Nueva Ecija.

"I think he was very sick," Bantog said when Jack asked whether he knew anything about his dad.

Jack figured that his dad might be in Cabanatuan. He and Ed Buendia determined to attempt an escape for the prisoners in Cabanatuan.

"Maybe we can link up with Captain Robert Lapham to get this done," Buendia thought aloud.

"Let's build a stockpile of weapons first!" Jack added.

They increased their hit-and-run ambushes and felt they were making constructive gains against the enemy. Their weapons cache was getting large. They visited with Captain Lapham and started looking at the logistics.

"How do you evacuate all those sick POWs?" Lapham asked.

"I was hoping you'd tell us!" Jack answered.

"After we take them from prison, where do we put them and care for them?" Buendia asked.

They sat around the table of a farmer's kitchen and discussed all the possibilities. They finally agreed they still lacked resources. They decided to have another meeting with more guerilla groups, so everybody could offer ideas.

In the meantime, they decided to ambush for more medical supplies. Just as they were becoming bolder, they received word from General MacArthur's command in Australia. MacArthur's order was for them to stand down; their task would mostly be intelligence gathering, and their collected information would be transmitted through a communication system dominated by submarines.

All units were supposed to coordinate with one another. Materiel and medicines would come too, although liberation seemed far away. By lying low, the U.S.-Philippine forces were supposed to maintain their structure and discipline. They had to set up a network for the future liberation.

Jack sighed. Somehow, there had to be a way to reach his family, to let them know where he was and ask how everybody was doing—and maybe somebody could tell him where his dad was.

The officers in their unit discussed the increasing persecution of civilians by the Japanese whenever an ambush occurred. It was like baiting the guerillas to come so they could be killed.

They limited their attacks to areas far away from towns, like the Japanese convoys on the highway or the reconnaissance patrols that came to the mountains.

After the first year of guerilla life, instead of wishing everyday for the war to be over, Jack grew stronger in resolve. There were rumors about collaborators, possible traitors, and tales of unsavory characters that swirled around the camp. Jack and Buendia learned to trust each other and watch each other's backs.

Jack missed Neneng and felt helpless as to where to find her. He heard that Dr. Mendez had been killed by a guerilla who would be king. That guerilla was later killed in a shootout in a struggle for power.

One day, a young Filipino guerilla approached him quietly. He thought he had seen Mrs. Mendez at the church in San Nicholas.

Nobody had seen either Mrs. Mendez or Neneng for a long time, and this report made sense. Jack took a good look at the guerilla.

"Thank you. Let me think of something," he said.

Jack had to observe first if the guerilla could be trusted. Then he asked Ed Buendia's opinion.

Clara Mendez kept her head low as she returned to her pew after receiving communion. She heard the early church service that Sunday, as usual, with Pilar. She noticed that an old man had looked her way more than once, and it was not one of their tenants. She did not sense danger; instead, she sensed a curiosity. When Mass was over, the stranger came purposely toward them as they dipped their hands in holy water. He bumped Pilar, and Clara also went off balance and dropped her missal.

"Pardon me!" he said. The stranger picked up the missal, handed it to Clara, and quickly disappeared in the early morning light.

Her heart was pounding with anxiety on the *calesa* ride home, but Clara waited to get inside her room before opening her missal. There was a note from Jack tucked between the pages, asking about Neneng. The next Sunday, she left a note on the pew where she had prayed. She answered that she would give the information only to Jack.

It was a week before Jack came. He waited for Clara in the shadows of the rice granary, disguised as an old man, stooping to disguise his height. Clara arrived with a scarf over her head, her path lighted by the half moon.

"Mrs. Mendez," Jack said.

"Jack," she said, holding his hands tight as she let out a sigh.

"Please tell me where Neneng is," he said.

Clara nodded. "She's in the Carmelite convent in Baguio, under the name Sister Agatha." Sensing him tense, she continued, "She's in disguise as a nun."

Jack sighed in relief.

"Your father was in the concentration camp in Capas, Tarlac. The prisoners were sick and suffering, but I don't know where he is now," she said.

"I hear reports that he might be in Davao, but we are not sure either," Jack answered.

"Be careful. God be with you," she said.

"Thank you!" Jack said. He gave her a hug, and then he disappeared into the night.

His hug startled Clara, for it was not their custom. Then she smiled—she would have to get used to it.

One late evening, after a Japanese patrol had just passed, Jack scaled the wall of the convent with a young guerilla named Agosto. It was not easy to stage this operation because he was tall and could easily be spotted. He had to wait for evening, and thankfully he found a reliable companion and lookout in Agosto.

A nun saw him coming down his rope and stifled a scream. He put his right finger across his lips and raised his left hand, palm open, toward the nun. He approached slowly.

"I need to see Sister Agatha," he said.

The nun hesitated, and as Agosto dropped from his rope and approached them, she pointed to the chapel. Agosto guarded the door, standing behind the column of a saint.

Jack went in and knelt in the back pew. In the first two rows was a group of novices standing up, chanting softly in unison. After making the sign of the cross, they formed a line in the middle aisle and walked toward the door with their heads down.

Jack stood up and watched the figures, looking for Neneng.

"Oh!" said the first novice who noticed his presence, disrupting the line formation.

"Oh!" echoed the other novices one after another.

Neneng's head shot up at the commotion, and their eyes met. She stood aside for the others to pass as though at a loss for what to do. In her mind, she had said that she did not want to see him ever again, and yet seeing him now, she realized she loved him still. The tears started falling on her cheeks.

As soon as the others were out, Jack walked quickly toward her. Without speaking, he caught her in his arms and kissed her passionately. The years of longing, anger, and frustration welled up in him, and he could not speak. Neither could she. She was hesitant only for a moment, then she melted in his arms and returned his passionate kiss, her arms around his neck.

"Darling," he said hoarsely. "I love you so much."

"Jack," she said with emotion, "I love you!"

"Let's forget our quarrel, darling. It's time to get married," he said, holding both her hands in his right hand and encircling her waist with his left hand. "We have to determine our own happiness and not allow other people to spoil it. We must!"

She could not speak as he kissed her again. Then, catching her breath, she nodded, smiling.

"Oh!" she said, a frown creasing her forehead. "The priest is here only for Mass and confession. He doesn't know about me."

Jack was only momentarily taken aback. He took her hand, and they knelt before the altar.

"I take you for my wife," he said.

"I take you for my husband," she followed.

"I'll be faithful to you always," he said.

"I'll be faithful to you always," she said.

"Until death do us part," he said.

"Until death do us part," she said solemnly.

They stood before the altar, and Jack kissed her tenderly on her lips.

"Do you feel safe here?" he asked, keeping her in his arms.

"So far, yes," she answered. "I hope the enemy will not bother us. I'm able to send letters to my mother, but I have to send them through Manila, and somebody brings them to her under a different name. We can't trust anybody."

Jack looked at her thoughtfully, realizing the pains they had to take to avoid being victimized. He had heard of the difficulties girls and women had to undergo.

"Your mother was able to see my dad when he was in the concentration camp in Capas. I wish we could do something, but the task would be so enormous."

"She wrote me," Neneng said. "Oh, Jack!" she exclaimed with dread, knowing that many prisoners were dying in concentration camps.

They sat in the front pew, talking for a while, getting their bearings with each other.

"Sir!" Agosto said in an urgent tone as he came in.

Jack looked around and heard some commotion from a distance. "We'd better go!" he said, giving Neneng a quick kiss. "I'll visit again!" he said, and he quickly hid in a bush with Agosto. Next, they scaled the wall, and Jack waved briefly; then they were gone.

"Be careful!" Neneng said after him.

Neneng stood in front of the Mother Superior the next day. She was going to ask for an audience, but she was summoned earlier than she expected. The whole night she felt happy, knowing that she and Jack loved each other, and that was all that mattered. Then it occurred to her that she had to explain to the Mother Superior, so she formed dialogues in her mind to explain the situation and defend herself. Round and round her reasoning went, logical or not, and she fell asleep without formulating what exactly she was going to say.

"Reverend Mother," she started, then she sighed. "I love Jack! We are going to get married!"

Mother Elena knew about Neneng's predicament because Clara Mendez had explained it before leaving her daughter. As Mother Superior, she planned to deliver a long diatribe regarding rules and regulations in this convent. Looking at Neneng so vulnerable and innocent, Mother Elena changed her mind. There was no need for a scolding, for Neneng's family came from the same side of the fence as hers. She was docile and obeyed the rules; she was here more to hide than to be a nun. "Just remember the rules," she said softly.

Neneng nodded, suddenly smiling through her tears, and half ran out of the room.

Jack was a happy man. Even if it took two days of stop-and-go hiding to reach the convent, he could hardly wait for the next visit. He knew, however, that aside from the job at hand, he must keep in mind the safety of everyone concerned. Because he was much taller than most Filipinos, he had to disguise his height and visits by scaling the wall after dark.

On his next visit, he happily kissed Neneng as soon as he saw her. He heard a series of sounds he could not figure out.

"Ahem! Ahem! Ahem!"

"What's that?" Jack said, looking around.

There was a nun sitting on a bench on the other side of the garden.

"Who?" Jack looked closer, then he added, "Hi!" He waved.

The nun did not say anything, but Neneng tugged at his sleeve.

She seemed to have thought this out ahead of time and explained calmly. "We have some rules to follow. It's 'Filipino custom, no touch,' Jack. You might think it's Victorian, but Filipinos are still old-fashioned. They frown on public shows of affection. Every now and then, you hear of a shotgun wedding. A father who sees a man kissing his daughter will demand that the man should marry her."

Jack was put off. Worse, Neneng was still wearing a nun's habit. He began to sulk. "Darling," he started.

Neneng gave his hand a squeeze and talked gently. "I'm still afraid. If somebody suddenly comes, this is my protection." Neneng said as though reading his mind.

Jack realized that he had to agree. There would always be a nun hovering around as a chaperone when he was with Neneng; he would have to live with it. It reminded him of the grandmother who was always there when he visited her home before.

On later visits, he was content to hold her hands, and even with that, it took a while for Neneng to be comfortable with the nuns around.

Jack was careful not to tell Neneng about their operations and other military matters. Once, his guerilla spies told him that Yoshiro was in a convoy going toward Baguio. Jack was worried, and his group planned to ambush the Japanese convoy. It was, however, a big, well-armed convoy and probably too dangerous to challenge. The guerillas sighed in relief when the convoy proceeded to the Cagayan Valley.

He longed to share with Neneng his successes and frustrations, but that would have to wait for quite a while. Neneng was tacitly attuned to this thinking. They talked instead about their families and their backgrounds, dreamed of a home together some day, and tried to resolve some points.

"I still hope to be a doctor one day," Neneng said, looking up at Jack thoughtfully.

"I think you'll make a good one," Jack answered. "I've realized you are a strong person. If you finish at UST after we are married, it will be easy to get help for our children's care. I know we need doctors, whether here or in the States."

"Oh, Jack! I'm so happy! Our family comes first, but I can be helpful in other ways too," Neneng exclaimed and embraced Jack.

Although he did not mention it, Neneng knew Jack worried about his dad. Finally, Jack heard that his dad might be in Davao.

"Oh, Jack! I'm so happy to hear that!" she exclaimed, and he kissed her.

"Ahem! Ahem!" the chaperone nun said.

"Forgot!" Jack said, releasing Neneng.

Neneng held his hands and guided him to a bench.

"I've explained to the Mother Superior that we would otherwise be married if not for this war. Be patient Jack. It is safe for me to stay here."

Jack sighed; he was living with it.

"Oh!" Neneng said and suddenly lighted up. "We had a good batch of strawberries that we preserved and were able to exchange for other things we need. Sister Jacinta is a real businesswoman, and she is the only one assigned to deal with lay people. I asked the Mother Superior, Mother Elena, if I could keep a jar for you and Agosto. Here it is."

Neneng took the jar from the pocket of her habit and handed it to Jack with a grin. Jack looked at her, and they laughed like children with little treasures.

XXXI

Clara has been in San Nicholas since leaving Neneng in the convent. She mostly remained indoors during the day. By her suggestion, her Kuya Emong had ordered that taller shrubs be planted around the perimeter of their home so that, in time, Clara could go outdoors without being seen by people.

The harvest of *palay* was less than usual, since only old farmers were left to till the land. Everybody's share had been reduced because they had to submit a huge portion to the Japanese garrison.

Emong managed their farms with Kulas, but since their bookeeper joined the guerillas, he trained the thirteen-year-old old son of a dead tenant to do it. This young man was good with numbers, and he did the account balances. Clara meticulously went over all the account balances when the tenants were gone and made due corrections where it was necessary, pleasing the tenants in her fairness.

The tenants supposed she was around, but they did not ask directly, thus letting them hide the possibility of this fact from the Japanese. Most people were aware she had to hide her daughter, and they realized the injustice of Dr. Mendez being killed.

Clara was safe only for so long. One morning, she started early gathering vegetables and fruits in the garden and brought a basketful of it to Celestino's family at the barn. The mango tree had been bearing a lot of fruit, and she reached for the ones that were almost ripe. She had big plans for the day. She would send word for a tenant to gather most of the ripe fruits by noon so she could preserve them.

I need more brown sugar, she thought, suddenly worried if their ration was enough and whether the errand boy could get back quickly from the market.

She pushed the back door open with her left hand, her right hand heavy with a basket of large mangoes. As a gust of wind blew her hair, she tossed her head, trying to return her tresses to their place. Her head was down when she stepped up, but as she looked up, she recognized the pair of shiny boots across the room.

She was flushed from being out in the sun or she would have turned pale when she saw Colonel Mifune. Mifune stood by the door to the living room, watching her.

"Good morning. You are looking well, Mrs. Mendez," he said.

She was startled and half-embarrassed, aware that her pale blue dress was her oldest working dress. She put her basket on the kitchen table and gathered her composure.

"Good morning, Colonel! Or is that a promotion?" she asked, noticing the different uniform. "This is a pleasant surprise!"

"Yes, I'm a General now," Mifune replied, walking halfway across the dining room. "May I talk with you, Mrs. Mendez?" he said as he preceded her to the living room, signaling with his eyes for Emong to leave.

Emong left the living room and sorted the vegetables in the kitchen.

"Pardon me, Colonel … I'm sorry, General. I was working in the garden," Clara said, referring to her homely clothes; then she blushed as she caught the way the general looked at her.

"You are fine, Mrs. Mendez," General Mifune replied. "I have come to ask you a favor," he said, pausing as he watched her closely. "I have so far been living in a Spartan and ungracious environment in Cabanatuan. Knowing your capacity for homemaking, I hope you can supervise some rearrangements in my lodgings and also in some of our other facilities."

Clara's heart was throbbing wildly in fear that he had come for Neneng. This request, she thought she could handle, although it could be just as dangerous. She spoke slowly. "General, it would be unbecoming of me as a Filipina. Also, I'm needed here."

"Perhaps I have to make myself clearer," Mifune answered. "My wife has died in Japan while I've been out here fighting this war. You are a widow. I do not deny that you might return my kind regard for you one of these days."

Flustered and sensing danger, Clara replied carefully. "This is all so sudden, General, you understand that I need to think this over?"

"Yes," General Mifune replied, "but not for long, Mrs. Mendez."

Clara nodded and stood up, looking grave.

Mifune looked at her and, stopping himself short, left.

Clara waited for the general to leave; then she rushed to the kitchen. "I must leave," she whispered to her Kuya Emong.

Faustina had just come from her bedroom and the three now went to the window and glanced casually outside. A Japanese soldier was watching the house.

Clara thought quickly. She started packing a few clothes and some money. At noontime, she called Pilar. "Bring bread and tea to the guard. Tell him also that he can use the bathroom."

Clara wrote a letter, finished her preparations, and waited for dusk.

She called Pilar and instructed her carefully. She also dabbed Pilar's wrist with *patis*, a fish sauce that had a strong smell. "Bring this letter to the guard and ask if he can take it at once to General Mifune. If he doesn't agree, tell him you will take it yourself on your bicycle."

The guard kept his distance from Pilar, put off by the fish sauce. He indicated that he did not want to take the note. He motioned that General Mifune was in town and would be back the next day.

Pilar motioned that she would use the bike, and the guard nodded. Soon, the old lady eased the bike out of the house and waved to the guard.

Clara had quickly put on Pilar's clothes, dabbed some *patis* on her hand, and with flour on her hair sticking out of the bandana, left in her disguise. Her money and clothes were tightly bound and wrapped in a poor cloth sack behind the bike seat. She had *galletas de patatas* and an assortment of wrapped rice sweets and preserved fruits, plus money, in her pockets.

She biked until she was out of sight from the guard, then she left the bicycle resting against a mango tree, where they had agreed she'd leave it. She hailed a *calesa* and went to the bus station. She took the bus to the Cagayan Valley, and then got off at the second stop. From there, she took a bus to Baguio.

The bus to Baguio was the last trip for the day. It was quite late in the evening. She had dozed off in the bus while traveling, but she had to find a spot to sleep. Clara was not usually short of ideas, but she could not risk being recognized, nor did she want to draw attention to herself. She feared for her safety.

She did not recognize anybody on the bus, but she hesitated coming down the bus steps, unsure for the first time on where to go. She could not go to the convent yet; she was sure they would not open the door at this time. She went with the crowd of passengers, and then made a right turn toward the houses near the plaza. She hid in the shadows and looked for a safe spot.

Several concrete benches lined the walkways from the plaza stage to the opposite pavilion of rose hedges. In between two of them was a large bougainvillea bush. The lights on the plaza illuminated the opposite side toward the church, which was farther on. Farther on still was the convent she had to reach.

Behind the bougainvillea was the only spot that could work. She decided to go the roundabout way, close to the houses, one at a time, almost tiptoeing, so nobody would see her. She made it to the spot, breathing through her mouth and trying not to make a sound. She spread her bandana on the ground at a spot shielded from the light by the bougainvillea bush. She took out an extra blouse from her sack and covered her chest and arms with it; her sack was her pillow.

Clara woke up when she heard cars motoring past the plaza. The birds were chirping, and the sun was already high. She realized that in her exhaustion, she must have slept too soundly. She felt stiff and numb, groaning as she straightened up.

She wiped her face with her handkerchief and combed her hair into a knot. With the cloth sack on her arm, she squinted in the bright morning sun as she walked exactly like an old beggar toward the convent. She knocked as most beggars did at the door; then, after some time, she was let inside. Mother and daughter cried when they saw each other.

General Mifune was very angry the next day, but like his son, did not punish Emong and Faustina, two old people who on questioning could not tell him anything, for they really did not know anything about Clara's whereabouts.

XXXII

Jack's guerilla group made strides in camp organization. They ambushed enemy convoys more selectively, usually for something strategically important. Their vegetable supply was steady, their pig and chicken farm was working, and the civilians took turns in community duties.

Escapees from the death march, misplaced soldiers, and Filipino soldiers who did not want to go home continued to swell their ranks. Every now and then, different groups quarreled among themselves. Sometimes, would-be guerillas could not take the hard life and would flip in and out of their units. Then, too, there were soldiers who got restless and ended up causing trouble, victimizing innocent civilians.

Major Howard Andersen was the highest-ranking officer in Jack's guerilla group. He was once a POW at Camp O'Donnell but, in a work detail to fix communications lines, his group was rescued by guerillas. After he was taken from house to house, he fell into delirium from the malaria he was harboring.

The guerillas hiding Andersen were already having problems hiding him when they heard that Jack's group had some quinine. They brought Andersen over. By then, Andersen was thin, and his recovery was slow. Dr. Yuson saw him and advised that he should just be given time.

"After his diarrhea clears up, the quinine, proper food, and rest should do it," Yuson said.

When Andersen did get well, Jack and Ed Buendia felt rewarded to have him, for Andersen was a good strategist. Their operations were smoother, and Andersen always laid out fall-back plans.

At one point, Jack's group inherited a captain from another group. He'd left for want of discipline and proved to be a helpful addition to Jack's group. Captain Blackwell proved to be a good captain, and Jack and Buendia were glad they had not let cynicism get the better of them. Their group was building a reputation for dynamism and fairness. Two more lieutenants and three sergeants also joined.

Major Andersen and the three captains took the time to enforce discipline and keep up morale. There was a risk of collaborators or Japanese spies among the men on the fringes, and the command structure was clarified, so each company knew each other well.

They had stopped raiding the garrisons in town in order to prevent reprisals against the townsfolk by the Japanese. There had been instances when little barrios were almost wiped out by retaliatory attacks. One of these occurred after a cornered, free-living U.S. soldier escaped from a town by killing several Japanese officers, including a colonel. That U.S. soldier had joined Jack's company.

At one time, their group received an SOS from guerillas' families in a town in northern Pangasinan. The town was heavily patriotic, but recently, their new mayor had indicated he was a Japanese collaborator. When a man was caught visiting his family at night, he was turned over to the Japanese authorities. Under torture, he divulged that he was a Huk, a member of the Hukbalahap movement. Not only that, he claimed it was their group that had recently ambushed a Japanese convoy in another town.

The Hukbalahap, or *Hukbo nang Bayan Laban sa mga Hapon*, meant "troops of the country against the Japanese." It started as a guerilla movement. There was, however, a strong undercurrent of socialism, inasmuch as they appealed to the masses that were dissatisfied with landowners. Since it was primarily a Filipino movement, there was no affiliation with the U.S.-Philippine government. There had been rumors that the leader of the movement had met abroad with other communist leaders.

Members of the Hukbalahap movement attacked the prison the next night to rescue the man. Several Japanese soldiers were killed, so the whole town was facing possible reprisal. A convoy of Japanese trucks was going to wipe out the entire town, except the mayor's family. Jack and Buendia's companies were to evacuate the civilians before the Japanese came, and they planned to leave the mayor behind. The wily mayor, however, played a dual card; he had notified both the Hukbalahap and the Japanese.

The two guerilla companies closed in on the town after dark. The Filipino guerillas had the task of calling on each house to pack and go. A trail was established through a rice field and on through a dense *cogon* grass and bamboo trees where vehicles could not pursue them.

As they were hurrying the evacuation, gunshots were fired, and Jack automatically dropped to the ground. He looked up from behind a *gumamela* (hibiscus) bush and saw Buendia's signal match flare. Both men crept out from their hiding places on either side of the dirt road, looking for where the shots had come from.

"You are going that way!" A man standing in front of the municipal building gesticulated with a revolver on his hand. He stood with his feet apart, a rifle slung on his shoulder, and the revolver in his right hand pointing to another direction. He was surrounded by a group of armed men in peasant clothes.

Buendia signaled for Jack to cover him, and Jack signaled back an OK. The guerillas came out of the shadows as they realized that a confrontation was about to happen.

"Friend, where are you taking them?" Buendia asked.

"To our camp!" replied the medium-sized dark man. "I am Captain Peralta of the Huks."

"I don't want to!" a middle-aged man answered vehemently as he stood with a blanketful of baggage, surrounded by his wife and two daughters.

"You are going to obey!" Peralta said in a loud voice, walking toward the protesting man.

"I don't like the Huks!" the man said.

Peralta stepped forward and slapped the man twice. The man fell from the blows, his lips bleeding.

Buendia did not wait. He grabbed Peralta's collar with his left hand, and his right fist landed on Peralta's jaw.

Just then, rumbling trucks full of Japanese troops arrived. Japanese soldiers started firing as soon as they came within view.

"Get them out of here!" Jack shouted as civilians started running on the designated route.

Other civilians were confused; some ran toward the direction pointed by the Huks. Peralta got up from his blow and aimed his revolver at Buendia. Jack shot Peralta's hand.

Jack turned when he heard another shot and only belatedly realized he had been hit.

I hope I don't die! Jack thought and looked at the direction where the shot came from. "Jose!" Jack said in surprise, recognizing Neneng's suitor who did the *harana*.

"Jack!" Jose said.

"What are you doing? We're fighting for your country!" Jack could not help but get angry.

"I know!" Jose replied as though in a daze.

More Japanese trucks arrived in the town square; the loud screeching sound of brakes accompanied the indiscriminate firing of soldiers even before they could get off the trucks. Panic broke out among the civilians.

"Let's go!" Buendia pushed Jack in the direction of their escape.

The sound of another shot was very close to Jack. He turned to see Jose slumped and bleeding. He got hold of Jose's collar with his left hand and dragged him into the bushes by the nearest house. A full-blown battle had erupted with the guerillas and the Hukbalahap against the Japanese.

The guerillas had the advantage of being hidden, while the Hukbalahaps had most of their men in the town square. The Japanese jumped off their trucks, guns blazing.

When the shooting was over, the guerillas had prevailed. It was a terrible sight of carnage as bodies littered the town square and the dirt road. Captain Peralta of the Hukbalahaps was dead, and so were most of his men.

Jose lay on a grassy patch under an acacia tree, looking very pale and thoughtful. He was stripped to his waist as his shirt was used as a pressure bandage on his chest wound. The shirt was soaked with blood. There was no doctor.

Jack was also stripped to his waist, but his shirt used as a bandage for his chest wound was not soaked. Jack wondered what this meant. All he knew was that he could still function, while Jose was fighting for every breath.

"Jack," Jose called softly.

"Yeah?" Jack said, moving from a chair contraption where he sat. He touched Jose's arm.

"I thought the Huk movement was the answer, now I am convinced it is not. Thank you for fighting for my country, Jack." Jose smiled wanly.

"We're all in this together, Jose."

Jose nodded and died.

They spent some time burying the dead among the villagers, including Jose. The mayor was dead, and his wife and two young sons put him in a marked grave. Nobody spoke to that family.

"You'll be alright," Jack said to the sons, breaking the ice.

Most of the Huks were left where they lay, so their relatives could find them. The Japanese were also left where they lay, because the Japanese reinforcements would come soon.

They commandeered three carts drawn by water buffaloes so they could take the food and medical supplies from the Japanese garrison, as well as other equipment from the Japanese trucks.

The villagers formed an uneven column as they retreated across the rice field and rested near a stream. It was past midnight, and they were making good time, in spite of the wounded. Ed Buendia had almost lost his voice answering questions from villagers. This was one time that Jack's inability to speak Tagalog gave him an advantage. Jack explained to the villagers in English, which they understood, while Buendia was having a harder time as he explained in Tagalog, for most of the villagers spoke the Pangasinan or Ilocano dialect.

"You can settle in the outskirts of our camp," Jack said, "or you can choose to travel to other places where you have relatives. Just remember, you are not safe in any nearby town where the Japanese could find out that you came from a village where a lot of people died. We have food, not much, but it should be enough."

It was two days travel to their camp, hiding mostly by day, and taking longer routes through friendly territories. Finally, the clatter of pans less carefully laid, signaled their arrival at the camp. Buendia and Jack wiped the sweat off their brows as other soldiers took charge of assigning spots for the newcomers.

Jack was glad their camp was deep in the mountains. A lot of the civilians they had saved in situations like this lived in settlements on the camp periphery. They were like lookouts. At the same time, they had to be trained to protect themselves as a first line of defense, and they were given arms.

Some were able to move to towns after establishing contact with relatives. That gave the guerillas a source of worry too, just in case the civilians divulged the vicinity of the camp.

Jack's wound was on his right shoulder, just below the collar bone. The bullet did not hit a vital organ, but Dr. Yuson put him on an arm sling, and his right arm felt limp for a while. Jack was out of the bigger action, but he stayed busy with other work.

Jack shook off his nagging doubt that Jose recognized him before he got shot.

Jose had been one of Neneng's most avid suitors. He was dark, not so tall, and handsome. He could easily be the poster boy of what a Filipino looked like. Jack became aware of his competition when Jose did the *harana*; and Jack realized that Jose was often Neneng's partner in the dance presentations. Jose's family consisted of a lot of teachers and writers, and they were well respected. They were not affluent, but they were comfortable.

Jack was glad that Jose realized the Hukbalahap movement was not for him. Sometimes, instead of fighting the Japanese, the Huks seem to be fighting the civilians, or they fought among themselves. There were also instances when the Huks seemed to compete with the U.S.-Philippine forces for sympathy. The socialist tendencies of the movement were opposite to the Fuentes and Luna families' way of life as landowners. As far as Jack could tell, Neneng's family and her relatives were fair with their tenants.

At one time, Jack's company thought they could work with the Huks, but they quickly changed their minds. Since their guerilla group was composed of U.S.-Philippine soldiers to start with, their rank and file realized that the Hukbalahap were focused on social discontent.

Jack could feel the stripping of his innocence regarding human nature. War tested the mettle of the best men, and some who turned out to be traitors were the last ones he would have expected.

The officers' meetings were becoming a little more frequent, and longer, mostly dealing with the logistics of an enlarging camp. So far, problems have been nipped in the bud.

Every now and then the officers would be given a treat like *guinatan, biko,* or *maruya* (fried ripe bananas with sugar) by some motherly villager. Major Andersen graciously accepted but tried not to encourage it. It would be bad if the women competed for influence, or worse, got too close to the married men.

One day it was not a motherly villager, it was a pretty young lady. The target was Jack.

He had to stop this at once. "Thanks a lot! My fiancé will be glad to hear we have nice people taking care of us," he said.

When the young lady looked at him askance, Jack was glad he made his point. The problem, however, was Buendia. The girl started going for him.

"Didn't you say you have a sweetheart in Manila?" Jack asked.

"Yes, but I haven't seen her for a while," Buendia replied.

"Well! Don't you think you need to make a clean break of it first?" Jack said.

"I'll visit my sweetheart soon and clarify things," Buendia retorted.

Captain Ed Buendia did go to Manila to settle things with his sweetheart. He was almost caught by the Japanese. Buendia escaped and killed two pursuers. He arrived in the camp with a wound in his thigh.

The situation was getting complicated since the girl wanted to attend to Buendia.

"No!" Major Andersen said firmly.

"I still love my Manila sweetheart. She's more beautiful than ever," Buendia said.

"Then stop seeing this girl!" Jack retorted.

Jack became aware that the girl was sneaking in to see Buendia. He was becoming disillusioned with his friend.

He missed Neneng, but Agosto, his lookout, had gone home to the Visayas to join his wife and family who was from there. Agosto asked permission to continue his guerilla activities there.

Seeing Jose from an opposite camp brought home the fact that Jack could not even confide to anybody where Neneng was. The only person right now he could trust completely was Ed Buendia, but Jack doubted that Major Andersen would agree to excuse two high-ranking officers at the same time. Jack would have to wait for an opportune time after his wound healed and someone he trusted could accompany him as a lookout when he visited Neneng.

By 1944, U.S. planes had enough clout to drop more supplies to the beleaguered guerillas. At first, the recipients were just the groups with access to the coastline. With radio communication, plus a little more daring, Jack's group finally got supplies too.

Jack was still recuperating and heard the excitement when the package was retrieved.

"The package fell on the river, luckily there was a material that kept it dry," Major Andersen said.

The packing had an inner layer of a synthetic fiber that looked impermeable to water. The package contained guns and ammunition, dynamite, quinine tablets, sulfadiazine tablets, jars of sulfa ointment, G.I. uniforms, olive undershirts, G.I. shorts, pocket knives, boxes of matches, and several books.

Dr. Yuson came as soon as he could. He wanted to try the new antibiotic on a private who had been suffering from a large, festering wound. In less than a week, there was marked improvement. Yuson was excited to use the medicine on a very sick patient in town. He asked for a dose from Major Andersen, and he was given some.

What a relief to know they had more quinine! There were even rumors of a stronger antibiotic called penicillin. The troop morale perked up.

Right now, their priority was intelligence gathering. Their guerilla group was a bunch of companies, short of a battalion. Jack's unit had a good network established with counterparts along the central plain of Luzon. They mapped out the garrisons, airports, troop movements, and supply lines.

Out on the eastern Luzon coastline, the group headed by Colonel Russell Volckmann was monitoring Japanese strength. They discovered a Japanese intelligence report in a plane that crashed. General Yamashita's plan was to control the Cagayan Valley food supply if it should happen that he had to fight a defensive war.

This information was discussed in their meeting. Major Andersen said it for all of them.

"That would have been a good idea, but coordinating guerilla units now know exactly how to disrupt that," he said.

Jack seemed to be hitting his stride with the intelligence. He glanced at the notes he had written as to where his units could later be used. Jack was in the interior, and he knew that the mountains of Baguio were a likely hiding place for retreat or resistance.

Things are looking up! he thought, and he looked forward to visiting Neneng soon.

Jack went to visit Neneng when his arm sling came off and he could scale the convent wall. He finally found someone trustworthy but felt guilty that his companion—a soldier named Pedro—was in harm's way by accompanying him. Jack did not want to seem selfish.

Neneng cried when she saw him. "Jack! I was so worried! What happened?"

He could not talk yet. He kissed her first, disregarding the frowning nun hovering in the doorway. Finally, he let go, and guiding her to a seat, he put his arms around her.

"It's a long story," he started.

Neneng was crying silently as he talked, so he interrupted himself.

"Darling, please," he said.

She looked up at him and wiped her tears. She kissed him gently and snuggled into his arms without saying a word.

He held her tight and finished telling his story. He noticed she was still thoughtful.

"I will count on your prayers to get me through. We don't know what will happen, I could only fight as best I could," he said, as though reading her thoughts.

"Just remember I'll always love you, and I'm so proud of you! Keep my rosary, Jack. I feel a lot better knowing you have it."

She put her rosary in his breast pocket and went back into his arms. She looked pained with anxiety, but that was all she said. He knew she wanted to say much more. They were beginning to understand each other quite well now, and they often thought things out together.

Jack looked at her. He expected her to say something about Jose.

"He was a friend, in a way, but I never could agree with his point of view. I suppose he thought he was fighting for freedom … at first."

There was no mention of whether she was going to pray for Jose.

On Jack's later visit, Clara Mendez was in the convent. Jack marveled at how Clara Mendez was able to pull off what she did. Clara talked to Jack briefly before he visited Neneng. She asked Jack to bring her a revolver the next time he came.

"For self-defense," she said.

War is hard not only on the men, he thought.

Jack realized that the Mendezes valued honor as much as life. They were probably quite rich, but they did not live ostentatiously. They did not waste their time on senseless socials; they were usually busy in a constructive way. They were careful with their emotions and selective with their company.

In a way, Jack believed their position in the community protected them from random, senseless accidents that happened to most civilians, but there was also a sense that the Mifunes had an eye on them. The Mendezes could be pursued, but Jack sensed that the Mifunes had not only put their priorities straight, but there was also a decency that had not left them yet in this war.

Let's hope this war ends before we have to see the worst of most people ... Could I have been friends with the Mifunes? he wondered, considering they were so different in their attitude towards women. Looking back, even during their forced conversations with Neneng, Jack had actually enjoyed the exchange of ideas with Yoshiro. Here was somebody Jack considered his peer. Too bad he and Yoshiro had been too busy competing for Neneng's attention.

Clara was actually like a fish in the water at the convent. Being a good organizer, with a good knowledge of plants and domestic things, soon she was supervising the novices. While Sister Jacinta had to take care of matters that dealt with the outside world, Clara helped a lot in smoothing out things in the convent.

Jack almost felt like it was old times when he visited. Every now and then, the convent had a bottle of fruit preserve for him and Pedro; sometimes, it was just a little dessert or treat they would be given while they sat during the visit. He had learned to abide by the rules most of the time, although he sometimes tried to elude the guards now and then to kiss Neneng. At one such time, he held Neneng's face in his hands.

"You have grown," he said.

"So have you," she said tenderly, and they both laughed, remembering their quarrels.

"Let's not get into a fight ever again, time is too precious," he said.

She looked at him with a raised brow.

"What?" he said.

"You sound like an old man," she answered.

"Yeah?" he quipped and embraced her as they laughed softly.

On one of his visits, Jack brought Clara Mendez a stolen Japanese 8 mm automatic pistol. He showed her how it worked and gave her bullets. He hoped she would never have to use it. He thought of taking them to live with the guerillas, but he decided against it. They could be too tempting for men when civilized ways were at a modicum. He sighed; he did feel like an old man sometimes.

XXXIII

For the POWs in the Davao Penal Colony, the days turned to weeks, then months, a year, and two years—then they wished they could stop hoping for freedom. Their only civilian contacts were the Filipino prisoners who taught them about important things that were peculiar to the region.

The forest that surrounded them was more intimidating than the flimsy barbed wire around their camp. Every now and then, they were reminded that escaping was not a good idea, for nobody could guess who among those left in the camp would end up being shot.

There was one unforeseen event they talked about for a long time. As they were clearing more forest for their farm, there was a sudden motion from the forest. A POW dropped his ax out of surprise and was suddenly running as fast as he could.

"Look out!" he cried as he dodged behind a tree.

"Ahhh!" Corporal Linley screamed as he was gored in the thigh.

It was a wild boar that had already been hit with a lance in the back. Some civilians must have been chasing it, but they abandoned the chase when the boar entered the penal colony grounds. The boar was bleeding, but it ran back and forth, charging whoever it saw. The POWs and the Japanese guards ran in different directions.

"Baboy sulop!" (wild boar) the Filipino prisoners cried.

They were not afraid of the boar. They chased after the boar with their ax and plows, hitting it with several blows.

"Ni ara! Ni ara!" (Here it is! Here it is!) two of the prisoners exclaimed when the boar dodged into a *cogon* patch.

The chase was on again as the boar ran toward their parade ground. Bleeding and dazed, the boar took another blow to its head before it finally collapsed dead on the ground.

The POWs and the Japanese did not know what to make of it, but the prisoners proceeded to butcher the animal and made a fire to cook it in the open. They spiced it with garlic from their farm and sprinkled salt on it. Their captors almost begrudged them their prize. When the scent of grilled pork permeated the air, the POWs and the Japanese started coming nearer and offered to help.

The prisoners grumbled, but they had no choice or they might be punished. Everybody was able to share the *sinugba* (cooked in the open fire), no matter how small the portions. For most of them, it was heavenly to eat fresh grilled meat after such a long time.

On a clear day, it was pleasant to farm while the sun was up, then watch the glorious sunset. They imagined there were more stars in this part of the world than where they came from. They learned of the ylang-ylang tree as the breeze blew the fragrance of the wild flowers their way. On rainy days, however, they tried to shake off the gloomy weather by hanging out in their club house.

Their social club was good for airing out their frustration and despair. It was a hodgepodge of support groups, false rumors, false claims, and bickering.

One night, a fistfight occurred between two private POWs. It was a dreary week of rain as a typhoon ravaged the eastern part of the islands. The argument was over whose fault it was that they were prisoners. Soon, officers and soldiers were arguing, and a free-for-all was about to happen.

Their chaplain went up their makeshift stage and raised his hands. "Please! Gentlemen, listen!" He could not be heard as the arguing voices were louder.

A corporal had a better idea. He started singing "God Bless America."

"Shaddup!" most of the soldiers hissed, but gradually others stopped arguing and they looked at each other.

John was on their makeshift stage, trying to prop up their hoarse chaplain. He grabbed his chance and spoke as loud as he could, saying, "Alright, I know whose fault it is!"

As the men paused, he explained quickly.

"You can't blame Roosevelt, you can't blame MacArthur! If it's not the Japanese, then it must be our tough luck! We are so far away from home, and we are in enemy territory. We did not have a chance to finish training more troops; we were caught by surprise, maybe we should not have been; and no reinforcements came as had been planned when we tried to hold Bataan. We were disorganized at the suddenness of the war; we were short of food and ammunitions. We were starved—but we fought, and most of us were ill by the time we surrendered!

"Instead of looking for blame, put yourself in the shoes of Roosevelt or MacArthur. What could you have done?" he said, pausing. "But the war is not over yet! Let us be the best soldiers under the circumstances, for one day we will fight again!"

The men fell silent. John sat on the lone, decrepit chair on the side of the stage, emotionally exhausted. The men went back to their quarters silent and forlorn as the rain poured. John looked up as the chaplain touched his shoulder, and together they left the club house.

The next day, the rain was unrelenting, but there was a change in attitude of the POWs. Most were silent as though deep in thought; the few who did talk began to see what it was like on the other side of the command. Overall, there was a friendlier atmosphere and a glint of hope in their eyes.

Their social club started making headway. Out of almost a hundred men who liked to sing, they formed several choral groups that would sing alternately for small evening programs, and all the groups were coordinated into one show for big events. They celebrated Thanksgiving and Christmas on the right dates, but for their Fourth of July celebration, they did some just-below-the-radar festivities, like pots and pans in the kitchen suddenly clattering with a noisy bang on the floor, or somebody belting out a song like "God Bless America" with a different tune, or one soldier passing another and saying a line from "The Star Spangled Banner" and the next soldier saying the next line, and the next soldier, another line, and on and on. Their captors looked at them but did not do anything.

They had several group leaders and one overall show director. He was a high school music teacher who was patient with making people work together. They discovered a really good tenor in their midst, and the director began dreaming of staging opera skits, only they had no libretto. They also had a good baritone, but he did not go for "serious stuff;" he just wanted to sing something for laughs that ended with a lot of banana peels thrown his way.

Somehow, the companionship blunted their longing for home and loved ones. Aside from music, they had rudimentary cards and other contraptions that worked as table games. John went four for two in chess against Captain Kirk Fielding.

"*I better watch out. This guy is smart!*" John thought.

In the midst of the noisy activity, they provided cover for the men who had been tinkering with whatever they could scavenge; for now they had the semblance of a radio, and they could listen to the news.

They had been hearing news of guerilla units in Mindanao. Not only that, a U.S. submarine had come recently!

"So where does that leave us? Nobody cares about us?" Corporal Linley complained.

"They know where we are. They'll find us," answered Major Richard Hoover.

John Stewart listened to the exchange. It was good to hear optimism, but deep in his heart, John was not sure. He had been here for almost two years. "*What has happened to the war?*" he thought.

On June 6, 1944, the Allies landed in Normandy. Corporal Linley was beside himself, and he ran from their makeshift radio room to tell the others.

"We've invaded Europe! The Allies have landed in Normandy!"

The POWs cheered loudly. Their captors were already anxious as it was, and now realized that the POWs have a radio somewhere. They searched for the radio and found it. Fifteen POWs were lined up bare-chested in the hot sun as punishment. They had not yet eaten breakfast, and they were not given water. It turned out to be a rather mild day however, for clouds covered the hot sun now and then; so most of them lasted until the afternoon. But then, one private wobbled and teetered, and after more swaying as though in a daze, he fell on the ground. The corporal beside him just looked far in the distance, still standing straight. Shortly afterward, however, he could hear the private snoring, so the corporal fell on the ground too, his eyes closed. One by one, the men fell, but some snored too loudly.

Sergeant Minamata got a baton and hit each man on the shoulder. "Get up!" he said. He could not hit them with strong blows—he himself was half-laughing.

In the distance, John Stewart watched, his apprehension changing to laughter and then to thinking. Maybe the captors were getting soft, or maybe they were just all human beings after all.

The POWs learned to hide their anticipation from their captors and again constructed a radio.

One morning, John heard the signal scratching sound just outside his window. Major Hoover was immediately beside him as they looked out to see Private Harvey pretending to stand casually.

"They're moving us!" he said.

John and Hoover looked at each other. They had been keeping their eyes and ears open while keeping their mouths shut. They had noticed their captors behaving apprehensively. There was no denying that U.S. planes had been buzzing overhead quite frequently over the last couple of days.

The Japanese lieutenant called out the units as they stood in groups in the hot sun. The groups that were going to leave had hurriedly gathered their few possessions and filled their canteens. The decrepit trucks were waiting. One after another, the prisoners boarded the trucks, grumbling louder as they were jam packed once again.

The trucks creaked and rattled as the drivers maneuvered down the dirt road. By now, the road looked like a cart road with deep ruts and a raised center. There were rocks in the road that made the trucks tilt this way and that, and when the bottom of a truck hit the raised center, the POWs would be tossed around, banging their heads together.

"SOB!" cussed Hoover.

Nobody minded him, for most of them had taken turns swearing as they got bruised from the rough ride. When the trucks arrived at the Gulf, their relief was replaced by misgiving. They imagined that any other prisoner camp would certainly be worse than DaPeCol. A sense of dread muted their grumbling.

The POWs squinted in the bright sunlight as the trucks lined up in rows to unload them; then they stood aghast as they saw the decrepit transport ship awaiting them on the wharf.

"Here we go again," Captain Fielding whispered as he marched closer to John.

PART FOUR

XXXIV

John shook his head. The memory of riding in one of these ships was a nightmare.

"That ugly son of a gun again!" exclaimed Private Harvey.

The chorus of expletives among the POWs was unprintable.

"Where to?" Some POWs asked aloud, while others left the question in their minds.

They were herded up the gangplank two at a time, straight into the bottom hold of the ship.

"That's enough!" hollered Corporal Linley as the hull filled up with more bodies.

But more POWs were being crammed in, with barely enough breathing space. Some POWs were being literally thrown in, crashing against the heads and shoulders of others who were already finding it hard to breathe.

John was quiet, bracing for the nightmare on the hell ship. "Please!" he said softly as he made a little more space for a private to stand between him and Fielding.

Five more bodies came down the stairs, and the other soldiers did not want to move.

"Please make room!" John spoke louder and with authority. He was glad Fielding stood right beside him, and Hoover was to his left to enforce discipline; otherwise, it would be more difficult to handle this chaos.

Grudgingly, enough room was made so they were all at least standing, packed against each other and guarding their breath. The door closed, and a silence followed. They were suffocating, and John did not even want to speak, but he thought it might help.

"Conserve your energy, men."

It seemed like forever before the ship finally moved. The men looked at each other, wondering.

"God!" somebody suddenly said.

The odor of somebody passing gas permeated the foul air.

"If you do anymore, I'll kill you!" a soldier said.

Silence again.

The ship slowly left the port, and the rhythmic sound of the engine was heard as they went into deeper waters. One hour, two hours ... the heat, the stench, the humming noise of the ship's engine and the inability to move started to affect the men with some kind of stupor. Most men were asleep or falling asleep where they stood.

John fell asleep and woke up to a nudge from Captain Fielding.

"My turn," Fielding said.

"OK!" John nodded, checking his watch. John felt sheepish that he fell asleep so quickly. The heat and the stench were terrible; sleep was an escape. The officers had to take turns somehow, and he had taken the first turn.

His eyes searched for Major Hoover.

"Eight hours? No water?" he said more with his lips than aloud.

"Yep." Hoover nodded.

Suddenly, the door above opened. Hands stretched down bearing a metal container with gallons of water.

"Water!" Hoover said.

He caught the bucket to avoid any spillage. Men woke up from their stupor to scramble for water.

"Easy!" he said as hands thrust canteens in front of him.

Fielding helped those who could not wait sip the water directly from the bucket. That way, they did not waste the precious water.

"Another one!!" John Stewart caught the other bucket.

The rationing was a bit chaotic, but at least everybody got a share.

When a metal drum was lowered back down, some of the men just stared at it. Those with dysentery or needing to use a bathroom quickly figured out it was for them. They made room for it in a corner, but it filled up too easily.

When it was full, they banged at the door for their captors to remove it.

Another day of the same routine followed ... or was it two? Most men could not care less.

"Maybe it is better to die," Corporal Linley said softly.

A sudden, deafening blast made the whole ship shudder. The impact of a bomb hitting its side threw most of the POWs off balance.

"We've been hit!" several voices chorused at once.

Before they could say more, water started rushing through the door of their compartment. Fielding hoisted Corporal Linley up on his shoulder to open the door.

"Quick!" Corporal Linley beckoned as soon as he was out.

Hoover got out and helped pull other POWs quickly. Those at the bottom were beginning to panic.

"Move faster!" John hollered as the water rose up to his chest.

He pulled the weaker ones by their shirts, and Fielding pushed them up as fast as he could.

The ship began to list, and John grabbed the last two necks within sight and pushed them toward Fielding. Fielding barely got the two men out. John and Fielding were underwater, but all the other men were out. Both men held their breath; then slowly released air as they groped along the ship's iron bar that went vertically upward, towards where there was sunlight. They reached the surface gasping and clinging to the first wood plank they saw.

John felt relieved yet sad to be among the lucky souls floating there; for among the scattered debris were also some POWs that did not make it. All too soon he heard shots. Turning, he saw Japanese soldiers in small boats shooting at the POWs swimming toward the shore.

With hand signals, he and Fielding decided to swim the longer route to the shore to avoid the gunners. John was thankful that he and Fielding were good swimmers. He felt like his lungs were ready to burst by the time he reached the shore. There were a lot of bodies there, all gasping for breath as the waves lapped their feet.

Exhausted, John wished he could rest for a while, and hoped Fielding was somewhere. But even as he looked back to see the ship beginning to sink, he saw Japanese gunners in small boats still intent on coming after them, firing shots.

The first shots hit the coconut trees.

"Ahhhh!" a POW screamed as he was hit.

More screams followed as shots rained on the POWs. This was followed by the sound of running feet as the men tried to escape. The POWs scampered inland, diving and zigzagging to the thicket of bushes and grass between trees.

A bullet whipped past John and lodged into a mangrove tree.

That was close! John thought as he ran away from the line of fire, farther inland to where he did not know.

Finally, the shots could not be heard anymore. John was exhausted. There were two other soldiers gasping for breath nearby.

"Let's get some sleep. I'll watch first for two hours," John said.

The two soldiers nodded and were soon asleep. It was only afternoon, but they had been through so much already that they were dead tired. John was glad the Japanese had returned his watch and wedding ring. This watch was from his father. He reflected on the two precious objects and looked at his empty left fifth finger. He would be in dreamland if he did not watch out. He slapped himself to stay awake until it was time to wake up the private beside him for his watch. John fell asleep very quickly.

XXXV

John dreamed there was somebody whistling while he was on top of clouds following the sound, creeping up behind a person. The sound grew louder and was followed by voices, and John woke up with a start, startled by the bodies near him jerking into consciousness.

A bare-chested Filipino boy was whistling and motioning for the POWs to follow him. The survivors sprouted from different directions and greeted each other as they followed the whistling guide. As the number of gathered POWs increased, John looked around at the familiar faces.

"Sir!" Captain Fielding said from behind him.

"Glad to see you, Kirk!" John said, patting Fielding on the back.

It was beginning to get dark, and without a lamp, the soldiers followed closely without question, too tired to worry or think. They walked and stumbled until the smell of food and burning leaves made them hasten. They arrived at a clearing surrounded by *nipa* huts. In the center, several torches illuminated a group of guerillas who greeted them warmly.

Most of the guerillas were Filipinos, their clothes equally dishabille as the newly arrived POWs. Their wide smiles showed white teeth against dark skin, but their eyes showed more than just welcome—and the POWs felt choked up with their greeting.

They sat anywhere they could—on the grass, on stones, or on benches—each man hungrily devouring the rice, dried fish, bananas, papayas, and vegetables that were served to them. Some drank water, but most preferred to share the coconut juice from the baby coconuts that had been sliced open. They could eat more, but there was just enough, and they profusely thanked their hosts and the young men and women who served their food.

"I am Colonel Wendell Fertig, welcome!" said the bearded American guerilla leader.

"Thank you!" the men chorused.

Colonel Fertig updated them about the war situation and tried to answer one question at a time. Several small maps were passed around.

"You are still in Mindanao," he said. "Your ship rounded this southern tip here, Sarangani Strait, went west on Mindanao Sea, came up north, and was bombed in the vicinity of Sindangan Bay."

"Whew!" was all Fielding could say as he pointed on the map.

"The Allies are planning the liberation, and MacArthur is in Australia. Yes, a U.S. submarine brought instructions, radio equipment, supplies, and medicines; it left with some people who had to be evacuated. It was an American submarine that hit your ship."

"No!" The POWs could not believe it.

"This is not unusual. The bombers did not know that U.S. prisoners were inside the ship. They were just bombing enemy ships," Fertig continued.

John watched some men grumble, but he had guessed that already. He looked around and hoped that the faces missing were still alive somewhere on this island, for this was less than half of those who got aboard the ship.

The exchange of information continued until almost midnight. The men were happy and excited at the turn of events. Their spirits were up, and they chattered among themselves and marveled about the progress of the war. Soon, however, they were too tired and slept wherever they could; some were accommodated in the huts, most slept on the grass.

Fertig invited John, the chaplain, and Major Hoover to his hut. It was larger than the usual *nipa* hut and perched atop six large posts. As usual, there was only one story, and the floor was made of rough wood planks instead of the usual bamboo slats. There were spaces between the wooden planks where you could see the earth below. The *nipa* huts thus appeared to be on stilts, and foreigners only realized why it was like that when it rained.

They climbed six wooden steps up into a fairly large room, with a kitchen on the right, a washing area a little off from it, and two bedrooms. They entered the room on the right, and Fertig pointed toward the corner.

"Help yourselves," he said.

Rolled tightly like posts and resting against the corner behind the door were several bright woven mats called *banig* by the natives. Each man rolled his mat open on the floor. They all promptly fell asleep.

It was late before the men stirred, oblivious to the uneven surface. They were just glad to sleep at last.

It had been a long while since John felt so good when he woke up in the morning. His senses were acute as he heard the chirping of the birds. When he heard the cock crow, his first thought was to eat the fowl, and he hung his head in embarrassment, only to find the chaplain also red faced.

"We are going to use it for *sabong*, or a cockfight," Fertig explained, amused at the embarrassment of his guests. "It is a form of entertainment here. Of course, we eat the bird that loses."

"We'll hope the younger cock loses then," the chaplain said.

The guests looked at each other, and they all laughed heartily. In Fertig's hut, they ate better than the regular troops. They had eggs with their rice for breakfast, and there was *bulad*, the dried fish that the natives used as a viand. John had learned to eat this salted dried fish that was called *tuyo* by the Tagalogs. This was the viand for most poor people who could not afford meat. Sometimes the well-to-do would have this for breakfast along with eggs, almost the equivalent of the American bacon. Fertig glanced at John eating his dried fish with tomatoes.

"Yes, it's good with tomatoes," Fertig said.

"I feel like a king," John said with a nod.

"Let me try that," Hoover said.

The portions were small and the coffee mild, but the guests agreed how delicious it was.

Feeling contented afterward, they talked with Fertig about future plans.

"I'd like to get into the next submarine and help in Australia," John said.

"OK, if we ship you from here, there will be room for the other injured POWs being taken cared of by some families," Colonel Fertig replied.

"Oh? I know Fielding wanted to go too, but OK," Hoover said.

"Among the rescued are Private Holt and Corporal Williams, and there's more," Fertig replied. "I'll send papers, maps, and other data with you."

"I'm thankful there were more men who made it!" the chaplain exclaimed.

"Yes! There are also U.S. civilians hiding on another island. They were caught here in the war and should be evacuated too," Fertig continued.

They got to see the *sabong* two days later. A man from the next barrio came early in the morning with a scrawny red and black cock that crowed noisily. The owner smoked a rolled cigar, and he blew the smoke right into the cock's face, talking to it at the same time.

"I hope that cock loses," the chaplain said, irritated by the cock that woke him up.

Fertig sat on a chair near the hut steps, content to pat his white cock and let it scamper forward and back. A rope was tied on one end at the cock's leg, while the other end was tied to an iron ring nailed on a small post.

The cockfight was in the square at the center of the huts. There was no fence or formal perimeter. The spectators merely formed a circle around the cocks and their owners. The usual number of bettors emerged, after first arguing on the pros and cons of each cock.

"I'm betting on the scrawny one. He looks mean!" a Filipino guerilla said.

"I'm betting on Fertig's, he's the strong, silent type," answered Corporal Linley.

The *tari*, or small knives, were tied to the cocks' legs, and the cockfight began.

"*Sa pula!*" (For the red!) the Filipino guerillas betting on the scrawny one shouted loudly.

"*Sa puti!*" (For the white!) the ones supporting Fertig's cock shouted back.

"Go! Go!" screamed the U.S. soldiers in a language they could understand.

The cocks were like prize fighters that first made circles inside the perimeter. Each eyed the opponent, scratched the ground, circled around, and made more cackling sounds.

"Phooey!" Corporal Linley could not help feeling disappointed.

"*Saba!*" (Quiet!) one of the Filipino guerillas retorted.

Suddenly, the red cock flew at the white one. The white one bled, but it got up and flew straight at the red cock. The fight was on with both cocks flying toward each other, the blades of the small knives on their legs cutting into the opponent. The feathers, blood, and dust flew, and the guerillas got hoarse screaming for their favorite.

Fertig's cock was bleeding, but the scrawny one was on the ground.

"Go! Go!" The bettors wanted a sure winner.

The scrawny cock stopped moving, and the Fertig bettors rejoiced. Then Fertig's cock went into a convulsion and stopped moving too. The men fell silent.

"We still won!" Corporal Linley exclaimed.

"Yeah!" chorused the Fertig bettors.

"Under the rules of the game," Fertig started to explain.

But John and some of the men had started laughing.

"This is ridiculous!" the chaplain said, protesting.

"Your prayer was answered," John said, still laughing, and Fertig laughed too.

True enough, they had chicken for supper, and the chaplain presented for debate the morality of cockfighting and betting. The men had mixed reactions—half of them liked it.

Before the week was over, the ex-POWs started feeling like they were on vacation. There was an abundance of *lanzones*, which most of the soldiers tasted, then there was the *rambutan*, which was like lychee. Instead of scrambling for survival, the ex-POWs were on the lookout to try *mangosteen*, *madang*, *nangka* (jackfruit), and the notorious smelling durian.

Fertig briefed John and the other officers.

Wendell Fertig was a lieutenant colonel, U.S. Army Reserve, who was working at Bataan with the engineering corps just before the war started. He was later sent to Mindanao to help Major General William Sharp. When Major General William Sharp, commander of Visayas and Mindanao, obeyed the order to surrender his forces on May 10, 1942, Fertig did not obey, thinking that the order was made under duress. Figuring that he was the highest-ranking officer in Mindanao, Fertig asserted his right to command all the Mindanao forces. Along with that, he proclaimed himself a general. In due time, there were about thirty thousand guerillas under his command.

The Allied Command Center in Australia worked to establish communication with the guerilla forces in the Philippines. Now and then, an American submarine would surface at a rendezvous point and unload radio equipment, medicine, weapons, and some uniforms. On its return, it took sick, escaped POWs and U.S. civilians who had been stranded in the Philippines at the outbreak of the war.

By this time, Fertig had also been reached by men under General Douglas MacArthur, and he was advised that he should not proclaim himself a general. Fertig took the correction in stride, obeyed, and continued with his work.

One afternoon, Colonel Fertig took the officers on an informal survey around the camp perimeter. The rain the previous night was not heavy, but it was enough to clear the humidity of the past days. The men took turns taking deep breaths of the fresh air. This afternoon was glorious, and the sun shone between the tall trees bordering the camp. From a distance, they could hear birds and other sounds, and they imagined there must be monkeys and other wild game out there.

The ex-POWs kept busy by improving the camp. They felled a number of trees and divided the labor between constructing housing, facilities, and preparing a farm. Stripped to their waists and sweating, the men could afford to whistle, for they liked what they were doing, and they were free.

Finally they learned that the submarine would be arriving, and John prepared to go.

"I'll see you when I come back," John said, shaking hands with the officers and men.

"Good luck!" Fielding said.

"Have a good trip!" Hoover and Fertig said.

XXXVI

John had carefully packed the papers and maps Fertig had asked him to carry to the commander of SWPOA (SouthWest Pacific Operating Area). Berting led the way on a narrow trail as the early morning light brightened their path. Alberto "Berting" Sim had been a young career lieutenant in Major General Sharp's army at the outbreak of the war. Fertig was among the officers the young lieutenant taught in his Tagalog class. When Fertig decided not to surrender, Berting was among the Filipino officers who went with him to hide in the mountains.

"We will be in Sindangan Bay two days before the sub arrives, so we can check the area and wait for the injured ones," Berting explained.

They walked at a brisk pace while Berting talked about the guerilla set-up. At noontime, they stopped at a shaded area, and Berting opened two packets of lunch wrapped in banana leaves. It contained rice, a small piece of pork, and a boiled egg. Berting then climbed a coconut tree, dropped two young coconuts with his bolo, and sliced off the tops. They drank the juice and ate with their hands.

At Sindangan Point, other injured POWs were brought by guerilla support groups. They slept there for the night, awaiting other POWs. Two boys arrived on the run the next morning. They had a message from their radioman that the submarine would be in Sirai Bay.

They all moved there, and indeed the submarine arrived that night. John and the other POWs were brought to the submarine by the outrigger canoes called *bancas*, the rowers glistening with sweat. The guerillas rejoiced as they unloaded boxes of ammunition, equipments, medicine, uniforms, and other supplies. From Sirai, the submarine proceeded to Negros Island and picked up more POWs and other U.S. civilians.

John resolved to study the whole set-up, incredulous that a U.S. submarine could be in enemy waters bringing supplies and evacuating people while he and the other POWs had languished as slave laborers.

John arrived in Australia full of hope and ready to fight. He was glad he got some rest at Fertig's colony, for he was debriefed as soon as he arrived.

"Major Jesus Villamor?" John asked, unbelieving as they were introduced. "Last I heard, you might have survived after being shot down, but I did not hear the follow-up reports."

"I am blessed with several lives!" Villamor bantered. "I never knew what fate awaited me that December 9 when I climbed on my P26 plane. I was congratulating myself for having shot down one of the Japanese bombers I was chasing, when suddenly I went down too. The swarm of enemy planes that took me out was on the way to bomb Fort Stotsenberg. Our men fished me from the Pasig River, and then I was awarded the Distinguished Service Cross. MacArthur included me in his staff when he left for Australia."

The captain of the lone airplane that fought back when the Japanese bombers arrived at the start of the war was in the group that exchanged questions and answers with Brigadier General John Stewart. The G2 officer was a serious guy named Major Craig Delsey.

"I am confident that Colonel Fertig's guerillas are well entrenched and dependable. I did not go with Fertig on his visit to Dipolog and the surrounding areas because we thought the submarine might come anytime. Captain Fielding reports that the network is more extensive than at first glance, and the morale is amazingly high," John stated.

"That's a relief to hear since we were first cynical when he proclaimed himself general, and he was not so forthcoming of progress reports from the Visayas group. How familiar are you with the Visayan Islands?" Delsey said.

"The area I knew mostly about was Samar," John said, slightly blushing at the thought of Balangiga and Clara. "My knowledge of the area has not been updated, however, since I was assigned to Balangiga shortly after I graduated from West Point. My recent assignments have been in Luzon. I can understand some Visaya dialect, but I have a harder time following the Waray dialect. I haven't met James Cushing, but I met Chick Parsons before the war in Manila," John finished.

"There has been a spontaneous desire by the people to fight back, with many would-be leaders springing up from different places. In the Visayas, specifically in Cebu, the guerillas chose James Cushing and Harry Fenton, a.k.a. Aaron Feinstein. Thinking that a higher rank gave them more clout, the two promoted themselves to major." At John's surprised expression, Delsey chuckled and said, "Yes, it happens."

He continued, "James Cushing was a mining engineer who lived in the Philippines. When war broke out, he joined the army and was assigned to the Corps of Engineers. Brigadier General Bradford Chenoweth, the commander of the Visaya force, commissioned him as captain.

"Cushing liked to blow up bridges and military installations, but he became disillusioned with military red tape. He went to Mindanao, but there was no action there either. When he got back to Cebu, the Japanese were just spreading their domination of the islands southward, and soon the U.S.-Philippine forces were in retreat. The civilians were torn between heading for the hills and staying in town. Most of the guerilla movement headquartered in the mountains. Cushing's was in Masurela; Fenton was in Maslog. General MacArthur learned of these movements and sent Major Jesus Villamor as a personal emissary." Delsey turned to Villamor.

"MacArthur sent me via the submarine USS *Gudgeon* to Negros, where I met with Cushing," Villamor said. "Cushing looked like a reliable guy, and I was happy to report my findings to General MacArthur. Unknown to us at that time, his guerilla partner, Harry Fenton, was becoming unstable back in Cebu. While Cushing was away, Fenton started behaving oddly and began executing some Filipinos for wrongs that were not proven. Soon the count of execution was sixty-six. Fenton also started having relationships with adolescents as young as fourteen, and he was accused of rape. A fellow guerilla got the upper hand, and suspecting Fenton of having raped his wife, executed Fenton.

"When Cushing came back, the Filipino leader was in turn executed, since there was the possibility he was about to turn Cushing in to the Japanese."

John sighed at the complex personalities, infighting, and events that shaped the war. Even Fertig has been chastised when he appointed himself as general. As radio communications got established between Brisbane, Australia, and Mindanao, there were instances when Fertig was not that forthcoming. Nevertheless, these guerilla networks worked, and he was one lucky beneficiary.

He slept well that night and dreamed about Clara. He woke up with a start and checked himself. *I should be worrying about Jack.*

Two weeks later, G2 headquarters was abuzz with excitement.

The next briefing explained why. Major Delsey could hardly contain his elation.

"The last submarine extraction of people and information from the Philippines brought us an unexpected gift. We now realized that we have the enemy's Z Plan. The Z Plan is the Imperial Japanese Navy's strategy that Admiral Mineichi Koga and his staff drafted after we shot down Yamamoto.

"Our intelligence surmised that when we attacked the Japanese toward Palau, we somehow pressured Koga and his chief of staff, Rear Admiral Fukudome, to board two Kawanishi planes en route to Davao, Philippines. A storm was brewing, and Koga's plane was never found. The plane carrying Fukudome crashed in the Bohol Strait. Ten survivors and Fukudome swam to the shore. The guerillas found them, and they were turned over to Cushing.

"Two of the survivors escaped the guerillas and were able to reach the Japanese authorities. Subsequently, one town after another was persecuted until Cushing had no choice but to give up the survivors to the Japanese authorities.

"A box carrying the Z Plan, however, surfaced in the sea and was recovered by two friends. The two handed over the box to Cushing's men and then fled with their families as the Japanese persecution heated up. This plan finally made its way to our command in Australia," Delsey said.

Cheers and loud applause erupted among the officers at the briefing. There was a palpable enthusiasm as they all looked forward to the day of reckoning.

Brigadier General John Stewart was in Hollandia, northern New Guinea. Allied forces had been moving north rapidly after their success in leap-frogging past the Japanese stronghold in Rabaul, on the island of New Britain.

He sat on his desk to study the briefing papers and remembered to flip the desk calendar to September 1944. Even if their briefings had been extensive, tension was rising among the officers, who were bent on winning without mishaps. With the tension and the hectic training of troops, John looked even leaner. There was more food around, but the soldiers burned up the calories quickly.

John put the papers down as he had practically memorized the strategy and its implications. He smiled when he caught himself holding his breath out of excitement.

XXXVII

The Southwest Pacific Area Forces coming from the Bismarck Archipelago and New Guinea were ready to attack. The Americans had 157 combat ships and 581 other vessels of the Seventh Fleet, protected by 106 warships of Vice Admiral Halsey's Third Fleet. Halsey had to answer to Admiral Nimitz. One hundred sixty thousand Americans who had trained in Australia and New Guinea had to be put ashore in the first phase.

The American plan was to land the troops on the eastern shores of Leyte, from the vicinity of Tacloban all the way south to the vicinity of Dulag. First they had to bomb the enemy installations. The frogmen and the minesweepers would follow to clear the area, then the big ships could come and unload the troops.

The navy, under the overall command of Admiral Chester Nimitz, had to provide protection for the troops to land. They anticipated a strong Japanese counteroffensive. Rear Admiral Jesse Oldendorf would be in command of the naval forces in Leyte Gulf until Vice Admiral Thomas Kinkaid could arrive there on October 20, 1944, with his Seventh Fleet. Kinkaid had to answer to MacArthur.

The Southern Attack Force (XXIV Corps), the Northern Attack Force (X Corps), four divisions of Lieutenant General Walter Krueger's Sixth Army, reserves, and logistical personnel could be landed only with the protection of naval cover.

When the Americans proceeded to bomb the enemy installations on the Gulf of Leyte, there was little enemy resistance. Starting at 10:00 AM on October 20 until October 22, 1944, the troops came ashore in a fifteen-mile radius from Tacloban to Dulag.

Guerilla units in this area were very active, especially since one of their leaders was USN Lieutenant Commander Charles "Chick"

Parsons, an American who had lived mostly in the Philippines. Prior to the bombing, the civilian populace had been warned to evacuate the area; thus, there were no civilian casualties.

The troops who came ashore were soon met by civilians coming out of hiding and singing "God Bless America." The lower-ranked soldiers may have been surprised by this, but the U.S. commanders who had been in communication with active guerilla units were not. Chick Parsons had come aboard the command ship to give his assessment.

On October 22, 1944, after lunch aboard the USS *Nashville*, General MacArthur, Philippine President Osmena (former President Quezon had died), General Carlos Romulo, and other senior commanders disembarked. They waded across the shores. MacArthur then declared on the microphone: "People of the Philippines, I have returned!"

Brigadier General John Stewart stood at attention among his men, who had just reached the shore. His lips were pursed to a thin line and his jaw was set, but the tears silently falling on his cheeks belied his countenance. He was not oblivious of the applause for MacArthur, nor was he lacking in identifying with it, but a surge of conflicting emotions choked his ability to speak. The desire for revenge, to right a wrong, had been paramount in his mind when he boarded the rescue submarine at Sirai; yet now, despite his joy that MacArthur fulfilled his troth with the Filipinos, John had a nagging sense of having been shortchanged.

Long ago, the war had started with the U.S.-Philippine forces using old, inadequate, and obsolete weapons, and the new trainees still needed time to be ready—yet they took a stand in Bataan to hold back the enemy, even if help would not come. Now the Allied forces had all new weapons for land and air, including the LST (landing ship tank), LCT (landing craft tank), LCI (landing craft infantry), and many other marvels. John had studied them all like a boy mesmerized by all the novelty.

He could blame nobody for the parsimonious attitude of the U.S. government then. The Great Depression had affected all levels of civilian and government life; the attitude was defensive, as the poor could not even think of fighting for their future. John shook his head at the irony that the war wiped out the unemployment rate, and the bonds made possible the financing.

The young soldiers were well fed, healthy, and enthusiastic to get on with it and win it. John knew he had to temper that with caution and wisdom, since it was his responsibility to protect his men.

In Australia, while training the young soldiers for the coming liberation, he sympathized with the greenhorns who had to learn to fight, kill, survive in jungles, overcome mountains, and thrive in all other elements. Even if some of them were aware of the humiliation of the Fall of Bataan and the ignominy of the Death March, their desire for revenge had to be tempered against the first shock of what a battle really was.

Captain Schroeder made his way toward him, and John smiled. There was so much hope and courage among these men; he would not fail them.

Waves and waves of fresh Allied soldiers came ashore ready to fight, the divisions looking like swarms of ants filling the shores of Leyte, but there was no fight that day.

It was pure luck that, at that time, the Japanese command in the area was in the process of moving their headquarters farther inland. There was only one Japanese division in Leyte. This was the Sixteenth, consisting of twenty thousand men under Lieutenant General Shiro Makino.

On October 21, 1944, Brigadier General Seichi Mifune felt a sense of dread as he left the Japanese headquarters in Manila. During the conference, he had listened to Lieutenant General Tomoyuki Yamashita respectfully airing his opinion that it might be better to make a stand against the Allies in Luzon. However, Field Marshall Hisaichi Terauchi, the Japanese field marshal for the southwest Pacific, had a different plan.

Terauchi had arrived in Manila on October 6, a providential occurrence Mifune was griping about. Apparently, the Japanese Central Command in Tokyo had figured out that the Allies would land in Leyte, and Terauchi ordered two divisions to be sent there. Yamashita, the commander for the Philippines, had to obey his superior.

Mifune absentmindedly ordered his driver to head toward Nueva Ecija. He had to collect his things, issue some orders, and then return to Manila to be deployed to Leyte. Tokyo had ordered SHO-1, the Japanese strategy for the defense of the Philippines, to be triggered as of October 18. Why did the order arrive in Manila only on the twentieth?

He worried that Yoshiro's company might also be sent to Leyte. Yoshiro had been sent on a mission to the Cagayan Valley by Yamashita. Yoshiro had reported good harvests and favorable future forecasts. This coincided with Yamashita's alternate plan, should a defensive war be necessary.

Mifune puffed at his cigarette irritably. He had been junior to Yamashita in military school. He had admired Yamashita's drive and brilliance as a military commander, as well as his integrity and loyalty to the emperor of Japan. Mifune had arrived early before the meeting so he could greet Yamashita as a friend and exchange opinions. The two men agreed that the reports of their naval and aerial victories in the Battle of Midway and over the Marianas were false. If the Japanese were winning, then why were the Allies now in the Philippines?

Now he would be with the two Japanese divisions leaving to reinforce Makino's division in Leyte. Mifune puffed at his cigarette and filled the car with smoke that his driver suffocated on.

The driver opened his window and hoped the general would not notice.

Mifune was lost in thought. He remembered the horrible premonition he had felt when he heard that SHO-2, the Japanese strategy for the defense of Formosa and the Ryukyus, had been prematurely triggered. That was because Vice Admiral William Halsey's fleet had been all over the Ryukyus, Formosa, and back and forth to the Philippines, taunting the Japanese to retaliate with naval and aerial firepower, causing their very own defense resources to be compromised.

Yet there was a glimmer of hope. The Japanese Navy had an ace up its sleeve: Vice Admiral Jisaburo Ozawa, a brilliant strategist.

On October 23, 1944, the Japanese Thirty-fifth Army's First Division and Twenty-sixth Division arrived in Ormoc, Leyte.

Lieutenant General Shiro Makino was surprisingly optimistic as he greeted Mifune and the other generals.

"It should be easy to dislodge the Allies from the Dulag area," Makino said. "They have been stuck in bad terrain. Between the beach, the jungle, and the mountains, they have been unable to get entrenched. They could not make headway with their airstrips."

Mifune hoped this was true. He was taking command of the battlefield in the Dulag area, and rain had started to pour already.

The next day, Mifune surveyed the battlefield with his binoculars. *The coming storm could be a disadvantage to us*, he thought.

True enough, the rains poured heavily. The battlefield was a quagmire of mud and blood as the machine gunners from opposite sides blasted the enemies indiscriminately. It was hard to see well when the strong winds and pelting rain made everything a blur. They could not even hear each other; they only heard the howling wind.

Mifune watched as a captain signaled to the machine gunner where to fire. He wiped his binoculars, but the rain blurred the glass before he could see well. Just the same, it was obvious that the Allies had dug in and could not be dislodged.

This is terrible, he thought. *This is a different enemy. They're young, strong, and well-fed.*

The fighting continued, with the well-equipped Allies holding their ground. The Japanese continued to lose soldiers as Allied aerial attacks became more frequent. By October 26, Makino's Division had lost 75% of his men. The Japanese airplanes dwindled in number after they were used to dive on American naval vessels in kamikaze attacks.

The Japanese generals' meeting was a time to air frustrations. The same lousy weather greeted them everyday, and the storm was supposed to get stronger still. To them, it did not make sense they were losing more men than the newly arrived Allies.

"I won't let them build their airstrips," Makino vowed.

Even during their meeting, they could hear an Allied aerial onslaught. The generals watched from their perch the attacking fighter planes coming from the warships in Leyte Gulf. They cheered when a kamikaze plane hit an Allied aircraft carrier.

A series of retaliatory bombs from another ship followed swiftly and hit the Japanese camp. The generals' smiles turned to apprehension and they ran for cover. Mifune heard a loud blast before he could reach the door, then the roof caved in.

Mifune had been propelled against the wall by the impact, and he sat up dazed, looking at the cement, wood and metal debris around him. In the darkness he discerned a few bodies that moved in pain; and as he felt a discomfort in his chest, he absentmindedly touched it. He had a chest wound, and he could not stop the flow of blood with his hand.

He thought of Japan, Yoshiro, and his daughter as he lapsed into unconsciousness, but it was not his dead wife's face he conjured next; it was Clara's face as she looked at him with a question and then suddenly looked down to hide her thoughts. *Stubborn woman!* He thought, and then he died.

It was late November 1944 when Captain Yoshiro Mifune arrived in Manila. He wept quietly as he read his father's letter. The general had written about the conditions in Leyte as though to warn him should Yoshiro be sent to Leyte. Uncharacteristically, his father had written, "*I love you and your sister very much, my children.*"

Yoshiro had never heard his father say that before. It was assumed, but never said. The war had humanized his father. Yoshiro suspected that it was partly because his father had indeed fallen in love with Mrs. Mendez. A week after he had written the letter, Mifune died. Yoshiro now felt the onus of responsibility to take care of his sister and carry on the family name. *How cruel war was!* Now he had to study the grim reports of how much they were losing.

For the Allies, landing on the shores of Leyte had been easy, but moving inland became difficult. They had to go through mountains, swamps, and jungles, and the soldiers trying to build airfields found the terrain unsuitable. Moreover, the continuous downpour of rain left them with quagmires of mud they could not work with.

John held his breath as he watched a lieutenant throw a hand grenade. It landed near the enemy's machine gunner, the one who had just killed soldiers from the lieutenant's platoon. From his right, a captain rose from a shallow dugout and pointed out the opening for his company to attack.

John's division advanced cautiously that day. The terrain was rocky so their foxholes were shallow. Mud and rainwater filled their foxholes, and some men who were soaked wet and shivering for long periods started to get sick.

On December 7, Lieutenant General Walter Krueger briefed the men with his decision.

"We are pulling out of Dulag and moving to Ormoc," he said solemnly, using a pointer.

He gave the pointer to Colonel Dalton to discuss the crucial points in their strategy.

Wonderful! John sighed in relief, impressed with the strategy.

However, more Japanese reinforcements had also arrived in Ormoc by December 1944. Along with the reinforcements, the total now numbered over sixty thousand soldiers. Yoshiro was among them. The incoming Japanese troops started counterattacking the Americans and their half-built airstrips.

Yoshiro focused his binoculars on a kamikaze plane diving on an American destroyer. The blast from the impact reverberated through the destroyer, and it was followed by the frantic running back and forth of men as they tried to put out the fire. Yoshiro bowed in sympathy with the suicide pilot now engulfed in flames.

Their battle the next day was at the edge of the airstrip. Yoshiro directed his gunners to attack the advancing Allied front. The Allies pushed forward as though oblivious of the gunfire from the Japanese. Suddenly, an American plane flew out of nowhere, and Yoshiro and his men took cover as they were strafed with gunfire.

Yoshiro got up from the airstrip shoulder and cursed under his breath. His machine gunner was dead, and the plane was returning. He ran for the machine gun and aimed it toward the airplane when he heard a bullet whiz by. The blood on his right shoulder told him something, but he refused to be defeated.

The Allies were running forward from the front. He reached for his right sidearm revolver, but his right hand felt limp from his wound. Clumsily, his left hand reached for it, and he aimed his gun at his temple.

"No dice, buddy," said a burly American corporal, unusually swift in leaping forward to tackle Yoshiro.

The corporal kicked his revolver away. As they fought, the corporal grabbed Yoshiro's hand and twisted his forearm backward.

"Damn you!" Yoshiro cursed.

"Tell that to the marines," the corporal answered nonchalantly.

Heavy fighting continued, but the Allies had won Ormoc by December 10. The Japanese lost sixty thousand soldiers—only four hundred became prisoners. By contrast, the Allies lost thirty-five hundred men, and twelve thousand were wounded.

XXXVIII

From Leyte, U.S. forces liberated Mindoro on December 15, 1944. They then prepared the airfield positions for subsequent Luzon landings. The soldiers could be heard whistling as the rains eased into a drizzle. Eager anticipation could be sensed among the men, even more so since it was Christmastime.

John sat contentedly enjoying the conversation with his fellow officers. They had eaten well at a dinner table laden with holiday trimmings. John had received letters from Jack and from his family in Virginia, and he beamed with paternal pride at how well Jack was doing. He resolved to focus his thoughts on his family and the war, instead of somebody else.

The war was not yet over, and they were about to face a tough battle against Yamashita. Yamashita's land forces numbered 262,000 soldiers, divided into three groups. The Allied Command was aware that Yamashita planned to fight a defensive war in Luzon, using food and resources from the Cagayan Valley.

MacArthur proceeded to liberate Luzon with Lieutenant General Walter Krueger commanding the Sixth Army, Lieutenant General Robert Eichelberger commanding the Eighth Army, Lieutenant General George C. Kenney commanding the Allied Air Forces, General Sir Thomas A. Blamey in charge of the Australian Allied Land Forces, and Vice Admiral Thomas Kinkaid commanding the U.S. Navy.

By January 1945, 175,000 American troops had landed in Lingayen Gulf. The Allies rapidly advanced toward Manila, the Bataan Peninsula, Olongapo, and Corregidor.

Brigadier General John Stewart was with the 37th Division that entered Manila from the north on February 3. They raced to free the foreign civilians that were interned in the University of Santo Tomas, the Old Bilibid Prison, and Los Banos. It took a day of fighting because 200 hostages were used by the enemy to forestall them. Finally they freed the 4000 grateful prisoners from the University of Santo Tomas.

John's face was black with soot from exploding oil barrels, cars, and other barricades that blocked the road to UST. Even before the Allies could rub their dirty faces with their sleeves, a messenger rushed to the officers' group.

"The Japanese Naval Defense Force is putting up a fierce fight in the Manila Port Area. Many civilians are getting caught in the crossfire," the guerilla captain said in between breaths.

Aside from the 37th Division, the Allies had planned to surround the Japanese with the First Cavalry Division approaching from the east, and Eichelberger's Eleventh Airborne Division from the southwest. Yamashita and his 150,000 soldiers fought their way out on the retreat toward Baguio and the Cagayan Valley; but Rear Admiral Sanji Iwabuchi felt it his duty to stay and fight. He deployed his 20,000 sailors and gave the order to blow up all military installations: bridges, water supply, electric power system, etc.

The resulting ignitions caused fires that blew with the wind. It first burned areas of bamboo shacks, then half of the city. The fire could be seen from 50 miles away.

By February 4, the Allies realized what a fierce fight it would be against Iwabuchi's sailors. Manila was circled with barbed wire fortifications and barricades of overturned trucks and trolleys. Houses were used as shooting positions for machine guns, there were firing slits on the walls, entrances were sandbagged, and stairways were barricaded.

On February 7, MacArthur was poised to enter Manila and he planned to have a huge victory parade; but this did not happen. Because Manila was heavily populated, MacArthur at first prohibited air attacks; then he reversed it when U.S. casualties increased. Artillery shelling commenced.

When the Spaniards first came to Manila, they built a walled city with fortifications: 'Intramuros'. On one corner of the one hundred fifty acre site was Fort Santiago. The walls of Intramuros were forty feet thick at the base, and it was sixteen feet high. The Japanese had dug underground tunnels to trap the advancing Allies.

Near Intramuros was a police station where the Japanese installed so many machine guns and placed obstacles. The Allies used Howitzers and tanks before sending the infantry in. Each room was manned with several machine guns, and the Allies fought room to room, and floor to floor, only to withdraw. After more shelling, the Allies tried again, only to withdraw again. Only after incessant shelling had reduced the building into a pile of rubble, did the enemy guns become silent.

The fighting to take back the government buildings southwest of Intramuros, and beyond into the Manila Club, the University of the Philippines, and the Manila Hotel, were all room to room, floor to floor debacles before the Allies could win it.

When the buildings were won by the Allies, the Japanese withdrew to Intramuros, and in the process, vent their fury on the civilians by bayoneting or burning them. When the Allies finally reached Intramuros, there were 4,000 Filipinos being held hostage. The Allies used a loudspeaker to plead for the release of the hostages. When there was no response, six days of bombardment followed.

By February 23, the 37th Division attacked Intramuros from the north and east. There was a respite when the Japanese released 3,000 hostages of women and children; then the fighting resumed. The male hostages had already been killed. When the fighting stopped, Intramuros was left in ruins.

Still the fighting raged on in other buildings: the Legislative Building, the Finance Building, Bureau of Agriculture, and the Bureau of Commerce. It had occurred to the Allies to just starve the enemy, but escaped hostages said that the enemy had enough food. So the Allies continued until the buildings were destroyed.

Even if Manila was declared free by February 26 (1945), the Japanese in the Finance building held until March 3.

The destruction was as bad as London. Out of over eight hundred thousand Filipinos living in Manila, one hundred thousand died. About one thousand Americans died, along with sixteen thousand Japanese.

Yet the Allies had a lot more work to do: pursue Yamashita and his soldiers.

Lieutenant Colonel Russell Volckmann's guerillas pushed from the north against Yamashita's forces while a portion of General Krueger's troops pressed from the south.

John was grim as he tried to shake off the memory of the Manila debacle. He heard it was as bad in Corregidor, where even battle hardened soldiers cried. He looked at the map of Balete Pass then focused his binoculars, surveying the troop movements. Four platoons were pinned down by enemy fire. They took cover among the stone outcroppings and ditches just vacated by the enemy. A reinforcement of enemy soldiers arrived to halt the retreat, and it was a touch-and-go attempt to retake their position.

The frontal assault team held their position and returned fire in a bloody exchange. John held his breath. There was some movement on the right flank, where platoons had been ordered to make a pincer movement. Suddenly, a burst of fire came from the camouflaged helmets, and the enemy was being shot down. The breakthrough was just in time! John sighed in relief. They had to pursue quickly to prevent the enemy from making a last stand.

The Allies finally took Baguio but still did not capture Yamashita.

Some Allied divisions were sent to liberate Bicol and the southern Luzon area. A portion of Eichelberger's troops liberated Palawan on March 1, 1945, but they were too late to save most of the American POWs, who were burned to death on December 14, 1944. The central Visayas region was liberated between March and April 1945.

In Mindanao, the guerillas controlled the airfield in Dipolog, making it easy for the Allies to move troops and materiel. Here, Colonel Wendell W. Fertig and his band of guerillas were of immense help. By March 11, 1945, a westward drive commencing from Mindanao moved toward Borneo, one island at a time.

Mindanao was a large island occupied by forty-three thousand Japanese soldiers. It was declared liberated by June 30, although pockets of resistance remained until July 27.

The liberation of Luzon was declared on June 30, 1945.

XXXIX

Sister Jacinta heard the news of the landing in Leyte from the middleman picking up their strawberry preserves from the door. The Mother Superior, Mother Elena, decided to tell the congregation.

Clara became very restless once she heard that news. Finally, she asked the Mother Superior if they could have a radio. She reasoned that since she and Neneng were lay people, they could listen and just tell the nuns what was happening. She added that she still had some money.

When the nuns agreed, Sister Jacinta sent the middleman to look for a radio. Now Clara and Neneng followed the day-to-day progress of the liberation. The nuns in the cloister were all beaming with joy and relief, and everybody had an appetite to eat now that the war was ending.

On April 12, 1945, the news of President Roosevelt's death caused sadness and anxiety. Clara followed the news and soon relayed to the nuns that things were going alright in the U.S.

By the end of April, Clara took the risk of sending a message to her Kuya Emong. She and Neneng were eager to go home, and they started preparing. Their Kuya Emong arrived one early morning with a driver in their old car. General Mifune had returned the car to the Mendez home before he left for Leyte.

"We cleaned the car," Kuya Emong said.

Clara just smiled. She knew how meticulous the general was.

Clara had never heard her Kuya Emong talk so much! He filled them in on everything he knew about the war.

"The prisoners were freed from Cabanatuan," he said proudly.

He told them about Captain Robert Lapham riding from behind enemy lines on horseback for several days to get to the American camp. Lapham advised the U.S. forces that they had to evacuate the sick prisoners in Cabanatuan very soon if they wanted to avoid what had happened to the POWs in Palawan.

This time, Lapham's plea was brought to the attention of the intelligence officer (G2), who then presented the problem to Lieutenant General Krueger. The task was given to Lieutenant Colonel Henry Mucci to supervise Captain Robert Prince in planning the mission.

Filipino guerillas augmented the 121 troops that were to rescue four hundred sick POWs. The POWs were rescued and put in carts pulled by water buffaloes. The mission was a success, although the raiding team had one fatality: the doctor.

"The mayor of Cabanatuan was placed under house arrest," Emong said. His narration of events jumped around, and Clara listened attentively so as not to miss anything.

The mayor of Cabanatuan had arrived when Mucci and his group were planning the raid. The mayor had been at his post for sometime during the war, which was suspicious enough. He also offered them a bottle of scotch, which was hard to come by in this time of war. Taking precaution against possible duplicity, Mucci had ordered that the mayor be placed on house arrest until the POWs were saved.

"By the way, Yoshiro Mifune was also sent to Leyte."

Clara bowed. They had heard on the radio about the fighting in Leyte, and they knew the high mortality on the Japanese side. She looked up to see Neneng torn with mixed emotions, then both of them made the sign of the cross.

Emong informed them that Celestino and his family had returned to Manila soon after the liberation forces arrived. Celestino felt that the Allies could use people to establish order. There were rumors of looting in some areas, and Celestino's house had been left unguarded when they had left Manila in haste.

Mother and daughter smiled as the car passed along the winding roads, and they could see the vast greenery of hills and vales and the newly planted *palay* (rice seedlings). They both took deep breaths and savored their freedom.

"Hmmm! How wonderful!" Neneng said.

Emong just smiled.

They arrived at San Nicholas late in the afternoon. Clara and Neneng rushed to Faustina, each relieved to have come out of the ordeal. They cried and hugged her for a long time.

Clara looked at her mother with a keen eye for observation, noting that her mother had visibly aged and looked thin. She wondered if her mother was getting too old to take care of herself, or whether she was just worried about them.

"I must make sure she eats well," Clara resolved.

Clara was reassured when the family talked about their finances. Faustina knew where their money was and how much they had. They had kept their U.S.-Philippine money and stashed it underground in several places, although most of it was in the car garage. They had kept the Japanese occupation money at a minimum and preferred to barter goods with others. Since the *palay* harvest was ongoing, albeit smaller, they were still accumulating assets.

At first, it was all happy chatter as the ladies exchanged news and observations with their Kuya Emong. Neighbors then arrived to welcome back Clara and Neneng. They exchanged news on everything that had been going on and felt relieved to be able to talk freely of things that could only be revealed now.

Clara welcomed the respite of graciousness returning to the troubled world. During these visits, women often brought gifts like fruits, delicacies that had been proudly cooked, or something from their garden. She was glad to have enough of her famous mango preserves to give away in exchange for the honey, *tapa* (dried sugary beef), and *chiesa* that the visitors brought.

Mrs. Edrozo told them about her son Luis being put in an execution line-up and the hooded informant letting him go. Later on, she found out that the hooded person was their farm tenant who had been coerced.

"Luis thought that he was about to be pointed out. Oh, how scared we were!" she said.

"Did you hear what happened to de Silva?" Mrs. Narciso said eagerly. "Mr. de Silva was suspected of being a collaborator. While most people were undergoing hardship during the war, he seemed to be doing well. On Holy Friday, he was in the procession. The next day, his car sped past the plaza and almost collided with a *calesa*. On Easter, he still had not returned home from Manila.

"The townspeople speculated that something bad had happened. When there was news of a guerilla ambush in Bulacan, they thought he was the target. Their maid who came to the market was confronted by gossip-mongers whether de Silva was the victim in the ambush. The maid, who was Visaya, did not completely understand the Tagalog. She thought that de Silva was ambushed.

"She came home crying hysterically to her mistress. The mistress, Rebecca, equally became hysterical. The self-important people led by Pacing wanted to convey their sympathies, the sooner, the better. Since de Silva's stone house fronting his hacienda was quite a distance from town, they thought of hiring a bus.

"'Why not just go in a *calesa*?' Belen Villar asked.

"'You will arrive there the next day,' Pacing answered sarcastically.

"The ladies wanted a more stylish way of arriving, but the occupation authorities had requisitioned most cars. Only de Silva still had his. After pooling their resources, the group went by hired bus to the hacienda.

"By afternoon, they could not leave because of the pouring rain. Loud thunder startled them, and lightning lit the skies as another round of tea was being served. Suddenly, there was a knock on the door. The maid went to open it and started screaming,

"'Ghost! Ghost!' she screamed and ran to the kitchen.

"Rebecca stared at the large figure wearing a coat and fainted. The visitors looked at the figure and ran to the bus, getting soaked in the rain. Only Belen had the sense to ask.

"'Are you alive?'

"'Estupida!' the drenched Spaniard answered.

"The ladies could hardly contain themselves as they shivered on the way home. They were upset and embarrassed. It was Humberto alright. He was in Manila and had sent word about being delayed, but his wife did not receive the message.

"'I don't care! If he dies again, I will not attend his funeral!' Pacing was so flabbergasted."

Clara and Neneng alternated between being amused and appalled by the stories, but some were like mysteries. Faustina told them about Juling in Cabanatuan. Faustina could not send money regularly because, although Kulas was available at first, Kulas had recently suffered from pneumonia. Faustina had given permission for Juling to sell the curtains in Neneng's room.

"It's good that it's peace time now, or we might run out of curtains!" Faustina shook her head.

Clara was a little baffled that the curtains had to be sold. She thought there was something else to the story, but she would have to solve this one later.

Pilar the maid was not around. Mrs. Reyes told Clara that Pilar's husband was taken by the Japanese for interrogation and tortured. Carding, the husband, was merely a Huk sympathizer, not an active one, but word reached the Hukbalahap that he needed to be rescued. In a difficult rescue attempt, he died in the crossfire.

Although Pilar was faithful to the Fuentes family, there were days when she could not come to work, saddled by the care of her children and her mother, who was often sick. Without work, there was no food on the table. Clara was sympathetic to the problem, so she sent for Kulas to bring some rice and money to Pilar.

Pilar came the next day, bringing her niece Rosa, who could do the housework. Pilar was very thin, full of apologies, and crying.

"I was ashamed to ask."

"We are here to help each other," Clara assured her.

She realized that Pilar needed help long ago and should have asked for help earlier. She wondered what other problems were there and looked around her. This bright, sunny day, she noticed what had eluded her before: the surroundings were so worn out.

They had cleaned the floors, wiped off the dust, and washed the curtains when she and Neneng arrived, but there was no wax, and the curtains were old and faded. What they accepted without criticism earlier was bothering Clara now. They cleaned cupboards and threw away spoiled food. They inventoried their stockpile of old clothing, but it was hopeless. There were no clothing materials available in stores, so the ladies were all busy darning clothes and making do with repairs. It was going to be a long wait before the stores got new cloth.

Emong had not bothered to get new help, since it was all the same to him. His concern was the vegetable patch, which was growing vigorously.

Pilar's niece, Rosa, was a good worker, and after a week of cleaning, the ladies resigned themselves to the result. Neneng now had a chance to read at leisure, while Clara did some darning of beaten-up clothes. It was then that Clara and Neneng could no longer hide their anxiety about their men. There had been no word from them.

"It is time to go to Cabanatuan and check our house," Clara remarked. "Is it safe yet?"

"It should be. The next day should be fine. We will finish with the tenant accounts tomorrow," Emong said. "I will send for Pablo to drive the car."

"Thank you!" Clara said.

Clara and Neneng cried silently upon reaching Cabanatuan and seeing the bombed-out remains of the government buildings and military installations. The church and school were mostly intact, but the plaza pavilion looked lopsided, with half of it in ruins.

They had brought rice, vegetables, fruit, and preserved pork. Once more, there was a large amount of fixing and repairing to do. Juling was so happy to see them. Juling had kept the house clean, but it was the same story of worn-out furniture, no wax, and not enough soap.

Clara went to market the next morning with Juling. She could not believe there was such a shortage of food and supplies, and what prices! The stores on Rizal Avenue did not have what she needed either.

Her pharmacy was also practically empty. She went to the hospital and inquired where she could order some medicines. Her mind raced with all the expenditures of stocking up her pharmacy from scratch. Somehow, she had to order supplies, even if the order had to be hand-carried to Manila.

Coming back to Cabanatuan meant that Clara and Neneng had to attend to so many things at once and also catch up with the news. Clara almost dreaded seeing the families from Carlos's side. Clara had heard stories from some townsfolk while in the market. The de Leon family was among those who signed up early with the Huks, and Jose had visited Cabanatuan secretly to recruit men.

Fermin and Pacing had a hard time keeping Andong from going with Jose, but later on, Andong joined a guerilla group ran by a less-than-stellar leader, and he was killed when they attacked a Japanese garrison. On the other hand, their daughter Linda showed a liking for Jose, and Pacing had to admonish her daughter to stop secretly meeting Jose.

Although it was known that Andong had died as a guerilla, rumors had been swirling that Fermin, Pacing's husband, was a collaborator. There were also other business dealings that other people were questioning.

Pacing's family visited Clara's home the evening after Clara arrived.

"Many people are mad at me! I merely helped so the rationing of rice and sugar would be orderly!" Fermin said belligerently as they ate supper. "Andong had already died, would I get along with the Japanese?" he added, shaking his head.

Pacing was crying, and Clara and Neneng started crying too; Faustina merely frowned. Linda was silent.

"Others just don't have anything better to do!" Emong said.

"Oh! I know so much about people spreading lies!" Juling said as she almost spilled the chicken soup she was serving on Emong's shoulder.

"You are lucky you did not stay in town!" Pacing turned to Clara.

Clara had heard this comment before, and she just smiled serenely. In troubled times, people sometimes twisted the truth, and Clara listened to their side of the story and hoped for the best. Secretly, she wondered what would have happened if she had stayed in Cabanatuan. Some of the councilmen and even the mayor were under a cloud of suspicion.

Clara and Neneng also brought food for Father Gabriel, and there they met Sister Antonia. Father Gabriel's older sister had come to visit with a plan to open a girls' school for her Order. Sister Antonia had been delayed in presenting her findings to her Order in Manila, for she was instead diverted to help in the hospital.

"Come help in the hospital, there's so much to do!" she told Clara and Neneng.

"Yes, Sister, as soon as we can!" Clara promised, wondering how she would divide her time.

One look at Father Gabriel gave the visitors cause for worry. The priest looked so old and thin. He had been serving his parish alone ever since Father Ramos went to San Miguel a year ago and never came back. Nobody knew what really happened. Some said that Father Ramos was abducted by robbers, some said it was the Huks, and others said he was tortured by the Japanese. Father Ramos was going to visit his dying mother, and Father Gabriel only found out that Father Ramos was missing after Ramos's sister notified him that they had to bury their mother without waiting for Father Ramos.

The burden of the world's sins seemed to have fallen on Father Gabriel's shoulder. It was not just the Masses, baptisms, weddings, and sick visits that he had to do, he found the confessions more taxing, and this left him with a cynical look and sadness in his eyes. Then there was the problem of sanctuary when a guerilla hid in the church. There were rumors that Father had been tortured by the Japanese, but other people said it was the Huks. Most people believed he had been giving information to the guerillas.

"There are a lot of evil people," Father Gabriel said.

Clara waited for Father Gabriel to open up, but he only exchanged pleasantries with them. She glanced at Sister Antonia, who just nodded. Father Gabriel had stayed in Cabanatuan throughout the entire war, and there was so much he saw and knew.

Clara's visits with friends kept her updated.

"Two of my children died from diphtheria," Mrs. Cortez said sadly. "The disease started among the market vendors and their families, and it spread fast. Now my only son left is the one who became a guerilla with Captain Lapham's group."

"I'm glad I mostly stayed away from the market," Mrs. Plata chimed. "I'm thin from eating the vegetables from my garden, for I can't even afford the sugar ration. You are lucky you did not stay in Cabanatuan."

"And there were no medicines!" Lina Salgado said. "Look at my wound! It's not healed still. I got this when the bombs fell near the plaza. I was in a *calesa*, the horse got scared, and it ran so fast that we crashed against the electric pole. That bomb killed Councilman Paredes, who many people suspect was a collaborator."

Clara was a little guarded when Mrs. De Leon talked about other people but did not mention Jose. Most people avoided talking about the Hukbalahap movement. At least Clara had the satisfaction of serving them tea with honey and lemon, which she brought from San Nicholas. She decided to give the other bottle of honey to Mrs. De Leon.

Some people did not have enough money to buy food. Mrs. Plata used to have a beauty shop, but it was hit by a bomb. Clara gave her some rice, and Mrs. Plata wanted to curl their hair in return. Clara and Neneng did not want it, but Mrs. Plata persisted.

"Just a little wave," Clara and Neneng both said.

When a shipment of textiles arrived at Tan Commercial, Juling cut short her marketing to report it to Clara. The store owner was glad to help the first comers as a sign of good luck. Clara had her pick of different clothing and curtain materials. Her money was going to be short, but Mrs. Tan had no problem with Juling coming back with the difference. A group of ladies arrived when Clara and Juling were leaving with their bundles.

"Good morning!" Clara greeted the other ladies.

Only a few answered her—they resented the fact that she had gotten the first pick. She shook that off and worried instead about how to measure each piece of cloth carefully. Her sewing machine still worked, and she was thankful, but she wondered how to apportion her time.

Emong was enjoying himself. He had allowed the ladies to persuade him to stay in Cabanatuan until the next *palay* harvest. He used the spare room, while Juling had to sleep on the sofa in the living room.

Emong would take a morning walk to the church; then come back to the plaza to play table games with other men outside the coffee shops. Although he mostly played *damas* (checkers), he was learning to play chess, and he was proud when he beat a fellow beginner. Part of his enjoyment was in hearing all the news, rumors, and innuendos that drifted among the men.

The plaza was near the market, so he knew what went on there too. Sometimes he would bring home fresh meat, fish, vegetables, or out-of-season fruits.

One day, Emong went early to the plaza. He was playing *dama* when loud screams could be heard from the market. He and his friends rushed there. In the middle of the commotion, two men were having a fistfight. The onlookers started to take sides, when suddenly the bigger man pulled a knife. The audience scattered with screams of horror.

"Police! Police!"

The smaller man was wounded and fled toward the crowd, right where Emong and his friends were. The aggressor pursued his victim and raised his knife. Emong and his friends ran in different directions.

Emong arrived home on a run, one of his slippers missing. "Haah! Haah!" Emong was pale and could hardly speak.

Clara was receiving some pharmacy orders and left the drug agent to attend to her Kuya Emong.

"Fan him!" Faustina ordered Juling.

Clara wondered if he should be taken to the hospital when Emong finally spoke.

"Water!" he said.

Faustina was flabbergasted that she forgot to give him water. Clara also felt sheepish.

"I thought he would stab me!" Emong blurted.

It was already lunchtime, and they sat down to eat while Emong told his story.

"Ask around about what really happened," Clara told Juling on the aside, and Juling nodded.

Juling went to the market after lunch and then reported.

"It was a love triangle. The aggressor was the loser in the hand of a maiden. He ran after the smaller man that ran to Emong's group, and stabbed the smaller man again before the arriving police could stop him. The aggressor is in jail, but the smaller man is serious in the hospital."

Emong stopped going for his morning routine for the next two days; then his curiosity got the better of him, and he decided to rejoin his friends. His friends had started to come back too.

At mealtimes, Emong would update the family. They could only half believe what was going on. One suppertime, his story was so long-winded that the exhausted Clara nodded off at the table. She asked to be excused.

Emong was only temporarily taken aback. He enjoyed finding out exactly what happened to different people. He told them of their younger maid before the war, Tessie. She had gotten involved with a Japanese soldier, and then she could not really return home, so she decided to go to Manila. Lacking money, she sold the Mendez curtains. In Manila, she met an American soldier who was planning to marry her.

Clara looked at Juling, who merely nodded.

Sometimes Emong could coax his Aunt Faustina to come with him in his morning stroll, which would shorten his excursion but give him more satisfaction. One time, the two arrived just before lunch, laughing together.

"I'm sorry we ate all the *lanzones*, they were so sweet," he admitted sheepishly.

Clara and Neneng laughed too. It was good to see Faustina having fun even as she grew older. She looked better now that she had gained weight.

Clara made a mental note. From now on, their family would visit her Kuya Emong more often. It was good for everybody. She wondered why she had missed that. They would stay with her Kuya Emong at harvest time, and Emong should come over for feasts. He had been so unselfish in looking out for the rest of his family, but there were a lot of times when he was by himself in San Nicholas. Maybe the other families could visit more often too.

Neneng helped in the hospital as often as she could, and Clara started helping there one week later.

Most people in town were striving to put things back in order and fix the damages caused by the bombs. Two buildings near the barracks were being demolished, and the plaza pavilion and market needed repairs, yet people had a spirit of joyful anticipation as most of them helped.

Neneng and Clara thought that being too busy was why they were getting thin. True, they were always exhausted, but underneath the bustle, with each passing day both were worried they had not heard from the men. As though by silent understanding, they did not talk about their anxiety—but a gloom hung over them, and they did not have the appetite to eat. Each evening, they prayed through the night and were visited with bad dreams.

"Eat!" Faustina passed the rice to Clara.

Clara would have refused another serving, but her mother was looking intently at her. She put some rice on her plate and passed the rice to Neneng.

"Eat!" Clara told Neneng.

Neneng looked up at her mother's tone of voice. It was like a plea, and she understood. She put some rice on her plate too and decided to get another serving of the pork dish.

Clara was remembering her struggle to find meaning in life after leaving Balangiga. Her mother had always been able to read her mind and now she knew she had to look out for her daughter too.

XL

When the liberation forces came, Jack and his guerilla group were absorbed into a battalion headed by Colonel Watts. They went on to liberate the Cagayan Valley and were rewarded by the joy in the faces of civilians who were finally able to return home. The Americans had liberated large segments of Luzon already, but something eluded them. Lieutenant General Tomoyuki Yamashita and a large group of men under him had not surrendered.

The Allies knew Yamashita had planned all along to make his stand in the Cagayan Valley, an area bordered by three mountain chains: the Sierra Madre on the east, the Cordillera Mountains on the west, and the Caraballo Mountains on the south. An intelligence report speculated that Yamashita and his men were hiding somewhere in the mountains, but it was vague.

The plane searches had serious limitations due to the difficult terrain and large areas. Since that did not yield a positive result, the Allies followed up on leads from interrogations and started sending reconnaissance patrols to different locations in the mountains.

Jack was in a group of officers who backtracked toward the Baguio Mountains. He thought of Neneng, knowing she was waiting to hear from him, and he planned to send word that he was still tied up here. This was not familiar territory. They found nothing. A gnawing dissatisfaction pervaded the search team.

Colonel Watts followed another lead that took his team beyond Kiangan, Ifugao Province. They stood on a cliff overhang for a better view. Their back toward the mountain, they looked down the steep precipice at the tiny village below, the houses looking like specks. Beyond the village was another mountain; a winding road snaked up its side all the way to the top, where it seemed to end among the clouds.

Travelers to this region complained they were unable to see much beyond the next mountain. In the higher elevations, clouds could seem so near, and visibility might only be a few feet on a cloudy day. Accidents could easily happen after it had rained, for the already difficult road became slippery. The local people would be glad to advise travelers, but a lot of travelers did not ask for help. Definitely, travel was advised for daytime only, and on a good sunny day at that; for fog and mist would descend once the sun set, making traveling dangerous.

Watts pointed to the nearest mountain while holding the binoculars in his left hand. "Our units have searched that and found nothing," he said, shaking his head. "A long time ago, if you told me there were thousands of men hiding here, I would tell you I could easily find them."

Jack scanned the mountaintops with his binoculars. There was still a large forested area they had to check. He pointed to an area above the other mountain. "That might be worth searching. Why don't we send a well-equipped reconnaissance patrol?"

"That would be the best solution! You up to it?" Colonel Watts asked.

"I'm going!" Jack replied.

"Me too!" Captain Buendia replied.

Just then, they heard the screeching sound of an arriving jeep. A lieutenant jumped out of it and quickly saluted them.

"Lieutenant Egan reporting with an urgent message, sir," he said, handing Watts a note.

Perplexed, Watts returned the salute and scanned the note. "Our spies captured the brother of Yamashita's mistress. Under interrogation, he revealed that Yamashita's forces are in this region and planning to ambush our troops. Hmmm ... maybe we should get out of here first!"

Colonel Watts's jeep led the group heading back. Jack's jeep was right behind him, followed by Buendia's, then Egan's.

"It's getting cloudy and dark. It's only 2:00 PM. Is that rain coming?" Jack said to the private beside him, noticing that Watts's jeep had slowed down.

Watts's hand motioned a stop, and they all stopped as the rain started to pour. They all stayed in their jeeps as a spray of wind-blown rain soaked them. Darkness had fallen prematurely except when lightning streaked the skies.

The winding roads were mostly narrow, with sections of one-way traffic. The runoff from the rain caused rivulets of water to erode the shoulder, and Watt's jeep happened to be on the shoulder.

Jack could hear the young private's anxious breathing beside him, but Jack was looking at Watts's jeep. They had kept the jeep headlights on as they figured out what to do, but only after the last lightning did Jack notice something unusual with Watts's jeep. He grabbed a flashlight and beamed it on Watts's jeep. It was askew as the right tires sat on the eroded shoulder. He flicked the flashlight on Buendia's jeep as a signal.

"Rope!" Jack said to the private as he ran to Watts's jeep. Together, they tied one end to the back fender of Watts's jeep. Buendia and the private from his jeep came running and caught the other end and tied it to Jack's jeep.

"Jump out!" Jack shouted over the rain as the lieutenant beside Colonel Watts was slow in reacting.

The jeep was beginning to slip. Jack grabbed the lieutenant's hand and helped yank him out through the jammed door. Next he grabbed Colonel Watts's hand.

"Colonel!" Jack screamed as the jeep slipped from the shoulder and dragged the colonel and Jack with it. Jack's eyes widened with fear as they were briefly airborne, then plunged below. With a loud thud, the jeep got caught in a tree that grew from the side of a cliff, and the two men were on top of it.

Jack quickly got up from his awkward position at the back seat and touched the bump on his forehead that had hit the iron side of the jeep. He looked around and saw Watts immobile and face down on the front seat. Jack gingerly moved forward and felt for a pulse.

"Help!" Jack screamed.

The jeep had been caught in an overhanging tree; but Jack realized their precarious position when the branches groaned and creaked from the weight. Jack caught a big branch with one hand and grabbed Colonel Watts's arm with the other. He held them in a fork created by two branches and closed his eyes as the rumbling sound of the jeep breaking through the lower branches was followed by a crashing sound to the chasm below.

"Let it go!" Buendia yelled to the private, who was trying to untie the knot on Jack's jeep. "Oh God!" Buendia said and jumped out of the way as Jack's jeep careened toward the cliff—it was still tied to Watts's jeep.

The private was on his knees, bruised and shaken but glad he was not run over.

Lieutenant Egan came running with a rope and threw it to Jack in the overhanging tree. He turned to the private from Jack's jeep. "Can't see, beam the light there!" He helped the private focus the light and threw the rope again.

Jack caught it on the third try. "Watts is coming first. He must have hit his head on the jeep when we fell!" Jack shouted in the rain, whether they could hear him or not. He placed the rope around Watts's waist. "Careful!" he added after he tugged on the rope to signal.

"He's unconscious, take care of him," Buendia told the lieutenant driving Watts's jeep as he helped Egan throw the rope to Jack.

"Can hardly see," Egan said. "Wind and rain is stronger."

"There! There!" Buendia said, then, "Get me another light!"

The first flashlight was waning, the second worked only briefly, then all they could see were shadows in the rain. Buendia tried his hand in throwing the rope to Jack, but the wind blew it away. They tried placing a weight at the end of the rope, then putting a loop on it, but even if Egan's aim was better, it still was not good enough.

Jack looked up from his perch and realized it was getting futile. "We might just have to wait until after the rain, or for daylight."

"Oh God!" Buendia groaned.

"Can you hold on, sir?" Egan said worriedly.

"I'll try, that's the only option," Jack answered resolutely, but even he was not sure. That meant more than sixteen hours of waiting in the cold mountain, hanging onto a tree that was not so big. He just hoped it would hold his weight.

Camp John Hay, Baguio, Benguet Province

"That's all, gentlemen, have a good evening," the general dismissed his team and stood up from the conference table.

A captain hurried in with a salute, bearing a message.

"Hold on. Please be seated." The general said with a wave of his hand. "Lieutenant Egan confirmed arrival three hours ago, a garbled SOS came afterward, and no news after that." The general looked from the message to the map and frowned.

"Right, sir. Colonel Watts's team sent the SOS to the camp there, and I think the camp tried to cope with it for several hours before notifying us. The weather report confirmed that sudden, heavy rain fell on the area and continued for several hours." The captain looked grim.

"Could Yamashita's men have ambushed them, or did they have an accident?" the general said.

"It could be an ambush, but if the weather report said it rained, I'm leaning toward an accident," a colonel beside him said.

"If I may, General," a newly appointed major raised his hand. With a nod from the general, Major Lauro Delgado pushed his chair back and walked toward the charts and maps. "Whatever happened, we need a well-equipped rescue team. I doubt if our smaller base in Ifugao will have all we need. We can start from here now because it takes about nine hours to drive from here to there under good conditions. If it has rained, we will be crawling slowly, but we will be taking better equipment, a medical team, and we could try to be there even before sun-up. Certainly, daylight will help, but I'm worried they might need help as soon as possible."

"Alright, it's your task then, Major," the general said. "By the way, we have a lieutenant who grew up in the area."

"Right, sir. May I take Lieutenant Joaquin Dunuan then?" Delgado asked as he picked up papers.

"Yes, and good luck," the general answered with a nod.

"Thank you, sir!" Delgado turned to the captain who brought the message. "May I see the list of the soldiers we are rescuing?" As he looked at it, he turned grim. "Oh no!"

Jack clung to the branch as another lightning bolt streaked by. He tried to think constructively. *If I move to that bigger branch, I can sit with my back to the trunk and have a better anchor with that other branch. It might not be as easy to see me.* He edged slowly to the spot.

He felt hungry, but he had no food in his pockets so he slurped rainwater from his sleeve. It was darker still when the rain and lightning stopped and an engulfing white mist made him shiver. *Wake up! Do something!* Jack did not even want to look at the nothingness below, but he would surely fall if he fell asleep. *Better act fast!*

He slowly took off his pants while clinging to the branch with one hand. He groped for the belt and circled it around his arm. He transferred the contents of his pants pockets to his shirt pockets. He tied a double knot with one pant leg and one end of the belt, then tossed the end of the other pant leg to encircle the tree trunk. He gingerly groped for the end until he finally found it. He then encircled himself with the pant leg and tied it to the belt so he was tied to the trunk. Next he reached for his pocket knife and sliced both his sleeves from the wrist to the elbow. He tied the sleeve ends around a higher branch. He interlaced his fingers around it and could rest his head a bit sideways, but it was not so comfortable.

Through the night, memories marched like silhouettes among the fog. He prayed the Act of Contrition and said good-bye to his family, then he let himself dream of Neneng.

I love you.

By 7:00 PM, the medical team was ready in two ambulance vans. Two army trucks with armed personnel and more equipment were to precede them.

"Sir, if we think General Yamashita is in the vicinity, we need communication and back-up troops as soon as possible," Lieutenant Dunuan said worriedly.

"Yes, we have already mobilized for greater troop strength considering that Yamashita still has thousands of soldiers under him. The troops will be right behind us. We need to be at Colonel Watts's site because if it was an accident, they might need our help urgently," Delgado said.

"A long time ago, I would not have thought this was doable, sir, but the extra lights rigged by those engineers focus brightly several feet right in front of the trucks. It's really a great help," Dunuan said eagerly.

"OK. Dunuan, take the lead truck, I'm on the next. We will also rotate drivers to be sure there is no fatigue factor," Delgado said as he motioned for them to go.

The rain had stopped, but the narrow, winding roads were treacherous and slippery. It was 4:00 AM, and they were within sight when the lead truck stopped, and Dunuan signaled with his flashlight.

Delgado was fully alert and beginning to sweat from the tension, in spite of the damp cold. He signaled with his flashlight for the team to come down.

The rescue team brought out the portable lights and flooded the area with light. The narrow road was obviously not passable because of the eroded shoulder.

"It looks like the tire marks go off the shoulder," Dunuan said.

"Let's look down there," Delgado said, pointing with his flashlight. "A jeep! That's an army jeep!"

"There's another jeep. That makes two!" A sergeant beside him focused the light beam below, a little perplexed.

"More light!" Delgado ordered. "Are there bodies there? Doctor, stand-by! Sergeant, take a group to explore the other end of this road."

"That tree! It looks like there is something there. Is that a cloth or a body? Beam it over there!" Dunuan said excitedly.

"What? Let me see!" Delgado looked at the overhanging tree. "I'm going down. Ropes!" he said, more from intuition than from anything he saw.

"May I come too, sir? We also need blankets, just in case," Dunuan said and hurriedly caught up with Delgado, who was already tying the rope to his waist and grabbing a blanket into a knapsack.

"Yes, let's go! Tie the other end to the truck now! Stand by if we need help." Delgado adjusted his headlight and was ready to go down the cliff.

Delgado's strong arms and sure footing got him there first. He appreciated how Jack had tied himself to the tree, even if it made him harder to see from the road. Delgado looked anxiously at the slumped figure and gently felt for a pulse. He wrapped a blanket around Jack's shoulder and looped the rope on his upper body. He motioned to Dunuan as the latter arrived.

"He's passed out and feels cold, but he has a pulse," Delgado said worriedly.

They wrapped another blanket around Jack's lower body and tied another rope around it. Dunuan held Jack while Delgado cut the sleeve and the pant piece to free Jack.

"Let's cover his head too, it's rough getting pulled up there," he added, and he tugged at the rope.

Buendia sat on the front seat of his jeep, dozing on and off, trying to come up with ideas, and feeling guilty because of their inability to help Jack. The men in the two remaining jeeps finally turned their ignitions off and shivered in the cold. Colonel Watts was in the back seat of Egan's jeep, half reclined and covered with the blankets they had, still unconscious.

Buendia blinked when he saw a flickering light, then he rubbed his eyes to be sure he was not dreaming. He stared at the light until it became a moving beacon coming toward them.

"Help! Over here!" Buendia shouted, jumping from his jeep.

The others woke up and ran to meet the rescue team, grateful for their deliverance.

"Captain Jack Stewart is down there on a tree, over the cliff! Colonel Watts has been unconscious since he fell with the jeep down the cliff. We have him in the back seat of the other jeep. Hurry!" Buendia said excitedly.

"Major Delgado is there trying to get a soldier from a tree," replied the nurse.

"Can you take care of Colonel Watts? I want to help rescue Captain Stewart," Buendia said and ran to the other side.

The rescue team checked Colonel Watts. They put him on a stretcher and carried him to the ambulance.

XLI

The hospital was improvised. The Japanese had previously enlarged the small municipal hospital and added a surgical wing on the first floor. When the town was liberated, the nuns urged the carpenters to add an upstairs room to add more beds for pediatrics and general medical, and to accommodate more supplies.

At the farthest end of the new, lower wing was the infectious disease ward. The hospital chief ordered that they put the beds for the diphtheria cases in this ward. There seemed to be a resurgence of diphtheria among people who had evacuated to other areas. There was a special access to that ward through a separate entrance. A lot of organizing was needed, and the transition from one wing to another was usually bumpy. There were several army surgeons now and other medical personnel. Still, they could use more help.

Neneng worked in the surgery ward. Every day, she worried about Jack, and every day she prayed he would come back. She resolved to lessen her worrying and better care for herself by eating properly.

"Have mercy on Jack, oh God!" she prayed.

One day, she was asked by Sister Antonia to dress wounds in the surgical ward. The army surgeon would work on the newly operated cases with her assistance, but she would have to do the rest by herself. One of the surgeons was leaving, but the replacement had not arrived yet. There were two other ladies who helped in surgery, but one had left for Manila to find out how soon she could return to study nursing. The other one, Mimi, was reassigned to the pediatric ward by Sister Antonia. Neneng figured out why already. Mimi was a flirt, and Sister had watched the goings-on with a frown.

Dressed in a white uniform, a white cap hiding her curls, Neneng arrived earlier than usual. She had been given more and more responsibility when Sister Antonia realized she could dress wounds just like a doctor, business-like with no squirming. Today, she had to dress the wounded in Ward A, and in the afternoon she had to help decorate in the church.

She was on her last patient, trying not to worry about Jack. She hid her anxiety with a smile and quickly put away the bandages and medicines as soon as she finished.

A corporal on the next cot was reciting a poem to her, but she kept her head down.

Alas, oh nymph! Let the moonbeam bathe your face

that I may see it from this distance!

Lift my spirits with a glance,

Vanish my sorrow with your smile ...

A figure appeared in the doorway and, as though by telepathy, Neneng suddenly turned. Neneng left her tray by the bedside and ran halfway down the aisle, where Jack met her in an embrace.

"Jack!" she exclaimed, choked by emotion.

Unable to restrain himself, he held her tight and kissed her passionately. "My darling!" he said.

"Oh, Jack! Darling, I was so worried," she said between breaths. She noticed a bruise on his forehead. She touched it gently, and a tear fell, but she said nothing.

"We had a problem in the Ifugao region, but I'm alright," Jack said and held her tight.

"Hey, I'm still here!" a soldier in one cot protested.

"I was reciting my poem! Aren't you going to hear it?" the corporal chimed in.

"Sorry, guys!" Jack laughingly apologized as he removed Neneng's cap. "Enough of that!" he added.

Neneng shook her head and smiled. They held hands and ran upstairs to see Clara. They almost collided with Sister Lourdes, who was carrying a pail of water.

"Excuse me, Sister!" Neneng said, catching her breath.

Clara saw them coming as she walked down the hallway with a pile of bed linens. She put them down on a hallway chair and ran toward them.

"Jack! Thank God you are safe!" said Clara as Jack hugged her.

The three held each other as tears of happiness flowed freely.

"We want to get married now," Jack said suddenly to Clara.

"Huh?!" Clara said, startled, and she looked from one face to another.

"We would like to do it now, knowing that we don't want other factors to interfere with our plans. It's our life." Jack said seriously.

Clara realized they had given this thought. She was suddenly happy for them, and she smiled through her tears. "Now?" she asked gently.

"Yes!" Jack replied and held Neneng by her arm.

Neneng smiled a little shyly, but happily nodded her head.

Clara caught the attention of Sister Lourdes coming their way. "Sister, I need to go!" she said as Neneng tugged her hand.

Clara allowed them to lead her down the staircase, and the three half ran the length of the Avenida Rizal toward the church.

They were breathless when they got there.

"Father! Father!" Clara called as soon as she reached the rectory.

"Good morning, Mrs. Mendez," said Father Gabriel. He had heard the commotion. He had gotten up from his office desk and was already standing at the door.

"The children would like to be married now, Father," Clara said.

"Now?" he asked.

"I hope there's no problem with that, Father? We can go to the church now," Jack said seriously.

Father Gabriel looked from one face to the other and thought for a moment. "Come," he said as he led them to the church.

There were a few people in the church scattered among the back pews, each in their own prayers. Father Gabriel led them to the front of the main altar and opened his missal. Jack and Neneng held hands. Clara stood beside Neneng, holding back her tears.

Father Gabriel performed the ceremony solemnly. The pair followed every word he said.

"I, Victoria, take thee, John Jr. as my lawfully wedded husband," Neneng said.

"I, John Jr., take thee Victoria as my lawfully wedded wife," Jack said.

The two looked confused as they realized they did not have any rings to exchange. Clara took off the rings from her hands; her wedding ring she gave to Neneng to give to Jack; and John's ring she gave to Jack to give to Neneng. She looked very solemn, but she smiled. The two looked at her.

"They're yours now," she said softly.

Jack and Neneng put the rings on. Jack gently kissed Neneng on the lips, and she returned his kiss tenderly.

"I now pronounce you man and wife!" Father Gabriel said.

Then the priest congratulated them, and they all hugged each other happily.

"Will you join us for supper, Father?" Clara invited.

"Yes, I'll be there, my children," Father Gabriel replied.

The three walked home briskly. The women seemed to have gotten used to hurrying most of the time, because there were always lots of things to do. Jack and Neneng held hands, and Neneng held Clara with her other hand. The newlyweds seemed to walk on air, but they still walked faster than Clara, for Clara was crying with mixed feelings of happiness and loss.

She was surprised by the sudden turn of events. When Neneng and Jack did not have rings to exchange, she had given her rings with the generosity of a mother giving unselfishly to her children, but she had given away the ring that made life worth living in her darkest hours. She was wiping her tears when Neneng and Jack suddenly stopped, and Clara almost collided with her daughter.

Clara looked with consternation at her daughter, but both Neneng and Jack seemed to be listening to something. She paused and listened too.

"Mama!" Neneng said and tugged at the hand she was holding.

Clara nodded. They turned toward the commotion.

From a distance, beyond the church, they could hear the approaching band playing "Hands Across the Seas." A parade of American and Filipino soldiers marched behind them on the street.

People came out of their houses, and the women shrieked with joy. Then most people ran back into their houses to bring out their American and Filipino flags. They waved the flags frantically at the victorious troops.

"Victory!" shouted the men, flashing the V sign.

The children ran alongside the parade, laughing and singing with the band. A lot of people were overcome with emotion and lined the street with tears in their eyes. The cheering got louder as the band played "Stars and Stripes Forever" with gusto. Toward the tail end of the parade were the officers in open jeeps—and among them was John Stewart in his general's uniform, scanning the crowd with anxious eyes.

"Dad! Dad!" Jack shouted and waved.

John stood up excitedly. "See you after the parade!" he shouted back.

The three hurried to the town plaza where the parade was going to end. The entire city seemed to be in the plaza, the din of noise caused people to shout. People were chatting, laughing, and crying at the same time.

Usually shy, the townsfolk mixed with the soldiers, thanking them and trying to share their adventures from the war. Some looked for loved ones, others exchanged news. Little children ran back and forth, not understanding what it was about.

Jack dragged Neneng and Clara along with him as he rushed to the end of the parade. John Stewart jumped out of the jeep as soon as it stopped and embraced Jack. The father and son could not speak for a while—then finally Jack brought Neneng close, and she kissed John's hand.

"We just got married," Jack said.

"Good work, son," John said, then he paused as he saw their rings. He smiled and hugged them both.

Now he turned his full attention to Clara, who was smiling in a calm way. Just then, the twelve noon church bells started to toll, and they looked at each other.

"The bells must stop haunting us," Clara said.

John sensed the confusion from Jack and Neneng as he took Clara's hand and kissed it. He looked long into her eyes.

"You brought me hope when I was ready to die," John said softly.

Clara looked steadily at him as a tear fell down her cheeks. "Thank God you are safe, John. May God be with you always." She paused as she was overcome with emotion. "Good-bye," she said tenderly, almost in a whisper.

John took a step forward. Then he nodded with his jaw set, unable to utter a word.

Clara took her hands from his and brought the conversation to the family beside them. She introduced the newlyweds and John.

"Oh, Doray, how are you? Here's Neneng, she just got married."

The family of Doray Gamez congratulated them. "Juan recovered from malaria! Thank God! We evacuated to Juan's family farm near Mt. Arayat, but then my husband caught malaria. We finally got quinine from the guerillas," she added.

John's eyes were on Clara, but he made an effort to converse.

"I heard that some of our men, Captain Delgado among them, joined the guerillas near Mt. Arayat," he said.

"We heard of him! They teamed up with the liberation forces early, but I don't know whose division. We got Juan's quinine from their group!" Doray was excited.

"Major Lauro Delgado headed the rescue team when we had an accident, Dad," Jack said. "Delgado said he knows you."

"Glad to hear Delgado was there," John said, trying to hide his worry.

"Jack!" somebody called, and Jack turned.

"Ed! How'd you get here so fast?" Jack asked Buendia, and without waiting for his reply, Jack introduced Buendia to the enlarging circle of friends.

A few feet away, Pacing and Fermin heard the good news and joined their circle. Congratulations abounded.

Clara turned to Jack and Neneng. "I'll prepare lunch so it will be ready when you come," she whispered.

Neneng and Jack nodded happily.

Clara fled from the scene blinded by tears. She hurried away as conflicting emotions besieged her. Somehow, she managed to get home and saw her mother and Kuya Emong watching the fun in the streets.

"Neneng and Jack just got married. I'm preparing lunch," she said to them.

They nodded in approval.

"I'll call Juling," Emong said as he went down the inside staircase. "I'll get extra dishes from Liong's."

Clara somehow put on the rice, got the food out, and started cutting vegetables, but her tears kept falling. She had prayed for them all to survive this war, but she could not hide the fact that it was John who had worried her most. All she asked was for God to let him live, for her long-lost love to be happy somewhere, even if she was not going to be part of that life. In spite of the war and all the hardships, the thought of her love for John had made life so beautiful. There was no doubt she had no right to a married man, but her love surged back unbidden when she saw him, and she realized how bitter it was to give him up.

My daughter will now have the kind of happiness that had eluded me, she reasoned. There was so much to thank God for.

But God! Dear God! she thought. *It hurts so much to let John go!*

Faustina came quietly into the kitchen, for she had seen John in the parade. One look at her daughter and she knew. Clara started feeling faint, and she barely made it to the kitchen chair before she burst into tears.

Outside, the fireworks display started, and the band started to play again as the town took on a fiesta atmosphere.

Neneng, Jack, and John would arrive soon, and Clara and John would avoid each other's glances so as not to cloud the happiness of the newlyweds.

War Statistics

General Douglas MacArthur proclaimed the Philippines liberated on July 5, 1945.

On July 26, 1945, the Allies (U.S., Britain, and the U.S.S.R.) issued the Potsdam Declaration demanding that Japan surrender. Japan did not heed the ultimatum. The possibility of a bloody, prolonged war to defeat Japan was on the mind of the U.S. president.

On August 6, 1945, the first atomic bomb was dropped in Hiroshima.

On August 9, 1945, the second atomic bomb was dropped on Nagasaki.

On August 15, 1945, Japan surrendered.

General Douglas McArthur accepted the formal surrender of Japan aboard the USS *Missouri* on September 2, 1945.

Over fifty million died worldwide, ten times more than the deaths from World War 1 (1914–1918)

Two-thirds died in Europe; one-third died in Asia.

Japan lost 2.25 million people.

The United States lost 290,000 on all fronts.

1,111,938 Filipinos died in the war, out of a 1941 census of seventeen million. The relatively high ratio was attributed to its being the Southeast Asian country that resisted the Japanese the most.

In the Philippine land campaign, 10,380 Americans died, and 36,631 were wounded.

Lieutenant General Masaharu Homma

Lieutenant General Masaharu Homma was in command of the Japanese forces in the Philippines at the outbreak of the war. He was supposed to conquer the Philippines in fifty days; instead, it took him 150 days.

He was held responsible for the atrocities in the Bataan Death March, although the mortalities were actually due to disorganization, unforeseen numbers of surrendering Allies, and the mind-set of lower-level Japanese soldiers who were trained to be merciless and looked down on surrender as disgraceful.

Homma was actually charged with being lenient to Filipinos and was relieved of his duties on August 1942.

In 1945, he was tried as a war criminal and executed on April 3, 1946.

Lieutenant General Tomoyuki Yamashita

Lieutenant General Tomoyuki Yamashita, the Tiger of Malaya, was responsible for the invasion of Malaya and Singapore.

In a decisive victory against the British, his force of thirty thousand soldiers won against one hundred thousand British troops. The Japanese had more airplanes, and they used tanks and bicycles to rapidly overwhelm the British.

He replaced Lieutenant General Masaharu Homma when the latter was recalled to Tokyo.

He was the general in Luzon, Philippines, when the Americans came to liberate the archipelago, starting in October 1944. He differed in opinion with Field Marshall Terauchi about how to fight the American liberators; nevertheless, he obeyed. The Philippines was declared liberated even before Yamashita was captured.

Yamashita retreated with his troops to the mountains of Baguio and the Ifugao region, and surrendered only on September 2, 1945. He came out of the mountains at Kiangan, Ifugao, where a Memorial of Friendship had since been built.

He held himself accountable for the atrocities of his troops, even if he had been known to allay the overzealousness of some troops to kill American POWs.

He was tried for war crimes and executed on February 23, 1946. He remained loyal to his emperor.

Jose Abad Santos

Jose Abad Santos was a *pensionado*, one of those promising young men sent by the U.S. government to study in the United States. He finished law school at Northwestern University in Evanston, Illinois.

He was the Supreme Court chief justice when WWII broke out. Philippine President Manuel L. Quezon left him as head of the Commonwealth Government when Quezon and his vice president, Osmena, were evacuated by the Americans to Australia, then to the United States.

Jose Abad Santos refused to cooperate with the Japanese invading army. He fled to Malabang, in Mindanao. He was caught and executed on May 2, 1942.

The Congressional Medal of Honor

Only one Filipino was awarded the Congressional Medal of Honor. He was Sergeant Jose Calugas. He was a mess sergeant in Bataan when the Japanese soldiers were advancing. In spite of a barrage of enemy fire, he ran to an artillery gun and engaged the enemy, giving his fellow soldiers time to retreat. He was awarded the Medal posthumously.

Lieutenant General Jonathan Wainwright

Wainwright was a major general when WWII broke out. When General Douglas MacArthur was ordered to leave for Australia, Wainwright was promoted to lieutenant general and became the commander of U.S.-Philippine forces, stationed in Corregidor.

He rallied his troops as Bataan fell, but no help was coming. He had to surrender Corregidor in order to prevent a massacre; then he had to surrender the entire Philippines.

Most of the high-ranking U.S. and British POWs became slave laborers in various Japanese camps. They were in Sian, Manchuria, when news broke that the war was over.

Some books after the war unfavorably depicted Wainwright because of the surrender. He was awarded the Congressional Medal of Honor by President H. Truman.

Malaria and Quinine

In World War II, malaria wrecked havoc among the soldiers fighting in tropical countries, especially where there were swamps swarming with infected mosquitoes, the vectors of disease.

Malaria is caused by a protozoa—a single-celled organism—of the *Plasmodium* genus. There are four species: falciparum (the most severe), vivax (recurrent), ovale (recurrent), and malariae (quartan). The plasmodium has a life cycle that rotates from the female anopheles mosquito to the human host and back again to the mosquito.

The female anopheles mosquito is the potential carrier of the plasmodium, and it feeds at night on the human host. If the mosquito is infected with the plasmodium, it injects the sporozoite stage of the plasmodium into the bloodstream as it feeds. At the same time, if it bites an infected person, the mosquito takes the gametocyte stage of the plasmodium from that person's blood. The plasmodium goes through the sexual stage of its life cycle in the mosquito and is in the sporozoite stage when the mosquito injects it to the human host.

The sporozoites enter the blood and attack the liver, where it multiplies, bursts out; then attacks the red blood cells. The cyclical fever in malaria coincides with this rupture of red blood cells, expulsion of debris, and presence of toxic materials circulating in the blood. The severity depends on which species is the cause, and sometimes a person can harbor several species. Fever, chills, headache, nausea, abdominal pain, jaundice, black urine, delirium, encephalopathy, coma, and death can occur. The liver and spleen are enlarged, the kidney can go into renal failure, and in falciparum infections, the brain is severely affected.

The treatment for malaria is quinine. Quinine is extracted from the bark of cinchon trees.

Long ago, the Indians in Peru used it for many purposes, including fever and shivering from cold. The Spaniards colonizing Peru were suffering from different tropical diseases for which they sought a cure. Agostino Salumbrino, a Jesuit Brother who was also an apothecary, was in Lima, Peru, when he observed the Indians using the bark as medicine. He sent the medicine to Rome, where malaria was wrecking havoc because of the surrounding, mostly stagnant water.

Whereas before, Popes and cardinals had succumbed to malaria, by 1631, quinine was used as treatment. The treatment became widespread after it was used on the Duchess of Cinchon and Charles II of England.

Quinine became a major export from Peru to Europe, the "Jesuit's powder" causing conflict between governments. Finding an opportunity to benefit from the huge demand, the Dutch bought prohibited seeds and planted them in Java; the British also smuggled prohibited seeds and planted them in India and Ceylon.

The Dutch dominated the trade, but when this asset fell into Japanese hands in World War II, the Allies' supply of antimalarials was compromised.

The Bells of Balangiga

The three bells from the church in Balangiga were taken as war booty. American soldiers returned to punish the town following the massacre of Americans in September 28, 1901. The church was burned to the ground.

Of the bells that were taken, the smallest bell was taken by the Ninth Infantry Regiment to Tongduchon in South Korea. The Eleventh Infantry Regiment, known as the Wyoming Volunteers, executed the reprisal ordered by Brigadier General Jacob Smith. They took the other two bells to Wyoming, where these bronze bells are on a brick monument at the main flagpole of the F.E. Warren Air Force Base in Cheyenne.

In 1997, then–Philippine President Fidel Ramos made a formal request to the U.S. government for return of the bells. There were previous requests for the bells from Filipino groups, but there had also been an adamant refusal to return them from groups who carried the torch for those Americans who had been massacred.

The American sentry, Adolph Gamlin, who was cut down by the police chief, survived. His daughter was reached by those requesting the bells be returned to the Philippines. Her polite answer was equivocal. Until her father died, he had recurrent nightmares and would scream, "They are coming! They are coming!"

Presently, a commemorative stone stands in Balangiga, Samar, to mark that event.

The 'Bells' have not been returned.

Japan

Japan, an Asian archipelago in the north Pacific, has four main islands: Hokkaido, Honsho, Shikoku, and Kyushu. Its people first came into contact with Westerners when Portuguese sailors washed ashore after a shipwreck near Kyushu in 1543.

From then on, trading ships started coming. At a time when missionary zeal was strong in the Catholic countries of Portugal and Spain, missionaries often came with trading ships and involved themselves in social relief work and medical care for the people. St. Francis Xavier, a Jesuit, arrived in Kagoshima in 1549 and stayed for two and a quarter years.

The exchange of Eastern and Western ideas was beneficial to both, and the Portuguese were able to persuade the local lords, called *daimyo*, to allow the missionaries to preach. Eventually, three *daimyos* and a number of peasants from Kyushu converted to Christianity.

The Japanese were a very proud people, and a transition from the period of shogun dominance was beginning. The Western powers were eager to open trade relations, even if most of Japan was unwelcoming of foreign influence. In 1853, Commodore Matthew Perry headed an American naval squadron that docked in Edo (Tokyo) Bay. U.S. President Franklin Pierce wanted to trade with Japan and also requested that hospitality be extended to shipwrecked sailors. Although the negotiations took time, the United States got its foothold in Japan.

In 1868, the Meiji reign marked Japan's emergence from the age of feudalism. Henceforth, the Japanese recognized an emperor they revered almost as a god. Their constitutional monarchy mandated the Diet as a legislative body, and the pattern of governance had a strong Western influence.

Among the privileged, however, there was dissatisfaction at the slow pace of modernization. The oligarchy recognized that for Japan to survive, it had to modernize fast. Along with modernization came industrialization, and an accelerating demand for steel, oil, and other imports. Japan got its steel from the United States and its oil from the Dutch East Indies. To assure its supply, the idea of expansionism took hold among the elite. Soon, Japan claimed the islands to its south: Okinawa and the Bonin islands.

Japan pitted itself against Russia for the Sakhalin and the Kurile islands to its north. In a compromise, the Kurile Islands went to Japan, and the Sakhalin went to the Russians.

By 1894, knowing that Korea was like a vassal to China, Japan agreed with China that neither of them would do anything pertaining to Korea without letting each other know first. When Korea notified China of a need to crush a rebellion, China notified Japan, and Japan sent troops to Korea to crush the rebellion. The Japanese troops did not leave after the incident was over; instead, the Japanese appointed a puppet government in Korea.

China was undergoing internal upheaval in the late nineteenth century, just as foreign powers were trying to get concessions from it. England had been granted a lease over Hong Kong; Japan got Formosa (Taiwan); and the Russians were given the right to Port Arthur in Lushan.

Meanwhile, in the West, Spanish colonies were hankering for freedom. The United States was sympathetic to the Cubans, who were trying to gain freedom from Spain in 1898. When the USS *Maine*, an American vessel anchored in Cuba, was sunk, the Americans blamed the Spanish and entered the war. The United States won, gaining dominion over Cuba and Puerto Rico.

Commodore George Dewey's Asiatic Squadron was in the Hong Kong vicinity, already primed for action by then–Assistant Naval Secretary Theodore Roosevelt. When Dewey received orders to engage the Spaniards in the Philippines, he was in Manila Bay by April 30, 1898, and by noon on May 1, he had defeated the Spanish fleet. His squadron guarded the Bay until the U.S. soldiers arrived three months later.

The Treaty of Paris in late 1898 settled the Spanish-American War. The United States paid $20,000,000 to Spain, and the Philippines came under United States dominion. The United States also obtained islands in the Pacific that used to belong to Spain. However, Germany was also interested, so Germany bought the Pacific islands the United States got from Spain: the Caroline Islands, the Marshall Islands, and two of three islands in the Marianas, Tinian and Saipan. The United States kept Guam.

While Spain was crumbling, so was China. In 1900, because of different foreign powers trying to dominate China, a Chinese rebel group formed. Called the Righteous Fist of Harmony (Boxers), they laid a siege to the foreign embassies, but to no avail. Japan led the rescue in Tientsin, and Russia led the rescue in Peking.

In 1904, Japan attacked the Russians in Port Arthur (Lushan, China), and in May 1905, they again attacked the Russians in Tsushima Strait and won.

Japan and Russia seemed to be mired in a war. U.S. President Theodore Roosevelt played the intermediary as the two nations finally settled in the Treaty of Portsmouth, signed in New Hampshire in 1905. For this, Roosevelt was awarded the Nobel Peace Prize.

In the settlement that followed, Japan got possession of Port Arthur and the southern half of Sakhalin Island. Japan was not awarded any cash, for which it was unhappy and blamed the United States.

When World War I broke out, Japan allied itself with England and the United States against Germany. When the war ended, the Treaty of Versailles assigned to Japan the trusteeship of the islands in the Pacific that used to belong to Germany. These were the Marianas islands, Tinian and Saipan (the United States kept Guam), the Caroline Islands, and the Marshall Islands. Japan also obtained German holdings in China.

The United States had Hawaii, Midway, Guam, and the Philippines in the Pacific, with islands under Japanese dominion in between. Pearl Harbor was the primary U.S. Navy base in the Pacific.

In 1921, a Washington Naval Conference was called by President Warren Harding. The idea was to limit the expansion of naval fleets. The United States, Britain, and Japan agreed on a 5:5:3 tonnage ratio for battleships, aircraft carriers, and cruisers. Britain had a total of 580,000 tons, the United States had 500,000 tons, and Japan had a total of 301,000 tons. There were grumblings in Japan.

U.S. Secretary of State John Hay pushed for the Nine Power Treaty in 1922. The agreement between the USA, Britain, France, Japan, Portugal, Italy, Belgium, the Netherlands and China sought to adopt an Open Door Policy whereby nations should have equal rights and access to Chinese ports. It reiterated a respect for the independence of China.

In 1929, Japan was in need of resources from China. China was in turmoil. Suddenly, the Manchurian Railway, which belonged to

Japan, was bombed. Japan used the excuse of protecting its citizens and property to invade Manchuria (1931). China complained to the League of Nations. The League of Nations agreed, but it did nothing.

Several radical military officers were not satisfied with the pace of Japanese Imperial expansion. In 1936, they staged a mutiny and killed two of Emperor Hirohito's advisers, a third was wounded.

Major General Tomoyuki Yamashita, a rising star in the military, negotiated the surrender of this radical group. Its members committed suicide.

By July 1937, heightened tensions between the Chinese and Japanese led to a shootout at Marco Polo Bridge near Peking. With an established springboard in Manchuria, Japan attacked China.

That year, even Admiral Yamamoto could not dissuade the hawks in the military from their planned expansion of the naval fleet. Diplomatic talks with the United States and Britain did not work, and Japan built the battleships *Yamato* and *Musashi*, each weighing seventy-two thousand tons.

FDR ordered the U.S. Navy fleet to stay in Pearl Harbor in April 1940.

Meanwhile, in Europe, Germany staged its Anschluss, or union with Austria, on March 13, 1938. Then the Germans marched on to Czechoslovakia. In 1939, Germany invaded Poland, provoking England and France to come to Poland's aid because of a prior treaty. In June 1940, the Germans marched into Paris.

Japan had proclaimed a Greater East Asia Co-Prosperity Sphere in July 27, 1940. As the war spread in Europe, Japan joined the Axis of Germany and Italy on September 27, 1940, signing the Tripartite Pact. Other countries that wanted to halt the communism being sponsored by Russia, signed with the Axis Powers: Hungary, Romania, Slovakia, Bulgaria, and Yugoslavia.

The Germans went on to take the Netherlands, Norway, and Greece. England was under constant bombardment. In early 1941, the Germans invaded Yugoslavia and northern Africa.

Japan kept its eye on China but was wary of Russia, so Japan and Russia signed a Non-Aggression Treaty on April 1941. By June, Germany turned against Russia.

On December 7, 1941, at 7:45 AM Hawaii time, Japan bombed Pearl Harbor. Three hours later, they attacked the Philippines.

The Philippines

The Philippines was an unwilling pawn in the Western world's intrigue for power.

In 1453, Constantinople fell to the Turks, interrupting the trading routes between West and East. At that time, the Europeans had become used to the exotic things that came from the East, including the silk and spices that had become part of their daily lives.

The northern and central routes were closed by the Turks, but they let the Venetians use the southern route for a fee. Aware of the lucrative return on goods from the East, European powers raced to find alternate routes.

As early as 1421, the Portuguese had been exploring the African coast. Encouraged by Prince Henry the Navigator, the Portuguese sailed west and south across the seas, ushering in the Age of Discovery.

In Spain, after Queen Isabella and King Ferdinand vanquished the Moors in January 1492, their power grew when Christopher Columbus "discovered" the New World. Columbus thought he was somewhere in the East, thus calling the natives Indios (from India).

Columbus landed on Watling's Island in the Bahamas on October 12, 1492, and from there, Spanish colonization of the rest of South America and part of North America proceeded.

In 1498, Vasco da Gama rounded the Cape of Good Hope. Soon, the Portuguese went by this route to India and the Far East, establishing lucrative trade routes, dominating the spice trade to Malacca (in present-day Indonesia), and establishing trading posts and colonies in Africa.

The honor and prestige of discovering new lands sparked a contest among the European powers. The rivalry for influence between Portugal and Spain was mediated by Pope Alexander VI in the Treaty of Tordesillas (finalized in 1498). Henceforth, the demarcation would be an imaginary line at 370 leagues west of the Cape Verde Islands, running from the North Pole to the South Pole.

All lands discovered west of this line would belong to Spain, and all lands discovered east of this line would belong to Portugal.

In 1518, Ferdinand Magellan, a disgruntled Portuguese, went to King Charles I of Spain. The monarch, called Carlos Primero in Spain and grandson to Isabella and Ferdinand, was known as Charles V throughout Europe. He was the Holy Roman Emperor after inheriting the Hapsburg holdings from his paternal grandfather, Emperor Maximilian I. Magellan brought a globe and convinced the king to give him ships that would reach the East.

Magellan left the Port of San Lucar de Barrameda on September 20, 1519, with five ships: *Trinidad, San Antonio, Concepcion, Victoria,* and *Santiago.* They went west through the Atlantic Ocean, then headed south toward South America and sailed into the Pacific Ocean through a strait that later would be called the Strait of Magellan. From the start, the journey was difficult. The *Santiago* was shipwrecked in South America and the *San Antonio* deserted.

Aside from these problems, the journey was also marked by mutinies, illnesses, lack of food, and misadventures on islands they passed. The remaining three ships crossed the Pacific Ocean and came across the Southeast Asian islands.

On March 17, 1521, Magellan "discovered" the Philippines. The Spaniards landed the next day and subsequently came into contact with the natives. Magellan called the islands San Lazaro because it was the feast day of Saint Lazarus. On March 31, 1521, Easter Mass was celebrated by the Spaniards with friendly natives and their chieftain. On this occasion, Magellan claimed the islands for Spain. As the Spaniards got to know the different islands, with their own tribes and chieftains, they spread Christianity. On April 15, in the island of Cebu, eight hundred natives were baptized. The Chieftain, Rajah Humabon, and his wife were given Christian names, Carlos and Juana. Magellan gave a statue of the infant Jesus as a gift.

In a short span of time, however, seeds of enmity spread among the natives against the Spaniards. Some of the sailors were accused of rape, stealing, and other abuses; some chieftains refused to be friendly. Oblivious of the smoldering dislike, Magellan got involved in a dispute between two chieftains. He offered to fight for one chieftain against another named Lapu-lapu. In a battle on the shores of Mactan, near Cebu, the natives led by Lapu-lapu prevailed, and Magellan was killed. The other Spaniards escaped by going back to their boats.

Whereas the natives once thought the Spaniards were invincible, now the Spaniards' vulnerability was exposed, and the natives united to continue the attacks. The Spaniards took stock of their chances and decided to scuttle the *Concepcion*. The survivors on the two remaining ships sailed southwest until they came upon one of the Moluccas Islands and loaded up their ships with spices. They decided to go back to Spain along different routes.

The *Trinidad* sailed east, got caught in a storm, and landed back in the Moluccas. There, the Portuguese captured the Spanish sailors and held them prisoners. The *Victoria*, led by Sebastian del Cano, sailed west, rounded the Cape of Good Hope, and arrived in Spain on September 6, 1522.

Thus was proven that the East could be reached by sailing west and that the earth is round. Moreover, since the spices gave a very good return, the cost of the expedition ceased to be a deterrent. The significance of the expeditionary findings gave Spain a large advantage, both in political sphere of influence and economics.

The Philippines, an archipelago of more than seventy-one hundred islands, was not a country then. Although there were dark, short aborigines who lived in the mountains, the majority of Filipinos were of the brown Malay stock. These later immigrants had come to the islands from Indonesia and mainland Asia in several waves of migration. Most inhabitants lived in villages run by tribal leaders. There was an ongoing trade with Chinese, Indian, and Arab merchants, and the intermarriage within these groups accounted for the varied traits seen in Filipinos.

The islands are lumped into three large regions: Luzon (north), Visayas (middle), and Mindanao (south). In Luzon, distinct groups of Malayan immigrants occupied specific regions with their peculiar dialects (Tagalog, Pangasinan, Ilocano, Kapampangan, etc.). Most of the Visayas could understand each other, but in the south, the later immigrants were Muslim, with stronger ties to their brothers in the south than to their countrymen to the north.

Several Spanish expeditions followed after the *Victoria* returned, but these failed to establish a foothold in the islands until the reign of Philip II, son of Charles I. Because the vast Spanish empire was still expanding, some decentralization required that subsequent expeditions to the Philippines would depart from Mexico.

Miguel Lopez de Legaspi sailed west from Mexico with four ships (*San Pedro*, *San Pablo*, *San Lucas*, and *San Juan de Letran*) and arrived in the islands in March 1565. They were not able to land in Cebu at first, as the natives were hostile. They needed food and landed in islands that were friendly: Leyte, Samar, Limasawa, Camiguin, Butuan, and Bohol. On each island, Legaspi performed a blood compact with the chieftains, thus establishing a mutual pact of friendship.

As their scouts reported there was abundant food in Cebu, Legaspi ordered his men to take Cebu by force. As the Spaniards prevailed, the chief, Tupas, burned his village and fled. The Spaniards started a settlement in Cebu and found the statue of the infant Jesus among the ruins. This is why the infant Jesus is the patron saint of Cebu.

Legaspi decided to send the *San Pedro* back to Mexico to report on their success. Father Andres de Urdaneta was to pilot the return voyage, and the priest ordered that they sail northeast in an arc. Upon reaching California, they sailed directly south to Mexico (October 1565). A new route was thus established and later would be used for the Galleon Trade.

Whereas other expeditions after Magellan had failed, Legaspi's leadership and fair dealings with the natives were invaluable in gaining their trust. Soon, the 380 Spaniards successfully established settlements, and the six missionary priests among them spread Christianity.

Legaspi enforced good discipline among his men, and they tried not to forcefully take food from the natives. When food supply became a problem, they scouted for food elsewhere and subsequently established another settlement on the island of Panay.

As they heard of richer Muslim kingdoms to the north, Legaspi sent expeditions under Martin de Goiti and Legaspi's grandson, Juan de Salcedo. Augmented by friendly natives, the two conquerors subdued the tribes to the north and south of Luzon Island. Of particular importance was the strategic location of a settlement facing a bay, called *may nilad*, meaning there were nilads, a plant that thrives in the bay. The chieftain was Rajah Sulayman. He fought against the Spaniards and was killed. Legaspi decided to make this area his capital and called it Maynila (Manila). Legaspi named the islands the Philippines after the Spanish King, Philip II.

Spain conquered lands, but it also spread Christianity. After three hundred years under Spain, most Filipinos were Catholic, except for areas in the southern region that were Muslim.

The foundation of Islam in Sulu was laid by the Arab missionary and scholar Karimal Mahdum, who arrived from Malacca in 1380. A prince from Sumatra, Rajah Baginda later invaded Sulu to further advance Islam. Baginda's daughter, Bramisuli, married another prince from Sumatra, Abu Bakr, who further spread Islam around Sulu. In mainland Mindanao, Sharif Kabungsuan, who came from Malaysia in 1472, spread Islam in Cotabato.

Under the Spanish, the Philippines was administered through Mexico, and communication in the vast Spanish empire took a long time. The Philippines was part of the Galleon Trade whereby the government traded Mexican silver for Chinese silk and other merchandise.

The Spanish governmental system was oppressive to Filipinos. Philippine lands were apportioned for the Spaniards to administer, and although the intent was paternalistic, greed and ineptitude caused the Filipinos to become tenants on their native lands. There was no organized public schooling for children until 1863, but then again, the church controlled the curriculum. The little teaching Filipinos received was mostly the recitation of prayers. They were not taught Spanish as a language; they were even discouraged from speaking in Spanish. There was no encouragement for ideas or active thought, just rote learning of published text. Most Filipinos did not have rights; most suffered injustices without hearing or appeal. Worse, a lot of the abusers were friars of the Dominican and Franciscan Orders. They used religion as a weapon to subjugate the ignorant.

Justice was very slow, if it came at all. Complaints hardly reached Spain; even those that reached Mexico seem to fall on deaf ears. Administrative corrections, grievances, and injustices took long to be redressed. The Filipino was far down on the scale of human rights.

After centuries of oppression, a middle class gradually developed. These were the families who somehow learned to prosper by working with what opportunities were available. They spent money for their children's education, and by 1880, some children were sent to Madrid or other places in Europe to study. Away from the Philippines, they realized the iniquities they had long suffered, and they agitated for reform.

They were joined by some Spaniards and Spanish mestizos, who disapproved of the injustices and had come to love the Philippines as home. Among these were three priests who were charged with treason, and in spite of an inadequate hearing, were executed in 1872. The death of the three priests, Fathers Burgos, Gomez, and Zamora (Burgomza), did not instill fear; instead, it awakened the fervor of nationalism.

Dr. Jose Rizal, a Chinese mestizo who studied in Madrid, was a physician (ophthalmologist), philosopher, linguist, novelist, essayist, and poet. Most importantly, he wrote two novels that painted in vivid scenes the oppression and suffering of his people. Rizal's family had also been persecuted. When he was ten years old, his mother was accused of trying to poison the wife of a cousin. She protested by saying that she was just helping. Without a hearing, she was made to walk ten miles from Calamba, Laguna, to her prison in Santa Cruz, Manila. It took two and a half years of appeals to the highest court before the case was resolved.

Rizal's older brother Paciano advised Rizal to change his last name from Mercado to Rizal to protect his family as he became more controversial. Rizal had seen people who were accused of crimes, real or imagined, being humiliated and not having a fair trial. All around him there were abuses and injustices that people spoke about in hushed tones.

Rizal studied mostly in Madrid but circulated throughout Europe. There were times when he lacked funds; and once, in despair, he threw the manuscript of his novel in the fire. As he came to his senses and hope returned, he retrieved it, labored on, and with the help of friends, was able to have the novels published: *Noli me Tangere* (*Touch Me Not*, Berlin, 1887) and *El Filibusterismo* (*The Filibuster*, Ghent, 1891). The fervor among Filipinos to fight for freedom became stronger.

Upon his return to the Philippines, Rizal formed a civic league, La Liga Filipina, on July 3, 1892. On July 7, he was arrested, and on the fifteenth, he was exiled to Dapitan on the southern island of Mindanao. There, he practiced his medicine, built schools, did some farming, and built a water system.

Rizal also started a relationship with Josephine Bracken, the stepdaughter of a patient. It is possible to assume they were not allowed to have a Catholic wedding because of Rizal's writings against the friars, his questions regarding Catholic teaching, and his association with Freemasons.

When Rizal was arrested on July 7, 1892, another group formed that same night. Although sporadic uprisings against Spain had been occurring as early as 1572, this group formed by Andres Bonifacio and his friends was more organized and getting ready for an armed revolt. They called it Katipunan. (KKK, Highest and Most Respected Association of the Sons of the Nation).

Rizal's idea was for a peaceful reform; but the KKK favored armed revolt. Rizal refused several overtures to join, but while he lived peacefully in the south, several skirmishes with revolutionaries were going on in Manila. To further avoid being involved, Rizal petitioned Governor General Blanco that he be sent as a surgeon to Cuba, where there was an outbreak of yellow fever. Rizal was on the way there, but before he could reach his destination, Governor General Blanco had been replaced by Governor General Polavieja, who was unsympathetic to Rizal. Rizal was instead brought to Barcelona and returned home to the Philippines. He was tried for sedition, found guilty, and sentenced to execution. He was imprisoned at Fort Santiago, and it was there that he wrote the poem "Mi ultimo Adios" (My Last Farewell).

On December 30, 1896, Rizal was brought to Bagumbayan (present-day Luneta) to be executed. He was blindfolded and told to face away from the firing squad, like a traitor. As the shots rang, he turned to face the rifle fire, proud to die for his country.

Although the rebel groups were becoming more cohesive, there was infighting, and the emerging leader was General Emilio Aguinaldo. In time, Bonifacio lost the leadership, and on May 10, 1897, Bonifacio and his brother were shot to death.

In May 1898, when Commodore Dewey won in the Battle of Manila Bay against the Spaniards, the Filipino rebels thought the Americans had saved them and would leave. Aguinaldo declared Philippine independence on June 12, 1898, at Kawit, Cavite. The provisional Filipino government had an inauguration in Malolos, Bulacan, on January 23, 1899.

The U.S. government however, had other plans. There had been some sense of expansionism when the United States took Midway Island as early as 1867, followed by uninhabited Wake Island in 1898. In the Treaty of Paris, signed on December 10, 1898, the United States paid Spain $20 million for the Philippines and groups of islands in the Pacific.

When the Filipinos realized they had new masters, they directed their rebellion against the Americans. Uprisings were widespread as there was now a more conscious nationalism.

The rebellion's commanders were mostly in the provinces of central Luzon, and the infighting among its leaders continued. General Antonio Luna was a good general, but he did not play politics. Some men loyal to Aguinaldo felt threatened by the other general's success, and Luna was assassinated by Aguinaldo's men in Cabanatuan, Nueva Ecija, on June 5, 1899.

The Americans established themselves in due time. General Arthur MacArthur (father of Douglas MacArthur) captured Malolos, Bulacan, on March 31, 1899. Aguinaldo escaped and moved his headquarters to Palanan, Isabella. A message from Aguinaldo was intercepted from a captured soldier by General Funston's men. After asking permission from the military governor (General Arthur MacArthur) to move in, Funston captured Aguinaldo on March 23, 1901.

Some Filipino generals continued to fight afterward, like General Miguel Malvar in Batangas and General Lukban in Balangiga, Samar. Atrocities were committed by both sides, but with limited resources, the Filipinos soon surrendered or were killed. The United States declared the insurrection over in 1902.

It took years of benevolence to win the Filipinos over. Whereas before, public education was limited, the church controlled the curriculum, and the sons of the wealthy had to go to Europe for further education, under the Americans, public education was more available, schools really sought to educate, and the University of the Philippines was open to the bright Filipinos who would be future leaders.

Teachers from the United States volunteered. They arrived with the zeal to educate, and they trained future teachers. By 1927, 99 percent of the teachers were Filipinos. Whereas the University of Santo Tomas was established since 1611, there was no public university until the University of the Philippines opened in 1908. The U.S. government also started a program to send promising young men as scholars (*pensionados*) abroad, and this bred future leaders of the country.

The U.S. government also took measures to build a country that could defend itself by training Filipinos for the armed forces and establishing facilities to make this possible. Fort (William) McKinley at the south end of the Pasig River was an army training ground. An air base and training ground for the Philippine Scouts was established in Fort Stotsenberg in Pampanga. There was Camp John Hay in Baguio; and there was Nichols Air Base south of Manila.

Laws were passed to give increasing autonomy to the islands. The Philippine Bill of 1902 allowed the Filipinos to form the Philippine Assembly. The Jones Bill in 1916 provided for a legislature with senators and congressmen, and it promised eventual independence. As early as 1933, the Hare-Hawes-Cutting Act was going to set a date for Philippine independence. It also would have excluded Philippine farm products from their previous tax exemption upon entering the United States. Manuel L. Quezon, then aspiring to be the leader, talked this bill down, and it did not pass the Philippine Legislature. Quezon then went to the United States, apparently to plead the Philippine cause. The subsequent passing of the Tydings-McDuffie Act in 1934, which was essentially the same as far as Philippine interests were concerned, made Quezon look like a hero to the less informed, and he went on to become the first president of the Philippine Commonwealth.

Quezon was evacuated by the Americans when World War II broke out. He died in the United States before the war was over, and he was briefly succeeded by his vice president, Sergio Osmena. After Philippine independence was granted by the United States on July 4, 1946, the first president of the Philippine Republic was Manuel Roxas.

The Japanese Timetable versus the Allied Counteroffensive

The Japanese plan for the domination of Asia had a timetable; yet even in the most carefully laid plans, unforeseen factors can cause an unpredictable outcome. At the time that the Japanese bombed Pearl Harbor, Admiral Yamamoto was already dissatisfied that, by some fluke, a few American naval vessels had escaped destruction. One of these was Admiral Halsey's.

Lieutenant General Tomoyuki Yamashita had overrun British Malaya and Singapore by February 1942. Yamashita's soldiers had used bicycles in some cases when road conditions warranted it. With a fierce lightning attack, innovation, and high morale, Yamashita's troops defeated the British ahead of schedule.

The Dutch East Indies was conquered in a step-wise progression, and with persistence, Sumatra, Timor, Bali, and Java fell. The Japanese now had the oil, minerals, rubber, and other resources they needed. Burma and Ceylon (Sri Lanka) fell by April 1942.

In the Philippines, however, Lieutenant General Masaharu Homma took 150 days to get the Allies to surrender, instead of the expected fifty days. In February 1942, Homma fainted at a conference that had been called to find out what the delay was all about. By March, Homma was in Tokyo for consultation with his superiors to determine why he was behind schedule in subjugating the Philippines.

He requested more supplies and more troops. With the addition of fifteen thousand fresh troops of the Japanese 4th Division, Homma's infantry attack force numbered fifty thousand and were supported by 150 heavy guns. At a conference with strategists, an outline of attack suggested by Colonel Hattori was approved. This called for an increased, almost constant bombardment of the Allies in Bataan, especially around Mt. Samat. This was a contributing factor to the Allies' final surrender.

Homma disavowed knowledge of the maltreatment of Allied POWs during and after the Bataan Death March. He thought there would be about thirty thousand Allied soldiers, but Major General Edward King had surrendered seventy-six thousand men, twelve thousand of whom were Americans.

Two hundred buses were supposed to help transport the prisoners, but only one hundred arrived. Some lucky POWs got into those buses and did not suffer like the ones who had to undergo the death march.

Feeding had been planned for three times during the march, but the Japanese did not know that there were twice as many prisoners, that they had not been fed on the day of surrender, nor that the malnourished, sick men would take so long to complete the march. The first leg of the march was nineteen miles, which could be done in one day by stronger men, but it took the POWs two days. The Japanese didn't believe in surrender and low-level soldiers were usually maltreated by officers, so the average captor had no sympathy for these prisoners.

Rather than a premeditated inhumanity by the captors, it was lack of planning for the unexpectedly large number of prisoners, a misunderstanding of facts, and the nature of those with the upper hand to abuse their power that caused the misery.

Admiral Isoroku Yamamoto had studied in the United States and was aware of the vast resources the United States had. Along with the Japanese High Command, he gambled on a quick, successful conquest. They thought that the United States would opt for peace before Japan ran out of resources.

Vice Admiral Chuichi Nagumo's fleet of six aircraft carriers, battleships, cruisers, and submarines left from the Kurile Islands and advanced east toward Oahu, Hawaii, in complete radio silence. The successful opening attack on Pearl Harbor was followed by almost simultaneous lightning strikes: east toward Wake Island (December 8–23, 1941); southeast toward Guam (December 10); south toward the Philippines and northern Malaya (December 8); and southwest toward Hong Kong (December 8–10). Hong Kong surrendered on December 25.

Based on an authorization from the Arcadia Conference in Washington on December 22, 1941, the Allies formed ABDACOM (American, British, Dutch, and Australian Command) on January 15, 1942. Under British General Sir Archival Wavell, the task was to protect the Malay Barrier: the Southeast Asia peninsula and the island chain of the Netherlands East Indies and New Guinea stretching to northern Australia. This area was rich in raw materials and resources that the Japanese should not be allowed to have, including the rich Tarakan oil fields in Borneo and the *chinchon* tree plantations in Java.

On February 25, 1942, ABDACOM was dissolved. By March 9, the Netherlands East Indies (Indonesia) surrendered. Japan had overcome the Malay Barrier.

In March 1942, the Japanese attacked the southeast islands: Rabaul in New Britain, Kavieng in New Ireland, and Salamaua and Lae, which are in the northeastern part of Papua New Guinea. From May to July, they seized the northern part of the Solomon Islands (Bougainville). Rabaul became the "principal Japanese naval and air base in the Southwest Pacific." The Eighth Army under Lieutenant General Hitoshi Imamura was headquartered in Rabaul, so the Japanese controlled the land operations in the Bismarcks, Papua, and the Solomon Islands.

The Allies reorganized, and MacArthur became the Supreme Commander, Allied Forces, Southwest Pacific Area (SWPOA). His command encompassed Australia, New Guinea, Netherlands East Indies, and the Philippines. Admiral Chester Nimitz was in charge of the north, central, and the rest of the Pacific areas.

Even before the fall of Bataan on April 9, 1942, the Americans fought back by harassing Japanese positions in the Gilbert, Marshall, Wake Islands, and Rabaul. On April 16, Lieutenant Colonel James Doolittle staged a raid of sixteen B25 airplanes that dropped bombs in Tokyo. Although the damage was minor, the Japanese were demoralized enough to cause Admiral Yamamoto to plan strengthening the south boundary of Japanese influence by attacking Port Moresby.

Unknown to the Japanese, however, by May 1942, U.S. forces had broken the Japanese Naval Code and the Allies knew of the coming attack on Port Moresby. The Allies engaged the Japanese fleet as soon as it was sighted, and the ensuing Battle of the Coral Sea on May 7 and 8 resulted in heavy losses for both sides. Admiral Fletcher and Admiral Takagi's forces engaged in a massive dogfight with airplanes taking off from carriers. Both forces suffered heavy losses, but it was an Allied strategic victory because it halted the Japanese advance.

The Japanese continued with their plan for control of the central and southern Solomon Islands from May through July 1942. They started building an airfield in Guadalcanal. The Allies counterattacked and got control of the airfield, which they named Henderson Field. The Japanese sent reinforcements to take it back.

For eight months, both sides fought back and forth, with heavy losses on both sides. On February 1 through 7, 1943, under cover of night, thirteen thousand Japanese soldiers were evacuated from the island. They were thin and sick, wearing only remnants of clothing. The death count was thirty thousand Japanese and seven thousand Allies.

Port Moresby, the Australian base in Papua, New Guinea, was just north of Australia. The Japanese were determined to take it because it would facilitate an attack on Australia, MacArthur's base for the counteroffensive. When their initial attempt in the Battle of the Coral Sea was foiled, their ships landed Japanese soldiers at Gona and Buna, intending for them to pass through the Owen Stanley Mountains and attack the city. Both sides fought in jungles and suffered illnesses and deprivations because of the tropical heat. Neither side made much headway until MacArthur sent Major General Robert Eichelberger with fifteen thousand troops on December 1, 1942. Eichelberger enforced discipline and boosted his men's morale by fighting along with them. The Japanese evacuated their surviving soldiers. Eichelberger lost thirty pounds in thirty days, but he won.

The initial Japanese naval strategy had three phases: 1) neutralize the Pacific Fleet and seize the southern resources area; 2) consolidate and strengthen the perimeter to inhibit an Allied counterattack, and; 3) defeat and destroy Allied efforts to penetrate the perimeter. *Dupuy and Dupuy.

The Japanese had conquered Malaya, Singapore, Hong Kong, Indochina, Burma, New Guinea, the Bismarck Islands, and the Southern Solomons by March 1942. Inspired by their astounding success, and keeping in mind the Doolittle Raid, the Japanese High Command changed strategy. They decided to extend their influence in the central and South Pacific. Under this Revised Strategic Plan, drafted April through May 1942, they planned to seize Midway Island in order to have a closer base from which to attack Hawaii. They also planned to seize southern New Guinea (Port Moresby) and the southern Solomon Islands to harass the Allied comeback effort in Australia and interfere with the trans-Pacific supply routes from the United States and the Panama Canal. * Dupuy and Dupuy.

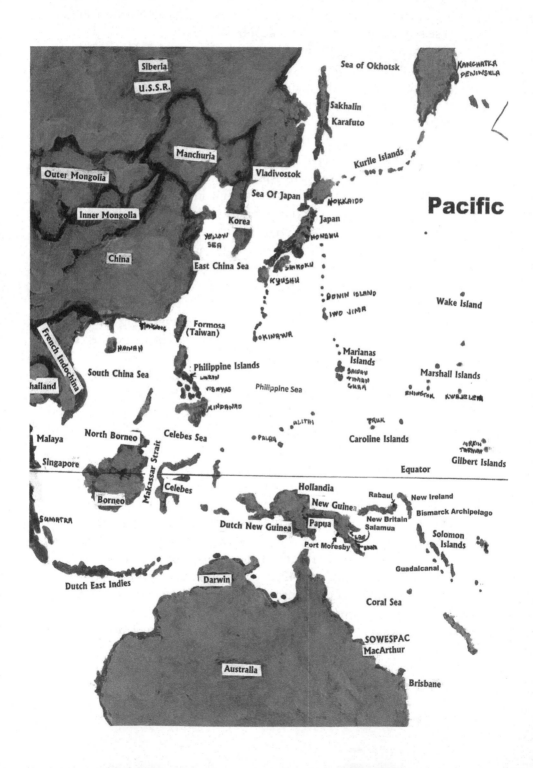

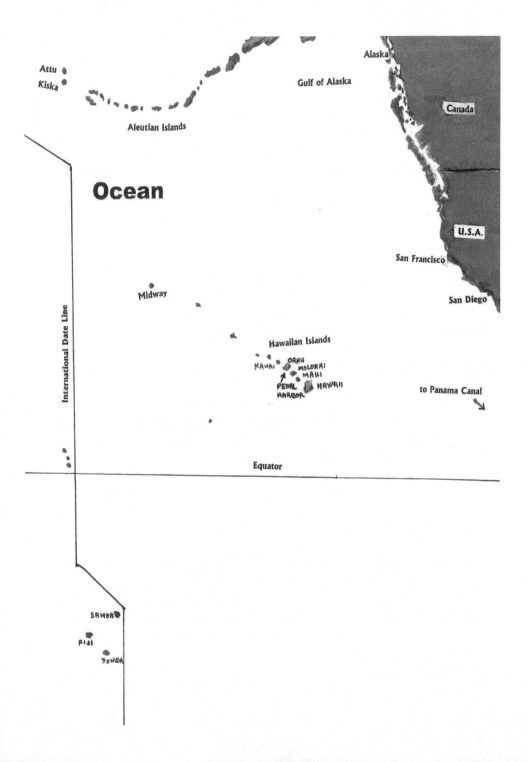

Although he was repulsed on his southern expansion at the Battle of the Coral Sea, Yamamoto continued with his plans to seize Midway. A diversionary tactic of attack on two Aleutian Islands, Kiska on June 6 and Attu on June 7, 1942, did not draw the Pacific Command into the trap because the Allies had already figured out the Japanese Naval Code. The Allies stationed on the two islands were quickly overcome. Back in Washington DC, however, Admiral Ernest King and some of the top brass did not believe this was a feint.

Yamamoto committed 165 warships for the Battle of Midway on June 4–6, 1942. The battle caused Admiral Nagumo and Rear Admiral Fletcher to lose their flagships. Fletcher had to put Rear Admiral Raymond Spruance at the helm.

The Americans lost the USS *Yorktown*, 132 planes, and 307 men; but the Japanese lost four carriers, one heavy cruiser, 275 planes, and thirty-five hundred men.

The Allies had been winning one naval battle after another, but when the United States won the Battle of Midway, the tide of battle turned decisively in favor of the Allies.

The order to retake Attu came from Washington DC and was executed May 11–29, 1943. The eighteen-day, intense battle cost the United States 561 lives, with an additional 1,136 wounded. Of the twenty-five hundred Japanese soldiers on the island, only twenty-nine were captured and the rest were killed.

On August 15, 1943, a tense group of Allied soldiers landed in Kiska ready for a fight. Surprised by the eerie quietness of the island, they crept from one spot to another, almost firing at each other. There were dogs scampering around, and hot coffee was still on the burner, but there were no enemies anymore. The Japanese had been evacuated.

"What does this mean?" Navy Secretary Frank Knox inquired.

"The Japanese are very smart, their dogs can brew coffee," U.S. Navy Chief Ernest King answered. * Sulzberger

World War II started with the United States as a Pacific power with dominion over Pearl Harbor, the Philippines, Guam, Midway, Wake, Kiska, and Attu. In between these were islands that used to belong to Spain, but were bought by the United States in 1898 and later sold to the Germans. After World War I, the trusteeship of the following islands was given to Japan: the Marianas Islands (Tinian and Saipan), Marshall Islands (Kwajelein and Eniwetok), Caroline

Islands (Truk, Palau, and Ulithi), and Gilbert Islands (Makin and Tarawa).

The Japanese proceeded to build formidable defenses on their islands with naval bases, airports, and fortifications. Admiral Yamamoto made Truk the headquarters of the Japanese Imperial Navy's Combined Fleet.

Early in the war, Japan invaded Guam. Add to this Bonin Island (southeast of Japan, north of Iwo Jima), Iwo Jima to Japan's south, Okinawa (southwest of Japan, toward Formosa), and Formosa, and the Japanese had a huge advantage in the Pacific.

In the first half of 1942, the new conscripts to the Allied war effort went four to one toward the Pacific Theater. Those assigned to the southwest Pacific Theater arrived in Australia for training to augment the Allied forces already there. When MacArthur arrived in Australia in March 1942, he was disappointed with the resources available. Later on, subsequent requests for more troops were denied as the Joint Chiefs gave priority to the European Theater. The southwest Pacific command of MacArthur was last priority.

MacArthur's problem with Washington DC was not only in their having a say in the command structure of war, but also with prejudice against him by some people because of a perceived arrogance. MacArthur liked to work with men he knew, trusted, and who had delivered positive results in the past. At first he was unhappy with the people he had to work with.

According to Gailey, "The overall strategy was developed by General Marshall and Admiral King and issued as a directive on July 2, 1942. The major goal was to 'isolate and capture Rabaul.'" This was Operation Cartwheel. Thus the Allies had to take control of the Santa Cruz Islands, Tulagi in the Florida Islands, and Guadalcanal in the Solomon Islands. To capture Lae and Salamaua in northeast New Guinea, the Allies first had to capture Gona and Buna (in Papua New Guinea, farther south) to provide air cover and have a supply base. Thus the Allied forces in Australia were directed to stage a phased operation, attacking one island after another and getting control, until they could take Rabaul.

Warfare in the Pacific islands was not just about the enemy, it was also about tropical heat, jungle, difficult terrain, diseases, and deprivation. Out of frustration, MacArthur told Eichelberger to take

Buna or not come back alive. Eichelberger won Buna. From there on, the Allies showed they could handle tropical warfare.

Beginning in October 1942, MacArthur developed a good working relationship with Vice Admiral William Halsey, commander of the South Pacific Area, and Vice Admiral Thomas Kinkaid, commander of the carrier force.

Halsey was a colorful man, brilliant and daring, his patriotism unquestioned. By order from Washington DC, a peculiar arrangement occurred whereby Admiral Halsey had to work with MacArthur but still answer to Admiral Nimitz. Halsey had no problem with that, however, and he and MacArthur were able to plan and get things done together.

Gradually, MacArthur was able to place under his command the people he could work with: Air Force Lieutenant General George Kenney (July 30, 1942), Rear Admiral Daniel Barbey of the Seventh Amphibious Force (January 10, 1943), and Colonel Charles Willoughby, G2.

On February 1943, MacArthur reinforced the U.S. Army Forces in the Far East (USAFFE) and established the Sixth Army. He requested for Lieutenant General Walter Krueger, who was at that time commanding the Third Army in San Antonio, Texas. Krueger would prove to be among the best U.S. Army commanders.

On April 18, 1943, the Allies found out from intercepted messages of the Imperial Japanese Navy that Admiral Yamamoto would be flying from Rabaul to Bougainville. His plane was shot down.

As the war effort accelerated, American factories worked full blast. Shipyards were building naval fleets; airplanes were being produced fast. The Lockheed P-38 replaced the Curtis P-40 and Bell P-39. On June 30, 1943, great examples of American innovation arrived: the landing ship tank (LST), landing craft tank (LCT), and landing craft, infantry (LCI). These marvels facilitated the Allied counterattack.

In his Central Pacific command, Nimitz sent the marines to take the islands and atolls in the Gilberts (Makin and Tarawa) on November 21, 1943, after first softening the targets with preliminary bombing. The U.S. Marines lost one thousand lives, and the Japanese lost forty-seven hundred.

By January 31, 1944, Marines were landing in the Marshalls (Kwajelein and Eniwetok) and bombing the Japanese in the Caroline Islands (Truk, Palau, and Ulithi).

Meanwhile, MacArthur proceeded on a northward campaign from Australia. The Allies won the Battle of the Bismarck Sea on March 2–4, 1943, and instead of attacking Kolombangara, they followed Halsey's suggestion and attacked Vella Lavella on August 15–October 7, 1943. This was closer to Rabaul.

The next plan was to take the Hansa Bay area in northeast New Guinea to move the Allies 120 miles northward of Saidor. Brigadier General Bonner Fellers, the planning chief, conceived of moving up five hundred miles instead, to Hollandia, which was on the northern part of Dutch New Guinea. This would bypass enemy strongholds, isolate those areas, and speed up the plan for liberation. Fellers's immediate superior, General Stephen Chamberlin, vetoed the plan. Fellers then went directly to MacArthur. MacArthur liked the idea and made Fellers his military secretary, rescuing him from General Chamberlin, who fired Fellers.

When the U.S. president and the Armed Forces Staff approved this "leap frog" strategy, MacArthur used the idea to bomb Rabaul, isolate it, then bypass the stronghold, the same way that Nimitz later bypassed the Japanese Imperial Navy's command base at Truk. Not only was the timetable moved forward, but there was also less mortality and less expense. The ninety-five thousand Japanese soldiers who were left on the island of New Britain, mostly in Rabaul, abandoned the base on November 20, 1943.

By sheer tenacity and in spite of heavy fighting, the U.S. Marines moved west from the central Pacific, and MacArthur's troops moved north toward the Philippines, both with the ultimate goal of reaching Japan.

When the war in Europe did not require as many ships and naval armaments as the war in the Pacific, these materiel were sent to MacArthur, along with more men to command. By April 1944, he was in charge of 750,000 men.

Finally, on June 6, 1944, the Allies landed in Normandy. The liberation of Europe was underway, and radio announcers trumpeted the news excitedly.

On June 15, 1944, U.S. forces landed in Saipan, one of the Marianas Islands. On June 19 and 20, the Japanese counterattacked, and the ensuing Battle of the Philippine Sea started. It was later called the Marianas Turkey Shoot. The battle was fought by airplanes from aircraft carriers. Within two days, four hundred Japanese planes and two carriers had been destroyed; while the United States lost 106 planes and no ships. The Japanese lost their biggest and newest carrier, the *Taiho*. On July 21–24, the Allies landed on the last two Marianas Islands: Tinian and Guam.

After the Allies took Morotai in New Guinea and Peleliu in the Palau Islands in September 1944, various plans were being formed as to how the war should progress. Nimitz supported attacking Formosa first, while MacArthur supported liberating the Philippines first.

While the military planners explored the most effective strategy, Admiral William Halsey, commanding Task Force 38, did a preliminary harassment of the Japanese in Luzon and Formosa. He then proceeded to do the same in Palau, Mindanao, Yap Island near Palau, Ryukyu Island south of Japan, and the Bonin Islands near Okinawa, closer to Japan. Because of this, the Japanese prematurely triggered SHO-2, their war strategy for the defense of Formosa.

In the ensuing air battle, the Japanese lost about a thousand airplanes, while the Americans lost less than a hundred. Since the Japanese were so propaganda conscious, they under-reported their losses and inflated their report of American damage. To their detriment, their own military planners had inaccurate estimates of their capabilities.

Admiral Halsey had noticed there was not much Japanese resistance in the southern Philippine island of Mindanao. He recommended that General MacArthur's planned invasion of the Philippines should start in Leyte, toward the middle of the archipelago, instead of farther south. Admiral Halsey's idea was enthusiastically forwarded by General MacArthur and approved by President Roosevelt and his advisers. Landing the liberating Allies in Leyte was going to be the biggest naval battle of all time.

The Battle for Leyte Gulf

The Japanese High Command had figured out that the Allies would be landing in Leyte, so they ordered the activation of SHO-1, the defense strategy for the Philippines. The order was dispatched on October 18, but it did not reach Field Marshal Hisaichi Terauchi and Lieutenant General Tomoyuki Yamashita in the Philippines until the twentieth. Terauchi was the field marshal for the southwest Pacific, and he had arrived in the Philippines on October 6. Even if Yamashita was the commander in the Philippines, Terauchi was superior. Terauchi ordered two divisions, the Thirty-fifth Army's First and Twenty-sixth Divisions from Luzon, to reinforce troops in Leyte.

Since previous naval and air encounters between the Japanese and the Americans had been reported by the Japanese as unqualified victories for propaganda purposes, this backfired because, instead of understanding they had suffered significant losses, some Japanese commanders thought they were winning. Terauchi was under the impression that the Americans were weakened, and his decision to make Leyte the decisive battleground was contrary to Yamashita's idea of making the stand in Luzon. Nevertheless, Yamashita obeyed.

As for the Japanese Imperial Navy, mobilizing for SHO-1 was delayed because of a supply problem. The Allies had become very effective in submarine warfare. Since mid-1943, U.S. submarines had been sinking Japanese oil tankers. By late 1944, two thirds of Japanese tankers and half of its merchant fleet had been sunk. The toll on the Japanese economy was significant, and the Japanese naval fleet had a fuel shortage.

The Allies had already landed the troops by the time the Japanese naval fleet arrived in Leyte; nevertheless, the Japanese could have inflicted a serious setback. SHO-1 called for four groups of Japanese counterattack. The first strike force would be led by Vice Admiral Takeo Kurita. Included under his command were five battleships: the *Musashi* (seventy-two thousand tons), the *Yamato* (seventy thousand tons), the *Atago*, and the *Takao*. His fleet had been in Singapore, then in Brunei Bay, Borneo. He left Brunei on October 22 and went through the Palawan Passage (from the southwest).

In the Palawan Passage, there was the danger of coral reefs and shallow water. As he arrived at the Palawan Passage on October 23, Kurita's fleet was detected by two U.S. submarines, the *Darter* and *Dace*. The *Darter* sank Kurita's flagship, the *Atago* (a heavy cruiser of 14,616 tons), and hit the *Takao*, which was heavily damaged. The *Dace* sank the other heavy cruiser, *Maya*. The *Darter* was later scuttled as she ran aground, and her crew went to the *Dace*. Suffering losses, Kurita proceeded to the San Bernardino Strait.

The second naval group would be led by Vice Admiral Kiyohide Shima. It had been in Ryukyu and then in Formosa. It sailed south on October 22, heading toward Leyte and coming from the northwest.

The third group would be led by Vice Admiral Shoji Nishimura. This group, originating from the south, left Brunei, Borneo, on October 22 and sailed for Surigao Strait.

The fourth group would be coming from the north and led by Vice Admiral Jisaburo Ozawa. It would be coming from the Inland Sea (Japan), where it departed on October 20, 1944.

Thus, from the Palawan Passage, Admiral Kurita's fleet was soon in the Sibuyan Sea, west of Leyte. Admiral Halsey was waiting. Halsey had three other groups guarding specific areas: east of Luzon, east of Samar, and the San Bernardino Strait. Halsey had sent a fourth group to Ulithi for supplies.

There, in the Sibuyan Sea, Halsey's fleet came under attack from Japanese planes based in Luzon. As one of the light carriers caught fire, the USS *Birmingham*, a cruiser, came to help. More aerial attacks followed, this time from Vice Admiral Jisaburo Ozawa's Fleet coming from the north. The USS *Princeton* and the USS *Birmingham* were lost. Halsey's fleet exacted its revenge, however, as they sank the *Musashi*, the seventy-two-thousand-ton carrier and former flagship of Yamamoto and Koga. This battle in the Sibuyan Sea (October 23–24) was the first stage in the Battle for Leyte Gulf.

Vice Admiral Ozawa's fleet attacking from the north caught Halsey's attention. Naval strategy usually had the mobile force as the main striking force. Surmising that Ozawa's fleet was the strike force, Halsey's fleet chased Ozawa to the north. Halsey had previously given instructions to form Task Force 34 when he said so, but this order never came. By some miscommunication, the naval fleet that was guarding the San Bernardino Strait went north too.

On October 25, Vice Admiral Kurita continued on to San Bernardino Strait, which was left unguarded. From there, he continued on to the Philippine Sea, east of Samar.

Vice Admiral Shoji Nishimura's fleet sailed toward Surigao Strait, where Vice Admiral Thomas Kinkaid was waiting. Rear Admiral Jesse Oldendorf's fleets were there, too, in the northern area. The battle cost Nishimura's fleet two battleships, the *Fuso* and the *Yamashiro*. Vice Admiral Shima's fleet arrived during the thick of battle, and when he saw the losses Nishimura's fleet was taking, Shima did not engage the enemy. The Americans continued to sink more of Nishimura's ships. The Battle of Surigao Strait on October 24–25 was the second stage.

Vice Admiral Kurita's fleet was in the Philippine Sea by October 25. It sailed southward toward Leyte Gulf. In his path, just off Samar Island, were three small groups of carriers under Rear Admiral Clifton Sprague. This was called Taffy 3, or Task Force 77.4.3. Their largest gun was five inches in diameter, and they were facing Kurita's eighteen-inch (Yamato) and fourteen-inch guns. At the time of impact, however, neither opponent knew exactly who they faced, nor what the other's capacity was. Taffy 3 became aware of the enemy only when the enemy fired on his search planes at 6:30 AM. Kurita thought he was facing Halsey's fleet. The Japanese used dye to mark where the hits landed.

"They're shooting at us in Technicolor!" a sailor exclaimed. * Nalty

Taffy 3 engaged the enemy with everything it could muster, even with some planes taking off in such haste they had no bombs. They also started making smoke to deceive the enemy. They sent messages to Admiral Halsey for help, but Halsey was far up north and engaging Ozawa's fleet. It could not help. Taffy 3 lost the USS *Hoel*, USS *Johnston*, USS *Samuel R. Roberts*, and USS *Gambier Bay*.

By 9:00 AM, Kurita was so shaken by the Americans' fierce counterattack, and not knowing that he was on the verge of victory, he withdrew and sailed toward San Bernardino Strait. The *Yamato* reversed course. The battle off Samar in the early morning of October 25 was the third stage.

While Halsey was engaging Ozawa's fleet at Cape Engano, he received the distress call from Vice Admiral Kinkaid. This annoyed him, but when Kinkaid specified that his fleet was low in ammunition, Halsey realized he had a problem. Next came a message from Admiral Nimitz that said, "Where is, repeat, where is Task Force 34? The world wonders." *Nalty

The latter part of the message was "padding" that the radio communicator added. Not realizing that, Halsey felt insulted and fretted for an hour before turning south. Ozawa had drawn Halsey to a place where he was not able to finish off Ozawa's fleet, and Halsey had missed the other battles. The Battle of Cape Engano on October 25 was the fourth stage.

Allied airplanes under Vice Admiral Marc Mitscher's command found Ozawa's seventeen retreating ships as early as 2:00 AM on the twenty-fifth, about two hundred miles east of Cape Engano. A one-sided battle ensued in the United States favor. Ozawa lost his three remaining carriers and one destroyer, including his sole fleet carrier, the twenty-nine-thousand-ton *Zuikaku*.

In the planning stages against the liberation forces, Ozawa was aware that Japanese resources were diminished. He had planned a ruse to remove the Third Fleet from protecting the landings so the Japanese could bomb the Allied troops as they landed. Ozawa wanted to bait Halsey's fleet to get them to head north, while Vice Admiral Kurita's fleet would go through the San Bernardino Strait and arrive at the Leyte Gulf from the north, and Vice Admiral Nishimura's fleet would go through the Surigao Strait and arrive at Leyte Gulf from the south. With this pincer movement against the Allies, and with Admiral Halsey hopefully out of position, Kurita's fleet would be able to bomb the landing troops.

As a war strategy, the mobile naval group would usually be the main strike force, so Halsey figured Ozawa's fleet would be the one. Actually, the strike force was going to be Kurita's fleet, and it almost got into position, but instead it left.

Thus, notwithstanding near mishaps, the Battle for Leyte Gulf was an American success. The Japanese lost twenty-six ships (four carriers, three battleships, six heavy and four light cruisers, and eleven destroyers) and about 305,710 tons of materiel. In contrast, the Americans lost six ships (one light carrier, two escort carriers, two destroyers, and one destroyer escort), and approximately thirty-six thousand tons of materiel. The Japanese lost 10,500 sailors and airmen. The Americans lost twenty-eight hundred lives, and there were one thousand wounded.

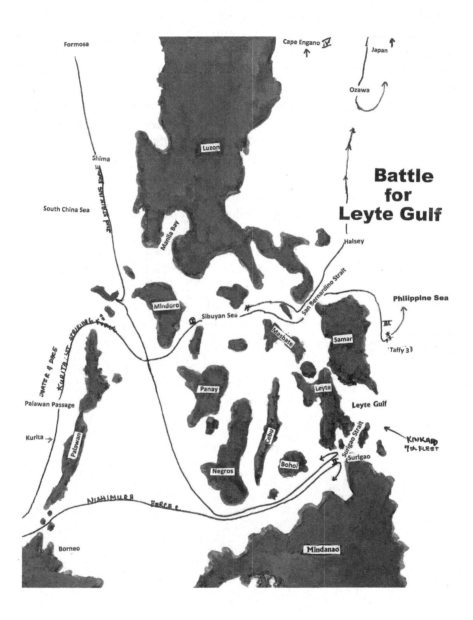

Battle
for
Leyte Gulf

On October 29, the Japanese made full use of another weapon, the kamikaze. The first ship that was sunk was the USS *St. Lo*, one of the ships belonging to Rear Admiral Clifton Sprague's Taffy 3. The kamikaze, or divine wind, was a suicide plane whose pilot would crash his airplane on an American ship or vessel, sinking or damaging the vessel. The pilot would die in the process. Vice Admiral Takijiro Ohnishi first realized the potential of this with some pilots who swore to die for Imperial Japan.

By the time the Allies gained the upper hand in the war in the Pacific, the kamikaze attacks had become so frequent that even when the Allies tried to shoot the planes down, there was still a lot of damage. It became so organized that, toward the end, the Japanese ran short of airplanes and pilots.

In December 1944, a misfortune struck Halsey's fleet. Since Leyte faces the Pacific Ocean, typhoons were frequent. At that time, technology for forecasting weather conditions was not adequate, and weather analysis was not accurate. On December 17, Halsey sent his fleet to Ulithi for refueling. On December 18, a typhoon hit, and the fleet lost three destroyers: USS *Spence*, USS *Hull*, and USS *Monaghan*. Seven other ships were damaged, 790 soldiers died, and 80 were injured. The ships and their remains were scattered across three thousand miles.

Bibliography

Alexander, Bevin. *How Great Generals Win.* New York: W.W. Norton & Co., 1993.

Black, Wallace B. and Jean F. Blashfield. *Bataan and Corregidor.* New York: Crestwood House (McMillan Publishing Co.), 1991.

Clausen, Henry C. and Bruce Lee. *Pearl Harbor:Final Judgement.* New York: Crown Publishers, 1992

Collier, Basil. *The War in the Far East 1941-1945 A Military History.* New York: William Morrow and Company, 1968.

Conroy, Robert. *The Battle of Bataan—America's Greatest Defeat.* New York: The MacMillan Co., 1969.

Cutler, Thomas J. *The Battle of Leyte Gulf 23–26 Oct. 1944.* New York: Harper Collins, 1994.

Dupuy, R. Ernest and Trevor N. Dupuy. *The Harper Encyclopedia of Military History—From 3500 B.C. to the Present.* New York: Harper Collins Publishers, 1993.

Elliot, Charles Burke. *The Philippines to the End of the Military Regime-America Overseas.* Indianapolis: Bobbs-Merrill Publishing Co., 1961.

Encyclopaedia Britannica, 15th ed., Vol. 4, 10, 14. New York: Helen Hemingway-Benton, 1973–1974.

Gailey, Harry A. *MacArthur's Victory: The War in New Guinea, 1943-1944.* New York: Presidio Press, 2004.

Harris, William, and Judith S. Levey, ed. *New Columbia Encyclopedia.* New York: Columbia University Press, 1975.

Humble, Richard. *Battleships and Battlecruisers.* Herts, England: Winchmore Publishing Services, Ltd., 1983.

Ireland, Bernard (Gen.) and John Keegan (ed.). *War at Sea 1914–45.* London: Cassell and Co. Wellington House, 2002.

Karnow, Stanley. *In Our Image.* New York: First Ballantine Books, 1990.

Knox, Donald. *Death March.* New York: Harcourt Brace Jovanovich, 1981.

Lacsamana, Leodivico Cruz. *Philippine History and Government 2nd ed.* Philippines: Phoenix Publishing House, 1990.

Lockwood, Charles A. and Hand Christian Adamson. *Battles of the Philippine Sea.* New York: Thomas Y. Crowell Company, 1967.

Matloff, Maurice (ed.). *American Military History,* Vol. 1 (pp. 335–342) and Vol. II. Philadelphia: Combined Books, 1996.

Maroon, Fred J. and Edward L. Beach. *Keepers of the Sea.* Annapolis, Maryland: Naval Institute Press, 1983.

Mason, John T. *The Pacific War Remembered-An Oral History Collection.* Annapolis, Maryland: Naval Institute Press, 1986.

Miller, Edward S. *War Plan Orange: The US Strategy to Defeat Japan 1897-1945.* Annapolis, Maryland: U.S. Naval Institute, 1991.

Miller, Nathan. *The US Navy—An Illustrated History.* New York: American Heritage Publishing Co. and the US Naval Institute Press, 1977.

Morison, Samuel Eliot. *Leyte: June 1944–Jan. 1945 (History of U.S. Naval Operations in World War II, Vol. XII).* Boston: Little, Brown and Co., 1975.

Morris, James M. *History of the US Navy.* Connecticut: Longmeadow Press, 1993.

Nalty, Bernard (ed.). *War in the Pacific: Pearl Harbor to Tokyo Bay.* London: Salamander Book, 1999.

Nunn, Stratton Heckler. *The New Grolier Encyclopedia of World War II: Vol. 3, War in the Pacific.* Connecticut: Grolier Educational Corp., 1995.

Oleksey, Walter. *The Philippines—Enchantment of the World, 2nd Series.* Connecticut: Children's Press, Grolier Publishing, 2000.

Parkes, Carl. *Philippine Handbook 3rd ed.* Chico, California: Moon Publications, 1999.

Pitt, Barrie (ed.). *The Military History of World War II*. London: Aerospace Publishing Ltd., 1986.

Polmar, Norman. *The Ships and Aircraft of the US Fleet*. Annapolis, Maryland: Naval Institute Press, 1978.

Prange, Gordon W., Donald M. Goldstein, and Katherine V. Dillon. *Dec. 7, 194, The Day the Japanese Attacked Pearl Harbor*. New York: Anne Prange and Prange Enterprises, Inc., 1988.

Sides, Hampton. *Ghost Soldiers*. New York: Doubleday, 2001.

Smith, Steven Trent. *The Rescue*. New York: John Wiley and Sons, 2001.

Steinberg, Rafael. *Island Fighting: World War II*. New York: Time-Life Books, 1978.

Stolley, Richard B. (ed.). *Life: World War 2*. London: Little, Brown and Co., 2001.

Steinberg, Rafael. *Return to the Philippines: World War II*. New York: Time-Life Books, Inc. 1979.

Stewart, Adrian: *The Battle of Leyte Gulf*. New York: Charles Scribner and Sons, 1980.

Sulzberger, C. L. *The American Heritage Picture History of World War II*. New York: American Heritage Publishing Company, 1966.

Toland, John. *But Not in Shame*. New York: Random House, 1961.

Tope, Lily R. *Cultures of the World-Philippines*. New York: Marshal Cavendish Corp., 2002.

van der Vat, Dan. *The Pacific Campaign: World War II, the US-Japanese Naval War, 1941-1945*. New York: Simon and Schuster, 1991.

Wainwright, Jonathan (Lt. Gen.) (ed.) by Considine, Robert. *General Wainwright's Story*. New York: Modern Literary Editions Publishing, 1945.

Webster, Donovan. *In Their Footsteps*. Washington DC: Smithsonian Magazine (March 2004): 81–87.

Whitney, David C., and Robin V. Whitney. *The American Presidents*. New York: Bookspan, 2001.